A Surfeit of Mirrors

also translated and introduced by Brian Stableford:

Anonymous: Sâr Dubnotal vs. Jack the Ripper; *Anthologies*: News from the Moon; The Germans on Venus; The Supreme Progress; The World Above the World; Nemoville; *Allorge*: The Great Cataclysm; *Bérard*: The Vampire Lord Ruthwen; *Bessière*: The Gardens of the Apocalypse; *Bleunard*: Ever Smaller; *Bodin*: The Novel of the Future; *Brown*: City of Glass; *Caroff*: The Terror of Madame Atomos; *Champsaur*: The Human Arrow; *Derennes*: The People of the Pole; *Driou*: The Adventures of a Parisian Aeronaut; *Dunan*: Baal; *Duvernois*: The Man Who Found Himself; *Eyraud*: Voyage to Venus; *Falk*: The Age of Lead; *Féval*: Anne of the Isles; The Black Coats ('Salem Street; The Invisible Weapon; The Parisian Jungle; The Companions of the Treasure; Heart of Steel; The Cadet Gang; The Sword-Swallower); John Devil; Knightshade; Revenants; Vampire City; The Vampire Countess; The Wandering Jew's Daughter; *Féval, fils*: Felifax, the Tiger-Man; *Haraucourt*: Illusions of Immortality; *Kahn*: The Tale of Gold and Silence; *La Hire*: The Nyctalope vs. Lucifer; The Nyctalope on Mars; Enter the Nyctalope; *Lamothe-Langon*: The Virgin Vampire; *de Lautrec*: The Vengeance of the Oval Portrait; *Le Faure & de Graffigny*: The Extraordinary Adventures of a Russian Scientist Across the Solar System (2 vols.); *Le Rouge*: The Vampires of Mars; *Lermina*: Panic in Paris; Mysteryville; The Secret of Zippelius; *Moselli*: Illa's End; *Nizet*: Captain Vampire; *de Parville*: An Inhabitant of the Planet Mars; *de Pawlowski*: Journey to the Land of the 4th Dimension; *Pellerin*: The World in 2000 Years; *Ponson du Terrail*: The Vampire and the Devil's Son; *de Régnier*: A Surfeit of Mirrors; *Renard*: The Blue Peril; Doctor Lerne; The Doctored Man; A Man Among the Microbes; The Master of Light; *Richepin*: The Wing; *Robida*: The Clock of the Centuries; The Adventures of Saturnin Farandoul; Chalet in the Sky; *Rosny Aîné*: The Givreuse Enigma; The Mysterious Force; The Navigators of Space; Vamireh; The World of the Variants; The Young Vampire; *Rouff*: Journey to the Inverted World; *Ryner*: The Superhumans; *Spitz:* The Eye of Purgatory; *Steiner*: Ortog; *Tiphaigne de la Roche*: Amilec; *Varlet*: The Xenobiotic Invasion; Timeslip Troopers (w/*Blandin*); The Martian Epic (w/*Joncquel*); *Vibert*: The Mysterious Fluid; *Villiers de l'Isle-Adam*: The Scaffold; The Vampire Soul; *Ward & Miller*: The Song of Montségur.

A Surfeit of Mirrors
Symbolist Tales and Uncertain Stories

by
Henri de Régnier

translated, annotated and introduced by
Brian Stableford

A Black Coat Press Book

Visit our website at www.blackcoatpress.com

ISBN 978-1-61227-076-0. First Printing. March 2012. Published by Black Coat Press, an imprint of Hollywood Com-
ics.com, LLC, P.O. Box 17270, Encino, CA 91416.

TABLE OF CONTENTS

Introduction

The stories here translated as "Symbolist Tales" all appeared in the collection *La Canne de Jaspe* [The Jasper-handled Walking-Stick] in 1897. Some of those in the section "Tales of Oneself"[1] had previously appeared in *Contes à soi-même* (1894), but that earlier collection had contained at least one other item, and at least one new item was added to the section reproduced in the later collection. The three stories in the section "The Black Trefoil" had earlier appeared in *Le Trèfle noir* (1895). I have reversed the order in which the three sections were presented in *La Canne de jaspe* in order to make the sequence contained here more nearly chronological.

The items translated as "Uncertain Stories" all appeared in the collection *Histoires incertaines* (1919). "L'Entrevue," here translated as "The Glimpse," had previously appeared in the *Revue de Paris* in 1917. I have not been able to trace periodical appearances for the other two stories, but it seems obvious that they, too, were written during the Great War and partly motivated by the same uniquely melancholy impulse of escapism. Again, I have changed the order in which they ap-

---

[1] The title *Contes à soi-même* is capable of more than one interpretation, the most tempting of which is perhaps "tales [written] for oneself," but the majority of the stories collected by Régnier under that title are introspective tales about introspection, variously clothed and distanced but mostly obsessed with mirrors, real and figurative, frequently arranged in such a way as to multiply their images illimitably. They are, in essence, allegories of the supposedly difficult, and probably futile, quest to discover or construct an identity—a far more elusive grail than anything merely holy, of whose attainment stern virtue is no guarantee. The implicit meaning is thus closer to "tales of oneself" than "tales for oneself."

pear in the collection to what seems to me to be a more rational sequence, and I have also taken the liberty of detaching the final part of the second story, "Marceline ou la punition fantastique," here translated as "Marceline; or, The Fantastic Punishment," and removing it to an appendix at the end of the section, because I do not believe that the author really wanted or intended it to be attached to the story, and inserted it under real or imagined editorial pressure. The reason for my action will be obvious to the reader. "L'Entrevue" and "Le Pavilion fermé," the latter here translated as "The Sealed Pavilion" were both reprinted separately in volume form in 1927.

"Le Veuvage de Shéhérazade," here translated as "The Widowhood of Scheherazade" was initially published in *L'Illustration* in 1925 and was reprinted separately as a booklet in 1926; it was reprinted again in the collection *Le Voyage d'amour, ou L'Initiatian venetienne* (1930). "Le Paradis retrouvé," here translated as "Paradise Regained" was published as the title piece of the posthumous collection *Le Paradis retrouvé: contes choisis* (1937); I have not been able to locate any previous publication, and suspect that the frequent attribution of the date 1936 to the story is a guess as to its date of composition, based solely on the fact that Régnier died in that year.

Henri de Régnier was born in Honfleur in 1864; although both his parents were of aristocratic descent—his mother's maiden name was Thérèse du Bard de Curley—both families had suffered the effects of the Revolution; his paternal grandfather, who belonged to a military family, had emigrated, and although his maternal grandparents had hung on in Burgundy, and had retained their aristocratic pretensions, they too had come down in the world. Henri's father was a customs inspector, but he had literary connections by virtue of having been a childhood friend of Gustave Flaubert. Régnier maintained aristocratic airs, always posing as a gentleman and ostentatiously wearing a monocle, but manifested little snobbery in his literary associations and had no hesitation in working for politically-radical periodicals.

His affectations were fed in childhood by his maternal grandparents, at whose home in Paray-le-Monial he sometimes spent vacations, returning continually to the house after its desertion, in search of isolation, observing its gradual decay. The nearby ruined Château de Cypierre was in an even worse state, and it was there that he experienced a kind of epiphany that cemented a lifelong fascination with the past in decay—a moment described retrospectively in "Le Pavilion fermé." In 1874, he was enrolled at the Collège Stanislas, which he hated, but where he met Egbert Vielé, who was later to change his name to Francis Vielé-Griffin, and formed a fast friendship that lasted for many years, until it fell apart in 1900 when Vielé criticized Régnier's first novel in terms he could not forgive. They provided one another with an audience for their first verses, and hung around *Le Chat Noir* after they both began half-hearted studies in law that were soon abandoned in favor of literary life.

Régnier published his first collection of poems, *Les Lendemains* [Next Days] in 1885. He and Vielé became involved in the publication of *Lutèce*, one of several periodicals that provided him with an early outlet; he is alleged to have published six short stories there as well as numerous poems, but the periodical is not available on *gallica*, so I have not been able to check its contents. *Lutèce* gradually became an early showcase for the Symbolist Movement, and Régnier was a participant in the movement's first meetings, held at the salon of the ill-fated Robert Caze, who was killed in a duel in 1886 by Charles Vignier, after being charged with cowardice for refusing to fight when called out by Jean Richepin. Régnier met and became closely involved with the other pioneers of the movement, including Stéphane Mallarmé—whose *mardis* became the new focal point of the group—and Gustave Kahn.

Régnier also frequented the salon maintained by the Parnassian poet Jose-Maria Hérédia, at which the doyen of the Parnassians, Charles Leconte de Lisle was a regular attendee, and he was seen by some critics as a hybridizer of Parnassian and Symbolist approaches. Indeed, he sometimes described himself as an "independent" first and a Symbolist second, but he was generally quite happy to be identified as a leading member of the movement; in 1890, with Vielé-Griffin and Paul Adam he founded a periodical dedicated to the movement's ideals, *Entretiens politiques et littéraires*, in which he published a good deal of work, including "Le Sixième marriage de Barbe-Bleue" (1892), here translated as "Bluebeard's Sixth Marriage" and "Eustase et Humbeline" (1893). Most of the other leading Symbolists, including Remy de Gourmont, were fellow contributors, although they all transferred their primary allegiance to more dedicated and resilient publications such as the *Revue Blanche*, in which Régnier published "Hermogene" (1893), "Hertulie" (1894) and "Les Diners Singulier" (1896; tr. as "The Singular Diners") and the *Mercure de France*, co-founded by Goumont and Alfred Vallette, in which Régnier published "Le Signe de la Clef et la Croix" (1897; tr. as "The Sign of the Key and the Cross"). The press associated with the *Mercure* published most of his books, including the two collections translated herein.

Régnier produced one of the Symbolist movement's key "manifestos" in *Le Bosquet de Psyché* [Psyche's Arbor] (1894), and the poetry he published in the 1890s warrants consideration as a core contribution to Symbolist verse; the relevant collections include *Poèmes anciens et romanesques* [Old and Romantic Poems] (1890), *Tel qu'en songe* [Whatever One Thinks] (1892), *Aréthuse* [Arethusa] (1895) and *Les jeux mystiques et divins* [Mystical and Divine Games] (1897). He did retain something of the formality of Parnassian verse, as well as its interest in antique themes—most obvious in *Aréthuse*, which is replete with the mythological creatures, including fauns and centaurs, that remained central to his personal symbolic schemas—but he also followed Gustave Kahn and Jean Moréas into experimentation with free verse.

Alongside his Symbolist poetry, Régnier developed a series of experimental exercises in symbolist prose that ran parallel to the similar experiments carried out by Remy de Gourmont (a selection of which in translation can be found in *The Angels of Perversity*; Dedalus, 1992), and which similarly helped form an exemplary core. That core might have expanded much further had other journals associated with the movement Régnier not folded—*Le Centaure*, which was primarily the inspiration of Mallarmé's loyal disciple Jean de Tinan, collapsed after publishing only two issues 1896—but there were enough to make up the two collections whose contents were eventually recycled, with new material, in *La Canne de jaspe*.

Although Régnier's literary work seemed to change character markedly after 1898—the year in which Stéphane Mallarmé's died—in which respect he was by no means alone among the stalwarts of the Symbolist cause, and he was often referred to thereafter as an "ex-Symbolist," he never abandoned the fascinations that had drawn him to the movement in the first place, but merely began to place them more discreetly in verses and narratives of a more orthodox kind. This obvious in the way that the same key symbols of the first phase of his career—centaurs and other mythological half-humans as well as the everpresent keys and mirrors—recur in the much later narratives of the "uncertain stories." Although it is by no means necessary to have read the symbolist tales to enjoy the later works, they certainly enable a fuller and more sophisticated appreciation thereof.

Régnier was by far the most popular of the self-declared Symbolists while the movement was in full swing; his poetry helped win the movement a much wider audience, and his prose fiction easily outsold Gourmont's, the latter eventually becoming much better known as a critic than as a poet or writer of fiction. As the movement's commentator-in-chief, Gourmont did not rate Régnier as highly as some of its other contributors, but in observing Régnier's tendency to monotonous repetitiveness, he carefully framed his remarks as faint praise rather than outright condemnations, and was right to do so. At any rate, *La Canne de jaspe* was probably the best-selling Symbolist volume of all, at least in its own era; it was reprinted several times in the last few months of 1897 and stayed in print until 1927. Many of Régnier's subsequent books also went through multiple editions—no mean feat when one considers that he was an unusually prolific poet and novelist, credited with more than fifty distinct volumes—and he retained his popularity, without undue prejudice to his reputation, for more than three decades. He was also a prolific journalist, although he never attained a reputation as a commentator to match Gourmont's and relatively little of his criticism was reprinted in book form.

Régnier was the only explicitly-advertized Symbolist to be admitted to the Académie, and although his election came after he seemed to have deserted the fold, it was undoubtedly construed as a belated endorsement of the Movement's aspirations. He first offered himself as a candidate in 1908, when he was the odds-on favorite to beat Jean Richepin and Edmond Haraucourt, both of whom had significant black marks on their reputations, but he lost to Richepin; swallowing his chagrin, he offered himself again for the next vacant chair in 1911, and was elected against the sole opposition of Pierre de Nolhac, whose credentials were very much thinner but still managed to muster 14 votes to Régnier's 18. Remy de Gourmont's comments on Régnier's admission were typically half-hearted, devoting far more effort to regretting the fact that so few of the leading Parnassians had been admitted to the august institution than celebrating the fact that a Symbolist had actually made it, but they were nowhere near as acidic as the speech of "welcome" made by Comte Albert de Mun, a Catholic writer who disapproved strongly of Régnier's apparent atheism, and who attacked the new member for the supposed licentiousness of his novels. Mun's speech is still cited on the Académie's website as the second most hostile reception ever accorded to a new member (that of Alfred de Vigny taking first place) but Régnier made no protest.

Régnier was more conspicuously aware of his aristocratic descent than Remy de Gourmont, but it is manifest in his work primarily as an affected lofty world-weariness, reminiscent in some ways of the pose adopted by Lord Byron, one of the key forebears of the Decadent style and Decadent worldview that became intricately interlinked with Symbolist technique. Although he was much les of a dandy than some of his more flamboyant contemporaries, Régnier did like to represent himself, not entirely tongue-in-cheek, as a man accursed by being born out of his time, spiritually anchored in the eighteenth century. He was never a happy man, partly because he was rarely a well man, much given to bouts of depression and illness. François Broche, introducing the edition of Régnier's *Cahiers* [Notebooks] (2002), whose publication Régnier had explicitly forbidden, summed up the first section of his introduction to the author, in which he quotes numerous acquaintances to establish the fact that Régnier was always "distant," by stating brutally that Régnier never liked himself, at any stage of his life—and his works certainly give the impression of a deep-seated gloom and self-dissatisfaction, without any real explanation of the fact.

That downbeat tendency is quite obvious in *La Canne de jaspe*, even though the contents of that collection were all published in advance of the event that some observers might have taken for the turning-point of his life—although Régnier did not seem to see it that way himself. His notebooks suggest that he fell in love with Hérédia's second daughter, Marie, in 1891, when she was only sixteen, but at the time she preferred his friend Pierre Louÿs, whom he had introduced to Hérédia's salon a few months previously. In 1895, however, taking advantage of Louÿs temporary absence from Paris, Régnier asked for Marie's hand, and was accepted. Louÿs, at first incensed, soon forgave him, however—and within two years of the marriage, Marie began a long affair with Louÿs that was not interrupted when Louÿs married Marie's younger sister, Louise, in 1899 (they divorced in 1899, but Régnier never divorced Marie).

Louÿs subsequently told acquaintances that he had found Marie to be a virgin when their affair began, but it is unclear what evidence he had for that assertion. Whatever the truth of the matter, Marie soon began a series of other affairs in parallel with her association with Louÿs, beginning with Jean de Tinan. Régnier seemed to take the situation in his stride, and when Marie became pregnant, apparently—and according to her own testimony—by Louÿs, he insisted that Louÿs accompany him to the Mairie to register the child's birth as Paul de Régnier, and that he be present at the christening to be inscribed as the boy's godfather; he also invited Louÿs to accompany the family on a holiday shortly thereafter. Régnier apparently took most of Marie's numerous other affairs in his stride in the same way, except for one particularly tempestuous fling with Henry Bernstein in 1910, which threatened to cause a scandal—but he refused to divorce her, and appears to have countered his wife's ever-increasing resentments after the affair with Berstein with a string of determinedly platonic relationships with married women, including the three dedicatees of the *Histoires incertaines*.

Exactly what the cause was of Régnier's unusual relationships, it is now impossible to determine—his notebooks offer not the slightest clue, turning a determinedly blind eye to the whole issue—but something was obviously amiss in his own eyes, and although his literary works make the mere fact obvious, they are as determined as his private writings never to specify any underlying cause. Nor do Marie's writings, when she became a successful poet, novelist and short-story writer in her own right, under the pseudonym Gérard d'Houville, offer any convincing clarification. It is not entirely surprising, however, given these and other circumstances, that Régnier conceived and nursed a bitter heartache that suited him very well, and might always been his manifest destiny. That dire self-disappointment, doubtless augmented by the depredations and deprivations of the Great War, is very obvious in the two long novellas that conclude the "Uncertain Stories" section of this collection and are, in effect, its principal showpieces.

As with all dedicated Symbolists, Régnier strove for literary effect in his early works to such an extent as sometimes to make it difficult to perceive his meaning, both at the syntactical level and in terms of the import of his stories. Many symbolist tales are formulated in the image of fables or apologues, but steadfastly refuse the conventional and simplistic morals that are traditionally attached to such tales; Régnier's are not only no exception to that rule, but occasionally take their deliberate perversity to unprecedented lengths. His early prose fancies, offered in straight-faced earnest, are mostly exercises in esoteric self-analysis, not so much of his own individual self as of the general nature of the self: an analysis riven with supposedly-inevitable disillusionments, whose occasional suggested solutions are—to say the least—eccentric.

As with many of Symbolist prose writers, although by no means as obviously as Alfred Jarry and Guillaume Apollinaire, Régnier's work in that vein strayed in the direction of surrealism, but it is probably more intriguing viewed as a series of exercises in offbeat existentialism. The success of *La Canne de Jaspe*, however—which far outsold the two volumes cannibalized therein—is probably due at least in part to the fact that the new material he added to it, which he placed at the front of the volume, was more playful in nature, and—to begin with, at least—more cheerful in tone. Indeed, it is not entirely obvious why "Monsieur d'Amercoeur" bears that name, as most of his reminiscences depict him as a devil-may-care individual blessed with a more-than-diabolical charm and luck, upon whom the misfortune he refuses to talk about only fell belatedly. As the black humor of "Marceline" and the addenda to the two collections demonstrate, Régnier was never incapable of playfulness, but even his playfulness became increasingly tinged with deep irony as his career and life progressed.

We have no way of knowing whether Régnier, when he became an old man himself, looked back on his own life in the same deeply embittered fashion that many of the old men who feature in his youthful work looked back on theirs. Perhaps one should be kind enough to hope not—but no serious student of probability would bet on it.

The editions of *La Canne de jaspe* and *Histoires incertaines* used for these translations were the copies held in the London Library; both date from the original year of publication, although the former is identified as a third printing and the latter as a fifth. I have not been able to compare the versions of "Le pavilion fermé" and "L'Entrevue" contained in the latter volume with the separate editions published subsequently, but the version of the former story reprinted (inappropriately) in the anthology *Vampire Story* (Fleuve Noir 1994) edited by Stéphane Bourgoin appears to be identical to the one in *Histoires incertaines*. The two addenda are both translated from versions reproduced on a website entitled *Miscellanées: une bibliothéque heteroclite*, located at *www.miscellanees.com*.

Brian Stableford

SYMBOLIST TALES

To the Reader
(The Preface from "La Canne de Jaspe")

I don't know why my book wouldn't please you.

A novel or a short story can only be a pleasant fiction. If it presents an unexpected aspect beyond what it seems to signify, it's necessary to enjoy that semi-intentional surplus without demanding too much of its consequences, considering them as fortuitously generated by the mysterious concordances that exist, in spite of everything, between all things.

That is how it is necessary to approach the stories making up the stories comprising "The Black Trefoil" or "Tales of Oneself," and to enjoy Monsieur d'Amercoeur's anecdotes. The baroque or singular adventures in which he figures represent him well enough, waist-deep in his semi-secrecy, and if the events they report don't succeed in amusing you, you will doubtless not remain insensible to the charms of the tender Herculie and will not be repelled by the speech of old Hermocrates. After all, even if "Bluebeard's Sixth Marriage" and "The Knight who went to Sleep under the Snow" don't amuse you every much, you might still like the landscapes haunted by those furtive and grave shades, the houses they inhabit and the objects weighed in their tenebrous hands.

There are swords and mirrors there, jewels, dresses, crystal cups and lamps, along with, sometimes, the murmur of the sea outside, or the breath of forests. Listen to the springs sing, too. They're intermittent or continuous; the gardens they animate are symmetrical. There, the statues are marble or bronze; the yew-trees are trimmed; the bitter odor of box-trees perfumes the silence; roses grow on the cypress; love and death kiss one another on the mouth; the waters reflect the shadows. Make a tour of the pools. Go into the labyrinth, spend time in the arbors—and read my book, page by page, as if you were a solitary walker, turning over a scarab beetle, a pebble or a dead leaf with the tip of your long, jasper-handled walking-stick, on the dry sand of the pathway.

Tales of Oneself

Instead of a Frontispiece

Of these tales, the title is still what pleases me most, being able to serve as an excuse if one is needed. If not, let each benevolent reader appropriate from these dreams whatever they can, and I shall have had, on top of that, the pleasure of obtaining something of my own.

I would have liked a few significant emblems for a frontispiece to these pages; one of my friends, a painter, could have designed them. They might have included, for example, a mirror or a seashell, or a curiously-ornamented water-bottle. He would have represented the last in pewter, because I like that metal, which is reminiscent of old humble silver, scratched and intimate: a slightly dull silver, as if tarnished by the approach of breath or if its sheen were tempered by moisture from having been held too long by a warm hand.

The allegory would doubtless have been further clarified by a conch shell. The sea deposits charming ones on the sand of beaches, among the sickly seaweed, a little water and cockle-shells. Mother-of-pearl, shining here and there beneath their crust, makes the luxurious scars iridescent, and their form has a mischief so mysterious that one expects to hear the Sirens singing in one's ear. Only the indistinct echo of the sea murmurs therein, and that is nothing but the flow of our blood, imitating the internal call of our destiny.

But a mirror would certainly be better still. I'm sure that my painter would have garlanded the oval frame with ingenious flowers, and that he would have been able to coil some caducean serpent around the handle.

My friend was unable to lend himself to my fantasy. His own is not to paint any longer but to live—as I have lived—the long hours of his silence, turned to face his dreams.

Bluebeard's Sixth Marriage

To Francis Poictevin[2]

The Church was completely somnolent. More than enough light came through its discolored stained-glass windows to distract attention from shade that was still inadequate for weeping, so the sparsely-scattered kneeling women seemed to be waiting for a deeper darkness. They remained taciturn beneath their protective headgear: the tall hats of the region, made of soft fabric, which sheltered the naïve faces of young women and almost buried the worn faces of old ones.

The sonorous concavity of the nave amplified the sound of a shifted chair. From the beams of the vault individual lamps were suspended, and the crown of an old crystal chandelier, its candles extinguished, swung almost imperceptibly. There were flowers and sculpted figures on the capitals of the pillars and on the font, around which droplets of holy water, reverently removed by fingertips in order to make the sign of the cross, wet the pavement.

An odor of incense conserved throughout the nave a memory of the recent vespers, and its permanence, simultaneously nuptial and funerary, evoked a more distant retrospection of psalmodic obsequies and joyful weddings.

---

[2] Francis Poictevin (1854-1904) was perhaps the ultimate Decadent Symbolist, in terms of his ornate prose and his flamboyant lifestyle. A dedicated dandy and aesthete, he was one of Joris-Karl Huysmans' closest friends and served as one of the models for Jean Des Esseintes in *À rebours*; his work became increasingly mystical and disjointed until he apparently went mad in the mid-1890s, but he was later hailed by the surrealists as a significant precursor.

Perhaps it was because of the time I arrived in Quimperlé that afternoon, when the bells were ringing with a silvery sound, like the cheerful name of the town, in a sunlit sky threatened by rainclouds on the horizon, but in my mind the idea of celebration was predominant, and that ringing represented to me the merriment of betrothals and processions at the crossroads and on the parvis. Sundays elsewhere in the region have a certain pomp and decoration about them, but here it is idle and requiescent instead. The houses are ancient, as if drowsy; people are in the doorways, as if awaiting the passing or return of some joy. The white winged head-dresses are suggestive of ceremony and complication. They sway as girls walk, and their disposition is indented with mischief and embroidered with coquetry; on the heads of the old women, they are simplified and fractured, and go to sleep, nonchalant and a trifle stiff.

The trees of the mall were aligned in a regular fashion; in the welcoming water of the river their mirage idled, in accord with the day of rest—which was also attested by the boatman sitting on the parapet of the bridge, his legs dangling down, who offered me an excursion on the Leta.

The languid river was not flowing. It extended between the quays and the trees, then turned slowly, attentive and torpid, between open banks, level with the grass of a meadow dominated, in the distance, by a shadowy forest set against a sky already nuanced by dusk.

The clock on the bell-tower chimed five o'clock; a leaf detached itself from a small elm, spun, settled on the water and remained motionless there. I went down to the boat and it cast off smoothly.

The two rowers cut into the smooth and compact water with the strokes of their oars; the angular wake of the boat broadened out to the banks. There, a single blade of grass stirred, or, in a patch of reeds, one alone—the tallest—oscillated for a long time.

In front of me was the silent avenue of the river, the quietude of its flow or the attraction of its bend; then, the landscape toward which I was heading separated its ensemble as I approached. It divided in two and slid by to either side, in files of trees and meadows, the foliage corresponding or alternating on one bank or the other. Their double passage was reconstituted behind me, if I turned my head to see them: a renewed orderliness and surprise, whose aspect was further modified as I progressed toward that which furnished the raw material of its variety and its changes, which was: meadows of vaporous grass brushed by wisps of mist; roads bordered with poplars, reeds and irises with flexible sword-like leaves. All of it was reflected in the precise water, and, although the daylight was only just beginning to diminish, the silence was that of the calmest of evenings. The marbling of the cloud-patched sky spread opaque metallic plaques over the water, which, weighed down, seemed to be descending between its banks.

It descended to the extent that the riverside verdure loomed up even more. The proximity of increasingly numerous tall trees imprinted them with an excess of gravity. Porches of shadow were hollowed out there; darkness roofed grottoes, on the threshold of which the final gleam of the sky on the water faded out, and the river went into the forest, all its water ebony, along with the boat, in which I could no longer see the wood of the oars in the hands of the rowers, whose gestures were now enigmatic, and seemed to be desperately imploring the subterranean terror of some Styx.

They had being rowing for a long time, and eventually stopped to rest, in accordance with the curiosity of the location. Then, the boat was neatly embedded, as if welded to its reflection in the petrified water, into which water dripped from the oars, the droplets counting out the silence measured by their scrupulous clepsydra, one drop at a time.

Perhaps the evening had not so much arrived as I had gone into it. It resided in the forest, and there seemed akin to the heavy riverside foliage. The location was taciturn, and the boat became obstinately sedentary, at a place where the river, broadening out into a lake, seemed to come to an end, black, formless and stable, and, without continuing its course, to deepen indefinitely, superimposing its waves upon one another and accumulating them within itself.

While the spectacle of my excursion had changed with the increasing dusk, and ended in near-darkness, my mental tranquility had degenerated, through all the nuances of melancholy, into a kind of anguish. I was about to instruct the boatmen to go back, and to quit that solitary basin, which only mirrored a silence that was the soul of shadow, when I perceived a house, off to one side in a little cove. It was sad, enclosed and charming, to the extent that I conceived a desire to go into the garden surrounding it to pick a few of the beautiful roses that were growing there. I would breathe in their odor during my return along the bleak watercourse that had brought me this far.

A woman came out of a small outbuilding and invited me to visit the dwelling, which she was looking after. Isolation and the difficulty of gaining access to the cottage had, she confessed, deterred purchasers—although, she added, people often came to see the ruins.

"What ruins?"

"Those of the château, Monsieur—that of Seigneur de Carnoët, Bluebeard."[3]

---

[3] Although Gilles de Rais is commonly offered as the inspiration for Charles Perrault's character *Barbe-Bleue* [Bluebeard], he has a more plausible rival in Breton legend in Commore the Accursed, Sieur de Carnoët, who allegedly lived near Quimperlé in the sixth century. The legend of his six wives was transfigured in a children's story by "Lizzie" Champney, "The Bubbling Teapot" (1883) before being more widely publicized by Ernest Afred Vizetelly in his book *Bluebeard* (1902). Although the latter was written in English, Vizetelly was one of Émile Zola's translators, and Régnier might have been acquainted with him. Régnier and Vizetelly might both have played a part in helping to inspire Anatole France's ironic

Her face was calm beneath her white peasant's bonnet, and her benign mouth wore a semi-regretful smile. The large cape that enveloped her body fell in grave folds.

With the immutable costume of the region, she resembled her forebears, and in that singular retreat on the threshold of olden times, she appeared to me as a contemporary of the Sire, legendary in his tragic history.

His abode!

And I thought about the high tower, the beautiful dresses with golden embroidery, stained with blood, the supplications of sweet pale lips, the brutal fist twisting the long tearful tresses, the fatal sequels to insidious and tempting wedding ceremonies, the echo of which I had heard in that day's festival bells, and of which I had respired the memory in the nave of the old Church, along with the incense.

It was doubtless in a dusk similar to this one that Sister Anne, who had only seen the sun through a dusty haze throughout the day, wept because no one had come for her, for whom the inexorable hour was nigh.

The high tower from the summit of which the anxious Watcher had interrogated the circuit of the vast horizon of the forest, the deserted roads and the two banks of the river, was the same one whose black debris I had glimpsed in front of me. It was the only part of the ancient château that had survived the collapse of the prideful dwelling, and of its own decrepitude, nothing survived but the section of crude stone wall that loomed up in the shadow.

It was standing on a mound of grass and moss, cloaked with ivy that was eating away at its base, climbing over it walls, penetrating its joints and spreading out in its fissures, and its solid mass impressed its image on the surrounding forest.

---

augmentation of the legend in "Les Sept femmes de Barbe-Bleue" (1909; tr. as "The Seven Wives of Bluebeard").

The surrounding ground was uneven, depressed or raised up according to whether there had been a moat there or a wall. Destruction is various in its character; sometimes, that which falls slowly fades away, gradually crumbling and disappearing, instead of lingering in recalcitrant ruins that resist time, disputing its disintegration and heaping up its fall in a brute mass whose raw material the earth cannot repossess without remaining hunchbacked, deformed by the difficulty it has in reabsorbing them or covering them poorly with its verdure.

The almost complete obscurity had become a presence, by virtue of the aspect that debris had taken on in order to gaze at me with all the opacity of the old granite mass, which summarized the darkness within itself and gave it form.

It was impossible that ghosts did not wander around those stones, and I could not imagine them as other than gentle, melancholy and naked: stripped of their dresses, hanging from the wall of the sinister redoubt, where the successive blood of five wives had reddened the flagstones!

How else could they have wandered than naked, since their beautiful dresses had been the reason for their death, and the sole trophy that their singular husband wanted to retain of them?

Had not one of them perished—the first—because her dress was as white as the snow that the unicorns in the tapestries of the bedrooms were trampling with their crystal hooves as they moved through gardens beneath castles, drinking from jasper bowls and kneeling before Ladies allegorical of Wisdom and Virtue? Had another not died because her dress was as blue as the shade of the trees on the grass in summer, while the garment of the youngest, who also died, gently and almost without weeping, imitated the hue of the little mauve seashells that one finds on the grey sand of distant shores by the Sea? Yet another had her throat slit. An ingenious artifice had disposed her adornment in such a way that branches of coral prettified the fabric with arabesques, changing the appearance of its shades, in order that a bright pink might be edged with vivid green, and that they might sharpen or soften when it became prasine[4] or glaucous. Finally, one—the fifth—enveloped herself in a sheet of ample muslin, so light that by means of overlapping or redoubling, it appeared according to its thickness or transparency to be the color of dawn or dusk.

All dead, the sweet spouses, with screams, beseeching hands or stupefied and silent surprise.

The bizarre and bearded Seigneur loved them all, however. They all passed through the door of the manor to the sound of flutes playing beneath the arcades of flowers where, in the evening, to the cry of clamoring horns among the torches and the swords, all come from distant lands where he had sought the out, all timid because he was arrogant, amorous because he was handsome, and proud to confide their languor or desire to the grip of his hand.

Whatever cheerful, melancholy or sweet memories they had left in the natal dwelling, where, from the bud of their childhood, their abundant youth had bloomed, neither their mothers' tears not the sobbing of their old nurses had been able to prevent them from leaving, in order to follow, at a distance, the fiancé of their destiny. One leaves everything for love, and, in drawing away, one scarcely turns back to look once again at some ancient palace on the river's edge, with its terraces in quincunxes, its lawns in guilloches and its trees in rows. Soon, they barely remembered an ancient and pompous house in the corner of the city's main square, but neither the medallions of the façade from which grotesque faces grimaced, nor the knocker on the old door, which was warmed by the midday sun.

They forgot the little manor in the midst of meadows, among the pools where the frogs croaked in the evening when it was going to rain, and also the beautiful château and its forest domain. There was even one, who came from overseas, who no longer thought of the abrupt and sandy island whose rocks were eroded and beaches battered by the sea, and which,

---

[4] The particular shade of green manifested by a leek.

in winter, was tormented by the wind, persistent against its solidity. She scarcely gave an occasional thought to a certain little sandy beach where she had played with her sister, when the tide was low, and where they had been so frightened at dusk.

Alas, he only loved them for their various dresses, those meek or haughty wives, and as soon as they had fashioned the fabrics that clothed the grace of their bodies, and impregnated the with the perfume of their flesh, communicating enough of themselves for them to have become, as it were, consubstantial, he killed the unnecessary Beauties with a cruel hand. By means of destruction, his love substituted for the worship of a living being that of a phantom made of her essence, of which the vestige and the mysterious delight satisfied his industrious soul.

Each of those dresses inhabited a special room in the château. The ingenious Seigneur shut himself up, for long evenings, alternately, in one of those rooms, in each of which a different perfume burned. The furniture, matching the wall-hangings, corresponded to the subtle intentions. For a long time, passing his hand through his long beard, sprinkled with a few silver threads, the solitary Lover gazed at the dresses hanging in front of him, in the melancholy of its silk, the pride of its brocade or the perplexity of its moiré.

Appropriate music was played outside the walls. Around the white dress (O tender Emmène, that was yours!) prowled the slow chords of a languid viola. Accompanying the blue (which was yours, naïve Poncette!) oboes sang. Near yours, melancholy Blismode, a lute sighed, because it was mauve, and your eyes were still lowered. A fife laughed shrilly as a reminder that you were enigmatic in your coral- spiced green dress, Tharsile! But all the instruments came together when the master visited Alède's dress, a singular garment that had always seemed to clothe a phantom; and then the music whispered, very quietly, that Bluebeard had loved Alède very much. She was Sister Anne's twin; it was possible to mistake one for the other, and it was both of them that he desired the new wife to resemble—for they are six, those ghosts, who wander in the evening around the ancient ruin, and only the last is clothed.

That is because, little shepherdess, you guarded your sheep on a moor of pink heather and yellow gorse, on the edge of the forest, standing or sitting among your flock, in your large cape of coarse wool, which sometimes sheltered a fearful lamb from the wind.

Beautiful eyes make the simplicity of a face more beautiful, and yours were such that the widowed Seigneur, having seen you as he passed by, loved you and wanted to marry you. His beard was entirely white then, and his gaze was so sad, O Shepherdess, that he moved you more than he tempted you with the adventure of being a great Lady, and living in the château where you tell the time by the shadow of the towers in the forest.

No hint of the noble Sire's bad reputation had reached the solitude of the little guardian, for she was humble and poor, so no one deigned to take to her, and, being proud, she did not interrogate those who went past her isolated thatched cottage between two old elms, against which her sheep rubbed themselves, wearing away an necklace of bark. In any case, she did not regret being what she was, since she was in love; although she would have liked to be able to buy a new dress for the occasion of her imminent marriage, she consoled herself with the thought that her lover never showed any sign that her woolen cape and cotton bonnet displeased him.

At dawn, a fanfare of horns awoke the forest, and four banners, deployed simultaneously at the summits of the four towers at the corners of the manor, undulated in the morning wind. A rumor of celebration filled the vast dwelling. The corridors were abuzz; in the courtyard, horses pawed the ground, some covered with gaudy blankets, others bearing complicated saddles, the strongest skirted with steel mail, and each of them having a beautiful rose mounted of the forehead. In a corner, a few musicians dressed in yellow smocks, were standing with their backs to the wall, quietly rehearsing flute preludes.

Finally, the drawbridge was lowered. The cortege emerged. In the lead, men-at-arms dressed in buff leather, carrying baskets of flowers on their long interlaced lances. Then came, in good order, a multitude of valets and braided pages, archers, slingshot-wielders and halberdiers, and virtuosos in groups, the first of whom were blowing into bizarre twisted horns. Their cheeks were inflated, that corpulence nourishing their rubicund faces. A few, agile or thin, were banging copper cymbals rhythmically; the rest played delicate instruments and marched with small steps, their eyes lowered and their expressions attentive. The last preceded an empty litter borne on the shoulders of mulattos and followed, on horseback, by the Lord of the Manor, in a white silk coat embroidered with oval pearls, over which his silvery beard descended. Behind him came a troop of pikemen and musketeers, and, bringing up the rear, the servants from the cellar, the kitchen and the stables extended the procession.

The little cottage at which all that pomp stopped was asleep, the door closed. The sheep could be heard bleating softly in the fold, and birds that had come to perch in the elms or on the roof flew away, frightened by that approach but reassured by the silence of the cavalcade that stood motionless all around. A light breeze stirred the plumes of the helmets, turned over the lace of collars and scattered the horses' manes, but the silence did not prevent a murmur running through the ranks that the person who lived there was a shepherdess named Héliade.

The Sire got down from his horse, knelt in front of the door and knocked three times. The door opened, and they saw the Bride appear on the threshold.

She was stark naked and smiling.

Her long hair matched the golden color of the flowering gorse; the nipples of her young breasts were as pink as the sprigs of heather. The whole of her charming body was simple, and innocence itself, so unaware did her smile seem of her beauty. In seeing her so beautiful of face, the men looking at her did not perceive the nudity of her body.

Those who noticed it were not astonished by it, and no more than a couple of valets whispered to one another. Then, in the ingenious cunning that had suggested to her that she should appear naked, she advanced, grave and victorious, though poor, into the ambush of her Destiny.

The entire town was excited by the ceremony announced for that day. Curiosity was augmented by the fact that, although they knew the harsh Seigneur by virtue of the rigor of his tolls and his demanding taxation, no one knew who was about to go through the doors of the Church with him, as his bride.

The Bishop had only been warned to have his altar dressed for the occasion and to order his most beautiful liturgies, so, without having replied to the imperious mandate of the châtelain, he was standing on the parvis with his miter and crosier, in full pomp, with his cantor and all his clergy, as soon as the bells had signaled, by their peals, the entrance of the procession within the walls.

The people, weary of waiting and considering the lamps lit behind the choir, counting the garlands strung between the pillars and numbering the episcopal entourage, uttered cries of joy when they perceived, at the far end of the main street, above the moving heads, the long lances of the cavaliers marching through the populace, pushing them back to form a corridor and driving them toward the already-crowded square—for good folk love ostentation and this, both martial and nuptial, had excited their curiosity and provoked their collaboration. Thus, they were already pressing around the escort surrounding the mysterious litter from which the strange bride would emerge.

They were amazed to begin with, and thought it some sacrilegious fantasy of the audacious suzerain; but as they were, for the most part, naïve souls, and they had seen figures that resembled this one many a time, painted on stained-glass windows and sculpted on porches,—Eve, Agnes and Virgin Martyrs, equally tender in their flesh and similarly embellished with soft eyes and long hair—their astonishment turned to admiration, in thinking that some celestial benevolence had sent this miraculous Child to reduce the intractable pride and cruelty of the Sinner.

Side by side, she and he advanced into the Church that I had visited a short while before, so peaceful in its meditative dusk. The nave was perfumed and illuminated by candles and sunlight. Midday was blazing through the rose-windows and incandescent stained glass, and the sly and glabrous Clerics thought, in seeing the naked girl pass through their midst, a stranger to their concupiscence, that the Sire de Carnoët was espousing, by virtue of witchcraft, some Siren or Nymph like those mentioned in pagan texts. Had the Bishop not ordered the thurifer-bearers to charge their incense burners, in order that their smoke might interpose itself between the Visitor and the eyes of God and humans?—thus isolating, with its thick veil, the unexpected group that could be seen, through an odorous mist, bowing before the altar: one golden-haired and one silver-headed, beneath the benediction of the long crosier, which consecrated the exchange of the rings.

The shepherdess Héliade, who had married in the nude, lived for a long time with Bluebeard, who did not kill her as he had killed Emmène, Poncette, Blismode and Tharsile, and that Alède he no longer regretted.

The sweet presence of Héliade cheered up the old château. She was seen sometimes, clad in a white dress like those of the Ladies allegorical of Wisdom and Virtue, before whom, beneath the castle walls, the pure Unicorns with the crystal hooves knelt down, sometimes in a dress as blue as shadows on the grass in summer, or mauve, like the shells that one finds on the sand of gray beaches beside the distant Sea, or glaucous and coral-spiced, or in muslin the color of the dawn or the dusk, according to the caprice of its folds, diminishing or augmenting the transparency, but most often covered by a long cape of coarse wool, wearing a cotton bonnet—

for, although she sometimes wore one of the five beautiful dresses that her husband had give her, she still preferred her cape and bonnet to their ostentation.

When she died, after having survived her husband, and the old manor had collapsed, of age and neglect, it was for that reason that she, alone among the ghosts who wandered amid the ancient debris, returned there fully dressed, and that she appeared to me, perhaps, with the features of the peasant woman who had had taken me there that evening, and who, standing on the bank, watched me draw away, to the sound of the oars, over the dismal water and through the taciturn Night.

Eustase and Humbeline

To Ferdinand Herold[5]

Of all those who were enticed to fall in love with the beautiful Humbeline, one alone remained faithful. He seemed to owe that to the perseverance of his passion, rather than to any recompense she might have given him. Nothing having intervened to diminish it, it remained the same, for it is not so much time that wears away our sentiments as the credit that one accords to it, and although the reasons for falling in love are in ourselves, it is from elsewhere that those which cause us to love no longer ordinarily originate.

Humbeline had doubtless held the presence of Eustase the philosopher in too much esteem not to have chosen the best means of conserving it.

Eustase excelled at explaining Humbeline to herself. To him, she was an abbreviation of the whole universe; they were both grateful for that. A gracious exchange was established between them in consequence, and to the extent that she was attentive and benevolent toward him, he was assiduous and circumspect toward her.

Some had been more and less to her than Eustase. They had tried to divert Humbeline from her taste for herself, to the profit of those who had a similar taste. The futility of their enterprise and the rejection of their pretentions had rendered them exceedingly sensible of the check to their demands.

---

[5] Ferdinand Herold (1791-1833) was an operatic composer best-known for *Zampa* (1831), one of several stories based on the mythical motif of a young man who puts an engagement ring on the hand of a statue, which then closes upon it with dire consequences.

Eustase amused himself by consoling his rivals, showing them by example, and trying to prove to them by subtle arguments, what an infirmity there was in wanting to possess the most beautiful things other than by thinking them beautiful, and, as he delighted in allusions, he made use of that means to clarify their folly.

If they came to visit him at home to consult him about their disappointment, he showed them, smiling, and with a delightfully renunciatory gesture, a marvelous item of glassware, which isolated, against the funerary backcloth of an ebony bracket on the wall of his bedroom, his visible prestige.

It was a fragile vase, complicated and taciturn, in a cold and enigmatic crystal; it seemed to contain a philter of some extraordinary power, for its swollen, seemingly respectful paunch was corroded; arborescent vitrifications streaked the interior in the crepuscular translucency of its walls; it was intact and intangible in its slenderness, brittle in its frosty hardness, and so beautiful that the mere sight of it filled the soul with gladness that it existed and sadness by virtue of its sacred reservation.

And to anyone who did not understand the gesture and the emblem, Eustase said: "I found it in the Domain of Arnheim;[6] Psyche and Ulalume have held it in their marvelous hands." And he added, in a whisper; "I haven't drunk from it; it was made to be only ever sipped by the lips of Solitude and Silence."

Dusk entered the spacious and cenobitic chamber. Through the clear windows, the setting sun reddened; it seemed to be doubled; outside, very close to the bloody and sulfurous clouds that were slowly scarring it, and also very

---

[6] "The Domain of Arnheim" (1847) is part of a sequence of stories by Edgar Allan Poe in which the wealthy protagonist creates wondrously beautiful psychologically-symbolic environments; several of Régnier's early stories are closely allied to the sequence. "Ulalume" is the title of one of Poe's best-known poems.

distant in an inclined mirror facing the window, which reflected it. The occidental fervor burned, coldly, in the crystal; it shrank there in miniature, cured of what had been too poignant in the distance, reduced therein to a glacial and mineralized aspect.

That was the moment when Eustase went out every day to visit Humbeline. She lived, alternately and according to the time of the year, in her garden or her drawing-room. The drawing-room, as large as a garden, and the garden, as small as a drawing-room, resembled one another. The soft lawn was smoothed out into a carpet. The water in the pond was reproduced, clarified, in the mirrors of the boudoir, and the wall-hangings represented in interior arabesques the shadow of the leaves outside on the walls of the cottage.

Every day, Eustase went there, as he had the day before, and the charm of the conversation that took place between the young woman and the philosopher was due to the honest exchange they made of the reciprocal utility that they had for one another.

Humbeline freed Eustase from mingling with life. The aspects to be found there were, for him, summarized in the instructive Lady, with all their contradictions and variety. That delicate individual was, in herself alone, an exquisite tumult. All the incoherence of passions existed in her tastes, reduced to minuscule dimensions, and to an infinitesimal but equivalent motion. Furthermore, she offered to Eustase the memory of all the landscapes in which that which our sentiments find in their image strives and extenuates. For their part, her dresses already depicted the nuances of the seasons, and the ensemble of her hair was simultaneously the whole of autumn and all forests. The echo of seas certainly murmured in the naïve shells of her ears. Her hands were florid with horizons whose flexible lines were traced by her gestures.

It was these resemblances that Eustase interpreted for her. He detailed their infinitesimal analogies for her, and gave her the pleasure of having, at every moment, a consciousness of what she was, magnified beyond what she seemed to be.

She thus made contact with the world through every pore of her charming skin and every point of her moist, friable and sponge-like egotism, loving nothing but herself in everything, but in a communicative and amalgamated fashion.

They lived happily thus; she only seeing of everything external to her that which constituted her, and that which she constituted, and he seeing entirety within her.

Sometimes they juxtaposed their steps in a stroll, if she happened to conceive the whim, one evening in spring or summer night, at dusk in autumn or midday in winter. Everywhere, Humbeline moved only through herself; Eustase walked not so much with her as within her. He made delightful voyages there, and on returning, gladly said to her: "The setting sun of your hair was a tragic golden hue his evening, Humbeline!" or gave her to understand that a sleeping serpent was coiled according to the torpid tresses of her gorgonian coiffure.

She laughed, and nonetheless preferred what was slightly enigmatic to her in Eustase's words to the all-too-clear conversations that the lovers she had sent away had imposed upon her.

They took revenge for their dismissal by denigrating the choice that had replaced them. All of them, loving too much, by virtue of jealousy or ill-temper, to admit the principle of reciprocal reserve that the two companions in spirit adopted with respect to the other, and supposing that intimacy to be very different, alleged, as if it were a reproach that menaced its duration, that Eustase had not always been like that.

To be sure, he had once been very different. I know that by virtue of having known him in an era when he believed in life. Like others, he had desired, seen and possessed, and then, weary of being dispersed in his desires, appropriated to their objects, possessed by everything he believed that he possessed, he had made dreams of them, of which perhaps the bitter aftertaste remained of being more identical to those that replaced them than what they had actually been.

Life had cooled and had been deposited within him like a sky in a mirror.

Having suffered from being the intermediary between himself and nature himself, he had made Humbeline his mediator. It was that to which the mirror in Eustase's room made allusion, and the enigmatic item of glassware on the bracket of funerary ebony, in which the vitrified matter fashioned by means of illusion the water of which it was empty—and that was also the referent of what Eustase said, at dusk, about the Domain of Arnheim, Psyche and Ulalume, and what he said about the lips of Solitude and Silence.

Manuscript Found in a Cupboard

To Pierre Louÿs [7]

...Perhaps there is no solitude, and, if solitary individuals are thinking about themselves, deliberately or apathetically, they are not alone. They are looking at themselves in the future or seeing themselves in the past; they are anticipating or remembering. Theirs is a hypocritical solitude. All solitude is hypocritical: is mine any more veridical for being that of someone who appears to be limited to himself? However, I sometimes seem to be alone: the most alone of mortals in the most solitary of dwellings.

I chose an abode in the most deserted of our provinces. Old maps give it a name; very old people still remember having known one. It is a long time after having left any road that one arrives there, and when I lost their last trace I had already passed through places singularly and irredeemably abandoned.

To begin with, along the twisting roadways, the milestones gradually petered out. Those still encountered were cracked and moss-covered. Then the roads changed into paths, which thinned out themselves, hesitantly, and disappeared. The routes exiting from moribund villages skirted villages in their death-throes, and ended beyond the final cottages.

---

[7] Pierre Louÿs (1870-1925) was the Classicist of the Decadent/Symbolist movement, elaborately extrapolating a Hellenistic sensibility in his poetry and prose, much of which is unashamedly erotic. When Régnier dedicated this prose-poem to him, he presumably did so because of its echoes of Greek mythology, but some readers, knowing how the relationship between the two writers developed subsequently, might find a certain ominous quality in it.

Sad and plaintive towns! Packed in a corner of their over-large boundaries, which encircle ruined towers with the superabundant braid of their gnarled walls, the pitiful emaciation of a residential area, they shrivel up in the bottom of the basket of their walls like fruits hardening in a dry and ashy putrefaction. The autumnal wind seems to peck at them, with its dolorous bird-cries, from the entire sky.

In the villages, old hands were no longer able to set the bells in motion in the belfries, which are cracked all the way to the roof, disintegrating stone by stone and tile by tile in the grass. Such collapses were slow and soft, for those ancient stones and old tiles, all furred with moss, made no noise as they fall. They were friable, and ready, on contact with the ground, to revert to the dust that they had been before.

There were still hovels here and there, so wretched that they buckled beneath the branches; their venerable thatch seemed to purr under the caressing fingers of the foliage, and the animal somnolence of their fur of crude straw crouched down.

Afterwards, I went through great forests where, the further I advanced, the trees became stunted before becoming widely spaced and sickly, increasingly rare until they were finally lacking on interminable heaths, all of the same short and shaggy grass.

The river that had bathed the towns, brushed the villages and reflected in its waters the trees of the forest and the reeds of open country, after the steeples and the roofs, ended up fading away through the sands. The sands had insidiously absorbed its course, divided up into arms that had thinned into meanders. Its ultimate waters stagnated in silent pools, a few of which were no longer any more than patches of cracked mud.

It is the plain and the dried-up river that one sees at the far end of the grounds of my domain, through a breach in the trees and walls. No one any longer passes that way who might look inside, at my forest or my house. What does it matter if its rotten shutters no longer close, any more than the windows? This province is deserted and this dwelling is so isolated! There silence here is such that I could almost believe that I'm alone.

Then I lean on the old tome, closed again, in which I have been reading, for hours on end, some scrupulous and baroque treatise, some Mirror of Time or Clock of the Soul. I fix a point for my dreams; my thought is incorporated in the invisible; it clothes itself in formless complacency and constitutes a reality beyond my desires, until my gaze becomes weary; then, eyes closed, I see the debris of the voluntary idol reduce my dream to dust, to the luminous ashes of its artifice, to end in a rain of prismatic stars, powdered gems, and eyespots similar to those which radiate and blink in the visionary tails of peacocks!

Today, I have watched leaves fall into a pool of water, one by one. Perhaps I was wrong to have had any other occupation in my life than that melancholy measuring of time, leaf by leaf, in some bleak and circumspect water. Thus, of the days of my life, I would only have had the memory of the same tree, augmented by a similar one and others in sequence, side by side and face to face, in an alternating and augural avenue, until the conclusion of my past, as far away as my past.

The leaves fall, more frequently; two at once oppose their fall. A slight wind that has got up weighs them delicately before letting them go, weary and useless, one by one. Those which fall into the pool float, then, gradually, become waterlogged, become heavier and partially sink. Yesterday's are like that; there are others wandering beneath the surface. They are visible through the transparency of the glacial water, clear until the bed, scaled by the fraudulent bronze of litter already submerged.

I know the destiny of all those leaves; I know how they sprout and become verdant, how they wither in the days of autumn in spite of the false adornment of the various shades of gold and the hypocrisy of their red patches.

The setting sun is red through the trees; the violet putre-faction of dusk corrodes the dolorous clouds. The hypochon-dria of the moment is almost aggressive.

The lamp is burning in a corner of the vast room with high windows, and I remain there with my face to the dull pane. I can no longer see the leaves falling, but now it is with-in me that I sense something becoming detached and slowly piling up. It seems to me that I can hear the fall of my thoughts in my silence. They fall from a great height, one by one, in a slow leaf-fall, and I welcome therein al the past that is in me. Their light, dead fall no longer weighs anything of what they would like to live. Pride is deciduous, and glory loses its pet-als.

Another day. There's the lamp! I have watched the leaves fall, one by one, and yet there are thyrses in the vi-neyard and the gardens. Lips have sucked the juice of the pears. A child carried golden apples in his hands, and, when his face turned, on the threshold, to face the dusk, a crown of laurels was visible around his temples, while horns sounded in the depths of coves.

In the old cedar in front of the house, near a massive stone table, I can hear the screech of raucous trumpets. The gold of their sound seems disjointed by some rift. The breath therein is sour and discordant. They are mocking the glory they are intoning; they are saying that something considerable within them is abortive, and their hoarseness includes, while falsifying it, a fanfare!

It is the peacocks that are screeching, from their perch in the large cedar near the stone table. They are outlined in black against the dusk, still sulfurous and red-tinted; they are jade against the Etruscan sky; they are black, less as if they were being carbonized by the ardor of the furnaces of the sunset than by the virtue of their own glare and the devouring incan-descence of their plumage.

Black and fateful, do they not seem to be keeping vigil over a tomb? And the stone table is funereal this evening. Its rough-hewn block is sullen and seems weighed down. Will you take apart the oppressive and analogous slab, finally, O mysterious lost one, O subterranean one, who, being more than life, can only be possessed in death, you who are named Eurydice!

It seems so good to me to have known the other side of the river that I have named Eurydice. That name pleases her and she smiled to hear it given, as if it reawakened ancient joys within her. Sometimes, however, she will sigh to hear herself so called, for ancient sadnesses perhaps abide in the depths of her dreams. She was standing between two sequences of echoes; I did not know where they led her memory, for I knew nothing of the avenues of her Destiny, and my love in the face of her beauty was uniquely satisfied therein. I do not want to talk about my love nor discuss sentiments instead of evoking images. There is none more precious in my soul than that of Eurydice. My solitude is made solely for the phantom of her presence, and my silence endures solely for the survival of her voice.

I see again the undulation of her hair on the cushions on which she gladly leans back, for her beauty, like all truly delightful beauty, is not without languor. They were cushions with large ornamental flowers skillfully denatured. Mingled therein were motifs of fruits, pomegranates and tulips. The beautiful fruits were swollen or bulbous and the slender flowers were not so much imitative as logical and rational. Some fabrics were light enough for the interior down to appear therein by transparency: the white down of the swans of Montsalvat, the black stuffing of the swans of Hades!

Toward evening, she untied the hyacinth ribbon that retained her hair, and we sometimes walked in the twilight.

Most often, she wore a bright pale green dress. Silver glints shone in the prasine lucidity of the fabric. Translucent enamel roses ornamented it, which weighed down the folds and imposed a statuesque, seemingly archaic rigidity thereon. A necklace of gems juxtaposed on the skin of her breast the bright droplets of emeralds with the spaciously dead water of opals. Her feet were bare; her dress trailed slightly on the warm sand of the pathways of the garden in which we were strolling. It was an ancient strand, fluvial or marine. Little tortoises with yellow and black shells were walking there. Dwarf lemon-trees grew there. Their fruits were fleshy, acid with a bitter aftertaste.

Eurydice's face was singularly beautiful. It is in all the mirrors of my dreams; it is in your own that it is necessary to look at her, for she is, in every one of us, the eternal taciturnity, the secret resting on its elbows.

We have often contemplated the dusk together, Eurydice and I. At that hour, her name resonated more softly, more melodiously, the syllables being a collision of limpid nocturnal crystal, a fountain in a cypress wood. It was the hour when her name vibrated in its most melancholy fashion. Sometimes, she talked. The soft slowness of her voice seemed to draw away to the distance of a dream. Her voice became very low, as if muffled and lost in the labyrinth of her self, from which her ordinary gentleness gradually returned.

She talked willingly about waters and flowers, often about mirrors and what can be seen in them that is not there. We would also compose strange dwellings, rooms or palaces. We would deduce their possible gardens. She imagined them charming and melancholy. There was one with porphyries that time seemed to have healed of the blood they had shed, marbles, pathways with a poignant geometry, lawns where jets of water spread out, as if broken on the wheel of the sun.

One evening, I remember—it was one of the last times I saw her—she talked to me about peacocks. She hated them, and could never bear their presence in the peaceful and silent places in which we lived so inexplicably. I remember that evening, our meeting and the bleak river on which my boat encountered hers. She was there alone. She was weeping. A peacock had perched on the prow, its head and neck mirrored in the water while its tail filled the entire boat with its dazzling profusion. The sad, pale passenger was sitting among the plumes. The longest were dangling in the water at the rear.

And as that memory, composed of bleak water between old trees, a slow boat, an imperial bird in the dusk, an unknown and silent woman, was dear to me, I put my head, for the sake of melancholy and tenderness, on Eurydice's knees. She supported it with her beautiful hands; she seemed to be weighing it.

I looked into her eyes; an immemorial sadness veiled them, and I heard her say to me, in an ancient voice, so distant that it appeared to be coming from the other side of the river, the other face of Destiny, she said, in an ancient and veridical voice, so faintly that I could hardly hear it, so faintly that I shall never hear it again:

"It was me who, on the river's edge, one evening, lifted up in my pure and pious hands the head of the murdered Singer, which I carried for days on end, until exhaustion halted me.

"On the edge of a peaceful wood where entirely white peacocks were wandering in the shade beneath the trees, I sat down and went to sleep, sensing through my slumber, with grief and joy, the burden of the sacred head that rested on my knees.

"But when I awoke, I saw the dolorous head directing the gaze of its red and empty orbits at me. The cruel birds that had pecked out the eyes were stretching their supple necks around me, and smoothing their plumage with their bloody beaks.

"My reaction was of horror and sacrilege, and as I started, they had rolled among the frightened and taciturn peacocks, which deployed and displayed, without being aware of it, the extraordinary prodigy that they had become, for their plumes bore, from then on and forever afterwards, instead of their whiteness, imaginary eye-spots and vindicatory gemstones, the veridical emblem of the sacred eyes whose mortal slumber they had profaned..."

Hermogenes

To Jean Lorrain [8]

As I entered the forest I turned my head, and, with my hand on the dappled rump of my horse, I paused to gaze over my shoulder through the first trees at the land I had just passed through, in order to try to catch one more glimpse of the house of my master, Hermogenes.

It should have been at the extremity of the bleak, briny and boggy plain that displayed its checkered salt-marsh, flat and far and wide, where roseate puddles reflected and crystallized the rays of the setting sun. The sun blinded me, for it was straight in front of me, and the whole of that broken ground, traversed in the dampness of a autumnal afternoon, was no more, at that hour, than a expanse of gilded mist upon a glitter. The vapor and the glare outside the forest were reemphasized by the demi-obscurity slumbering in the interior of the covert.

Tall pines loomed up from a dull and felted ground, their slender trunks sunlit to mid-height, the shadow increasing as the sun descended over the sea. I could see the sea, smooth on the horizon, beyond the bare plain checkered by the pools in which, so brackish was their lukewarm water, my horse had refused to slake its thirst. It pawed the russet ground of the

---

[8] Jean Lorrain (1855-1906) was a central figure in the Decadent Movement, as a critic, poet and prolific short story-writer; forced to produce at speed when he became dependent on writing for his living he tried out various stimulants, including—with eventually fatal consequences—ether. A sampler of his prose work in translation is *Nightmares of an Ether-Drinker* (Tartarus Press, 2002).

underwood with its hoof, causing the pine-cones with which it was strewn to roll gently down the slope.

They reminded me of those that were burning in the hearth of my master, Hermogenes the other evening, whose delicate scales, where tears of resin scintillated, I manipulated with my fingers, while my host, sitting beside me, told me his story, so quietly that his voice seemed to come from within myself, as if it were to the depths of my own being that he was speaking.

Oh, how often I had thought of him again while riding along the little crackling paths alongside the salty mash-waters. The dampness of the spongy air was so impregnated with salt that my tongue could taste it on my lips. Hermogenes' sadness could certainly not have been sharper or sour-er. He had seemed to me to be retracing the path of his days and I told myself, as I resumed my route through the place that was already darkening; "May I be able to enter the twilight like him! May I be able to sit down at the spring, where there is a hearth for all the ashes of my dreams!"

I had arrived in a part of the forest where it appeared to me in its supreme autumnal beauty. There was a clearing be-tween the tall trees. The foliage was red-brown and gilded, and even though the sun had disappeared, it seemed that a gleam continued in the treetops, where the illusion of its sur-vival persisted by virtue of the tint of its presence. None of the leaves was moving and yet one of them, dull gold in color and already dry, or bright gold and still living, sometimes fell, as if the tiny melancholy sound of the spring in which their suspen-sion was reflected had sufficed to determine, in the silent in-difference of the atmosphere, the pretext for their fall.

I watched those which were falling into the pool of the spring. Two, then others, and one that I felt brush my hand. I shivered, for I was waiting, anxious in the silence, in order to continue my progress, for the cry of some bird to break the immobilizing spell. Everything fell silent, from tree to tree, to such a distance that I felt myself going pale, perhaps less be-cause of the solitude than the caress of the leaf that had brushed my hand, lighter than a dream on the lips of memory itself.

I went closer to the water, instinctively, in order to look at my face in it, and, seeing it pale and perplexed, aged by all that a ripple can add to the nocturne of that which is mirrored within it, I thought of Hermogenes, of my master Hermogenes. I heard his voice again in the depths of my inner being, and it repeated the melancholy story that he had told me, the story that also began at a crossroads in a forest, near a spring in which he could see his face.

By what mysterious ways, Hermogenes said to me, through what pitiless adventures must I have passed, only to have acquired the sentiment of a sadness so immense that it has veiled, by the excess of its bulk, the memory of its origin and the progress of its estate. It oppresses me with the total oblivion of its causes and all the weight its consistency.

Nothing in that dark and secret past is illuminated. Golden blades among the cypresses, rings of joy and alliance lost in seductive waters, torches, on the threshold in the night-wind, smiles in the depths of twilight: nothing illuminates that invariable shadow from which I had come, by laborious paths, to the point at which, weary of a march of which fatigue alone caused me to feel the distance, lost in the forest, I sat down on the edge of a spring, as one rests next to a tomb.

All that I had suffered was dead within me, and I breathed in the odor of the ashes that my memory exhaled. It was certainly mingled with flesh, flowers and tears, for I found therein a triple perfume of regret, melancholy and bitterness. There were echoes in the depths of that interior taciturnity, but they were torpid, and that formless and mysterious past surrounded me with its dolorous darkness. Without knowing its circumstances, I still felt regret, melancholy and bitterness. I would have liked its lips to murmur the cause in my dream; I would have liked to drink from its Lethean lake a memorial youthfulness, as in the water of that spring I perceived myself coming toward me, as silence comes to solitude, each with the desire to learn from the other the secret of their accord.

Was nothing of myself going to appear in my face in the intermediary water, then? My hands reached out their wounded palms toward the reflection. *O my shadow, who appears to me thus, you seem nonetheless to have come from the depths of my past. You must know its ways, mysterious or ordinary, its adventures pitiless or otherwise. Speak! Smiles in the dusk! Golden blades among the cypresses, or perhaps the torch, or the rings...*

A fallen stone had destroyed the mirror, and caused me to raise my eyes. They met those of the Stranger who had thus interrupted my reverie, and who seemed to be following her own, without perceiving my presence.

She was standing in her torn and ash-stained dress, which surpassed the bare foot with which she had pushed the perturbatory stone. A singular curiosity led me to speak to the newcomer. It seemed to me that I would only have to hear what she would say to me to remember. Our Destinies must have touched their lips and hands before separating for some inverse circuit in which they were finally meeting again at a point of their duration. They were two halves of a whole, and my sadness could only be the understanding of her silence.

Yes, my son, Hermogenes continued, she spoke to me. She told me why she had left the town. The life she had led there was loquacious, bombastic and frivolous; a futile slumber. The eve did not fructify any tomorrow therein, and the transient flowers of every day perished. The town was immense and populous. Its innumerable streets intercrossed in a thousand junctions, and all of them ended, via some that opened thereon, in a vast central square paved with marble.

Odorant trees grew here and there between disjointed paving stones, and sculpted a delightful shade there; fresh water sprang forth there amid the moist silence in a crystalline atmosphere. But the square was always deserted; it was forbidden to pause there, and even to cross it. One would have been able to dream there under the trees, drink the water and confront the solitude, but the crowd had to wander incessantly through the labyrinth of dusty streets, between the tall stone houses with bronze doors, amid the different faces and the superfluous speeches.

Oh, sad town! One wandered desperately there, in search of oneself—those, at least, who were not satisfied with arguing on the street-corners, making speeches on the boundary-markers, trafficking over the counters or dancing to the music of tambourines.

The majority were content with that. They came and went without coming together save for the agreement of a bargain or the satisfaction of a desire. A few sages walked there, with mirrors in their hands. They looked at themselves obstinately, trying to be alone, but spiteful children smashed the evidential looking-glasses with thrown stones, and the crowd laughed, thus imposing the authority of its despotism...

As she spoke, it seemed to me that the vision she evoked with disgust was reconstituted in me. I heard it, like a distant interior buzz. It raised memorial and analogous rumors from my past, and I said again, as the Stranger had said: "Let us leave the town, let us abandon the frivolous and vain life..."

She had left one morning, weary of wandering amid the composite and uniform crowd, amid the dust of sandals and the sweat of faces. She passed others beneath the postern, who were coming from elsewhere to increase the number of those living there, and when she was outside the walls, she heard a bird singing in a tree. The pride of being alone exalted her, and she felt herself grow as she isolated herself further.

The hem of her dress brushed flowers, while she descended by charming roads toward the sea. Sandy shores bordered it, roseate in the dawn, which melted into gold at midday and became violet in the dusk.

Oh, dusk on that first day of dreams! Her shadow on the sand told her that she was alone, and that the residue of herself was no more than a phantom at her feet, and it was to her shadow that she sacrificed, thrown into the sea as night fell, the stones of her necklace, which tinkled more melodiously than tears. Her necklace was made up of three kinds of stones, all valuable, and the whole was inestimable. There was, all night, a star over the sea—a star over the sea, until morning!

But I paid even closer attention to what the Stranger was telling me when she told me how the satyrs and fauns stripped her and left her naked in the forest. I understood that her actions and outcomes each represented my thoughts. I understood how I had lived the emblems of her adventures internally. They were what constituted my sadness.

The satyrs had first surrounded her, dancing. The long lush grass had hid the lower halves of their bodies and their prancing bestiality, while their hands offered bunches of grapes, fruits and odorant apples—but their hands had soon become bolder.

It was afterwards that she became a wanderer, entirely devoted to some mysterious and desperate quest: a philter to create souls within the hairy flesh of prowling goat-foots. She lifted up enormous stones with her frail hands but, instead of a balm or talisman, there were toads or stagnant water sleeping there. Snakes slithered under the dry leaves, hatched from golden eggs, which she believed to be those of peacocks or doves; a seething poison, where a remedy had been promised...

My son, Hermogenes said to me, I finally knew the origin and the substance of my sadness by virtue of all that the Stranger had told me. It was necessary for her to come to me for me to obtain, through her, consciousness of my misery. It had seemed immense and confused before; then I found it immeasurable—but, in seeing it more clearly, I recognized that I had deserved it.

One can no longer find oneself once one is lost, and love does not return us to ourselves. Why had I not been one of those cautious sages, who walk about the town with a mirror in hand, in order to try to be alone, facing themselves because it is necessary to live in one's own presence?

Such was the tale of my master Hermogenes and his encounter with the Stranger. He had taken curious lessons from it, because his mind was rational, but he loved to invigorate his reason with allegories. Perhaps he had wanted to make more impact upon me by mingling a fable with his instruction.

His apologue was ingenious and certainly had not been fruitless, for I exclaimed: "Fortunate are those who, like Hermogenes, meet themselves on the path of life through the intermediary of a dream; more fortunate still are those who have never quit themselves, and for whom their own presence has taken the place of the world!"

Night had fallen; my horse was walking over the dry leaves and stumbling over roots. I did not know how to find my way out of the forest and searched the stars, through the trees, for the road to the dawn.

The Tale of the Lady of the Seven Mirrors

To Jean de Tinan [9]

My father's decrepit old age went on for years. His neck oscillated. His shoulders became stopped. Gradually, he bent further over. His legs trembled. He withered away.

Every day, however, he went out alone into the gardens. His footfalls dragged over the shingle of esplanades, the tiles of terraces and the gravel of pathways. He could be seen, minuscule and shriveled, at the far end of avenues, with his thin cloth cap and his vast fur-lined silken overcoats, impaling a fallen leaf with the tip of his long walking-stick or straightening the stem of some flower as he passed alongside a flower-bed.

He slowly made a tour of the fish-ponds. There were square ones, with pink porphyry rims; circular ones, bordered with olive jasper; and oval ones rimmed with blue-tinted marble. The largest of all was surrounded with yellow breccia, and the golden gleams of tench glided therein. The others held red goldfish, carp and strange glaucous fish.

One day, my father could not go out for his accustomed walk. He was sat down in a large red leather armchair and it

---

[9] Jean de Tinan (1874-1898) died tragically young, while apparently *en route* to becoming one of the core writers of the Symbolist school, heavily influenced by Stéphane Mallarmé's aesthetic theories; he was closely involved with the short-lived periodical *Le Centaure*, where this story first appeared in 1896 as "Confession Mythologique" [Mythological Confession]. Régnier did not take offence when Tinan was seduced by Marie, and bemoaned the fate of "*pauvre petit Jean*" with all sincerity.

was dragged to the window; the castors grated on the checkered mosaics, and the old man considered the vast perspective of the gardens and water features for a long time. The sun set, reddening over the monumental gilt of November. The park seemed to be an edifice of water and trees, intact and fugitive. Sometimes a leaf fell into one of the ponds, on to the sand of a pathway, or the balustrade of a terrace; one, driven by a slight breeze, scratched its fleshless bird's wing against the window, at the same time as a bat scraped the darkening sky with its flight.

At dusk, the invalid sighed deeply. Footsteps were audible outside on a nearby pathway; a black swan beat the darkening water of a pool with its palmate feet; a magpie took off from a tree, chattering, and perched, hopping up and down, on the rim of a vase; a dog howled hoarsely in the kennels. Inside, a huge and taciturn item of furniture creaked dully in its skeleton of ebony and ivory, and the thong of a whip with a horn handle, set horizontally on a chair, uncoiled and hung down all the way to the parquet. No breath emerged from the old breast; the head sagged as far as the hands clasping the tortoiseshell snuffbox. My father was dead.

I spent the whole winter in the constraint of mourning. My solitude ankylosed in silence and regret. The days went by. I lived them in a scrupulous attention to that melancholy memory. The time passed without anything being able to distract me from my dolorous and funereal meditation. Only the approach of spring reawakened me to myself, and I began to observe the singularities that surrounded me, and which exceeded the reports that were given to me.

As if the paternal presence had imposed around itself, by its duration, a kind of attitude to people and things, the effects of his disappearance expanded through the surroundings. Everything came apart. Invisible joints cracked in some occult dislocation. The oldest servants died one by one. Almost all the horses in the stables perished; the old dogs in the pack were found eternally torpid, their eyes vitreous and their muzzles buried between their furry paws. The château deteriorated; the roof became dilapidated, the sub-basement cluttered; the trees in the park fell, blocking the pathways and putting horns on the bushes; frost broke the stone of the fountains; a statue fell backwards; and I found myself, in the unusual solitude of the deserted dwelling and the disordered gardens, as if awakening from a long season in which I had slept through the hundred years of the fairy tale.

Spring arrived in gentle showers, warm and precocious, with high winds that shook the closed windows. One of them opened under the exterior pressure. The perfumes of the earth and trees entered in a suffocating gust. The window flapped like a bird's wing; on the wall, the mythological wall-hangings quivered; the jets of water in the tapestries oscillated, and a wrinkle in the fabric made the Nymphs smile unexpectedly and the woolen visages of the Satyrs snigger. I breathed in deeply and I stretched away all the lassitude of winter; my numbed youth shivered, and I went down the stairway of the terraces to visit the garden.

They were admirable in their spring sap, and every day, from one hour to the next, I witnessed the blossoming of their beauty. Foliage accumulated in the crowns of the trees; the golden fins of the tench brushed the swollen water of their ponds; the blue-tinted carp circled the green-coated bronze of the central figure that twisted in the dulcified metal the slenderness of its voluptuous curves; sturdy mosses climbed the smooth legs of statues and secretly insinuated their flesh into the marble; the split sleeve of the Hermes was garlanded; their hollow eyes became velvety with a somber gaze; birds flew from tree to tree, and the composite charm of spring was unified into the harmony of an estival beauty.

Gradually, the azure of the adolescent sky deepened and hung in suspense over the extent of the park, over the grave anxiety of the foliage and over the circumspect dream of the water features. The water of switched-off fountains became still, drop by drop, in the silence; from the beds of the ponds, growths of bright green vegetation enlaced, on the surface, around solitary floating flowers; the flower-bed overflowed into the pathways; the branches of the trees were interwoven over the avenues; green lizards crawled over the warm balustrades of the terraces; and the heavy scent of vegetation was exhaled everywhere.

A kind of superabundant life animated the disorderly park; tree-trunks twisted into near-human statures. Hares appeared; rabbits pullulated; foxes showed their slender muzzles, their oblique march and their plume-like tails; deer took aim with their horns. The old gamekeepers, dead or disabled, were no longer destroying the inoffensive or carnivorous vermin. Winter had broken the fences that separated the gardens from the surrounding countryside, densely forested, chosen by my father because of the very solitude that safeguarded his retreat. It surrounded the grounds with an abundance of enormous trees, uncultivated fields and unknown places.

I wandered along the pathways. The summer was flamboyant; my shadow was so black in the sunlight that it seemed to hollow out before me the effigy of my stature; the grass of the avenues came up to my waist; insects buzzed; dragonflies caressed the water opalized by their reflections. There was no wind; and, in the immobility of their stupor or the posture of their expectation, things seemed to be living inside themselves. The day burned its beauty until the dull consumption of sunset; every day announced itself hotter than the last and suspended in slow dusks the end of its suffocating languor.

A malaise overtook me; I walked more slowly; I interrogated the avenue I was about to venture, the corner I was about to turn; an anxious round-point halted me at the center of its bifurcations, and without going any further I retraced my steps.

Once I had been wandering all day, and was sitting by a pond, gazing into the green-tinted water at the vague Medusan faces configured by the eddies and the serpentine tresses of the water-weeds: fluid gorgonian medallions divined and dissolved, bronzed by the reflections of a green-gold dusk, redoubtable and fugitive. The moment was equivocal; the sta-

tues sank back into the angles of hedges; the silence clenched ⟨
mouth after mouth with a paralyzing echo.

Suddenly, in the distance, far away, a cry rang out, gut-
tural and reduced by distance to a minuscule and almost interior perception: a scream both bestial and fabulous. It was
remote and unusual, as if it came from the depths of the ages. I
listened. Nothing more; a leaf stirred imperceptibly at the top
of a tree; a little water trickled drop by drop through a fissure
in a bowl and moistened the surrounding sand. Night fell, and
it seemed to me that someone behind me laughed.

The next day, at the same time, the cry rang out again,
more distinctly, and I heard it again almost every day; it was
getting closer. For an entire week it had been silent when it
burst forth again, directly to one side, terrible and vibrant,
followed by an abrupt gallop. It was still bright, and I saw,
protruding of a thicket, the naked torso of a man and the leg of
a horse, scraping the soil of the pathway with its hoof. Everything vanished, and I heard in my memory the singular voice,
which seemed to unite in its ambiguity laughter and whinnying...

The centaur walked placidly along the path. I stood aside
to let it pass; it went by, whinnying. In the dusk, I made out its
dappled horse's rump and its human torso; its bearded head
bore a crown of ivy with red berries. In its hand it held a
gnarled thyrsus terminated by a pine cone. The noise of its
amble was stifled by the long grass; it turned round and disappeared. I saw it once more, drinking from a fountain. Droplets
of water pearled its red mane, and that day, toward evening, I
also met a faun; its yellow-haired legs were crossed; little
horns protruded from its low forehead; it remained sitting on
the pedestal of the statue that had fallen over during the winter, and it was tapping its goat-like hooves together, making a
clicking sound.

I also saw nymphs, which lived in the fountains and the
ponds. They raised their blue-tinted upper bodies out of the
water and plunged in again as I approached; a few played on

the edge with algae and fish. Their wet footprints were visible on the marble.

Gradually, as if the presence of the centaur had reanimated the fabulous ancient people, the park furtively filed up with singular beings. To begin with, mistrustfully, they hid from my sight. The fauns ran away briskly and I never found anything in the places where they had stood but their reed flutes, with half-eaten fruits or a split honeycomb. The water of the ponds swiftly covered the shoulders of the nymphs and I was only able to divine their presence by the ripples of their dives and their hair floating among the water-weeds. They watched me coming, their little hands shading their eyes in order to see better, their skin already dry and their long hair still dripping.

The others became bolder too; they circled around me or followed me at a distance; one morning, I even found a satyr lying on one of the steps of the terrace. Bees were buzzing over its hairy pelt; it seemed enormous, and was feigning sleep, for as I passed by I grabbed the hem of my dress with its hairy hand; I freed myself and fled.

After that, I no longer went out, and stayed in the deserted château. The excessive heat of that terrible summer was fatal to my last old servants. A few more died. The survivors wandered around like ghosts; my solitude was increased by their loss and my idleness augmented by their inertia.

The vast rooms of the palace awoke at my footsteps and I lived in then one after another. My father had assembled sumptuous marvels there; his taste delighted in rare and curious objects. Tapestries dressed the walls; chandeliers suspended their proud scintillation of crystalline flashes from the ceiling; groups in marble and bronze opposed on carved pedestals; the squat feet of tall golden sideboards clenched their quadruple leonine claws on the parquets; vases in opaque or transparent substances stretched the sinews of their throats or swelled the amplitudes of their paunches; precious fabrics filled cupboards with tortoiseshell or copper doors. The clutter overflowed. There were glaucous or wine-colored silks, woven algae and embroidered grape-clusters, plush velvets, wrinkled moirés, pale satins sparkling like wet skins, misty and sunlit muslins.

I soon wearied of the spectacle of the tapestries; they represented the singular guests that had invaded the park; porphyry and pewter groups also depicted Nymphs and Fauns. A centaur sculpted in a block of onyx reared up on a pedestal. With their moist grace, their grimacing bizarrerie, their Thessalian robustness, those which had troubled the tranquil waters, those which had haunted the rustic forests and grassy avenues, all of them—all the monstrous life that was laughing, bleating or whinnying outside—were reproduced on the walls in flesh of silk and manes of wool, or lay in ambush, huddle in corners, in the solidity of metal and stone.

The scorching and furious summer had melted in rainstorms when summer arrived. My forehead pressed to the windows. I watched the gold of the park dripping in the sunlight in the intervals between downpours. The numbers of the monstrous guests seemed to increase further. The centaurs now broke cover in herds on to the pathways; they chased one another, prancing or racing. They had been joined by some that were very old, whose mossy hooves stumbled on pebbles; they wore white beards; the rain lashed their hairy rumps and hollowed out the thinness of their torsos. The satyrs, in flocks, gamboled around the pools where the nymphs swarmed in a mingling of blue-tinted flesh and russet hair; I heard the fracas of kicking, the swift trot of little capripedal hooves, the whinnyings, the cries and the discordant concert of muted tambourines and shrill flutes.

In an attempt to thwart the anxious enervation that was irritating my solitude, I tried to distract it by putting on fine clothes and ornamenting myself with jewelry. The trunks contained a considerable quantity of them. I walked through the vast galleries, dragging the sumptuous weight of velvet; but its touch reminded me of the fur of hairy beasts, whose eyes seemed to be watching me through the gems that I wore; I sensed that I was fascinated by the ocular fixity of onyx, palpated by the caress of silks, clawed by clasps, and I wandered, miserable and adorned, through the solitary sequence of the long illuminated rooms.

The autumnal rain and wind grew one evening into a tempest. The old château shook. I took refuge, on my own, in a heptagonal room with walls made of seven huge mirrors, limpid in frames of bright gold. The gusts outside slid through the cracks in the windows and under the doors, causing a large adamantine chandelier to swing, amid the tinkling of its crystal pendants and the vacillation of its candles. I thought I could feel the rough tongues of the wind on my hands; I felt myself gripped by its icy invisible talons.

It seemed that, suffocating in my glaucous satin dress, I was becoming by virtue of its contact one of the fluid and fugitive nymphs that I had seen undulating beneath the green waves, in the transparency of the pools of water. Instinctively, in an interior struggle, I tore away the insinuating fabric in order to defend myself against a mysterious penetration that was making me utterly listless; I gripped handfuls of my hair; my hands drew it out it like floating algae, and I appeared to myself, standing naked in the limpid water of the mirrors. I looked around at my sudden and fabulous statue, standing around me seven times in the silence of the looking-glasses, animated by my reflection.

The wind had fallen silent. The stridor of a claw scratched the glass of one of the tall windows, through which the abruptness of a lightning-flash designed the phosphoric track of the furtive scrape and vanished. I recoiled with horror. At the windows, attracted by the light or chased by the tempest, I saw faces and muzzles stuck to the glass. The nymphs were applying their moist lips, their wet hands and their dripping hair to the crystal; the fauns were putting the lips of their mouths to it and the mud of their fleeces; the satyrs were crushing their pug-nosed faces to its frantically; they were all pressing, climbing over one another.

The vapor of nostrils was mingling with the drool of teeth; fists were clenching bloody fleeces; the grip of highs was squeezing the breath out of flanks. The foremost, climbing on to the sub-basement windows, braced themselves under the pressure of those coming from behind and below; some were crawling and insinuating themselves through the hairy legs that were trampling them, and, in the terror of its silence and the mêlée of its effort, the host of fabulous flocks was kicking and leaping and laughing, collapsing under its own weight and reconstituting itself, only to collapse again; and that horrible bas-relief was swarming behind the fragile transparency that separated me from its sculpture of darkness and light.

Then I evoked, in the tumultuous night, the pikes of gamekeepers, the fists of valets, lashing that bewildered and muddy horde with whips, the great hounds of the pack biting the calves of fauns and the ankles of centaurs; I summoned the horns, the knives, the blood and the entrails of kills, muzzles digging into torn flesh, the measuring gestures, the fresh pelts...

Alas, I was naked and alone in that deserted château, beneath the furious night!

Suddenly, the windows cracked under the monstrous pressure; horns and hooves shattered the windows into shards; a bestial odor invaded the room violently and entered with the wind and the rain, and I saw, by the flickering light of the half-extinct chandelier, the unified rabble of fauns, satyrs, and centaurs hurl themselves upon the mirrors, to extinguish therein every allusion to my beauty—and, in the fracas of the smashed and bloody looking-glasses, hands extended to exorcise the horror of that terrifying dream, I fell backwards on to the parquet.

The Knight Who Fell Asleep in the Snow

To Madame Judith Gautier [10]

I didn't know my father, he said to me, one evening. Someone else took care of me in my childhood, but the first years of my youth were spent in the château that he inhabited and where he lived to old age, mad and hypochondriac, occupied with architectural and hydraulic schemes, the imagination of gardens, summer-houses and fountains. He ruined himself with the structures in question, and when he died, I came to establish myself in this room, which I have scarcely ever left since then. It's there, he added, that a man lived who had no adventures for having been too much a contemporary of a non-existent époque. Hence my solitude, and the appearance of being disdainful of the dictates of fate.

The baseness of its offerings justifies the abstention in which I reserve my condescension. I rapidly limited my desire to certain objects that are more symbolic than material. I arrange flowers here and there. They have no other meaning than themselves, and I like them better for it. I also have a few items of crystalline and prophetic glassware on pedestals. One vase is not sufficient to evoke all the springs from which one has not drunk, although I can see through the windows the icy arabesque designs of shores on which I have not landed and forests in which I have not been lost.

---

[10] Judith Gautier (1845-1917) was the daughter of Théophile Gautier, the great propagandist of "art for art's sake" and pioneer of "Decadent style;" her own works mostly display a lapidary Orientalism; Régnier refers to her as "Madame" because she was married (unhappily) to Catulle Mendès, although she retained her maiden name as a signature.

I also have this portrait on the wall. It is, behind an emblematic and dreamlike appearance, the face of a Destiny. It is in him that I see most profoundly into myself. He is the one who alerted me to myself and it is from the eloquence of his sadness that I have learned the lesson of my solitude. His voice has animated its silence; his hands have locked its doors with invisible keys. They are under the safeguard of his armed gesture and his peremptory eyes. Look at him as I have looked at him, and perhaps he will speak to you as he spoke to me. He is taciturn but he is not mute, for portraits speak, and if they do not express themselves by means of their painted lips, one hears them nonetheless. They are, in a mirror fashioned by the frame around their reflective glass, the almost-supernatural duration of someone who is behind us when we gaze at his appearance, who is perhaps within us, pale and a flower of dreams!

For a long time I have scrutinized that bleak and naked face, that dolorous face with the sad eyes. The slightly-inflated lips are swollen by a grave sulkiness. A meditative face of desire and mortification, in accord with those hands, gripping their lassitude in the crucial hilt of the long sword. The feeble, melancholy hands will never lift it again. Their gesture of exhaustion has renounced twisting the torpid flash of metal that runs gently along the ridge of the triangular blade.

There is no justification for the warrior costume whose breastplate stiffens that sickly torso. The shiny gleam of the polished armor seems to melt into long white tears, and beneath that bellicose clothing, beneath all that false appearance of continued strength, from the depths of being, life and destiny, one senses the suffocating moisture of a sob rising to that naked face, so much so that the hands on that superfluous sword manifest an attitude that is resigned not to persist in handling the useless burden any longer, heavier than strength and taller than the stature of the man who is measuring himself against it and succumbing thereto.

For a long time I have thought about that face and that body, which is only still rigid because of its inflexible accoutrement of armor, only upright because of the sword on which it is leaning. Even his helmet, which lies beside him, demonstrates that at least he did not want to die behind the mask of its visor, giving passers-by the illusion, by means of his bearing, that he was what he seemed to be; that he did not want to die in that rigorous posture of iron, the lie of which he would have cast down had he not been too late in breaking its irreparable spell; that he did not want to die without revealing himself to everyone by means of the veridical nudity of his face!

What was he, in his time, that authentic human being whose emblem survives in the appearance of what he had been? The old Chronicles cite his name and record his history: that of his deeds, which it is sufficient to interpret to have a sense of his soul. He lived in a century of violence and guile. He acted by means of speech and the sword. He sullied himself simply with all human actions, without being more avaricious or less brutal than those he robbed or vanquished. If defrauded or deceived, he altered the weight of the false balance. He employed himself in that which life demands of any man, to that which is called living, and the narrators of his deeds say, after having described and evaluated the epoch, that he died in consequence of languor for having, one cold night, in the mountains into which he had led his soldiers, lain down in the open air in the snow...

O my brother of the olden days and the present, it is that night of your life on which I shall meditate forever, that night when you were the man who slept in the snow. It was then that you understood the meaning of your past, the ignominy of your desires and the opprobrium of your sad days.

You have the face of someone who has looked himself in the face. The pure, cold and chaste snow taught you the regenerative lesson of its whiteness. It infiltrated the steel joints of your pride; its brought tears to the iron visage of your pride; it buried within you, beneath its shroud, the primitive and rugged mass of your faults as it leveled around you with its slow fall the facial cracks of old stones and the sharp blades of sterile grass.

Woe to the man who gambles his life on his desires. There are sometimes mysterious encounters in destiny; there are mirroring spaces beneath our footsteps in which we see ourselves entirely, instead of the dull disturbed marshes that were the color of our eyes; there are within us snowflakes of purity and dream, which extinguish the lukewarm ashes of the fires at which we warm our chilly and scabrous hands.

Alas, pure knight, at the dawn of the night of redemption, you were unable to bear the intimate bounty, and before the all-white landscape, tranquil and purified, you shivered forever at your past; you trembled in the wan fever of that which you were, and felt growing within you, as on a supernatural tomb, the internal and funeral lily, whose evangelical sap your being could no longer nourish and whose stem extended its blossoming flower, visibly, outside your armor, in the morbid and desperate grace of your visage: its flower with the cold petals of your naked hands.

It was then that, brought down again from the snow of the mortal summits and returning to the dead cities of your ancient dreams and the deserted palaces of your old desires, among the luxuries and vainglories of your former ideas, you languished for days in the slow death-throes compounded of the shame of that which you were no longer and regret for that which you could not be.

Your pernicious past survived too well in you for any contrary future not to perish by the contagion of its contact, and you suffered thus, ensheathed by the base of brutal substance of your self, overcoming it nevertheless by means of the pure visage of your sadness.

You were suffering thus when the painter represented on his anonymous canvas the emblem that you had become. It is that portrait which ornaments the wall of my room. It has alerted me to myself; it has spoken to my solitude the entire doctrine of its sadness. It is that which has instructed me not to adventure outside oneself—for all footsteps march over the snow, and are effaced there so quickly by the slightest wind that one cannot return to one's point of departure.

So, when evening comes beyond the icy windows, in the arborescence of forests and the arabesques of imaginary shores, and an imperceptible regret saddens me, never to have landed there and never to have slept there, I gaze, while delicately handling the prophetic and empty glassware in which my dreams of thirst and philters amuse themselves, I gaze, at the wall above the flowers on the sideboard, at the taciturn antique portrait, upright in the icy arms of his frame of tortoiseshell and ebony, with his pale face and his sword, of the knight who went to sleep in the snow.

The Living Doorknocker

To André Lebey [11]

I was born and grew up in this house. Nothing has changed since the most ancient times of my memory: always those vast bedrooms and spacious halls, those same bizarre corners, all that singular labyrinthine complication of vestibules, corridors and landings in a solid architecture, behind the long façade of gray stone overlooking the square, indifference gleaming in its windows and the precise blinking of its skylights. On the vaulted and tiled ground floor two unequal stories were superimposed, the first with arched ceilings, the second with its mansards.

That is where I was born, and where I lived. The curiosity of my childhood and the desires of my youth develop there, step by step. I have climbed those stairways a thousand times; I have opened all the doors. No, though! For two remained closed, at either end of the house: those of the rooms where my mother and my father died before I knew them, she put to sleep in the flower of her youth by the surprise of Death, he not before having slowly suffered meticulous tortures.

No portrait of them remained to me—nothing except, of one of them, a study full of books, mirrors and swords, and of the other, a gallery filled with display-cases of seashells, with cupboards full of lace and embroideries, and tables with mosaic tops. As for the keys to the mortuary apartments, they had

---

[11] André Lebey's writing were mostly political and historical, although they include a long account of the Breton legend of Mélusine; he eventually became a socialist *député*, but in his early days, he was a contributor, alongside Régnier and Pierre Louÿs, to *Le Centaure*.

long ago been thrown into the deep pond in the middle of the garden.

That garden is singular too; you shall see it shortly, very nearly as it has always been. High walls surround it on three sides and weld it to the house. It is not vast; it is square; arcades of old box-trees line the wall and form two niches at the far corners in which there are two figures, one of a Faun crushing a bunch of grapes under his hoof, the other of a Centaur rolling a waterskin with his. In the center there is a pond, also square, with raised edges of green-tinted stone, in the middle of which, on a pedestal set in the water, stands a green bronze statue of a naked man who seems to be listening attentively to the surroundings.

As there are neither trees nor flowers in the garden, dead leaves and petals do not fall into the water; it shines, bright, profound and black; when one walks around it one can see therein the mirage of the statue, which follows you, and always seems to be looking at you, for it has four identical faces on four bodies, which, by an artifice of optics, are the same one, taking turns.

I have often wandered in that garden; the sun scarcely gets into it; the rain makes the box-trees green and enables snails to crawl there. The place was always sonorous and extraordinarily silent; the water stagnated there without the noise of a fountain. I spent many hours walking between the high walls of that promenade; on leaving it to go back into the house, I found the same solitude from room to room.

During the winter months I sat by the fireside. The warmth of the flame shriveled the bindings of old books or melted the wax of seals at the bottom of parchments. Sometimes, I got up in my isolation to go to visit, in the rooms they filled, the swords and the seashells; I took one of them down from a panoply or took one of them out of a display case.

The sword was heavy or light; the blade, drawn from its sheath, bright or sharp, flat or sinuous; I stood there for a long time, weapon in hand, upright, immobile, lost in a violent reverie.

The shells were interesting; I weigh their fragility care-fully; some of them were cunning and confidential; some still contained grains of sand; they were bizarre and eloquent; I applied my ear to them, listening to the sound of the sea there-in, for a long time, indefinitely, until dusk. The murmur seemed to come closer, to grow, and ended up deafening me, filling me up entirely, to the extent that once, I had the impres-sion of a wave enveloping me, submerging me. I dropped the shell, which broke.

I did not go back again to the gallery, and similarly neg-lected the study with the swords, because of a mirror in which, having seen myself face to face, I had instinctively crossed swords with myself.

From then on, I did not go down to the garden as fre-quently, and spent my days at the windows of the façade, gaz-ing into the square.

The inhabitants went by without even glancing at the house. No one knocked at the door, knowing that it was in-exorably closed; only vagabond beggars or colporteurs occa-sionally lifted the knocker. The merchants in question sold popular images, gaudily colored, romantic and brutal, of fam-ous adventures, dramas in *complaintes*,[12] all of life. They let the wrought-iron hammer fall back with all its weight; the dwelling resounded with the blow; all my solitude shivered, and, in that dull reverberation I evoked the provocative sound of a horse's hoof, the departure, the gallop, the foam of the bit, the wind in the mane...

That doorknocker was rather remarkable, more so by vir-tue of the rumbling summation in its knock of some abstinent Destiny than by its form and singularity. It represented, in iron, the upper body of a woman, terminating in spirals. She

---

[12] *Complaintes* were intimately associated with the uniquely French institution of the *images d'Épinal* that were a key ele-ment in the stock-in-trade of *colporteurs*, providing the cap-tions for the pictures reproduced on the cards, in verses adapted to the tunes of popular songs.

had an expression of dolorous fury, her hair scattered, her bosom heaving, her throat suffocating, her lips twisted; she clenched her mute anger in the somersault of the metal, and stiffened her frantic and captive expression therein.

The days succeeded one another; my solitude, a prisoner of itself, stuck its face to the windows; with my forehead against the glass whose immobile transparency separated me from outside, I sometimes thought I felt the glass melt like ice, and my tears ran down my cheeks; sometimes, too, it seemed that all the crystal cracked and shattered as if struck by a stone from a slingshot.

One evening, at dusk, when no beggars or colporteurs had come into the square all day, and the knocker had not resounded once, as I was about to quit the window from which I had been following the fluttering of a bat, flying in the twilit sky or skimming the paving stones like a temporarily dead leaf. I saw a woman passing by. She looked at me.

I followed her, I followed her, I followed her! Oh, Monsieur, I can still hear in my memory the sound of the door which, having hurtled downstairs like a madman, I slammed behind me. It seemed to me that, in response to the impact, the house collapsed into rubble forever, that nothing existed any longer but that passer-by walking along the deserted street, who turned round and smiled at me.

Her gaze was like a sword-blade, her voice like the profound sound of the sea in a shell. Sometimes, she laughed, prettily. Her naked beauty was the statue of love; her flesh seemed as if it were standing over an eternal dawn. We went from town to town; with her I walked through wheatfields; I bathed in icy lakes and lukewarm rivers. There were great storms that ripped the sky apart with lightning, as if its overheated and sulfurous tresses were exasperating the congestion of the clouds and determining their crisis.

Her smile had all the beauty of spring. She scorched me with the embraces of summer and corroded me with the rust of autumn.

Through her, I knew all tenderness and all suffering. She put the song on my lips, the wrinkles on my forehead, the wound in my heart; she was my life.

We sat down in dives where the redness of the wine in the glasses announced that blood was about to flow. Desire rumbled around us. One night, by the light of torches, in front of the seated drinkers, I kissed her on the mouth. Swords were drawn; someone was killed. The murder peppered her face with droplets and she laughed, standing upright in the sanguinary coquetry of that ferocious adornment.

All the angers entered my soul; insidious or violent, they would whiten my hypocrisy or redden my brutality.

I have dragged her by the hair! How she wept, that evening! It was beside a green-tinted marsh, near yellow rushes, beneath a gray sky. We were waist deep in the mud into which we had rolled. The water reeked of rotting reeds and moss. The rain washed the mud of our embrace from our faces; but when we returned to the palace, the muddy footprints on the floor-tiles followed us like toads crawling on our heels.

It was a festival of gold and joy! She danced until dawn; a thin fabric stuck to the sweat of her breasts. All of her flesh subsided, breathless and hot; she roamed the streets drunkenly and, as I loved her, I struck her in the face.

Then we lived on the bank of a river. She cultivated a little garden where a few roses and gladioli grew; she was as sweet as happiness.

I followed her—I also followed her through the back streets of a foreign town, one evening when she hugged the walls furtively. I had been on the lookout for her treason. Her hand already on the secret key and her foot on the adulterous threshold, on perceiving me she turned round so abruptly that her mantle came undone and uncovered her breast; she backed up against the door, arrogant and spiteful, her hands forming claws. I seized her by her throat, arm with lust. We fell silent; her body clenched; she choked; her eyes grew wide, her mouth twisted and became moist with pink saliva. An occasional convulsion. The toe nail of her bare foot scraped on the stone.

73

When I sensed that she was dead, without ceasing to strangle her, I kissed her bloody lips.

I let her go. She remained upright for an instant, then collapsed. The folds of her mantle covered her again of their own accord, and she was no more than a gray mass from which a pale hand emerged, the fingers open, in a little pool of blood.

I walked for a long time through open country until I arrived at the edge of the sea. I had never seen it before but I did not even look at it. It seemed to me that I already carried it, in its entirety, within me, with its rumble, its sigh, its bitterness, its changing hues, from the soft pleated lips of the waves licking the cheeks of the sand to its foaming mouths, biting the contracted face of the rocks. The more I walked beside its murmur, the further it seemed to draw away from me; peace entered into me.

With every dawn it increased; I wandered for a long time; the wheat turned yellow, the trees lost their leaves, winter came; I wept when I saw that the snow was falling and took the road back to the house where I was born.

I found the large square again, the gray faced, the door.

The knocker was tensing its female torso there. I recognized it. The figure seemed to me to be a simulacrum of my past, hardened there, miniaturized in its metallic effigy. It was surely the same figure that had once, warm and living, on a tragic evening, agonized in my grip; the bare breast was swollen by the same sigh, the dolorous and frantic face was suffering there, but the mouth and eyes were closed in a definitive and minuscule repose.

With an indifferent hand I lifted the cold torso of worn metal. The hammer resounded, and I went back into my dwelling forever.

That is why, Monsieur, I shall die in the house where I was born. I can see it, tranquil in my mind's eye. I have been exorcized of myself in being summoned outside. It is necessary to have kissed life on the lips and to have seized it by the throat to be free of its phantoms.

I answered the appeal of my Destiny; it has ceased to summon me. Now that I no longer look out of the windows, I no longer handle the swords. I no longer listen to the shells; I no longer hear anything therein. My deafness is full of the intimate voices of my silence.

At dusk, I stroll in my garden. The green stone Faun who is crushing a bunch of porphyry grapes seems to have fallen asleep in his drunkenness; he has fallen over. The Centaur who was kicking a water-skin is also broken; his rump destroyed, he remains a smiling man; and the quadruple bronze statue that stands on a pedestal in the middle of the pond no longer seems attentive to anyone but itself.

The Unexpected Cup

To Fernand Gregh [13]

Passer-by, accept this cup from my hand. The crystal is so pure that it seems to be fashioned from the very water it contains. Drink, slowly or swiftly, according to your thirst. The day was hot, for the dusk remains so warm that one might believe that the day is not dead. By which road have you come? Did you come via the river-bank, or the salt-marshes, or the beaches of the sea? Have you broken reeds, marched through mud or trodden soft sands? You've been a long time coming; that's why you've encountered me. I dread the daylight. Only travelers in the dusk encounter me. I dread the daylight.

My dress falls in less harmonious folds along my emaciated body; if my hair still seems rich and red, it's the adornment of its autumn. The make-up on my face makes it resemble an overripe fruit; my smile no longer completes itself without becoming a wrinkle. Don't look at me; drink and turn away. I'll shut up; you can listen to the spring running. If the beverage I offer you refreshes you, be grateful to the spring.

Sit down for a moment on the stone rim and think about the Nymphs that inhabit it. Don't think that I'm one of them,

[13] Fernand Gregh (1873-1960) was at the very outset of his career when this dedication was made, although he had founded a periodical, *Le Banquet*, in 1892, which published early work by several of his school-friends, including Marcel Proust. Régnier could not know when he made the dedication that Gregh would explicitly renounce Symbolism in 1902 in order to found his own (far less successful) "humanist" school of poetry.

and know what I have been. It's not a vain tale; you'll learn one of the secrets of happiness from it, and perhaps the true meaning of love. Listen to me speak without raising you eyes, weary traveler, and when I've finished speaking, you'll no longer be able to see me. Darkness gathers quickly; I'll retreat into it as it grows, and you'll be able to continue on your way under the stars, while remembering meeting me by the spring in the forest.

Every year, the birds, in their autumnal migratory flights, passed over the town in which I lived. It was a few days after their annual departure—perhaps they had already crossed the sea—when the man who loved me died, slowly. The patience of his smile lasted until his death. A sadness spread over his dear face. The hypocrisy of his generosity could not survive him, alas, and I understood that he had not been happy.

We had fallen in love gradually. Our houses faced one another. For a long time he passed in front of my windows, and as I was beautiful, I gazed at him. One day, not seeing me, he came in. I was spinning yarn in the little interior courtyard. The hum of the spinning-wheel mingled with the cooing of doves on the rim of the roof; sometimes, a feather fell; above us, swollen clouds filed across the square of warm blue sky.

He came in and at down beside me; he came back every day. He was my entire soul. He knew that, and we talked about it. He possessed all the keys to my thoughts and we lived in the communal divination of ourselves. He was my spiritual master, but our lips, which said everything, never touched. His, however, gradually became paler; his smile became painful, but retained its moistness, and if it had persisted on is dead face, I would have been forever unaware of the irreparable wrong of my crime and my folly.

I discovered it, but too late, alas. I injured his expectation with useless gifts. Love is similar to itself and the reciprocity of our sentiments annulled its prize. The effigy alone would have differentiated the same metal whose vain coins we blindly exchanged. What did the connivance of our thoughts matter? Is there nothing in a woman's soul that does not exist in a

77

man's mind? Why did I refuse his caresses? Why did I not animate with my breath the mysterious statue that our mutual love fashioned, gropingly? Oh, how he wished for that in the silence of his desire and the secret of his covetousness!—but I had not understood the mute demand of his lips, which only touched mine when dead, dead to them forever!

It is my mouth that I ought to have offered to his, and my flesh and my hair and my fingernails. He would have savored the freshness of my skin and the perfume of my beauty. Naked, I would have inhabited his dreams after having shared his bed, and I would have left in his memory something akin to an imprint of my body in sand.

Oh, sands, sands, sands of the Styx, black sands of eternal shores, you shall soon cover my slumber when I descend toward your banks, of which I already hear the fatal and subterranean sound beneath my feet.

My life is ending; I have lived, day by day, in the horror of redeeming my sin. To punish myself for an imbecile and involuntary refusal, I have abandoned my body to the vulgar arms of passers-by. All those traversed, within my sight, by a flash of desire have slaked it freely on the offer of my kindness.

They were numerous, those who tasted the repentant gift of myself. Some of them were heavy with wine, which confused their kisses with the hiccups of their drunkenness; others, emaciated by hunger, gorged themselves on the fruits of my breasts. Some embraced me at hazard, on the impulse of their caprice; others exhausted the tenacity of their obstinacy on me. I satisfied the hastes of passion and the persistences of lust. The bright dawn has deposited dew on my naked body, and the sun has warmed my dry skin.

Now dusk has arrived; the passers-by no longer turn round. I have quit the towns; no one holds me back by the frayed hem of my mantle. I have fled the town for this remote wood. It is vast and solitary; roads intersect here around this spring. The water in it runs continuously clear. If anyone comes I bend down, and in this crystal cup I extend to his thirst that which I would once have offered to his desire: the unexpected and delightful cup that I once tried to be for anyone covetous of convivial refreshment.

That, O traveler, is why you have encountered me here. I have spoken to you to inform you of the error of a dolorous life.

The night is gathering; continue on your way, and when you rap with your staff on the door of the woman you love—to whom, as you unfasten your sandals, you will elate the incidents of your journey and the singular encounter—instead of listening to the questions of her curiosity or solicitude without reply, close her mouth with a long kiss.

Words are vain; I shall shut up; adieu. Love is a mute god, who only has the statues that are formed by our desire.

The Black Trefoil

I. Hertulie; Or, The Messages

To Madame de Bonnières [14]

From Hermotime to Hermas

By the time you are handed this letter I shall already be far away; I shall have walked all night beneath the stars. I had, however, believed that I would never leave our beautiful gardens, O Hermas. We walked there together; it was there that I met Hertulie; it is there that you will tell her about my departure. She will blame my love, and if I am leaving her, it is because of love.

Love alone makes us what we are; it renders us as we shall be, for it becomes what we are. So, the manner in which it develops is subordinate to our way of being, and they both testify to their reciprocal imperfection. The stature of love is equal to the dimensions of our shadow. Alas, the contagion of our infirmity discredits it; the origin of its effects is attributed to it; it is elsewhere, it is within us. Love is beautiful. Only the ugliness of our souls grimaces on the mask that represents it. Its aspect is fashioned in our image, and we see our interior resemblance therein. No matter how wretched we may be, and

---

[14] Henriette de Bonnières was the wife of Paul de Bonnières, one of Régnier's closest friends, who served as a literary critic for *Le Figaro* for many years (a job Régnier eventually inherited in the 1920s). Henriette was famed for her beauty and her portrait was painted by several of the leading artists of the day; she was one of the women with whom Régnier had a long adoring but platonic relationship.

even though it participates in our wretchedness, its insufficiency and deformity are still desirable. Love is still love. We love it no matter how deformed it is.

Imagine its beauty, then, O Hermas, if, instead of grimacing in tenebrous hearts, it strips bare in radiant souls. Love ought to be the host of wisdom, but its torch ought to illuminate marvelous vaults inside our dreams, covering with diamonds the stalactites of silence in the grottoes of anxiety; then, everything will gleam in a chaste festival of light, and in subterranean dawns between the precious stones, inflexible lilies would grow. Ordinarily, its uncertain lamp only haunts tombs or lairs; owls dip their talons in funerary oil and obscene satyrs mimic gods, in bestial shadows on the walls.

Love is the host of wisdom and I am going away to prepare its dwelling. I have consulted the past and the present; you have reproached me for not consulting myself sufficiently, of having read too many books and of having knocked at the doors of sages in haste. Wisdom, you said to me, does not wander; it abides, and assumes a semblance of sleep; it does not sleep in a castle of stone in the middle of a forest. Its attentive patience listens within us; it responds to our interior auscultations.

Alas, my friend, I have remained deaf to my own ear; I need someone to speak in order to hear my silence, and I have been obliged to be a transient in order to go to meet myself. There are ways; there are keys hidden in mysterious hands. Oh, I'm sure of it; there are doors that are opened, and a strange and hazardous sowing produces the consecrated crop of our own fecundity. Mourn for me, Hermas, for having recourse to the aid of sages in order to become one of them. It is necessary, in order to love, for wisdom alone can exorcise love from the spell in which it atrophies.

I love Hertulie, but I refuse our love the fate of parody. I'm leaving; there are stars in the sky and I'm weeping. Hertulie will weep. I shall return. Let her come to see you sometimes in your silent house Talk to her about me, as we have talked to one another about the grace of Hertulie.

Oh, I can still see her in the garden. It's there that I met her, there that you will read me her letter. Adieu.

Hermotime, thanking you in advance.

Narcissus' Stairway

Hermas returned alone, the following day, to the beautiful locations where he had so often conversed with Hermotime. The hours seemed sweet to them in that vast space of trees and flowers. It was an ornamental and solitary garden. Nothing remained of the château that had once been there, except the charm of imagining it for oneself, in accordance with the surroundings that had survived it.

Three streams of water radiated from an octagonal central area, and, at the end of each of them, amid various artifices of architecture and hydraulics, a fountain animated a different figure. One represented a man, laughing as he poured out the contents of a bronze amphora, another a weeping woman whose tears filled a golden crater. The one in the middle was the most beautiful. A sheet of water overflowed from a basin from which emerged, upright, a hermaphrodite statue. On porphyry side-panels, alternating faces of Tritons and Sirens spat out, by the inflation of their convulsive mouths, a suffocating draught of crystal. Sometimes, when the fountain was switched off and the enigmatic marbles embalmed with their triple nudity the arbors of silent trees, one saw a dove perch on the edge of the draining bowl in order to drink from it.

Around the octagonal basin, bronze statues alternated with yew-trees sculpted into pyramids and cypresses shaped into obelisks. Their reflection was metallic in the calm water, where that of the statues seemed to half-dissolve, to melt into a kind of other-worldly appearance, less their image than their shadow—for all water is slightly magical, and if it is utterly tranquil, one never knows what might lie dormant within it.

The rest of the garden was disposed in squares of woodland; a solid and close-cropped box-tree palisade framed them. Inside, beneath the tall trees, one was always walking over dead leaves. All these squares, two of which faced either side of the basin, were enlivened by something surprising. Here a little spring ran, one drop at a time; the hour was marked there by the natural clock. There one heard an echo; the voice came back from far away, and curious equivocations resulted from the fading syllables. In the other two one found circular benches with seats of marble or stone, with sphinxes or dolphins for armrests.

Superimposed on the garden was a terrace with a balustrade. It displayed its yellow sand pathways bordering embroidered flower-beds and flat lawns. One went up there by means of curved ramps, and one also descended, in the middle by means of a staircase, from which one could see oneself down below in a pool, in such a way that, from one step to the next, one seemed to be approaching oneself. That staircase was known as Narcissus' Stairway.

The extent of the pool was continued by the three streams of water that diverged there. They were like the routes of memory, in which remembrance seemed to march at a gentle pace over their long tremulous mirrors. The sun, hidden behind the trees, still warmed the stone of the step on which Hermas sat that day, savoring the pleasures of being entirely devoted to his dreams. The memory of Hermotime mingled them with a little sadness and a certain amount if irony. He discovered in front of him, on the sand, bizarre and irregular figures whose incoherent geometry the absentee had traced, while leaving the day before, with the tip of his ebony cane: lines cross-crossing broken circles, and spirals analogous to those that a little silver snake describes with the arrangement of its slender black spine.

That cane almost formed a sort of mundane demi-caduceus, of which Hermotime habitually bore the attribute, but the emblem was still lacking one of the two serpents and the young sage seemed to be waiting for the opportunity that would complete its exactitude. Thus, he seemed circumspect with respect to himself, and that precaution burdened his

slightly austere grace with a gravity that, in order to be perfectly elegant, required a final polish.

Hermas thought about Hermotime's wisdom, and heard
his words again. Almost every day, the two friends had come
to enjoy the beautiful garden. Hermotime slightly regretted the
fact that the château no longer existed; its bookshelves, its
cabinets of medals and its galleries of antique busts would
have been a refuge from the summer rain that sometimes oiled
the bronze of the statues and the metallic verdure of the yews
with its downpours, and dripped from the heavy leaves of the
trees like dissolved diamonds. Hermotime deplored all that,
extrapolating the beauty of the dwelling from that of the gardens.

A noble decorative taste was manifest therein, although
their authoritative and syllogistic orderliness denoted that they
had been designed by a specious and domineering mind, and
imagined, because of their meditative assembly of bronze and
water, by a dreamer, perhaps something of a hypochondriac,
who liked to compose methodical reveries there and plumb the
depths of some lofty, peevish and morose delectation.

Hermas and Hermotime often rested there, usually on
that last step, at the bottom of Narcissus' Stairway. The beautiful garden extended over depths of silence. The gaze followed the flight of the water beneath the trees. Only occasionally, when the sun was very bright, did they seek the shelter
of the woods, their cool and shady interior. Hermotime liked
to pause next to the little spring. Hermas preferred to lean
nonchalantly on the marble sphinx or caress the arched scales
of the porphyry dolphins. The echo never repeated anything in
falsifying what the two friends said to one another in low
voices. Their agreement matched their differences.

One day, they followed one of the watercourses as far as
the fountain where the singular statue smiled, Hermas saw a
dream therein; Hermotime assumed that it was a symbol. They
came back without talking, for dusk was already falling and
the waters, having been switched of, invited silence.

Habitually, Hermotime gladly related to Hermas, along with his thoughts, the details of what they had suggested to him. He spoke about them ingeniously, with scholarly divisions. His youth was given to that. Often, he carried under his arm, by way of mania or allusion, a closed book. In any case, he could speak better off the cuff better than one might have thought, and his eloquence produced ore pleasure than surprise.

Travels had taken him to strange places—or, at least, to places which seemed so to Hermas, because of their sonorous or languorous names. He had known illustrious and wise men. Hermas did not press him for tales of those meetings, for those masters appeared to him more curious in their understanding of life than their knowledge or wisdom, but Hermotime, subordinate to precepts, turned out to be short of anecdotes. Although he had forgotten the voices, he had retained all the doctrines, in order to search therein for the substance of his own. Wisdom is everywhere, he said; from his thousand scattered and mixed-up pieces, he had to reconstitute a figure that utilized them, its form, determined by the coincidence of their parts only making sense in their totality.

Hermotime sought these disparate pieces in the world. Above them was infinity. Hermas allowed him to say it, for his rather taciturn thoughtfulness lent to those words an inattentive and indulgent silence that he animated with the gesture of picking a flower or throwing a little gravel into the calm water of the basin next to which they were seated.

Large fish wandering there in a melancholy fashion, slow and almost vegetative, so old that moss was oxidizing heir scales. They were furred by old age and glided unctuously through the heavy water. Hermas and Hermotime sometimes watched them silently, becoming entirely torpid as evening approached, and incorporating themselves in the water, where they were no longer anything but an opaque and vague stupor.

The garden became even more beautiful in those degenerescent hours, in its composed solitude. Sometimes, a young woman would pass alongside the stream. Hermas, without knowing all those who lived in the town, esteemed some for coming to wander thus in the calm of the noble place. They, at least, were perhaps not without melancholy and they took on a certain tender grace there, which completed their beauty. Some doubtless came there to get a glimpse of him. His wealth and taste for solitude made him seem odd. No one was admitted to his sumptuous house. He hardly ever left it except to walk in this garden or his own, which was also vast and over-refined. He had wanted to know the names of these pass-ers-by, and when Hermotime asked one of them, he was able to learn that her name was Hertulie.

Hermotime loved her. He met her one the very morning of her arrival while walking on the terrace, where he was wait-ing for Hermas. Although it was not long until midday, bloated storm-clouds were already filling the sky. The sun shone at intervals and the young woman alternately opened and closed her umbrella. Their paths crossed several times; then they talked, and it was a grand amour that Hermotime confessed to his friend. To him, too, he had given the task of informing Hertulie of his departure, and telling her the me-thodical reasons for it. Hermas was therefore thinking about those things when he saw Hertulie coming toward him from the far end of the stream.

She came toward him slowly, smiling, perhaps because she was holding a beautiful mauve iris with a long stem in her hand. She and the flower resembled one another mysteriously, by virtue of a similar slender blossoming, a matching accord of delicate grace. Her pink and white dress, which had been green and yellow a little while before because of the reflection of the trees and the water, seemed to be a naïve and precious finery. The detail of it was exquisite, for the foliage interwo-ven in arabesques in the glaze of the fabric spangled it with silken frost—and the young woman stood like that in front of Hermas, slightly astonished that he was alone and did not re-ply to her greeting.

After a brief hesitation, as if not to show too much insis-tence, for decency's sake, nor, out of politeness to seem disappointed, she asked, while gazing at the flower: "Where's Her-motime today? Still dreaming over some book?"

Hermas contemplated her gravely, in silence, with gentle pity in his eyes. She seemed to him so slim and frail that he was anxious about having to tell her the unexpected news. She seemed to him to be entirely similar to the delicate iris, whose deportment was inclined by the weight of the flower—so simi-lar that he was about to break its flexibility with an imaginary thrust of his long blackthorn cane. The silver coiling serpent of the demi-caduceus would envenom love with its anxious fang.

Without saying anything, Hermas handed the letter to Hertulie.

He watched her read it, sitting on the last step of the stairway. She read it with minute application, her elbows on her knees, on the crumpled stem of the iris, whose flower hung down sadly. The thin paper, unstirred by any wind, trembled in her hands. She pushed back a curl of hair with one of her fingers.

A great silence had fallen over the entire garden, for the fountains had been shut off at the end of the watercourses. The silenced murmur drained away into an almost imperceptible drip, and its incessant duration could be heard in that fashion all night. The surfaces of the bowls, tarnished by a crepuscular leucoma, became fixed. The clumps of trees were petrified. Everything took on an attitude of supreme hardness before abandoning itself to the darkness. There was one last resis-tance of things, wanting to retain their diurnal appearance. They retracted themselves, as if suspicious of the dissolving insinuations of shadow.

Hermas was sadly thoughtful, not daring to look at Her-tulie. They stayed like that for some time. The dusk was moist and mild when, with a tacit accord, they rose to their feet. Tall and slender in her long dress, whose pleats were fluted all the way to the ground, Hermas saw her reflected in the bleak wa-ter of the pool, her pale face transfigured by the beyond of dreams and sleep, which possessed every face seen therein. That and the silence were so similar to death that Hermas felt it necessary to interject a few hopeful words, however futile, into the suspense of that anguish, and he pronounced them one by one, slowly.

"Hertulie," he said, "tender Hertulie, you are too beautiful not to have sometimes looked men in the face. Human faces are almost all sad, with the figuration of their past, and the ashes remain in the depths of all of them of that which they have tried to be, but only glimpsed through a dream. I won't tell you mine, there are too many singular desires therein; their solitary burning consumes me from within; they're the dusk of my own darkness. The simplicity of yours at least preserves hope. Night is falling, though, and we must go home. The fountains have been shut off; their laughter dead, the imperceptible drops that survive them are expiring one by one. It's the same with us; at certain moments, things seem to fall silent and to continue by occult perseverance. Your solitude has an echo, that of footfalls that are going away and will come back; one returns from all wisdom, and interrupted flowers bloom again."

Hermas bowed ceremoniously to Hertulie. She remained alone, on the water's edge, her broken iris in her hand, but the threads of the breach weakened, and the flower, too heavy, fell on to the sand. The silence absorbed that slight impact, for Hermas' footsteps could no longer be heard; and above the tall trees, in a clear patch of sky, a star was faintly revealed.

Emblematic Premonitions

That morning, Hertulie awoke in tears. That often happened since Hermotime's departure; her slumber melted thus into a plaintive and moist sadness. After spending all day wearily holding back her sobs, the night lavished the beneficent effusion of her tears without her knowledge. Darkness is secret and delicate; it takes care of wounded souls, and the anxious Hertulie, in the wake of its mysterious tenderness, often woke up gently saddened and almost smiling.

That morning, by contrast, she felt more troubled. In her sleep she had sensed, at length, with pauses and repetitions, some ambush of shadow behind the night, heard distant and delicate flutes singing in her ear, their melody mingling with a kindred sound of fountains which lent it an analogous liquidity, in such a fashion that the water seemed to be rhythmic, akin to the hydrophony of musical instruments. The silence in which one believes oneself to be when one is asleep had quivered, animated by inexplicable murmurs; all the melancholy of the past and the apprehension of the future had whispered to the sleeper and without a voice with which to formulate meaning, everything had spoken by allusion of the departure of Hermotime and the dangerous outcomes in which destiny goes astray.

Hertulie, sitting up in bed with a start, looked around the room in which she had gone to sleep. The sun was tinting the tulle curtains at the window and the muslin curtains of the bed, as if their light immobility were in suspense. The bed imitated the form of a boat and the copper swans that ornamented its corners seemed to be made of gold in the morning light. Their gently splayed wings drew the nocturnal ship over the imaginary river of the carpet, where arabesques stretched out complex and languid algae. Here and there, large rose-blossoms gyrated in its eddies.

Sonorous and youthful voices were audible outside; it was the noise of a market facing the house. Flowers, herbs, exorbitant fruits, rare vegetables and exotic poultry were sold there. From the window, Hertulie amused herself with the spectacle of the little crowd. Beautiful ladies frequented the market, singly or in commentating groups, carefully testing the maturity of some fruit in their ungloved hands or selecting the most beautiful flowers from an odorant sheaf. Donkeys passed by, shaking the warm and worn velvet of their long grey ears, indifferent to the efforts of the wings of tall pink flamingoes tied in pairs by supple reeds, which paralyzed their long jointed legs, as tall as bulrushes.

In the midst of a circle of listeners, an astrologer in a tall kabbalistic bonnet was predicting the future. Hertulie would gladly have interrogated him, but she thought about Hermotime. Without having quite grasped the meaning of the great things he was undertaking, she admired his ambition. Her respectful soul, attentive and tender, was suffering from his absence, and the resentment of a naïve pride in thinking about it did not compensate for the pain it caused her. In spite of that, remembering the young sage in all his learned and vagabond grace, she was ashamed of the frivolity of her impatience.

Ordinarily, the spectacle of the little square was less distracting. Three solitary elms were holding a long conversation with the murmur of their foliage directly opposite Hertulie's window. Sprawled in her armchair, she watched them swaying. In the evening they could be heard shivering, one by one—or sometimes, all three together.

The nights when she could not sleep seemed interminable. For something to do, she re-read Hermotine's letter, and tried hard to penetrate its meaning, for she had difficulty imagining the wisdom of which it spoke as a difficult and necessary thing. Although it spoke of miseries of love, she sensed the keen instinct within it without understanding how one could subordinate its enjoyment to such mysterious precautions. Her amorous simplicity dreamed in a more natural and less initiatory manner.

Oh, Hermotime, Hermotime, she thought, *when you return, will your eyes be more beautiful? Will your smooth long hair have a more graceful curl?*

That was all of her wisdom, and although she knew that he would come back, the anxiety of that return left her involuntarily desperate.

The days passed. As they did so, she marked them off on her calendar. The little red crosses followed one another there, composing weeks and already touching the confines of summer and autumn. The air became cooler; things were aggravated by a kind of heaviness, and were imperceptibly paralyzed by a meditative somnolence. Hertulie lived alone in her house, contracting there an indolent stupor in accord with the immobile attitude of her thoughts.

One day, dreaming thus while looking out of her window at one of the last lukewarm skies of the season, about midday, she saw, to her surprise, an arrow launched from outside catch momentarily on the curtain, vacillate there, and then fall vertically on to the carpet.

In the deserted street no one was running away. Where had the arrow come from? Its triangular steel point gleamed ironically. What did the message mean?—for Hertulie understood that it was one, and did not doubt that it came from Hermotime, just like the naked dagger that her trembling hand discovered one evening on the table.

That singular present frightened her, perhaps by its premonition of some tragic adventure, but the poor girl knew little about allegories and, from day to day, she became even sadder, more desolate in the anxiety of her waiting. That night, she did not weep again, for she did not sleep and insomnia deprived her of the gentle weakness of tears. The wind blew outside with a noise of discordant flutes; autumn inclined toward winter; it arrived.

For months she was without any further news of Hermotime. Spring reappeared; the clouds fled northwards. Again, the little market in the square cheered up the silence of the town. Hertulie went out to buy flowers. They were the first of the season, naïve and as if improvised; their petals seemed to be made of snow, sunlit and melting. Almost no one was walking past the barely-furnished displays. The kabbalist was missing and the donkeys were pawing the ground, still peevish in their winter coats.

Hertulie chose a few primroses in haste and, on going home, was greatly surprised, for on the sideboard where she was about to put them in a vase, someone, in her absence, had placed a pewter flask and a little mirror on the marble top. For a long time she meditated upon these attributes; the flask was badly dented, as if it had traveled a long way.

The days grew longer and the swallows returned. Hertulie liked to watch them flying around; their vivacity amused her; in rapid flight, they wheeled around the house from dawn until the time when the bats succeeded them in the crepuscular sky, hastily seeking to imitate them, awkwardly, with their uncertain wings. Then she turned away, almost in fear; their flight sketched out the shadow of a bizarre alphabet.

One evening, when Hertulie lingered for a little while, watching their zigzags inscribe the hieroglyphic flourishes of their apocryphal legend in the sky, when she finally closed the window and went to light a candle, her foot bumped into a sonorous object on the carpet. It was a key.

The next day, the young woman woke up in tears, as if the darkness had taken pity on her again. Her poor soul was agonized by the interminable absence and maddened by the mysterious signs whose enigmatic incomprehensibility increased her distress. Once released by the tears, however, she felt weak and hurt. The summer dawn was brightening the enshrouding whiteness of her curtains and, posed there while she was asleep, on her breast, there was an ear of ripe wheat.

It was then that she thought of going to find Hermas, to ask him for an explanation of these singular allegories, but, she being very tired and weak, the road very long and the afternoon very hot, she did not reach his house until after middle of the day.

The House of the Self-Contained Sleeper[15]

Hermas lived alone in an isolated house at the end of an old garden, not far from immense ponds, at the place where the grounds gave way to forest. Through the stagnant waters

---

[15] The original chapter title is *La Maison du bel-en-soi dormant*, which plays on the familiar title of Charles Perrault's "La Belle au Bois Dormant" (usually translated, a trifle dubiously, as "The Sleeping Beauty [in the Wood]") in a fashion that cannot be reproduced in English.

of the marsh and the lateral woodlands, an interminable avenue of ancient trees led to a round-point at which one had the sumptuous dwelling straight ahead, beyond a vast courtyard that preceded it. The grey sandstone paving stones were mingled with a few that were slightly pink. The sun made the mica within them scintillate, and after the rain, a coolness emanated from them. Then the gilded ironwork of the high gate gleamed more brightly and the two lanterns suspended to either side of the gate oscillated in the slightest breeze. Their forged gilt framed the beveled edges of their crystal; at night, they were no longer lit, for Hermas was not hospitable.

Nothing was known about him, and as a haughty and taciturn being constitutes, in the eyes of human baseness, an infraction of its customs and a kind of magic from which it is differentiated by its servitude, that reserve as envisaged with a malevolence scarcely contained by a reputation for extreme wealth. That double sorcery of gold and silence constituted Hermas.

In fact, preceding his installation in that dwelling, carriages had brought magnificent furniture. One of those carriages laden with rare crystals and inestimable glassware, which collided at the jolts while traversing the town at the heavy tread of the horses, had left behind the memory of a mysterious clinking. The next day the silverware passed through, and Hermas reveled in a solitary luxury.

That was his right, having been able to forbid any admixture between himself and things, for it is sufficient, to make an enjoyment innocent, to conserve beyond its reach an intangible point that can be kept forever intact. Hermas was one of those people who have a right to everything, by virtue of the superiority that enables them to neutralize slavery; so he adapted to his solitude an environment of silent magnificence, akin to his dreams; then the doors closed on those marvels, without forgetfulness being able to eclipse their passage through the streets of the little town.

There was much comment on the attitude of that retreat, which no one was allowed to penetrate; so the advent of Her-

93

motime produced some astonishment at the privileged position he enjoyed, to the point of familiarity, with respect to the reserve of the haughty young man who, from the miraculous crystal glass from which it was said that he drank, suiting alone at his sparkling table, seemed to have drunk, forever, with the silence, one of those philters that separate someone permanently from his fellows and no longer allow him to in conformity with anyone but himself.

That situation of having confiscated for his own usage what is normally a pretext for ostentation, was concordant with the solitary retreat of a man to a place whose disposition and architecture seemed to comprise the entourage of a sort of select popularity, domestic or amicable.

The curious were disappointed to find the habits of the fantastic master so contrary, not only to their curiosity but also to the obligations that apparently ought to have been imposed upon him by the almost princely appearances of the château in which he lived apart.

The aspect of the place was, however, embellished by that intentional contrast. It had a sort of fateful gravity, that kind of superfluous grace that places discordant with their original destiny acquire. Their inutility and disproportion seem no longer adapted to anything but the spiritual mania of the master who resides in them. It is in him that the concord of their disparity is forged; he is the point at which the junction of their mysteries equilibrates; and, without any further attribution than satisfying some melancholy singularity that is emblematic in them, no longer coinciding with life, one senses them becoming proportionate to a dream; and they take from that something fictive and imaginary, which raises him up and immobilizes him.

Hermas' abode consisted of a ground floor surmounted by a second story, the whole being vast. Tall and broad windows with large panes alternated with small latticed windows on the façade, separated from one another by flat columns in various marbles. Above each window, sculpted in the stone, smiled or grimaced a satyresque mask or a Heliconian face.[16] That façade loomed up at the back of a spacious, slightly convex courtyard.

Hertulie walked slowly over the uneven paving stones. Having come to consult Hermas, she hesitated now to go in. Last year, however, she had familiarized herself with him by virtue of having met him in the old garden where, with Hermotime, the three of them had sat down at dusk facing the watercourses. Hermas had always addressed himself to the young woman with ceremonious politeness, but, on the evening when he had handed her the letter and spoken to her at greater length, she had sensed something in his voice so distant that the melancholy interlocutor of her despair had withdrawn in her thoughts to the confines of dream, to a kind of distance beyond life of which she retained a sibylline apprehension, as if it ought to be outside the reach of Destiny itself.

She hesitated, not knowing on which door she ought to knock. All three were closed and bronze knockers clenched their ornamental projections thereon. Finally, she decided on the middle one. The blow reverberated inside. The prolongations of that echo in the vast house permitted the divination of its long corridors. The limpid polished marble of the tiling reflected the stucco walls of the vestibule. A delightful coolness further increased the beautiful proportions. Galleries extended from it, at the end of which one saw, through glazed doors, various perspectives of trellises in porticos and arcades; yew-trees garlanded with roses displayed their obelisks at the intersections of pathways. It was simultaneously grandiose, elegant and sad.

The staircase that Hertulie went up led to a series of rooms, all curiously furnished with the same bleak and sumptuous taste. The objects were immobilized there is a sort of anxious or indifferent solitude. In the rooms, in conformity with some taciturn visitor, the wooden mosaic floors did not

---

[16] Mount Helicon was the mythical residence of Apollo and the Muses.

95

creak underfoot. The silence there, although absolute, seemed to be in suspense rather than definitive; there was no imperceptible life to disturb its glacial lethargy, and yet, there was something apparent and superficial cracking its stability.

Among those rooms, one was distinguished by its charming wall-hangings. The bolts of cloth retained an imprint like the moist shadow of the touch of flowers over which they had long ago been folded, and because of that very pale green fabric, the forms of the furniture, in pale yellow and old gold wood, became languid, and the sideboards huddled in the corners, on which upright jade vases congealed.

In another of the rooms, Hertulie saw with astonishment a great many mirrors hanging n the walls. Held in frames made of gold, tortoiseshell, ebony or burgau,[17] they were opposed to one another, exchanging their reflections reciprocally and the combinations of their incidences; some of them, mounted in stone borders, resembled bowls of water, and Hertulie appeared very pale in them as she passed by.

She continued to search for Hermas from room to room. Doors with worn locks separated some of them, while others were arranged in long sequences. Heavy door-curtains in silks and satins brushed her with their fringes, which trembled behind her for a long time. They were all empty.

The solitude of these vast apartments was further enhanced by the lack of any portrait on the walls; no human face, gracious or sad, witnessed, in its memorial past, that apparatus of wealth, devoid of any visage to testify to its delicate or ostentatious solidity.

Old crystal chandeliers, complicated and sparkling, were suspended from high ceilings by silken cords or silver chains; their frosty adamantine crowns consecrated the absence of some invisible majesty, and their luminous congelation froze the silence and iced the solitude into which the pendants of

---

[17] Burgau is a kind of shell, produced by the mollusk *Monodonta lineata*, sometimes used for inlaying snuff-boxes—but not, in the real world, for framing mirrors.

their artificial stalactites extended. Some were iridescent with phosphorescence, as if by allusion to the setting sun that was tinting the sky outside; they assimilated the imaginary colors of occidental autumns to their crystalline fructifications.

The day wore on, and through the windows, Hertulie saw the illusory onyx of the clouds become stratified.

Still searching for Hermas, she finally arrived in a spacious hall where, through the wide-open casements, a light wind was scattering moist leaves on a writing-desk; next to the notepads was an arrow, a naked dagger, a flask and a key, which Hertulie recognized as identical to her own. The beards of the ear of wheat were caressing the mauve silk tablecloth on the desk, whose folds half-veiled the ebony foot whose twist was tumefied by a sculpted chimera.

Hermas' garden was visible through the window. There was a vast esplanade tiled with green-tinted marble. In spite of the hardness of its substance, its color gave the illusion of a moist and spongy surface. All around, hedges of holly were dotted with little red fruits, seemingly carved from blood-red jasper. A bowl of water, covered in green algae, was ornamented by a pink ibis standing on one leg, reminiscent of a sick flower. A line of conical cypresses closed the view of that strange and artificial marsh of stone and foliage; above it, the decaying residue of a setting sun, copper oxide and vitrified blood-flecked lukewarm saliva.

Suddenly, behind each cypress, a discordant flute sounded; then, one by one, they emitted the note of their isolation; afterwards, they began to harmonize, and eventually attained unison; they played, distant and delicate, on the threshold of the night, in some ambush of shadow. Their melody was interrupted by pauses and augmented by repetitions. Hertulie recognized therein the flutes of her slumber, but more mortal and further beyond hope. Everything they said made allusion to the absence of Hermotime; they consecrated its irrevocability, and Hertulie understood the meaning of that melancholy concert.

Hermotime would not come back. She had known that for a long time, by means of the broken iris and the hieroglyphs of the bats; she had read it in the grimoires of their flight; the flutes had whispered it to her and it seemed to her that Hermas was telling her again. As before, by Narcissus' Stairway, he murmured: "Hertulie, tender Hertulie, the fountains have been shut down; they have wept every night more sadly; they were weeping in your life; they are weeping in your destiny. O Hermotime, you will not come back; I have the evidence in the traveling arrow, the cruel dagger, the flask, all significant of the distant road, and the key by which you have locked the past behind you. Hermotime will not come back; he cannot come back. The ear of wheat will not flower again; wisdom will not become love again."

The flutes had faded away while it seemed that Hermas spoke, and Hertulie silently put a finger to her lips. The garden of green marble turned black; the clouds of the sunset were extinguished. Slowly, walking backwards, Hertulie drew away into the depths of the room, then turned round and disappeared.

Behind her, a heavy black curtain striped with gold fell back, its creases stirring momentarily, and became immobile in its grave and sumptuous funereal folds.

The rooms through which the fugitive passed again seemed to her more spacious; the extinct chandeliers suspended above her head the pendants of their crystalline silence; from room to room went, breathless and weary, until she stopped in the one where the mirrors were.

Her image was multiplied there to infinity. Around her, Hertulie could see into the utmost depths of a dream, in which she lost the sensation of having produced so many phantoms identical to herself; she felt that she was dispersed there, forever, and, by dint of seeing herself thus, elsewhere all around her, she was fragmented to the point at which, dissolved in her own reflections, exorcised from herself by that surprising magic in which she imagined herself indefinitely impersonal, her knees buckled and she collapsed softly on to the parquet, inanimate—while, in the solitary room, above the closed eyes of her pale face, the mirrors in their frames of gold, tortoiseshell and ebony continued to exchange between them the illusory aspect of the reciprocal vacuity.

From Hermas to Hermotime

It is true, then, that you have marched toward your Destiny! I anticipated that outcome. One is evasive with respect to oneself, but whoever caches a glimpse of himself searches thereafter forever, and the presents you have sent me told me that you have found yourself. Here they are, on my desk, and when I look at them I think of you. I see you again as you were when we met in the old garden.

I do not know where you have been, O Hermotime, what stones you have rolled before you on the roads with the tip of your blackthorn cane. How have you come to the wisdom in conformity with your dreams? It is to oneself that one is initiated. It was to you that it was necessary to return via vain doctrines.

Hertulie taught you more than the books of the philosophers. She had charming eyes and was able to hold a flower in her beautiful hands, which she resembled. We should only respire that which has flourished within us, and it is in the color of our eyes that the beauty of things is nuanced. One searches too far afield. Your scrupulous, didactic and formalistic soul wanted to follow its error to the end. Love is the host of wisdom, you said, but you searched for it where only the affectation of its presence is paraded. Dolor will show you the falsity of doctrines—what can they do to heal us?

I understood the meaning of the messenger arrow, made of feather and steel; it lightens in us that which can fly, and kills that which ought to die. The naked dagger already signified your mortal desire to be another man, and the flask represented your thirst to know yourself in the emblematic mirror in which one appears outside oneself; but when I received the fateful key, I divined that it had opened the access to your Destiny—and the ripe ear of wheat, O Hermotime, represents you in my eyes.

That is all well and good. Love gave you the instinct to conform your soul to the beauty of the sentiment for which, with the evils that it involves, you conceived the welcome that it merits. You wanted to adorn your soul for its triumph and disarm your victory, and, in giving love to wisdom, give wisdom to love. You have seen what was in you, where the secret of another lay: obligation, our mysterious sleeper, which is awakened neither by the subtlety of methods nor the noise of controversy, or anything that is not congeneric to its mysterious silence.

That is all well and good, Hermotime, and I imagine in the gardens where we walked a part of the miracle by which you have transformed yourself. Do you remember Narcissus' Stairway? Places act of their own accord on our dreams; it's there, now, that yours rediscover the best around them.

Come back, then, my friend, for, at the end of the watercourses, you will find Hertulie's sepulcher. It is there that she rests. We shall rest there too, one day. Where three statures were raised, three tombs will be seen. Hers is already in the middle. The monument is in pink and black marble, the place forever silent, for I have had the fountains destroyed. In their stead, flowers have been planted, the freshest and the most naïve—others will grow for us—and one might think that the dawn placed its bare foot upon them. Was Hertulie not the dawn of your true knowledge, the spring of your wisdom, of which you now savor the opulent summer? Perhaps you will know its bitter autumn; that is the season of my soul, and that is what has also come to the old trees in the garden.

It belongs to me now; I have bought it in its entirety and combined it with mine. My solitude is vast, you see, and we shall at least be able to walk there bare-faced, having both disdain the masks with which humans disguise themselves— we who bear forever the sole visage of our Destiny.

II. The Story of Hermagore

To Saint Julian the Hospitaler [18]

For a long time the Poor Fisherman had been seen standing motionless in his boat on the estuary of the river.

The water flows slowly between the banks and, as it comes from far away, from the depths of wooded or verdant lands, its current carries leaves, wisps of straw, and the occasional flower, vegetation that catches on the boat or swirls in the eddies. The sky is gray over a pale sea; the sandbanks join up with the dunes of the shore; the boat oscillates imperceptibly; weary and suffering, it moans; the plaint of its joints mingles with the sigh of the rigging, and the thin arms bring up nothing but an empty net.

For days and years, he had very often lifted it in vain. No fish were caught there, even though the Fisherman was patient and attentive in consulting the wind, the season and the tide, taking great care that his shadow did not extended beyond the boat, and not once did he see his face in the water.

Sometimes, weary of his futile station, he rowed out to sea. The stronger waves rocked his melancholia, heavily; the deep water took on a green tint. From the sea he looked back at the sandy shore and the estuary. The wind whistled in the rigging and, all day long, the fisherman persisted in his task.

---

[18] In making this dedication Régnier surely had in mind Gustave Flaubert's short story "La Légende de Saint-Julien l'hospitalier," which recycles one of the more peculiar tales from the Golden Legend. The (wholly fictitious) original seems to be influenced by the Greek myth of Oedipus, in its unusually convoluted and enigmatic account of an accursed child who acquires power and wealth but eventually repents the evil deeds that he has been led to commit.

To those harsh and fruitless days he preferred the mediocrity of a derisory prey, the small fry of quiet waters, the calm of the river, its indolent swaying, and its unctuous and monotonous flow, where leaves, wisps of straw and flowers passed by, one by one.

Birds, having no fear of him, flew around him. There were grey gulls with adventurous wingspans. He liked the wagtails the hopped on the sands better. With them, his thoughts went to vast interior regions where no other waters murmur but the springs where shepherds drink; the soft mud around the pools is trampled by livestock; the perfume of hay mingles with the odor of barns; there are beehives in gardens and hayricks lined up on the thatch; from the little square field where one digs in the sun one has nothing in front of oneself, above the living hedgerows, but the sky. Sweat trickles down the face in warm droplets, and the shade of trees is so cool that one imagines one drinking from a fountain.

One evening, when he was daydreaming thus while laying out his nets on the sand around his beached boat, he heard someone speak to him. It was a stranger; his tall figure was leaning on a staff; with is weary features and his monkish habit he resembled the dusk. The man asked to buy the equipment and the boat and, while talking, counted out gold pieces one by one in the shade.

At dawn, Hermagore the Fisherman paused in the midst of a vast sandy plain where blue-tinted grasses grew. The river had reappeared by virtue of a caprice of its meanders, and his glaucous eyes ran between the islets that were reflected there and seemed to be rooted there by the crowns of their inverted trees. A bird flew out of a bush; butterflies fluttered with their wings of dormant silk, gray and pink, some as yellow as gold. Hermagore felt the money that he was carrying in a canvas bag and resumed his route. Dusk fell, and every evening, the walker counted his humble treasure.

At the end of one day when he had traveled over soft meadows, Hermagore perceived forests. They striped the entire horizon with their massive line; in the interior, there was deep darkness, silent spaces. Sometimes the forest seemed to be ending and thinning out a border; then he began to run—but the woodland recommenced on the far side of some ravine whose crest and the trees, in interstices against the sky, had simulated the clearing from which one could see the continuation, in the distance, of the undulating crowns.

For a long time, in this wilderness, Hermagore heard nothing but the wind, but one day he recognized echoes that sent back the sound of an axe, and, having got his bearings, he found woodcutters felling beech-trees. Further on he saw a roof smoking, and finally perceived that land of which he had dreamed. The hills undulated smoothly; meadows alternated with fields of wheat, alongside which poplars were aligned. Sometimes, the music of a flute could be heard. Clothes were drying under the willows and, in the evening, everything seemed so calm that one dared not walk on the grass.

The little field was situated on the slope of a hill, square, with hedges surrounding it. Hermagore cultivated it with care. In the profoundly-worked ground he sowed his crop. All winter long he was happy, but when spring came he saw that the neighboring fields were much more fertile than his own. That was the way it was. His harvest was scarcely sufficient for the next sowing. The next crop promised to be even more meager; the birds were relentless, and Hermagore could be seen standing amid the scattered ears as he had once stood in his flat boat, gesticulating and throwing clods of earth at the marauders.

Sometimes he deserted his post and wandered around the country; everywhere lush crops were ripening, and the privilege of is poverty seemed to him more bitter still. Flocks went by, and he watched them from a distance as he had once watched ships disappear over the horizon; their sails knew all the winds and they traveled by distant seas to rich counties from which their holds came back impregnated with the odor of cargoes to enrich powerful masters, who, in dwellings ornamented with coral and maps, calculated ports of call and tides.

The next year was so bad that Hermagore gleaned in order to be able to sow. He went through the fields, bent over, beneath the sun. Finally, his seed prospered; his field too was vermilion, and he was watching it prepare his prosperity when the sky clouded over. The storm broke as hail; not an ear remained standing, and Hermagore, pale and silent with anger and despair, went away across the plain, his face bruised and his hands bloody from the hailstones that had wounded them.

As he approached a spring in order to bathe his injuries, he saw man lying on the edge, sleep. It was the same stranger who had once counted out pieces of gold in order to buy the boat. He had abandoned the oars and the net, then, and as Hermagore, went to wake him up in order to enquire as to his fortunes, noticed beside the sleeper an open purse; coins were scintillating within it; a few shone between the fingers of the closed hand. He must have started throwing them in the water, for some could be distinguished through the transparency, resting on the sandy bed of the spring. The man was still asleep. Hermagore picked up the purse and, having walked all night and part of the morning, he arrived at midday within sight of a town.

The houses were grouped around a vast dome accompanied by other smaller ones. Palaces bordered a large river traversed by hump-backed bridges. Trees were mingled with the houses; sometimes they lined up in long avenues or spread out in gardens. Waters shone therein. The streets were empty, deserted because of the heat.

Immense cemeteries surrounded the town; one might have thought they were forests, because a cypress stood at each corner of every tomb—which were all pyramidal or square blocks of stone. The first ones, those of women, were ornamented with roses. The perfume of the place, by virtue of the mixture of flowers and foliage, was simultaneously bitter and sweet, like death itself.

In the distance, a solitary visitor moved slowly between the tombs. Her long yellow veil sometimes caught on the branch of a cypress or the thorns of a rose, and then her face became visible, which was delicately made up. One she leaned over to read a name, and the medallions of her bracelet clinked on the marble; then she sat down and wept.

Hermagore drew closer. "Why are you weeping?" he asked hr.

"Where have you come from, then, transient," she replied, "to be unaware of my celebrated grief? The news has spread far and wide, and you're the only one who knows nothing about it. Do you not know that Ilalie was in love? She loved someone who left her. He has gone, and since then I please myself wandering in these places. He left one evening and abandoned me for poverty and wisdom, and it's said that he's now a fisherman on the edge of a river, near the sea."

"I have also been a fisherman on the edge of a river," Hermagore replied. "I've worked an arid land, but I'm weary of the ploughshare and the oar, and I've come toward gold and love."

Hermagore, who had lain down naked among the reeds of a river and slept with his head on a stone in the furrow of his field, who had been scourged by the wind, stung by bees and barked at by dogs, lay down on bronze beds and slept on woven silks. He was fanned by palm-leaves and lulled with songs; perfumes fumed at his bedside. There were astonishing amours. He became famous and sought-after, for there is a secret and cowardly dolor, for those repelled by it, in frequenting at least the happy lovers of the woman one desires, and Ilalie haunted the dreams of young men like a haughty statue. One morning found her naked on her bed, whiter than marble, smiling as if she had died of joy.

Hermagore did not shed any tears. He was admired for the superiority of his indifference, and the rumor of the elegant renown that she had brought him reached the queen. She lived in a palace surmounted by a vast dome surrounded by other, smaller ones. Hermagore was introduced into it in secret, and often entered it in the evening only to emerge again at dawn. The queen loved him and, as there is a mysterious contagion in destinies, he became king, the rightful one having died, idiotic and blissful, in the solitary pavilion where he dragged himself over the tiles, drooling. The sepulcher of the deceased consecrated the advent of the usurper; a few beheadings consolidated the adventure. The arrogance of the upstart made him believe in his predestination. People prostrated themselves before him; he grew bored.

One day, when he was crossing the main square of the city in broad daylight, with the crown on his head and a scepter in his hand, he noticed a man dressed in rags who was standing there looking staring at him and laughing. Again he recognized the stranger who had bought his boat and the sleeper whose purse had tempted him one evening by the spring. On the king's orders, the tatterdemalion was brought to him.

"Why are you laughing?" asked Hermagore. "What do you want from me—speak."

"O King," replied the wretch, "I'm looking at the shadow at your feet, cast by your glory."

The King looked down at the shadow. Composed of a crest, by virtue of the tall crown, a beak, by virtue of the scepter, and wings, by virtue of his cloak, it was squat, deformed and monstrous; it seemed, with its chimerical wingspan, to be some peevish and crippled animal, crouched at the feet of the conqueror and preceding him.

King Hermagore understood the beggar's allusion. It seemed to him that he had seen in the parody of his body the very image of his soul, and he wept. That evening he left the city furtively, and after having thrown his scepter and his diadem into the spring where he had once robbed the sleeper, as he passed by, he arrived at the little field that he had once worked, and, lying naked on the hard ground, he allowed himself to die there.

That year, an extraordinary crop announced itself throughout the land. Children got lost in the wheat. Only one little field remained sterile; it extended over the slope of a hill, uncultivated and full of brambles, green against the surrounding yellow, but when the wheat all around it had been cut, it became evident at close range that a single enormous ear had

106

grown there, and a skeleton was discovered underneath it. Its arms were outstretched in a cross, and the miraculous marvel was growing out of the skull.

A stranger who was working for hire among the harvesters came forward, cut the ear, and then knelt down, leaned over and kissed the ivory mask on the mouth. The others watched him do it in silence, and, when he did not get up again, they perceived when they touched him that he was dead.

III. Hermocrates; Or, The Tale That Was Told to Me at His Funeral

To M. le Comte de Clapiers [19]

I was woken up in the morning by an unaccustomed sound of voices. Everything fell silent. A horse struck the pavement of the courtyard with its shoe and, as I got out of bed and opened the window, someone knocked at my door. Without waiting for a response my valet came in, a letter in his hand. I broke the large black seal and read that Duke Hermocrates was dead.

The weight of the sigillary wax inclined the unfolded manuscript slightly. Outside, there was a clink of iron on sandstone and I saw the courier, urging his dappled horse to the gallop, going through the gate. He went along the avenue and I followed the unexpected, abrupt and diminutive figure with my eyes, gradually reduced to the proportions of a vignette, as if at the top of the page whose leaf I held between my fingers.

---

[19] Lazare-Alfred, Comte de Clapiers Collonges, was a cousin of Régnier's mother. Resident in Marseilles, he is nowadays remembered primarily for his coin collection. His elder brother held the hereditary title of Marquis de Clapiers, worn with distinction by some notable figures of the *Ancien Régime*.

In the green tunic with silver braid, the helmet with yellow plumes and the horn-handled whip, I saw once again the old duke's domestic and seigneurial retinue, the château, all the livery of the antechambers, stables and kennels, lackeys, squires and grooms, some sturdy and active, others booted and slim, crossing the gravel of the courtyards or the sand of the schooling-grounds, and, standing on the perron, flexing their calves or loosening their basques, or seated on the benches of the vestibule, knitting-needles planted in their powdered wings, the household servants, arrogant, obsequious and affected.

The vast château reappeared to me in the midst of its forests, at the end of interminable avenues, among its orderly or magnificent gardens, with coins or bouquets of water. One autumn, I had been a guest there. The Duke, by no means expansive, hardly communicated with the young relative who had come to pay his respects before leaving for the army. I went there as a companion to his son Hans, and, linked by amity, we were to join our ensign together.

We ate in the immense dining-room. Tapestries dressed the walls all the way to the ceiling. A Diana among the reeds of a river-bank was allowing her dogs to slake their thirst in the mud of a spring. One could hear the water splashing in the intervals between the rare words. The odor of wines and spices seasoned and swelled the silence. The sugar-frosting on the decorated cakes seemed to crackle. A fruit rolled from a bowl and during the scrupulous ceremony of the long meal, I was able to consider the thin, white-haired, clean-shaven, hard-faced old man at my ease, through the silverware and the crystal, better than I had been able to do face to face on arrival. His extraordinary life rendered him an object of admiration and curiosity to me.

The next day, at dawn, we left; then years had passed, and now he was dead. In the note, Hans asked me to come.

For the obsequies of the day after next it was necessary to get under way as quickly as possible, in order to arrive at the château on the previous evening. I gave orders for the trunks to be packed and the carriage to be prepared. The horses were tugging at the reins; the whip cracked. At dusk, a hare ran cross the road between two fields of clover and lucerne; the grey sky took on a hint of pink between the poplars.

The inn where we stopped for the night was good. The bedroom with serge curtains overlooked the main square; the clock chimed the hours; I slept badly.

At the edge of the town the highway resumed, between two rows of trees. Toward midday we were going alongside a canal. Its strip of flat water continued indefinitely, sometimes rigid between straight banks, sometimes flexible between curved shores. Hauliers were dragging heavy barges, a small donkey assisting them. During the long journey through that bleak landscape, almost identical to its reflection, nothing had distracted my thoughts. They were occupied with Duke Hermocrates. I reviewed the stories told about the course and aspect of his surprising life, which was already amplified in legend, and was now terminated.

Destiny resembled a fiction therein. Everything in it was ordered, as if in accord with a mysterious intention, and that mixture of everything made it unique and singular. Adventure risked disaster there, and the theft of its glory. A life both turbulent and methodical, the abundance of its events providing the opportunity for the most constant god fortune. That hand had lifted the sword, raised the scepter and pulled the strings of thousands of human marionettes. Aladdin's lamp mingled a drop of its oil with the molten wax of the torch of Eros over the flesh of a two-faced Psyche and awoke Fortune at the same time as Voluptuousness. The affairs of the time, with their enterprises, their ups and downs and their outcomes had furnished the man with the experiences of his diplomacy and the occupation of his power. From his youth to old age, everything—love, power, honors—had been given to him in a servile fashion. He knew human happiness in its excesses and its minutiae, the favors of fate in its connivance and its enslavement. Life had offered him all its circumstances, to the point of permitting him every opportunity, from noble deeds to underhanded intrigues—and now he was dead.

Dead! And what did he regret, in dying? During the twenty years of his retreat in that solitary château, to what reassessment of himself had he devoted his silence, while awaiting the eternal silence? He was said to have been living there in proud isolation, with the prestige of power voluntarily abdicated, save for the reserve of certain honorary, ceremonial and noble prerogatives. Etiquette is the mummy of grandeur, glory atrophies there into a doll. He amused himself with the scrupulous miniature of the efficacious pomp of his life. Alas, wandering in the sumptuous galleries, alongside those magnificent waters, upright and ill-tempered, doubtless self-absorbed, what had he reheard of the past in the echo of the halls, the voices of the fountains beneath the memorial oaks, which seemed, with the structure of life, the very voice of Destiny.

The approaches of the forest announced that of the château. The road cut through admirable woodlands and turned around the ridge above a vast pond. Frogs were croaking there. The triangle of still water, tiled here and there, in places, by water-lilies, plunged its point into the reeds. At each of the crossroads, an obelisk of green marble irradiated the star of the roads. One of them, which we followed, finally broadened out into an avenue; two parallel paths ran alongside it; between the quadruple range of trees, the carriage rolled more quickly. I put my head out of the window.

In the dusk, the château was visible; it was massive and sumptuous, monumental and delicate, with its windows, its frontons, its attics. The wheels became quieter on the sand; a wrought iron gate opened its passage between two stone pillars encircled with copper. We went through the vegetable gardens; little square basins glistened like the iron of spades; low buildings with fire-pots on their cornices surrounded a circular esplanade whose portal allowed a glimpse of the main courtyard, ornamented by trees in tubs. We stopped at a flight of steps. At the doors, lackeys held up candles, and one of them preceded me into the vestibule. Everything there was draped in black. A large crystal lantern swung from the ceiling, its flame flickering, and the butler, his long cane in his hand, bowed his bald head before me, with a clink of his silver chain.

I was lodged in the right wing of the château; a candelabra was burning on my table; a list of the people who had already arrived had been placed there. I ran my eyes over it while I was awaiting the return of the valet who had departed on my orders to enquire of the new Duke when he would be able to see me. The guests were already numerous. All the relatives were included among them; then the dead man's friends, and dignitaries who had come to pay their funereal respects, the majority for reasons of duty or politeness, some for the advantage of vanity, of which there would be no shortage. My former comrade Hudolphe de Haubourg would certainly be one of them.

Someone knocked. Hans sent word that I was to join him in the mortuary chamber, where he as keeping vigil, at ten o'clock. The clock chimed eight, and I decided to dine alone in my apartment, apprehensive of risking the communal meal, especially of encountering Haubourg there and having to put up with him. His conversation, all etiquettes, prerogatives and qualities, even wearied inattention. The sentiment of his dignity, exaggerated into a mania, persisted in the slightest actions. He laid claim to what was due to him to the point of making one doubt that one owed it. An honest man, but conceited; the erudition of his rank rendered him exact in demanding his precedences. Ceremonies, nuptial or funerary, pleased him; he never missed one, and took great delight in criticizing their faults, mocking those who insulted others, punctilious with respect to those who had insulted him. The obsequies of the old Duke and that for which they would provide a pretext must have preoccupied him for years, and he would do no less, I imagined, than put on a admirable performance,

I had pushed away the wedge of bread and was dipping quarters of spiced lemon in sugar when I was summoned. Via interminable corridors I arrived in the vestibule. The staircase went straight up; its wrought-iron banisters bordered its stone steps. Lackeys preceded me through drawing-rooms, some of them dark, where one bumped into items of furniture; groping forward, I sensed myself avoiding the pelts of tapestries or the flesh of satins; sometimes, on lifting up a curtain, silken tresses brushed my hand or face. Elsewhere, chandeliers were flaming; the palms of brackets displayed their hands by candlelight. The gilded wood of sideboards clenched to sustain tablets of rare marble or, bronze busts rested on onyx pedestals, backing on to tall mirrors which, in their burgau or rococo frames, reflected the tonsures of emperors or the napes of goddesses, the hair of queens or the fleeces of fauns. In the middle of one of these drawing-rooms, circular and painted with garlands, a single candle burned on a jade side-table. In a vast gallery, mosaics sounded beneath my footfalls. Between interlacing fruits, flowers and seashells, faces and emblems were visible; a zodiac displayed its prancing Sagittarius and its creeping Scorpio.

Finally, a door opened and I went in.

It was the Duke's bedroom. He was lying on his bed, at the head of which two candles were consuming themselves. I would have recognized him, as before but as if shrunken. His white hair seemed sparser and his face more glabrous. The human flesh retained a statuary quality in that harsh marmorized face. He had stiffened into a sort of dry mortuary sculpture.

Hans embraced me. While talking, he went back and forth, opening cupboard doors or drawers, shuffling papers or items of jewelry; finally, from a little enameled gold casket he took a large envelope and swiftly broke the seal. The silence was profound I looked at the little key in the lock of the casket, which was one of a bunch, the rest of which were oscillating. Hans sat down and indicated that I should do likewise. Time passed, and when he handed me the piece of paper, this is what I read in my turn:

"I shall not tell you my life story, my son; you have doubtless learned it through the rumors in which the memories still remain of those who saw me live it. They are already rare, for I am now old. The stories describe parts of it; some note the details curiously; a few trophies perhaps attest to future glory. The heavy plough, in turning the soil, will disturb medallions on which my profile will survive between two memorial dates. A laurier-rose will grow over my tomb; the epitaph will recall my deeds; a few of them were great, it's said. That renown is part of the inheritance that I am leaving you; you will benefit from it if you ever acquire a taste for diffusing yourself among men and getting mixed up in their Destinies. Might I also be able to bequeath you wisdom; listen, at least, to the particular truth that I have taken from the experience of a long life. I do not know what yours will be, or whether you will take part in the century's games; your temperament is little disposed in that direction; it requires desires that you do not have, and I suspect that this château, where I have spent my old age, will be the abode of your maturity. They see in the courtyard the monumental boudoir of someone who has brought regret and with him into retirement, when it is only the natural place in which a man remembers that he has lived.

"Oh, let live in the intended sense of the phrase; content yourself with being; but before you take possession of his dwelling, my son, it is necessary that you know, at least, on what thoughts my sepulcher will be closed.

"Be at ease, my son, have no fear that my shade will ever recross this threshold. I shall not come to test the weight of the sword I once carried in battles on its panoply, nor to consult among the dust of archives the titles of my glory, nor to recount the gold of which the cellars are full, not to accomplish spectrally the phantom simulacra that were the actions of life. I shall be a tranquil corpse, entirely dead, and no regret for what I have been will cause my ashes to quiver; there would, however, have been matter in my past to create a proud and obstinate ghost.

"I have made war; golden clarions have preceded me and all the winds, by turns, have shaken the creases of my flags. Great armies overstepping mountains, crossing rivers; I have even crossed the sea. I have organized countermarches and victories. Triumphal arches have been raised to me in bronze and foliage, from which an eagle or a dove flies from time to time. Thanks to me, the imperceptible ended in the prodigious; it is a few handfuls of oats, at the right moment, that make the charge; it is a morsel of bread, likewise, that makes the assault. By my efforts, thousands of men converged at the same crossroads, and the star of roads became the star of Destiny itself. I have known great enterprises, the abruptness of adventures, the unexpectedness of successes, all the infinitesimal detail of expeditions, all the impulses of improvisation. My name has been joined to the names of battles, and the territory of my dukedom counts more than one bloody encounter.

"A conqueror by force, I remained a master by intrigue. State secrets and the traffic of consciences were discussed in my study; the doors of my antechambers opened and closed with the dace-steps of covetousness. In hours of anxiety or anticipation, I have followed in thought the gallop of couriers over distant roads; their speed was the key to consequences. I have allied hopes, dissolved rancors; my seal had charged the conclusion of treaties; each of them added to my wealth an endowment or a snuffbox, a domain or a trinket.

"Rich, powerful and victorious, I had love. In mirrored chambers I have laid celebrated beauties down on cushions. They arrived, furtive or impudent, to offer or deliver themselves; their kisses were a stake or a salary. Highnesses and schemers brought their caprices or the calculations thereto. The mirrors reflected to infinity the postures of my victory in the facets of my vanity. Marvelous lips satisfied my vilest desires.

"I have tried to live in these lies, to enjoy them and be content with them, but the day came when I understood the deceptiveness of my illusion, when I wanted to relive them in that preparatory solitude in which a being summarizes himself, already weighing his own ashes.

"Alas, my son, during the twenty years of my retreat in this solitary château, I have found nothing of myself in all of that, which I believed to be my entirety. Oh, my thoughts were elsewhere! Around me, things maintained the countenance of my past. Guards stood at my door; lackeys encumbered the antechambers; women clad in finery sat at my table; curious and learned men slept under my roof in pilgrimage to the ancient idol, exemplary of their ambitions. Etiquette alone articulated the armature of my appearance, and I condescended to remain the simulacrum of the hero of so many stories, battles, successes and amours.

"People were able to imagine that, a proud and repetitive old man, I reviewed, with the pageantry of my glory, the deeds of its origin, that my brain ruminated battle plans or diplomatic ruses, and when, on the smooth sand of the pathways, my cane traced patterns and symbols, it was respectfully assumed that my obsessive memory was distracting itself by simulating plans for maneuvers or ciphers of correspondence.

"Oh, my son, I was not thinking about wars, nor about business affairs, nor about powdered princesses in mirrored retreats. The mental architectures that my efforts were striving to build in columns, domes and labyrinths were crumbling in the depths of my memory. The palaces, having become catacombs, were buried in the dust of forgetfulness, and, instead of the entire mass of enterprises, schemes and measures, all that remained as testimony of myself were a few fugitive impressions: transient, involuntary and furtive aspects of life. Those sparse moments, of the ruins of long years, seemed to me, in addition to the sole happiness, to have been the sole evidence. That is the whole of ourselves; that is all we regret: those seconds, felt almost unconsciously in the soul and the flesh, so briefly, which have a duration in memory akin to that of dust in the fissures of its rubble. That alone is worth something! The rest is whimsy, the empty, stupid life of our ambition, the covetousness of our brutality, subterfuges and affectations.

115

"Yes, my son, of great wars, all that I remember is some glint of sunlight on a sword, a little flower beneath the hoof of a horse, a frisson, an occasional gesture: minimal events mysteriously incorporated in my memory. I remember an open door, a rustle of paper, a smile on a mouth, the warmth of a skin, the odor of a bouquet; infinitesimal details, which are what life has of the rapid and the furtive, truly made to the measure of our nonentity.

"My hour is approaching; I sense that I am about to die and die entirely; perhaps there are afterlives for those who have known other joys; mine limited my destiny.

"A tomb stands at the far end of my gardens, in a solitary place. You shall lead me there with the appropriate pomp. My frivolous dust will lie there. A massive pyramid of black marble marks the spot; the epitaph will contain the lie of my existence, for the hero that it will exalt was but a paltry ephemeral sensibility, who, in circumstances in which others see a magnificent destiny, tasted only the miserable and humble joys of any perishable flesh.

"My child, I shall not return to haunt this dwelling; I am one of the dead who cast no shadow on the beyond. The few petty memories of hours and moments that I am carrying away will dissolve with my ashes. I am one of the dead who have no shadow; I shall not haunt this dwelling; you may live here tranquilly and smile when anyone mentions Hermocrates to you and exhorts you to imitate his endeavors; you know what remains to him of his thoughts and works. Smile, and think of him sometimes, at dusk; he loved a few of them."

It was then broad daylight. Hans opened the windows. I returned the singular manuscript to him, which he silently locked away in the golden casket. Gusts of fresh air came in. One of the two roses that were blooming in a crystal vase shed its petals. I took the other and went to the bed where the old duke lay, rigid, with gnarled hands. I put the flower between his fingers.

At midday we gathered in the great gallery on the ground floor. The relief of trophies bulged beneath the mourning-sheets, whose drapery was swollen in places by the corner of a pedestal surpassed by the toenail of a goddess or the hoof of a satyr. It was crowded, uniforms mingled with courtly costumes, and the noble host stood still beneath the chandeliers, lining the walls, backed up against the windows.

Hazard placed me close to Hudolphe de Haubourg. He came up to me and asked how I was related to the deceased, subsequently admitting his anxiety on the subject of obsequies. Universal ignorance of the ceremonial renders any ceremony dangerous; the difficulties of rank appeared to him redoubtable; certain cases presented themselves there of a nature that one would need recourse to an authorized competence; nothing of the sort had been done, so would even the best-established precedences be respected? He swelled with pride, prognosticating hitches and upsets.

Finally, the ushers announced Duke Hans. He came forward; a circle formed; there were bows and condolences and the flow commenced; I was the last to leave.

The coffin was lying in the vestibule beneath a catafalque, under the lights. The guards' swords gleamed; halberds rested on the tiles; eight porters lifted the heavy bier. Everyone followed.

The château displayed its monumental façade facing the grounds. The windows were quartered by their clear panes. The balconies were protruding their contorted ironwork; the niches were sheltering their statues; the marble columns were flourishing their sculpted capitals.

The gardens were deserted, their carpets of grass covered with large sheets of black crêpe; bronze tripods were burning between the trimmed yews; the lines of the pathways, sanded with jade, intersected at stucco obelisks; the avenue of water, tinted with floating ink, stagnated like a black marble slab.

There was a momentary pause; then the horses' plumes oscillated; bald heads were covered by caps. One group became agitated, from which Haubourg emerged, red and gesticulating, scandalized by some injustice, up in arms and brining is elbows into play.

A muffled drum-roll resounded, and the cortege traversed the park, alongside the lawns and the ponds, frightening the black swans that had been released on to the funereal water.

Monsieur d'Amercoeur

To Gabriel Hanotaux [20]

I. Monsieur d'Amercoeur

I have no intention of writing Monsieur d'Amercoeur's life-story here. Others are working at that fine project with infinite care, and I make no claim to be following them in the delicate investigations by means of which they desire to elucidate, point by point, an existence no less singular in its circumstances than the posthumous attention that it has excited.

There is, in fact, among those people who concern themselves with the particularity and causality of events, a keen curiosity regarding the individual in question. An investigation has begun, followed in various parts, and the exertion of so much laborious research cannot help but cast light on the enigma of his destiny.

Nothing passes more rapidly into oblivion than a glory like the one that Monsieur d'Amercoeur knew during his lifetime. Much in view then, because of his adventures, in war as in gallantry, by virtue of his status as a man of fashion and his exploits as a bold partisan, he seemed to be a more apt subject for the pastimes of novelists than the surveillance of historians, and it was not at all surprising to hear of his occult intervention in the most serious events, and that he not only par-

---

[20] Gabriel Hanotaux was a statesman and historian; in the former capacity, he was France's delegate to the League of Nations; in the latter, he produced a history of the Third Republic, a nine-volume history of the Great War and a seventeen-volume history of France.

ticipated in them but that he got to the bottom of them and orchestrated their ups and downs.

The initially-tentative entrance of Monsieur d'Amercoeur into a story is confirmed as his presence within it turns into precedence, and he dispossesses of their false attributes famous faces that become no more than apocryphal masks, behind which one distinguishes, magnified by reluctant mimicry, the thin smile of their mysterious instigator. Here is, therefore, a man who directs his times. One discovers one of his secret actions, and it seems, after all, that one is right to see him as one of the hidden springs of the epoch. If not, at least there remains a case of unique concordance by virtue of the almost marvelous fashion in which the facts of his life adapt, as if of their own accord, to the direction and range that can be attributed to them. They are, at the end of the day, merely singular coincidences. The probable builds up therein to the point of becoming the architecture of the truth.

I would not wish to make any injuriously surprising modification to a memory that is dear to me in more than one way. I have admired Monsieur d'Amercoeur since childhood. Connections existed between his family and mine, and the status that was afforded to him gave me the pleasure of seeing everyone adopt an opinion that was in part that of my relatives. They often talked about that remarkable man, and the stories of his adventures of every sort, which they did not hesitate to discuss in front of me, delighted me. The interest that I took in them never faded from my memory and it is to the tenacity of that childhood fascination that I owed the subsequent honor of becoming acquainted with the hero of so many fine stories.

Monsieur d'Amercoeur spent the last twenty years of his life in reclusive retirement—sufficient for the newspapers that reported his death to do so without commentary. He left the country after the shocking disgrace into which he fell. He traveled, he was forgotten. He left nothing behind, save for the noise that his mysterious escape had once generated, but a superficial renown, a few notable deeds in love and war, and the memory of certain eccentricities that preserved a vague celebrity, which later gave rise to the research whose successive discoveries were to end up attracting so much attention.

An adolescent during the interval of silence that preceded Monsieur d'Amercoeur's death, it was in the inn of a distant small town that I heard the name pronounced to which, for me, an entire intimate legend was attached. I made enquiries, and acquired the certainty that the Amercoeur in question really was the celebrated Marquis of whom my youth had dreamed. I sought him out; he granted me the requested interview, and I did not hesitate to visit him.

From the far side of the square I perceived Monsieur d'Amercoeur's house. It was a vast Portland stone building. Three windows beneath a fronton opened on to a balcony with bulging railings, supported to either side of the door by a projecting caryatid. The other windows were closed by shutters, those on the ground floor furnished with iron bars. On the fronton, one of the fire-pots ornamenting the roof-trusses projecting over the façade was an oblique triangle, the others little patches of broken shadow. In the middle of the deserted square was a fountain, its jet falling back into a low basin. A dog sleeping in the sunlight caught a passing fly. Others were buzzing around; a few, settled on the wall, seemed encrusted there; three flew away from the door-jamb when I rang the bell.

The torpor of the square made me appreciate the coolness of the vestibule. Arabesque stucco decorated the walls around green and yellow marble tiles. The limping valet led me through a dining room in which the table was already set. Pieces of orange peel were curling on a silver plate. Wine, in a cut-glass decanter, reddened the tablecloth with a bloody shadow. It exhaled an odor of pepper, sweetmeats and tobacco.

"Monsieur le Marquis isn't here," said the man, lifting a door-curtain. "He's taking a walk. I'll go and fetch him."

I found myself in a long gallery whose French windows opened on to the garden. A few roses were overflowing from bushes that must have been climbing the outer wall. The delicate flesh of the admirable, red and pompous petals of one of them was stuck to the window-pane; another, small and white, seemed delicately faded through the green-tinted glass, through which flower-beds could be seen framing a pool, surrounded by a semicircle of tall carefully-trimmed box-trees. Three groves of various trees ended there, the perspective of which was inversely reflected in three large mirrors placed at the back of the room in gilded brackets, between wooden panels, Here and there, antique busts stood on pedestals. The massive stools and monumental armchairs of a set of tapestry-upholstered furniture were set against the walls. In the center, a table supported a beautiful veined agate vase, next to a casket from which a pair of gold-rimmed spectacles protruded.

The Marquis is still nimble on his feet, I had been told, in spite of his eighty years; he plays a game of *boule* every day. He had abandoned one in order to receive me. He came from the far end of the central pathway. His tall figure was stooped over a walking-stick. The flaps of his embroidered silk coat came down to his calves. As he arrived at the French windows, the gesture he made to open them caused the rings on his fingers to sparkle. He looked at me without seeing me because of the glare of the windows, with which the handle of the stick held under his arm collided.

As he came in, the felt hat he threw on to a chair disclosed a small head with close-cut white hair. The olive-tinted face was illuminated by bright blue eyes. The active hands were still agile, not gnarled and fleshless, extended by lassitude, or perennially retracted, as often happens in old age.

When my name was pronounced the Marquis greeted me. "Welcome," he said. "I knew your great uncles, the Admiral and the Ambassador, very well."

As he spoke, he took a slender pipe from the agate vase on the table, which he stuffed and lit, and began walking back and forth with a light step, sometimes pausing in front of me. I also remained standing. Puffs of smoke punctuated his sentences as he passed.

"I can still see the Admiral," he told me. "He and his brother don't resemble one another, either in stature or corpulence. His is astonishing. I served under them, and if there's some honor in having done so, it's because following their enterprises required boldness and recklessness. If they didn't spare themselves much, they didn't spare anyone else at all. Their squadron and embassy were hard placements; I was subject to both, and the naval disciple was equal to the demands of diplomacy.

"Yes, I can still see your uncle with his green jacket and his crimson stockings, standing on his deck, his vessel leaving in its wake an odor of gunpowder and cooking. The able seaman and the scullion rubbed shoulders there. The succulence of the meals made the fury of the battles worthwhile. Neptune's trident shared the trophy cabinet with Comus' fork.

"And the other, with his priestly attitude and his prim old wife. All means seemed good to him. He made use of all kinds of trickery. Didn't he take ventriloquists with him to imitate his voice in the interviews he wanted to disavow, in which a sort of double counterfeited his person? His wardrobe contained the costumes of all kinds of masquerades, his pharmacy make-up and poisons; he used the skill of policemen, the agility of acrobats and the smiles of women.

"I met them both for the last time when they were very old. One was living in a little town, the other in a rural retreat. The Admiral had gout and the Ambassador was deaf. One had devoted himself to colleting seashells, the other to growing tulips. They had all sorts of them, very beautiful, and every year, one of them would send the other a shell resembling a tulip, or a tulip resembling a shell, and so on until they died, each without quitting his display-cases or flower-beds to clasp one final time those hands that had so rudely and delicately manipulated people, whose last gesture was to label a conch or number a bulb."

"Yes," I replied, "they were singular individuals, and it's a pity that they didn't write down what they knew. Did they ever recount the details of their maneuvers or their schemes?"

The Marquis had replaced his extinct pipe on the table, and the ashes of its little black urn poured on to the marble.

"What!" he exclaimed, almost going red with anger. "To write a life, substituting destiny for the hazard that assembles in human memory what it needs to fashion the imprint of a medal or the relief of a sarcophagus! Some people have that defective and pretentious impudence.

"To write a life is to recover the order of our statures, the motives of our actions, the place of our sentiments, the structure of our thoughts, to reconstitute the architecture of our Shadow! But nothing is gained by the perspective, in which hazard disposes the fragments in which we survive. Destiny envelops the circumstances that it appropriates. There is a mysterious choice between the decrepit and the durable within us.

"Awkwardness and clumsiness often prepare perfect actions. The deadly sword-thrust that touches and pierces might require a disgraceful torsion of the muscles. A clenched fist directs the flashing blade. Everything is perspective, and episodes. Of many intermediate gestures, a statue only fixes the decisive one.

"What a mediocre memory you would retain of me, if you knew everything about me! You would be less astonished to see me old and alone in this house—me, Polydore Amercoeur, who has frequented the beds of princesses and the courts of kings, who has borne the sword and worn the mask—if I told you why I'm here. I would destroy a necessary disparity.

"It is known that I have spent five years of reclusion in a solitary prison, but no one knows why I went into it or how I got out. My disgrace remains a mystery and my escape a miracle. The accessories of the deed do not exist. The archives do not contain any record of my connection and nothing was found of the instruments of my escape.

"Every man who explains himself diminishes himself. One ought to keep one's own secret. Every good life is composed of isolated moments. Every diamond is a solitaire and its facets only match others in the gleam they radiate.

"One can, for oneself, live each of one's days again; to others, it is necessary to appear intermittent. One's life story does not tell itself, and it is necessary to allow everyone the freedom to imagine it!"

The Marquis was striding back and forth across the room. The end of his walking-stick was tapping the floor. A ray of sunlight sparkled on the rings of his fingers. I watched him march. His long coat brushed the corner of the table, scattering the grey ash from his pipe, and I thought about his singular life of alternatives and contingencies, of balls and battles, full of fits and starts, and of which he retained, deep inside, permanently, the rumors and echoes.

Such was my first meeting with Monsieur d'Amercoeur. That was exactly what he said to me. Since then, the pattern of the life of which the celebrated marquis made a mystery has been reconstituted. The silhouette has become a statue. The few anecdotes reported here relate to his youth; Monsieur d'Amercoeur talked about it willingly, and gradually abandoned his reserve in my company. My prudence never ventured to disturb his. I listened to hum without interrogating him. That discretion won me his confidence, and he went as far as to allow me to copy a long letter of which he was the subject, which related an episode of his adolescence that pleased and amused me. The reader will find it among these stories.

Save for that document, the other memories came to me in our conversations, in which I heard them narrated by the illustrious storyteller. I do not pretend to be doing anything more than reproducing, precisely enough, the turn that he gave to them, both in relating the substance and in placing the story in his own mouth. Perhaps these brief stories, the circumstances of which seem curious to me, will serve, without my knowledge, to fill in some lacuna in the study made of everything concerning his character. I do not think so, however, and I would much prefer to see them as ingenious fables in which the mind of an old man obtained enjoyment in placing his past life in a ornamental perspective.

The events that he reports and the deeds he attributes to himself present a curious mixture of truth and fiction. Both are detectable there, and their combination is not devoid of artistry. I have savored the pleasure of these adventures; others might perhaps give them meaning and scope, but I prefer to hear the tone and imagine them as allegory: that of a masked man playing the flute at dusk, beneath the arcade of a clump of holly- and rose-bushes.

II. An Amorous Adventure at Sea

My turbulent childhood soon gave way to a difficult youth, but the former was forgiven when the latter brought me to embark, at the age of seventeen on the *Sans-Pareil*, which bore the flag of your uncle the Admiral. The squadron was about to sail when my father took me to the harbor. From the inn, I followed him through the streets, where he sometimes turned around to make sure that I had not given him the slip, for he feared some escapade that might thwart his opportunity to get rid of me.

The quays were overflowing. Stevedores, bending their backs beneath the weight of boxes, were elbowing their way through the crowd. Sweat was pouring from sunburnt foreheads and saliva dripping from the corners of mouths. The corpulence of barrels protruded over the flagstones where the obesity of sacks collapsed. People stepped over chains only to get tangled in ropes. The long gangplanks connecting the ships to the shore were sagging in the middle under the feet of porters. Vessels filled the dock.

Here and there, amid the network of yard-arms overlapped, a hoisted sail inflated, and the masts were oscillating imperceptible against the blue of the sky. There was an assembly of ships of all kinds, painted red, green and black, shining with varnish or dull with wear. Bulging hulls brushed against sleek flanks, the former swelling like goatskins, the latter tapering like rockets. Figurines were profiles at the prows, grimacing masks fashioning emblems. Carved into the wood, one could see the face of a goddess, the visage of a saint or the muzzle of an animal. Mouths were smiling in the snouts, the whole being barbarous, naïve or ridiculous. Holds exhaled the odor of food-supplies and the perfume of spices; the cargoes mingled the sharpness of pickling-brine with the perfume of tar.

A small boat picked up my father, me and my luggage, to take us to the squadron anchored outside the harbor. We wove our way through the inextricable clutter of the docks; the rhythmically-plied oars sometimes brought up a piece of sea-weed or peel. The stagnant salt-water was adulterated with all kinds of filth, marbled by oily patches, sticky with viscosities. Gradually, progress became easier, the obstacles more widely spaced; we went around a few large vessels with pot-bellies. Squatting heavily, streams of dirty water dribbled from the muzzles of their prows; the smoke of galleys rose in spirals around the masts; a cabin-boy perched in the rigging threw a rotten apple at us as we passed by. I picked it up and saw in the purulent flesh the marks of the teeth with which the joker was laughing at us, sitting astride a yard-arm.

The boat began to sway gently, and once the pier had been doubled we perceived the squadron; it was gathered there, high on the blue sea. Four ships, and one larger one, slightly apart. We steered for the *Sans-Pareil*. A flag bearing a coat of arms was flapping at the top of the mainmast. The muzzles of the cannon were gleaming in the gun-ports. The masts cast slender shadows on the calm water. A bell rang.

The rowers made haste, bent over their oars. A little foam splashed my hands. We were spotted, and climbed aboard by means of a rope-ladder. We were just in time. The anchors were being raised by rotating capstans; the ships were about to get under way. I was left alone; my father hurried off to talk to the admiral. The departure cut short our goodbyes. Whistle-blasts overlapped; commands were shouted through a loud-hailer. The extended sails inflated. My father got back into the launch. We waved to on another; we never saw one another again.

A brutal altercation, my exit, slamming the door, a day of anger wandering through the countryside, the asperity of the landscapes neighboring the château, the high winds of that scorching summer, the promptitude of an arrogant character, the impetuosity of an intractable pride, all came back to me, along with the paternal insult whose ineptitude I grasped: the lost head, enraged hands and furious fanaticism that had broken, methodically and angrily all the windows on the ground floor of the château with hurled stones, so that a shard of glass struck the head of the cellar-master and broke the cup that my father was holding, at the table from which the women got up in fear and fled.

The gardeners found me the next day, lying in the bushes, nursing the intoxication of my folly. Those worthy men, who had grown old in our service, were not unduly surprised by the outburst. They doubtless saw it as a continuation of my precocious misdeeds: opened bird-cages, trampled flower-beds, broken fences and, once, the most beautiful roses in the garden savagely cut and scattered on the path.

I was seven years old then. I had been removed from the care of the women and tutors succeeded one another, intermittently, from one month to the next. I saw their strange faces again. There were fat ones and thin ones, bulging bellies and rigid spines, in ecclesiastical garb or with a learned deportment, the worn faces of aged deacons and the hollow faces of young laymen, some reeking of the sacristy and others of the library. Of them all, the memory remains of looking forward to my liberty, a little Latin, not much Greek, no mathematics, a few shreds of history, and of one of them, whom I rather liked and ended up as a poet somewhere, precise notions of mythology, with a knowledge of the gods, their attributes and their amours.

Mine soon commenced. Mansards and barns sheltered the enterprises. Chambermaids' straw mattresses and pastoral bundles of hay lent themselves to my first frolics. I remember summoning bells interrupting the games and barking dogs disconcerting the positions. I put my arms round ancillary waists and fondled rustic breasts. The affectations of ladies' maids varied the naivety of shepherdesses. To the jargon of the former and the patois of the later I soon preferred the daughters of the nearby town.

It was one of them, and the scandal of an excessively loud love-making session, that occasioned, after an ill-tempered reprimand, the altercation whose consequences I could mull over at leisure aboard the *Sans-Pareil*, and in the fresh wind that raised her up, along with the swell, on the high seas.

Sculpted on her prow, the *Sans-Pareil* bore a mariner's face, winged and scaly, painted in gold, and on her poop, each holding aloft a lantern with swirling flame, were four genies blowing the breath of their gilded mouths into twisted sea-shells.

Birds the color of oriental waters and the white grebes of icy seas whirled around our errant beacon lights. The mariner's head was mirrored in calm waves or splashed by tumultuous waves. The tropical sun cracked its horny gilt and the moon of polar nights silvery its icy smile. Its staring eyes saw the curves of gulfs and the angles of capes; its ears heard the nonchalant harmony of waves lapping sandy beaches and the crash of surf on rocky promontories.

Many strange peoples came aboard. We received bearded men in garments of oily leather. Without saying a word, they brought us reindeer horns, seals' teeth and bears-kins. Ceremonious yellow dwarfs presented us with silkworm cocoons, bright ivory, lacquer-work, and insects and grotesques carved in jade like frogspawn. Natives offered us feathers lightly powdered with gold, and, on one isolated island, we saw green-tinted women coming toward us dancing and juggling red sponges.

For four years I traveled the seas in that fashion. The anchor bit into the coral of madrepores and the granite of reefs. The wind that inflated our sails had the odor of sunlight or snow. We took on fresh water on every shore. The salt water of marshes and the clear water of stony brooks left their mud or sand in the bottom of goatskins in their turn.

I visited many ports: those which swarm under the sun, those which get bogged down under the rain and those which go to sleep under the snow, which contain great ships, protect painted boats or only shelter a few bark canoes. Cities appeared to us at dawn and dusk, magnificent or lamentable, heaping up the rows of their palaces or crowding the huddled mass of their shacks, those from which one heard the sound of orchestras by night and those in which one heard the voices of fisherman hauling in their nets at dusk.

We saluted doges in marble dwellings and obis in mud huts. In sordid dives we slaked ourselves with black slaves; in luxurious bedrooms we courted bejeweled women. Smoky torches and bright candelabras shone over our sleep.

Thus I came to know all the seas. We escorted princes and joined merchant convoys. Sometimes our gun-ports roared. Sulfurous smoke floated, unleashing golden lightning. I felt the quivering of broadsides and the shock of cannonballs smashing into the hull, torn sails hanging down from broken masts. I saw ships sunk, by pirates' fire-ships as well as corsairs' grapnels.

The sea is even more terrible than those who bloody it. I've seen all its faces—its infantile morning face, its gold-streaming midday face, its Medusan evening mask and its shapeless nocturnal aspects, the insidiousness of calms succeeded by the vehemence of tempests. A god inhabits the changing water; he sometimes rises up, taking hold of the mane of the waves and the tresses of the algae, in the rattle of the wind and the rumor of the swell; he fashions himself out of foam and mist; his mysterious hands clench like claws; and, standing up, with his waterspout torso, his mantle of fog, his face of cloud and his lightning-flashing eyes, he works his magic on the waves and the squalls and, innumerable, collapses in the monstrous baying of the waves, the howling of muzzles and the laceration of talons, succumbing in the racket of his fall and reborn in the dribble of his own fury.

The sea was uniformly calm and mild when we arrived in the vicinity of the island of Lérente. We had come from far away, a long crossing over misty waters. The ice-floes were melting as we entered that warmer region; the sky gradually cleared and the sun reappeared. The crimson flag was rippling in the breeze; the figure on the prow was reflected in a mirror continually broken before it by the rapidity of the course that dispersed its crystal. One day, at sunset, the lookout cried: "Land!" The coast appeared momentarily, in green and roseate glory, and as dusk fell a damp fog enveloped the vessel and covered the sea around us. We were sailing slowly over violet water in the gentle moistness of those airborne tissues, translucent and crumpled.

The pilot steered with circumspection. The landing was dangerous, the point notorious for shipwrecks. A vague superstition surrounded the famous and charming island, divine and once siren-haunted.

Suddenly, the *Sans-Pareil*, her sails hauled in, completed her course and stopped; the anchor bit; the fine spidery mist clung to the masts, hanging down in curtains.

The island was almost invisible. Gradually, an exquisite odor of trees and flowers spread.

The order that everyone had to remain aboard cut short our curiosity. No one was to go ashore that night. The island's noises reached from a distance, as if filtered by the mist.

My companions went to bed, one after another. Everything went quiet. I learned on the side, listening to the imperceptible oscillation of the masts and the footsteps of a sentinel, and kept my ear cocked toward the shadows. Later, it seemed to me that I could hear music. It sang delightfully in the dis-

131

tance, in an intermittent fashion, as if insinuating itself through the pores of the fog, which muffled the spongy darkness. In the end, I distinguished a concert of flutes.

My resolution was quickly made. The pilot told me that the ship was anchored in the center of a sandy bay, five hundred fathoms from the coast. I went down to my cabin, hung a small compass around my neck and ran to the prow of the vessel, above the figurehead. Undressing rapidly, I took my bearings one last time, and let myself slide silently down an uncoiled rope into the sea.

The water was warm and calm, and I swam without making any noise. Soon, the ship disappeared from view. The waves murmured in my ears; sometimes, I floated on my back in order to verify my direction. Soon I heard the rumor of the breakers on the beach. The fog cleared and became a transparent vapor. I found my footing. Floating seaweed brushed my bare legs. The odor of riverside flowers mingled with the aroma of marine plants.

A little wood formed a black mass. It came down to the sea, where the whiteness of a marble terrace was visible. A stairway went down to the water. The steps were draining slowly. A statue of a woman stood up to either side; as the ebb-tide uncovered their waists it made two sirens of them. The polished scales of their tails moistened my hands. I approached each of them in turn and, hoisting myself up, kissed each one on the lips. Their mouths were cool and salty.

I climbed the steps. At the top, I stopped. A star was shining above the trees; wide pathways opened in their thickness. I followed the middle one; it ended at a round-point bordered by arcades of bushes, under which the jets of fountains fell back.

In the center, in a large nacreous shell, a woman was asleep. The water that was running down a rocky wall behind her left pearly drops on her cheeks and breasts. She was lying down, one arm beneath her head, stretched out in the shell, appropriate to her marine slumber. There was a nocturnal half-light, in which her long glaucous dress sparkled. She was smiling in her sleep.

Her smile awoke beneath my kiss. The undulant shell was soft to our united bodies. I took her; a sigh inflated her throat, her hair came loose and silently, in the translucent and perfumed shadows, to the murmur of the fountains, spontaneously and for a long time, she possessed, perhaps the naked image of her dream, and I the mysterious goddess of the embalmed isle.

"Who are you?" she asked me, in a whisper, as she put up her hair again, the damp end of which had stuck to her excited breasts. "Who are you, who comes mysteriously into private gardens in this fashion, to awaken nonchalant sleepers? Where have you come from? Your lips have the salty taster of the sea and your body a divine nudity. Why did you choose the darkness to appear?

"The marine gods have long been masters of this isle, so survey your domain. I have constructed this retreat to the glory of Love and the Sea. From my terrace, one can see everything. The high tides mingle their fleecy foam with the dove-down of my trees. The wind seems to unfurl in the harmonious treetops. One might think that the raucous and iridescent waves were cooing like turtle-doves.

"I have ornamented my gardens with sea-shells and fountains and erected on the steps of my threshold statues of the Sirens that once dwelt here. Was it them who sent you to me, their sister? I am terrestrial, alas, but the swell of my breasts moves to the rhythm of the waves, the waves of my hair imitate the undulation of algae, my fingernails resemble pink seashells. I am smooth and saline, and this glaucous dress is so limpid that I appear in it as if it were water running continuously over my body."

She smiled as she spoke thus, and then fell silent, and put a finger to her lips.

At the same instant the flutes sang in the illuminated boscage; lanterns lit up in the trees; footfalls and laughter were heard.

We both rose to our feet; something drew me to her ankle and I picked up a long strand of seaweed, which I coiled around my waist. The end of the pathway brightened. Capering torch-bearers preceded a procession of richly-costumed men and women. Silken hoods inflated to the beating of fans. The masquerade spread out into the gardens. The torches were reflected by the fountains. The jets of water scintillated like vaporized gems. The entire wood vibrated with music.

The beautiful nymph had put a hand on my shoulder and, extending the other toward the bizarre crowd surrounding us, she cried out in a clear voice:

"Honor the god, our guest; he came from the stairway to the Sea, to the pious courtesan Sirena de Lérente, who was asleep. He kissed the Sirens of the marine portal on the lips, and his mouth whispered his name to me. He is our guest."

And both of us, interlaced, preceding the musicians and the assembly that was acclaiming us, went along the pathway where the fountains and the flutes were singing to the palace, as dazzling as a magical submarine grotto, where the foam of silverware unfurled on sumptuous tables, and crystal chandeliers hung like stalactites from the ceiling.

And, naked, grave and joyful, I raised to my lips, after she had steeped her own there, a beautiful golden cup worthy of Amour, which had the form of a breast.

III. Monsieur de Simandre's Letter

I'm taking the opportunity to write to you, my dear cousin, provided by the leave of absence of one of my men, who is coming to your region, and I'm simultaneously taking the liberty of recommending the fellow to you. He's a lusty fellow, and you'll doubtless be able to make use of him. He shows in all circumstances an admirable resourcefulness and discipline, and I wish that your son resembled him in that respect, for it's your Polydore who is the subject of my letter, my health remaining good and my age preserving me from the kind of adventures of which he has too many.

Thus, I shan't talk about myself. You know me from top to bottom, through and through, thrust and parry. I'm just the same and I'd scarcely notice the years if the difference between the men of our time and the boys of today didn't make me feel the distance that separates us. Our youth didn't resemble theirs and our old age is even further away.

Polydore notified me of his arrival and his intention to come by water because of the smoothness of the road and the beauty of the banks. The slowness of boats pleased him more, he said, than the haste of the mail-coach; the sound of oars seemed more harmonious than the gallop of horses. That was, at least, what I gathered from his contorted and laconic note, the odor of whose wax seals made me feel ill, and which stunned me with its galimatias and its amphigory, while the pretentious intricacy of the writing exasperated me.

I took off my spectacles and put them down on my table. I lit my pipe and, while waiting for the dandy to come downriver and disembark at Pontbourg. I resumed smoking, gazing at the sky through my window-panes, while stroking my dog and letting the day go by.

You would be familiar with that corner of the sky, my dog Diogenes and the place where I live, my dear cousin, if you had ever decided to do as Polydore has done, but the abode of my captaincy, and the old château where I represent the authority of the Prince whose whims you counsel, have nothing to tempt a schemer like you. You're in position at court, and wouldn't risk missing the windfall of some opportunity by coming to visit an old codger like me in his lair. Besides which, you're not much younger than me, and it's said that you're not as nippy, for bowing, pirouetting and kicking and kicking your heels are more crippling than the guard-duty, sieges and ambushes to which I've returned, while you're still running around in fancy dress, taking your tobacco from the diamond-studded boxes of courts while I take mine from the stone pot in the guard-room, and you read with an enameled pince-nez while I'm writing to you with the aid of horn-rimmed spectacles.

Although a trifle long-sighted, my dear cousin, my vision remains good and I love to see what I contemplate every day. The objects that surround me are familiar. I know my lieutenants, and every one of my soldiers, by name. I recognize every sentinel by the way he drops the butt of his rifle on the old stone of the rampart. My window overlooks a hornbeam plantation arranged in quincunxes, where I go for walks; then, leaning on the parapet, I can see the high wall; to the right and the left, stout towers inflate their corpulent masonry. They support the vast fortified terrace on which the château rests, simultaneously elegant and military, among trees and a few flowers. It's truly a beautiful place. From there, one overlooks the entire town, with its houses, its narrow streets, its sprawling squares, its angular bell-towers and its quays along the river, traversed by the bridge.

One day, about four o'clock, I was watching quartermasters passing by, returning from expeditions with big bales of hay; some of them were laughing, chewing the stems of flowers, when I was notified of the arrival of some boats.

They were at the bend in the river, behind the large isle of poplars. I went down to the harbor to see them come in. They approached gradually, steering through the buoys marking the channels between the sandbanks. There were four of them, in convoy. They were all carrying furled white sails, their hulls painted in beautiful colors. They were no longer rowing; the boatmen were maneuvering them with poles. Finally, they arrived; they were moored to the key and gangplanks extended.

Polydore got up from the cushions on which he was lying at the front of the boat, sheltered by an awning—a silken sheet extended from four silvery poles. He lifted the flap with a hand laden with rings. His costume astonished me; he was wearing a loosely-fitting striped jacket, and one of those variegated tulips knows as "parakeets" was sticking out of his buttonhole. The boat, moreover, was also an aviary.

I jumped on to the deck, perhaps a trifle abruptly, for the curious birds in the cages took fright, with a clatter of wings and cries, just as the toe of my boot collided with a mandolin lying there. Piles of books over which I stumbled fell into the water and sank under the weight of their bindings. The blues, gilts, greens and purples of their smooth morocco leather or imbricated hides seemed, seen through the water into which they disappeared, to became fickle minnows, glaucous eels or orange goldfish. To complete the disorder, a little monkey, on whose tail I stepped, climbed the rigging of the mast, squealing and sat at the top on its behind, blinking the eyes in its hairless face.

Polydore pretended not to have noticed anything, and invited me to sit down; he seemed more ceremonious than expansive but invited me to dinner with scrupulous politeness.

The boats were moored in a line and one could easily pass from one to another. A laid table awaited us on the second. The evening was mild and beautiful, the fare excellent. The little monkey came down from the mast and frolicked around us, juggling with glass balls that emitted odorant scents when they broke.

At the end of the meal, which had put me in a good mood, I suggested to Polydore that I had no doubt that the third boat secretly contained some beautiful woman with whom he was in love. He smiled and, taking me by the hand, invited me to follow him. The boat in question was fitted out with boudoirs and couches. Precious silks were extended there, crystal and copper chandeliers swayed imperceptibly to the gentle inflexion of the river. In the middle there was a rotunda of mirrors.

To my offer of accommodation at the château, Polydore preferred the abode of his boats. The fourth, where I left him, contained comfortable bedrooms. I wished him goodnight and withdrew.

A few days later he came to see me. He had a book under his arm and a parasol to protect him from the sun. I took him to visit the château. He took a keen interest in the mosses covering the old stones. He seemed pale, and I reproached him for the softness of his life. My officers, good lads who lived heartily, would have distracted him from his solitude. He refused.

"No, Monsieur," he said to me, "I prefer my floating dwelling. The river is amenable to slumber; it scarcely rocks the boat; one no longer hears anything going by but life, and one feels as if one is being carried without being carried away. I like my sedentary solitude; I like the sharp and charming shadow that your château casts upon the water in the evening. Through the great arch of the bridge I can see the poplars on the island; we're close enough to the sea for a few gulls to come this far, and I like watching them fly. The flight of swallows distracts me too. The bats cross paths, and my little monkey watches them in the evening. They are to birds what he is to humans—dubious kin."

As I could see that Polydore was committed to his eccentricities, I ceased to combat them, and returned to my affairs without paying any more heed to him. I was getting ready to leave for a tour of the region.

On the appointed morning, I went across the bridge with my escort and saw Polydore, who waved to me from his boat. He had just been bathing in the river and was still naked and dripping wet. He was not, as I would have assumed, thin and sickly. The sun made the droplets on his white skin glitter, and he appeared, in the morning light, slender and wiry, his flesh firm and slyly muscular. I returned his greeting; he dived, and the water splashed around his fall.

On my return, I was amazed by the rumor that greeted me. Polydore had killed two men in duels and was cutting an unexpectedly frantic swathe through the entire region. The town and its surroundings were abuzz, their ordinary tranquility seemingly under a spell. The decency of a century of rigor had melted away like a church candle on the devil's altar. A crazy wind was blowing; the serious meals of yore were changing into orgies; orderly quadrilles were ending up as sarabands; the intrigues of yesterday were being transformed into scandals.

The imperturbable Polydore was leading this vertiginous whirl with a smile on his lips and a rose in his buttonhole. The contagion had spread to the countryside. One by one, the châteaux, calm at the end of their tree-lined driveways, torpid amid their ponds, correct in the depths of their grounds, were lighting up. Ballrooms were reopening. Their chandeliers were garlanded. Festooned carts and traveling berlins crossed paths on the roads, for the sake of ostentation or elopement. There was building in progress. Masons' ladders leaning on walls facilitated amorous climbs. There were masquerades.

One morning, the boats to which the elegant folk came every day to obtain the orders of the day remained mute. The gangplanks were not lowered; the little monkey did not climb the mast, grimacing. Everything seemed to be asleep. By midday, no one had appeared. People began to get anxious. The handsome gentlemen chatted between themselves animatedly. The absence of Polydore astonished them less than the desertion of his servants.

Finally, the decision was made to visit the boats. Having been consulted, I gave the order. The first was empty: not a bird in the aviaries; the strings of the mandolin broken; one book open at a torn-out page. In the dining room, a glass had been tipped over, reddening the tablecloth.

We reached the rooms. Doors locked. They were broken down. Everyone crowded forward to take a look. We went in. No one there. But in the great boudoir in the rotunda, where their anger had broken all the mirrors, we found the nine most beautiful women in the town crouched or lying alone, their hair untidy. Doubtless they had each come in secret, and had encountered one another there, by virtue of the singular caprice of their unique, multiple and alternate Lover.

139

IV. The Singular Diners

They were curious dinners that the Princesse de Termiane held every week.

A tall iron gate closed the entrance to the noble dwelling with its golden lances. In the distance, at the far end of the avenue that led to it, one saw the robust ironwork clench its ornamental defense and erect the arrogance of its portal. Wrought iron flowers garlanded the bars and spread over the fronton, where two vast lanterns swelled like duplicate fruits of crystal and bronze, each on the end of its chain.

The carriages of visitors stopped at that gate. It was necessary to get out there; no wheel ever scored the sand of the immense courtyard, as deserted as a sandy shore, flecked here and there by the velvet foam of sparse moss. Only a side door gave access to the interior. If the weather was fine the guests traversed the sandy area on foot; if not, they found a sedan-chair there with porters. No one ever disobeyed that order.

The façade of the palace slumbered behind its closed shutters. Swallows skimmed the grey mass of the edifice with their flight. The part inhabited by the Princesse was on the opposite side, overlooking the gardens, and only took up one corner of the dwelling, the rest of which remained empty.

She lived alone there, the Prince being resident abroad. He had been pointed out to me once at the baths in Lorden, where he came to cure himself in the springs of the humor that broke out on his face in painful red patches. He was a small, thin man with fox-like features, eccentric in every way, nervous, with a narrow waist striped by the sash of some order, which he never took off. Enjoying that society, whose language he did not speak, and where he was welcomed on account of his high status, he paraded his arrogance and mutism there before returning to his villa in Termi, from which he scarcely ever emerged, except for his annual cures and rare trips to see his wife. He only spent a few hours there each time.

The Princesse received him in the large drawing-rooms of the palace, opened for the occasion. He always left before nightfall. Then the drawing-rooms were closed again; the untied curtain-loops allowed the heavy curtains to fall back; the door-curtains hung down stiffly in their recovered creases; the snuffer put out the candles; the numerous domestics summoned for the circumstance immediately disappeared, returning to the quarters where they lived, only a few being sufficient for ordinary service. The fountains in the garden, which had launched their prismatic sprays, fell silent one after another, and in the courtyard, instead of the splendor of liveries, no one was any longer to be seen but the old gardener, picking up a leaf with the end of his rake or trimming the rounded heads of the orange-trees on the steps of the perron.

It was in that dwelling, fallen silent again after the pomp of those arrivals and ceremonial departures, that the Princesse received, every week, the few individuals making up her intimate circle. She lived, however, not so much solitary as reticently, not failing to put in an appearance, on certain festival occasions, to show off her elegance and beauty, smiling with the arrogance necessary to discourage familiarity, while nevertheless acting in accordance with the customs that the favor of her presence satisfied. That condescension concluded, her life became a closed book again.

Curiosity had admitted the secret without any longer attempting to penetrate it. It was mentioned to me in the early days of my sojourn, and if the hazard of encounters had not established a relationship for me, at first courteous and gradually friendly, with one of the guests at those mysterious dinners, I would never have given any thought to the desire to be admitted to one of them. My friend never missed attendance there, and nothing could deflect him from his assiduousness, even once.

On the appointed evening, he told me, when I interrogated him regarding the ritual of that singular cult, every guest got down at the gate and, having crossed the courtyard, found an old white-haired valet in the vestibule. Everyone received from him a small lighted lamp. Without anyone accompanying the visitor, he headed for the Princesse's apartment.

The long journey was complicated by the intersection of staircases and corridors. Footsteps sounded on the pavements of landings or the mosaics of galleries, rattled on the parquet of large halls or were muffled by the carpets of drawing-rooms. It was necessary to part draperies, open doors and operate catches. The light of the little lamp illuminated rows of statues and busts, the smile of a marble or the gravity of a bronze, a nudity or a pose. In passing, the light swelled the paunch of a vase, awoke the gilt of a sideboard, caused the crystal of a chandelier to sparkle. Empty corridors ended in deserted rotundas and, moving from step to step, and door to door, one finally arrived at the apartment of the Princesse de Termiane.

On the day when I was to be introduced there, I went to the home of my friend, Monsieur d'Orscamps, in good time. He had arranged that I should take the place at the Princesse's table left free by his departure. He was leaving the next day; his luggage was cluttering the vestibule. The stables open, the domestics dismissed, the whole house had already taken on an air of abandonment.

I looked for d'Orscamps on every floor and was about to go down into the garden when the sound of bagpipes guided me to the top of the house. I reached the attics and, opening a door, I discovered him in a small unfurnished room, squatting on the tiles and blowing into the mouthpiece of an instrument doubtless left there by some clown of a flunkey. He didn't hear me come in and continued inflating the obese bladder, from which he extracted a raucous melody. When he saw me, he got up, throwing away the instrument, which deflated with a plaintive sigh.

"I'm getting ready for the journey," he told me. "Tomorrow, the carriage will take me to the coast; a boat will take me across the sea and I'll see my birthplace again." He added: "I'd never have had the strength to leave, but for this old pipe and its poor music. I've seen my homeland again therein, its grey and pink moors, its woods, its shores, the dancing in the clearings, the complexion of the girls, the faces of the boys. I've breathed in its odor of sugar and salt, flowers and seaweed, bees and seagulls. Once I'm there, all of that will seem insipid.

"What will boredom make of me? A maniac, like the Prince de Termiane. You know him, you know how he lives at Termi. It's a sinister town, immense, with its abandoned palaces, its ruined houses among greenish marshy hardens, its inextricable side-streets, its perfume of fever and water, but it's there that he finds the only amusement that pleases him. He hunts cats. Those animals pullulate there. One sees them wandering everywhere, half-savage, stretching themselves on the crests of walls, sleeping in the sun amid the pebbles. At night, they mewl furiously.

"Monsieur de Termiane has killed thousands of them; he sets ambushes for them, likes in wait for them, and slaughters them. A singular pleasure. Perhaps they're the puppets of some visionary tragedy. Their smallness is a safeguard against their ferocity, and the mime of their death-throes evokes terrible masques. Who knows! All life is inexplicable. The imprint on the reverse does not allow the face of a coin to be deduced. One only sees in a mirror the inverse of what is reflected there.

"As for the Princesse, what can I tell you? You'll find out soon enough—and if it's necessary for you to leave one day, like me, you'll understand my anguish and why I tremble at the idea of that separation, at the thought that I'll never again see that gate, the vestibule, the vast halls, that I'll never again hold the little lamp in my hand, which makes my shadow crawl by my side. There are marvelous things that one never gets over. It's getting late—come on, it's necessary to be punctual."

We had set down our lamps, which we extinguished.

Five people were already gathered in the drawing-room where the Princesse came to meet us. I bowed down over her hand, which I kissed. Immediately, she took my arm and we went to the table, where she indicated that I should sit down facing her. D'Orscamps took the place to her right and the other guests arranged themselves as they pleased. I took advantage of the initial silence to look around.

The oldest of the guests was named Monsieur de Berve. He lived in a château in the vicinity and was reputed to be very knowledgeable, well versed in the sciences. His neighbor, whose name I didn't know and only learned subsequently, was a foreigner who had retired after long voyages overseas. He had bought back weapons, algae and corals therefrom.

I knew two of the others, men of intelligence and quality. The last and youngest seemed almost adolescent, but the age of his face contrasted with his precociously white hair.

The meal was exquisite in its meats, fruits and wines, embellished by the luxury of its silverware and the perfection of its porcelain. Two old valets supervised the service. A basket in which rare flowers surrounded a block of ice perfumed the room with its freshness, and high-set vermilion candelabras, one at each end of the table, erected the architecture of their candles.

Gradually, the conversation got under way. Each of the interlocutors took party in it with intelligence and verve. The Princesse listened attentively. Her hair, swept back from her forehead, was gathered at the back of her head. The beauty of her face was comprised in its form, the curve of the nose, the exquisite line of the mouth and, above all, her admirable eyes.

We finished the meal, and I noticed that the attention of the guests was consulting a clock fixed on the wall. The pendulum was swinging regularly; the conjoined hands parted, and an hour chimed in the silence the fell around it. The final stroke vibrated for a long time.

D'Orscamps and all the others had risen simultaneously to their feet. The Princesse, also standing, was motionless, a glass in her hand. I heard the clink of her rings against the crystal. She was trembling. D'Orscamps was very pale. She raised the cup to her lips and held it out to him. He finished it off.

"Adieu," she said to him, when he had drunk. "Adieu, then. You're leaving, by necessity. I won't try to stop you. The hour has sounded. Every hour sounds. Keep as a souvenir the little lamp that enabled you to come to me; let it keep watch on your beside table. Have it placed in your tomb. Adieu. May the light be with you."

D'Orscamps bowed, one last time, before the Princesse, shook hands with each of us, and disappeared through the door, which was still open. We heard him go downstairs, and then a sound of breaking glass—and when I went out in my turn, in company with the young man with white hair, we found the debris of the little glass lamp at the bottom of the last step on the stone, the pieces of which crackled under our feet.

By virtue of a rather bizarre custom of which the Princesse informed me when I parted from her, each of her Sunday guests came, without fail, alone, to visit her on one of the evenings of the week. As I was the latest recruit, my turn came on the Saturday. D'Orscamps, in our conversations regarding the singular woman, had warned me about that oddity of her caprice and the manner in which these meetings passed.

Madame de Termiane received her guests at nightfall, more or less, according to the season. She did so in a round room, illuminated through vitreous walls by a diffuse light. There were long hours of conversation, as if with a living shadow. My friend had told me impassioned tales of these intellectual adventures, which often went on until dawn. One felt that one was in the presence of a mysterious being in whom an unknown voice was speaking, about which one remained permanently anxious, Without explaining the nature of these oracles he gave me to understand that their beauty surpassed the human and was forever linked to a desire to hear them again, and forever—and the approach and promise of that secret divinity caused me to wait impatiently for the moment of my access to that revelatory Eleusis.

While submitting, in my turn, to the communal fascination that had gathered around Madame de Termiane those that her appearance on the threshold drew into the grotto of her solitude and mystery, I pondered the dangers. She seemed to be to be a flower opening at the entrance to perilous subterranean paths. She appeared to me as a fissure to the beyond, in which souls were engulfed, imperceptibly and furiously, by the admirable witch who could no longer be exorcised. I breathed in the cavity of the magic spiral. All week I was anxious and nervous. Insomnia exhausted me. Finally, the long-awaited day arrived.

From the morning onwards it seemed interminable. To distract myself from my thoughts I want out of the town and roamed the countryside. Summer had come to an end. I went along the river; it was running green and smoothly through long bent grass; I followed it. It passed not far from Madame de Termiane's palace and the idea came to me to prowl around it. Having arrived at the end of the avenue leading to the gate, however, I stopped, and sat down on a boundary marker.

It seemed to me that dusk fell rapidly. The grey mass of the old house loomed up. I heard myself ring the bell. The sand of the large courtyard squeaked beneath my feet. I watched myself and listened to myself. No one in the vestibule.

I lit the little lamp set aside for me. I examined the shape of its black crystal with roseate streaks. All the doors opened of their own accord in front of me; the galleries resounded with distant echoes. I arrived at the Princesse's apartments. I called out.

The empty drawing-room led to the sibylline rotunda that d'Orscamps had mentioned to me. I searched every last corner of it. My effort was wasted. Darkness fell.

I saw myself, lamp in hand, in a mirror; it seemed to me that I recognized in that image of myself someone that I ought to follow, the fraternal guide of my dream. Room by room, we made a tour of the immense palace.

I lost myself, and found myself again. The dust of the attics succeeded the saltpeter of the cellars. My lamp went out. I groped around for interminable hours. Finally, the darkness became gray; a white line filtered under a door.

As I headed in that direction my foot collided with an object. I picked it up. It was a cold, heavy mass. Kneeling down, I pushed the batten of the door, which opened, and the white light of dawn illuminated the head of a marble statue in my hands.

It was smiling, and resembled Madame de Termiane. I looked at it, and felt it gradually become lighter, and dissolve between my fingers, leaving nothing but a slight dust, which a slight wind dispersed.

I wrote to Madame de Termiane, describing the dream that I had had, which had kept me asleep until dawn outside her palace. She never replied to my letter and I never tried to see her again. The memory remains dear to me of having glimpsed her face, which is doubtless the very face of Beauty.

V. The Death of Monsieur de Nouâtre and Madame de Ferlinde

The crimson sunset bloodied the large red rose blooming behind the panes of the French windows. The petals were trembling and the thorny branch clawed the crystal. There was a big wind blowing outside, and beneath a black sky, the irritated water of the garden pond was darkening. The old trees were swaying and groaning; the bodies of the trunks threw out the elongation of branches, and suspended the palpitation of leaves. The draught filtered through the joints of the doors. The Marquis, sitting in a large armchair with his elbows on the marble table, was smoking in a leisurely manner. The smoke of his pipe rose vertically until, caught by the eddies of the draught, it swirled, its rings uncoiling in sparse trails. He had gathered the florid flaps of his coat on to his knees. Dusk did not pacify the squall. The large rose moved, clenching the wrath of its thorns. A little bat fluttered back and forth in front of the window, errant and bewildered.

"In order to get back to Ochria," Monsieur d'Amercoeur continued, "it was necessary to take one of two roads. I didn't like the shorter of the two, the sea-road. By the other it was six days on horseback. I made my decision. I had been assured of the bounty of the inns, and the next day, at dawn, I set off over the plain. High ocher-tinted mountains rose up on the horizon; I reached them rapidly. My horse went at a good pace and I let him go.

"The greater part of the journey passed without incident. No encounters, either in the empty hostelries or on the deserted roads. I drew nearer, and on the morning of the sixth day I had only had the remains of the forest to traverse. The place seemed to me to be singularly wild. A landslide of monstrous rocks heaped up broken rumps there, thrust up hairy breasts and extended deformed paws. The stains on the stones imitated the marbling of flesh; pools of water shone like eyes; and the velvet of moss resembled animal fur. The yellow sun hollowed out trails and showed up shiny spurs in places. Reddish pine-needles furred the ground with a russet fleece.

"At the exit from the forest one overlooked a desiccated plain, a landscape of brushwood and hillocks. I paused momentarily to contemplate its monotonous extent, limited by a rocky crest behind which Ochria lay. I was about to set off again when I heard galloping behind me, and a rider mounted on a chestnut horse accosted me, saluting. He was clad in a brown leather hunting costume, which amplified his medium corpulence and stature. His brown hair glittered in places in places with fawn reflections and his pointed beard reddened slightly. The sun, already in decline, gilded him all over, and the color of his body matched the ocher of the horizon and the gold of the surrounding foliage. He seemed exhausted after a long ride. We went down the rather steep slope side by side.

"Having ascertained that I was going to Ochria, he proposed to go there with me, to take me by the shortest route. The day was coming to an end. We were now moving between emaciated hedges enclosing the aridity of stony fields. At a crossroads we encountered a herd of goats. They were grazing dry grass, their beards were pointed and the movement of their little hooves making their slack udders dance. In their midst, a billy-goat with twisted horns paraded obscenely, pretentious and reeking.

"'He really is the image of an old satyr,' my companion said, with a brief, quavering laugh. He had stopped to consider the beast, which was looking at him curiously.

"The sun was setting. Objects were tinted with pale gold light. The ground we were covering was rank and ingrate, and behind us, the bitter mountain stacked its ocher-striped masses. My interlocutor continued: 'Yes, this land is mysterious and surprising things happen here. Vanished races are remade here; I almost have the proof and am on the lookout for the certainty.'

"Carefully, he took from his saddle-bag a lump of yellow-tinted clay and handed it to me. It crumbled slightly in my hand.

"'Look at that imprint.' He showed me a mark that was almost effaced. 'It's that of a faun. I've also been notified of the presence of a centaur. I've lain in ambush for several nights hoping to catch it. One doesn't see it, but one hears it whinnying. It must be young, its torso thin and its rump still rough. At full moon it comes to look at itself in pools of water, in which it no longer recognizes itself. It's the last survivor of its race—or, rather, its new beginning. The race has been hunted and destroyed, like those of nymphs and satyrs, for they existed.

"'It's said that once, shepherds surprised one in its sleep and took it to proconsul Sulla. Interpreters interrogated it in al known languages. It only replied with a quavering cry, like whinnying. They let it go, for the people of that time still knew a little about truths that have since become obscure. But everything that has existed can be reborn. This land is propitious for the fabulous work. The dry grass has the color of fleeces; the voices of spring murmur ambiguously; these rocks resemble unfinished beasts. Humans and animals live in sufficient proximity for there to be consanguinary exchanges between them.

"'Time has dispersed forms once conjoined. Humans have isolated themselves from their surroundings and withdrawn into their solitary infirmity: a retrograde step taken in the belief that they were perfecting themselves. The gods once mutated themselves into appearances of their choice, adopting the bodies of their desire, eagle or bull! Intermediary beings participated in that divine faculty; it is dormant within us; our passion creates and intermittent satyr there, only incorporating the desires that rear up in us! It's necessary to become what one is; it's necessary for nature to complete itself and rediscover the phases it has lost.'

"My companion talked incessantly and feverishly. I had difficulty following his speech, which he appeared to be continuing without being aware of my presence. In the meantime, the sun had set and, as the darkness became more intense the singular individual seemed gradually to fade away. He lost the russet gleam with which the daylight had impregnated his tanned leather coat, his beard and his hair. His whole appearance deepened; then his excitement calmed, as the landscape changed.

"Soon, we saw the water of a river shining. The moisture that it spread made its banks verdant. A bridge bestrode it with its arches. Night fell rapidly. My companion was no longer talking and I saw his black form beside me, sculpted from the surrounding shadow. When we arrived at the end of the bridge, whose gravel sounded loudly beneath hooves, he stopped abruptly, in front of a lantern hanging from a pole.

"As I looked at him I wondered whether the man who held his hand out to me was really the strange speaker of a little while before. His face seemed different to me, his dark hair and beard no longer ruddy; he appeared slim and elegant and he wore a smile full of politeness when, as he left, he told me his name, in case I might like, during my stay in Ochria to renew my acquaintance with Adalbert de Nouâtre."

The first person that Monsieur d'Amercoeur visited in Ochria was not Monsieur de Nouâtre. Even the memory of that singular individual soon faded from his memory. He gave no thought to renewing his acquaintance and did not run into him. He did not see him while out walking, nor in the taverns, nor at the homes of the courtesans he frequented, to whom access was quickly granted to a young man of his name, well-equipped with horses, clothes and jewels. Two of the most lustful fought over him determinedly. One was brunette, and stole him from the other, who was blonde, and who took him back, although he found it easier to satisfy them both by turns than choose between them.

His appetite for debauchery and gambling rapidly associated him with the most elegant young people in the town. He was soon invited to all the parties. He enjoyed himself there and, as greybeards love to get mixed up in the disorders of youth, came to make the acquaintance there, through the intermediary of the pleasures everyone sought, many serious individuals whom it would otherwise have been difficult for him to meet.

That commerce established him squarely in the best society in Ochria. After meeting him so frequently in their mistresses' houses, those gentlemen went on to introduce him to their wives, and Monsieur d'Amercoeur was soon familiar with the large silent houses at the back of their paved courtyards. He sat down at sumptuous tables, savored the dishes of knowledgeable cooks, drank wine from centuries-old cellars and saw the important personages and beauties of the city paraded in their finery beneath crystal chandeliers.

He found one among them particularly seductive. Her name was Madame de Ferlinde. She was slim and red-haired. Her long supple body supported a pagan head, crowned with tresses whose wavy cascade concluded in spirals. The incandescent mass of that hair seemed both fluid and sculpted, with the boldness of a helmet and the grace of a spring. She had the attitude and the bearing of a warrior Nymph. A widow, she lived in an old house amid beautiful gardens. Monsieur d'Amercoeur was soon going there assiduously, spending whole days there, arriving at all hours without the shepherd's hour ever chiming for him.[21]

That chaste Diana loved to adorn her beauty with creased tunics and lunar crescents, and merited the name of the goddess. She loved invisible orchestras, the shadow of love and the murmur of water. Three fountains gushed harmoniously in the midst of an arbor. The garden also contained a little grotto in which Madame de Ferlinde often came to rest. Hanging ivy veiled it from the sunlight, creating a pale green light within.

It was there that she first talked to Monsieur d'Amercoeur about Monsieur de Nouâtre. She depicted him as a man of manias, but erudite and charming, with a prodigious knowledge and refined tastes, who led a solitary life, frequently absent on travels, a great collector of books, medals and engraved stones.

Without revealing the details of his meeting with Monsieur Nouâtre, Monsieur d'Amercoeur spoke about it as an occasion when the latter had been very obliging, and accepted from Madame de Ferlinde the offer she made to visit him together, so that he could thank his traveling companion and she could see a friend who had neglected her for some time. On the agreed day, they therefore went to Monsieur de Nouâtre's home.

As soon as they went in, they saw an antique bronze in the middle of the vestibule representing a centaur. The broad torso was bulging with muscles, the rounded hindquarters gleaming; the flanks seemed to be palpitating; the raised hoof

---

[21] *L'heure du berger* [the shepherd's hour] was a euphemism employed to indicate the fulfilling moment of a lovers' rendezvous.

was at the ready, and the equestrian monster was raising an onyx pine-cone above his vine-clad head.

Everywhere their host took them, Monsieur Amercoeur admired an exclusive choice of objects concerning the history of terrestrial or marine demigods and the magical mythology of the ancients. Their effigies were modeled in earthenware, their legends evoked by bas-reliefs, their cults rememorized on medallions. Harpies with sharp claws, poisonous or winged Sirens, club-footed Empusas,[22] Tritons, Centaurs—each of them had a figurine or statue there. The bookcases contained texts relating to their origin, their existence and their nature. There were treatises on their species and their forms, enumerating all the kinds of Satyrs, Sylvains or Fauns, and one of them—the rarest, which Monsieur Nouâtre displayed with a certain pride—contained a description of the Papposilenus,[23] which is a horrible monster entirely covered in hair. Manuscripts in admirable bindings, retained the recipes for the Thessalian philters by means of which the witches of Lucian and Apuleius changed humans into owls or into donkeys.[24]

Monsieur de Nouâtre showed off his collection marvelously. Sometimes, a slight smile stretched his mouth. In his exceedingly dark eyes, coppery streaks scintillated at times,

---

[22] The Empusas of Greek mythology were malevolent female spirits that supposedly lured male travelers from beaten tracks and drank their blood; they were akin to lamias, but generally considered to be uglier, often one-legged or limping.

[23] *Papposilene* [Papposilenus] is a rare pleonasm, in that sileni are already, by definition, aged satyrs, and adding the prefix *pappo* [old] is therefore redundant. The author evidently feels that the reinforcement is functional in this case, in order to suggest a further level of exaggeration to the existing image of the satyr or silenus.

[24] Apuleius' Latin proto-novel *The Golden Ass*, which describes the extravagant exploits of a witch named Pamphile, appears to be based on an earlier prose satire in Greek attributed to Lucian, most commonly known as "The Ass."

and three golden threads glinted in his brown beard. When they parted, he squeezed Madame de Ferlinde's hand between his sharp-nailed fingers, and while he looked sat her, Monsieur d'Amercoeur saw metallic yellow gleams multiplying in her eyes, like a kind of furtive lightning, impassioned and violent, which vanished almost immediately.

That first visit was did not remain unrepeated. Monsieur d'Amercoeur often revisited the stucco vestibule where the bronze Centaur stood, hoof upraised, on its marble pedestal, the onyx cone shining in its hand. Monsieur de Nouâtre never explained the origin or the objective of the singular collections assembled in his house. He only talked about them in order to comment on the rarity of a book or the beauty of a trinket. Neither did he make any allusion to the circumstances of their first meeting. His reserve was matched by Monsieur d'Amercoeur. Their relationship of ceremonious amity kept the secret of the former and did not authorize the curiosity of the latter, and they both seemed to be in agreement in feigning a reciprocal forgetfulness.

"Madame de Ferlinde had been anxious for some days when she asked me to come to see her. I responded to her appeal and found her nervous and preoccupied. When I pressed her to tell me the cause of her disturbance, she replied evasively, but ended up confessing the singular apprehension in which she was living.

"She told me that the dogs howled every night, more out of fear than anger. The gardeners had discovered traces of footprints on the sand of the pathways. The grass, trampled in places, revealed a nocturnal presence—and to my great astonishment, she showed me a clod of earth on which a bizarre imprint could be seen. It was a rather clear impression. On examining the hardened print at closer range I perceived a few yellow hairs embedded in the clay.

"An invisible marauder seemed to be haunting the garden and spying on the house. Traps had been set in vain, and nocturnal patrols were being undertaken. In spite of every-

154

thing, Madame de Ferlinde could not help feeling an insurmountable apprehension. I did the best I could to calm the fearful beauty and, on quitting her, promised to return the following day.

"It was late Autumn; it had been raising; the streets were still muddy, the trees losing their leaves, red and yellow in the twilight. The main gate was open, the gatekeeper asleep in his lodge. I went into the vestibule and waited for a valet who could announce me to Madame de Ferlinde. Her bedroom, which overlooked the garden, was at the end of a corridor. I waited for some time. There was no movement in the vast silent dwelling No one came, and time passed.

"A faint noise reached my ears; I listened more attentively and it seemed to me that I heard muffled sighs, and then the fall of an item of furniture that had been knocked over. I hesitated; there as total silence. Suddenly, there was a heart-rending scream from Madame de Ferlinde's bedroom. I ran along the corridor and crashed into the door, which opened wide.

"It was already dark, but this is what I glimpsed: Madame de Ferlinde was lying on the parquet, half-naked. Her hair spread out is a long golden stream; and crouching on her breast was a kind of hairy beast, deformed and spiteful, embracing her and devouring her with its lips.

"As I approached, the mass of yellow hair bounded backwards. I heard its teeth grinding and its nails scraping the parquet. An odor of leather and horn mingled with the sweet perfume of the room. Sword in hand, I rushed upon the monster. It spun around, overturning the furniture, clawing the wall-hangings, evading my pursuit with an incredible agility. I tried to trap it in a corner.

"Finally, I made contact with its abdomen; blood splashed my hand. The brute sank back into the dark corner and then, with a sudden bound, knocked me over, leapt out of the open window into the garden, to the sound of breaking glass.

"I went to Madame de Ferlinde; warm blood was running from her torn throat. I lifted up her hand, which fell back limply. I listened to her heart, which was no longer beating. Then I was gripped by panic; I fled. The vestibule was still empty, the house seemed mysteriously abandoned. I went past the sleeping gatekeeper again. He was snoring with his mouth open, in the inertia of a lethargy that subsequently seemed suspicious, as did the absence of any servant in that isolated house, where Madame Ferlinde appeared to have sensed something bestial prowling in ambush around her beauty.

"It was dark. I wandered the streets in an inexpressible disorder. Rain began to fall. That lasted for some time. I was still unconscious of where I was when, raising my eyes, I recognized Monsieur de Nouâtre's house. I knew that he was a friend of the chief of police and the idea came to me of consulting him, and of informing him of the tragic event of that frightful night. Given the unexpectedly deserted hotel and the sequence of inexplicable facts, my presence at the scene of the crime constituted a monstrous accusation against me, of which it was urgently necessary to divert any suspicion.

"I rang. A domestic told me that Monsieur de Nouâtre was in his bedroom, to which he had been confined for several weeks. I went upstairs precipitately. A clock chimed eleven. I knocked and went in without waiting for an answer—and stopped on the threshold.

"Darkness filled the vast room. The window must have been open, because I could hear rain outside on the deserted street that he house overlooked at the rear. I called out to Monsieur de Nouâtre. No reply. I went forward into the shadows, hesitantly. A few embers were glowing in the fireplace. I lit a torch therefrom that I had found on a table with which my hand had collided. The flame sputtered.

"A body was lying face down, extended on the parquet. I turned it over and recognized Monsieur de Nouâtre. His wide-open eyes gazed at me vitreously, like unpolished onyx. There was pink foam at the corners of his lips. When I felt his hand it filled mine with blood. I parted the black cloak that enveloped the cadaver. There was a deep wound in the abdomen, made by a sword-thrust.

"I felt no terror; I was gripped by a violent curiosity. I looked around attentively. Everything in the bedroom was in order. The white curtains of the bed were open. There were muddy footprints on the polished diamond-patterned parquet; they extended from the window to the spot where Monsieur de Nouâtre lay. A bizarre odor of leather and horn infected the air. The fire crackled; two adjacent brands reignited, and I then perceived that the wretch had fallen with his feet in the fireplace, and that the flame had burned his shoes and charred his flesh.

"That double death caused great excitement in Ochria. I was summoned to the high court, but no one challenged me on the statements that I made. The connection of the tragic facts remained forever doubtful, and in suspense. Madame de Ferlinde left no heirs and her wealth reverted to the poor, along with that of Monsieur de Nouâtre, who was similarly devoid of family, although he had made a will in which he left me, in memory of him, the bronze Centair ornamenting his vestibule, holding an onyx pine-cone in its hand."

The valet came limping in and, one by one, lit the candles in the brackets and those of a large candelabra, which he placed on the table. Then he opened the French windows in order to close the external shutters. The wind was still blowing; an odor of roses and box came from outside and, attracted by the light, a little bat flew into the vast room. It flew around the ceiling as if it were trying to draw a circle there, incessantly recommenced and broken every time by an abrupt deflection. Its delicate wings were beating rapidly.

The Marquis remained huddled in his embroidered silk dressing-gown, and we watched the agile beast patiently persisting in its mysterious task, interrupted by the hitches of its haste and spoiled by the captious meanders of the inextricable thread of its flight, signing the air with the magical flourish of its intermittent incantation.

VI. A Voyage to the Isle of Cordic

The door, noisily slammed, caused the echo asleep between the two caryatides at the far end of the long corridor to resonate. Stone sheaths swathed their pale marble torsos, shining as if with an eternal sweat, and the tension of their raised arms supported the high golden ceiling. The mosaics of the pavement sparkled, and I walked at a slow pace through the sonorous emptiness of the place, thinking that the soul of the Prince was surely as slippery and perilous as those tiles, similarly painted with bizarre figures and interlacing arabesques.

The recent altercation between his highness and myself had left me anxious. My obstinacy had collided with his caprice. For an hour he had persisted in trying to relieve what he called my interment. I could still see him in his vast study, furnished with weapons and dolls—for he liked handling iron and playing with grotesques. He knew a great deal about swords and puppets, loving the panoplies and mannequins of which he had a whole collection of the former and a whole assembly of the latter.

Deep down, however, his armory preoccupied him less than his marionettes. Their faces of painted wax, their chiffon bodies, their wickerwork arms lent themselves to games of make-up, ornamentation and poses, meekly accommodating uniforms, dresses and liveries, and their small stature enabled the Prince to carry out trials in miniature to which he would subsequently adapt the costumes of his troops, the smocks of his servants and even the clothing of the ladies of the court. He thought them excellent, and sometimes borrowed them, less for amusement than in the unconfessed hope that the grace of his disguises and the elegance of his masquerade would be admired.

I could still see him, therefore, manipulating his figurines and discussing, with the harshness of a maniac combined with the cynicism of a diplomat, the conclusion to which he wanted

158

to lead me. Sometimes, as he paused in front of a mirror in order to adjust his attire, I perceived his pale face and his large nose. His coat-tails flapping his thighs, he returned to me, perhaps more determined than before to overcome my will and bend me to his own.

The Prince's character was sufficiently familiar for me to be able, usually, to find some ruse by which to evade his whims or the traps of his moods, but this time, his anger rendered him clairvoyant, and nothing deflected him from his endeavor—not even the ridicule I manifested, driven to the end of my tether and at the risk of a dangerous upsurge of his vanity.

It was all in vain, and I understood by a little tremor of his lips and an evil glint in his yellow eyes that contradiction had brought me to a crossroads at which roads opened that might lead to disgrace.

I went home to reflect on the difficulties of my sticky situation, and was still searching for the means of getting out of it when, the following morning, I received a message. His Highness ordered me to depart immediately for the Isle of Cordic, to leave my crew behind at to disembark alone in order to go to an indicated spot, where I would find his further instructions.

After due reflection, my perplexity decided to take the turn that events had taken as a good omen. The sovereign anger seemed to me to be a release, and I conceived the hope of escaping the consequences that his fit of temper had momentarily caused me to anticipate. A tedious voyage with, at the end, some joke to which I would lend myself with a good grace, seemed to me to be the probable outcome.

Such adventures often work out of their own accord, and there was rumor of some in which very serious individuals had been obliged to submit as a punishment to the buffooneries of the maniac prince, whose fits of rancor were satisfied by a burst of laughter or a disillusionment, and I resigned myself to adding, at my expense, one more tale to the legends that made our bizarre master the subject of novelist's sketches and story-

159

tellers' tales. At any rate, he gave rise to more anecdotes than history. His little court was singular. Its falls resembled clownish stumbles; acrobatic ambition was closely akin to the pirouettes of vanity.

The large horses with braided tails were tapping their hooves on the pavement. The coachman was upright in his seat. I climbed up; the door clicked; the wheels turned; the carriage went through the gate. The Palace loomed up on the far side of the main square, gray in the morning light. The great courtyard was deserted. Behind the pane of a window in the north wing, where the Prince's apartments were, I spotted him on the lookout for my departure, his hand on a curtain, which he allowed to fall back as I passed by.

The route went from tree to tree, milestone to milestone, town to town. Relays alternated with inns; humpbacked bridges rattled; gradients slowed the horses down, and they hastened down descending slopes; a ferry took me over a river.

I had never been to the Isle of Cordic. Perilous currents separated the coast from its fishing ports and uncultivated land. On the morning of the third day I scented the approaching sea. The trees were inclined, stunted and gnarled, as if their dwarfish musculature enabled them better to withstand the assaults of the wind. The air freshened; I caught side of the water at a bend. It displayed its grayness beneath a pale sky. Soon, the road went on to a narrow peninsula or stone and sand, which extended its nudity as far as a humble village at its tip. The carriage stopped there and I got down.

The sea was retreating before me over a thin soft stand unmarked by any footprints. A few boats were moored in a cove; one of them consented to take me to the island. I embarked, armed with a portmanteau, and watched my motionless carriage with its painted panels slowly dwindle in the distance, along with the green-liveried coachman and its plumed horses scraping the damp sand with their feet, where the muted waters of the sea had begun to rise again.

The boat swayed slowly; the water around it became blue beneath the clear sky. The waves inflated their glaucous swellings; sometimes one broke into foam, but the majority extended their humps in an invisible spine. A profound internal movement animated them. The mast groaned. The anchor, still streaming after being raised from the depths, clenched it crustacean claws; it lay on the deck, like a gnarled animal. Seabirds wheeled around.

Finally, a coast appeared on the horizon, low at first, which grew by degrees as we approached it, emerging from the sea. We soon saw its high vaporous cliffs, which solidified. We were sailing close to the island, on rounding a point the harbor appeared. Once on land, I set out in quest of an inn and then came back to wander along the shore. The ebb tide uncovered the mud of the bay; algae hung from the walls of the quay, smooth, sticky and dripping. Children were playing, interminably rolling pebbles over the flagstones. An old man was smoking while patching a sail.

I decided to go up the path to the cliff-top. It was steep and grassy. A fur of russet broom covered its back, and its bare flank plunged vertically into the sea. The fierceness of the heat was roasting the rock. From the topmost point of my walk a part of the isle extended before me. It seemed to be oblong, treeless in the terrible desolation of its pelt of moss, pierced by stony napes—the skeleton of its harsh nudity.

The reddening sun was setting; the entire island became violet, as if aged by a sudden crepuscular autumn. On the sea, a scattered fleet of boats was returning. The ocher sails resembled dead leaves, the only ones the wind every dispersed around the treeless isle. I wondered what the Prince had sent me here to do. By virtue of the annoyance I felt, his rancor was already taking on the appearance of a vengeance. The ocher sails were still wandering over the violet sea. Heraldic clouds blazoned the sky. The boats were coming into port as I went back down to it—for my inn overlooked the harbor. That evening, going up to my room, I heard them, captive in the bay, groaning dully on their anchor-chains.

When I awoke the next day, the sky was gray and compact, a violent wind dragging racing clouds across it. The green-tinted sea was flecked with white foam, while the surf of waves battered the cliffs. I obtained a guide to take me to the place where the enigma of my voyage would be resolved.

The place was on a table of rock situated at the southern tip of the island. We went through interminable heather, passing flocks of black sheep, each one—for the flocks did not mix—attached to a fence by a rope. They were browsing placidly. Our approach frightened them, and we then saw them go round and round their stakes, as if seized by folly, and the sorcerer sheep seemed to be tracing malefic circles on the wild heath.

I interrogated the man who was guiding me. He told me about the terrible winters in the island, the tempests racing to assault its coasts, the doors ajar, the houses squat, the inhabitants forced to crawl by the strength of the wind: all those poor animal people opposing their bestial posture and woolen clothes to the bad weather. We continued walking; the wind increased as the terrain became bleaker. Its grip was tangible, its slyness becoming brutal. Its sneak attacks were cunning; even its lapses were disconcerting.

We were now on the plateau of a crumbling spur of the cliffs, which fell sheer into the sea assaulted by the tide. There was a double tumult, one incoherent, the other petrified. Flecks of foam passed over our heads.

The high stone table was standing there. Under a fragment of rock, as I had been notified, I found the princely order. I read it, amazed. If my resistance remained obstinate, exile to this cruel land would attempt to reckon with it. It was necessary to choose immediately. The conciseness of the instruction demonstrated its seriousness. The anticipated joke took on a tragic mask. The flash of the yellow eyes had not lied.

I looked around. Enormous waves were unfurling on the horizon. Their force burst into white foam as the peevish rocks stood up to the furious tide; muzzles and rumps confronted the rush of the waves, steaming or dribbling. The wind blew through the coarse grass.

My pride was excited; the tumult of the sea entered into me; I walked all day. I knew the prince's police too well to think that I could escape them. My fate seemed inevitable. I understood the error of my boldness.

By going against the maniac's caprice I had collided with the despot's vanity, and in the dangerous mannequin with which I amused myself too frequently, my bravado had revealed the hereditary man, the descendant of the rancorous antique race whose fragments still survived, dormant, in the depths of the baroque Highness. I had forgotten that, in the collection of dolls and panoplies, isolated, to one side, beneath the golden eagle with outspread wings, the rude fist an ancient ivory hand of justice clung to the wall—that of a founding ancestor.

I walked all day. I went down to little beaches frenziedly hollowed out in the cliffs. The sand there was tinted pink, blue or gray, sometimes almost red; I found green and gold grottoes full of pebbles, shells and seaweed, with stalactites that made the resemble the interior of fairy coaches.

My whole life came back to me in memory, with its festivals, masquerades and pleasures. I heard the laughter of women. Their nude bodies emerged, one by one, from the sea. I understood then the grace of love and the joy of beauty. I felt myself summoned by all the forces of my youth, of which an unexpected order had so untowardly demanded a choice between pride and desire.

I went back to the little port. The evening was miserable.

Again, I saw the black sheep turning around their poles; they seemed to be tracing magic circles around me, as if they were putting a spell on my destiny with the fatal sign of their vertiginous captivity.

The captive boats were still groaning at anchor. They had not been able to go out today. The mariners were idly gathered on the quay, sleeping or playing dice. One of them, who was very old, watched me going back and forth for some time, then turned away scornfully and spat on the ground.

Perhaps he divined the baseness of my internal weakness. The dread of exile was causing my pride to buckle; the desires of my youth were dragging me far away from the frightful island, whose meaning I had not understood and whose bitter grandeur I had not felt.

The next day, I went back to the coast. The plumed horses of my carriage were pawing the ground; the green-liveried coachman whipped their shiny rumps; the braided tails flicked; the painted panels reflected the road, tree by tree, the gate of my house opened for my return, the mosaics of the corridor interlaced their figures and arabesques beneath my feet, and in the vast princely study, full of dolls and swords, facing the antique ivory fist whose weight I had felt on my shoulder, in front of the sniggering and stunted marionette balanced on his meager caves and strutting like a peacock in his coat, whose eye-spots were diamantine plates, I bowed over the hand that His Highness held out to my submission, and kissed the sigillary ring whose imprint I had recognized on the letter that the furious wind had snatched from my fingers to carry it away into the sea that foamed around the bare, rocky and solitary isle of Cordic.

VII. The Sign of the Key and the Cross

As I wandered through the streets of the town, one of the stories that Monsieur d'Amercoeur had once told me came to mind. Without naming the place where the adventure had happened, he had described it to me carefully, so well that today, I seemed to recognize it, at the same time as I saw that old town looming up before me, noble and monastic, crumbling in its dismantled ramparts along its jaundiced river, facing the bare mountains of the horizon, with its sunlit and shadowed streets, its old enclosed houses, its churches, and its numerous convents with alternating bell-towers.

164

I found it again, just as he had described it to me, that town, an old heap of stones, somber or luminous, numbed by warmth and solitude into a powdery ossification, and retaining by means of its surviving monuments the skeleton of its past grandeur. It had been stripped, little by little, losing its outlying parts, retreating within its walls when they were no longer overfull. In the center, it heaped up its houses in a compact block, still vast; elsewhere, it scattered its buildings, and slept everywhere in a torpor, with the occasional start at a sudden buzz, or the carillon of a set of bells.

The streets, paved with flat stones or hardened with cobbles, intersected eccentrically to end in squares where markets were held. The local flocks were gathered there to be dispersed again on the whim of the purchasers. The auction and the mass were, by turns, the sole occupation of the inhabitants. The town remained rustic and pious. The swift feet of sheep trampled the same paving stones on which the sandals of monks resounded. Shepherds and congregations crossed paths. The reek of fleeces was confused with the odor of monks' habits. The wind smelled of incense and sweat, sheep-shearers and tonsures, shepherds and priests.

I had arrived at the junction of two streets. A drinking-fountain ran there into an eroded basin. I remembered that fountain. Monsieur d'Amercoeur had praised the freshness of its water. The street straight ahead of me had to lead to the convent of the Black Friars. I followed it. Its tortuousness insinuated it into the very heart of the town.

A few poor shops opened their displays. Rosaries hung there next to knotted whips. The street suddenly broadened out, bordered by the high façade of an old house. I had seen others like it here and there, but this one stood out by virtue of the peculiarity of its appearance. It rose above a sub-basement of coarse masonry. The windows, far from the ground, were barred. The foundations must have been those of a primitive dwelling, on which the severe architecture of the present edifice had been superimposed. At the corner of the house, the street made an abrupt turn and descended a curved slope, carved into steps. The descent went around the rear of the house, uncovering its foundations, which were those of an ancient fortified château whose rump of smooth stone was buttressed at the base by the living rock.

I recognized the Hôtel d'Heurteleure.

The street came to an end; trees appeared. An avenue continued it, bordered by poplars. Old stone sarcophagi, now empty, were lined up in the long grass where footfalls had marked out a narrow path. It went straight along a wall, in which a small door opened. I shivered on seeing it. It led to a medicinal garden maintained by the Friars, whose convent was advertised at the end of the path by a gateway. Before continuing, I went to the little door in the wall. It was massive, and studded with iron. The entrance to the lock was shaped in the form of a heart.

Having arrived at the porch I rang the bell. The doorkeeper introduced me to the monastery. Immense corridors led to vast rooms. We climbed staircases; the guardian brother lifted up his robe. We did not meet anyone. The chapel, which I did not enter, was buzzing with the chanting of psalms. I was shown several cloisters; one of them, charming, square and full of flowers, was inhabited by doves. They perched on the friezes, like a natural and torpid bas-relief.

From there, the belfry of the church was visible. The clock was just chiming. A tall yellow sunflower gazed at itself in the deep water of a well, which mirrored its monastic face.

Nothing had changed since the day when Monsieur d'Amercoeur had visited the old town. The same aspect confirmed the endurance of the same habits. The crack of whips still mingled with the clicking of rosary-beads; the convent bells ringing their changes as in the time when Monsieur Amercoeur, staff in hand, his feet bare within his sandals, a cowl on his shoulders, had come to knock on the monastery door.

He asked for the prior, who was then Dom Ricard. I was shown his mitered tomb among the anonymous sepulchers that surrounded it. He had retained strong links with the world from which he had retired, holding out one hand there for alms and lending himself in exchange, when needed, to delicate mediations in which his prudence and wisdom were solicited. Monsieur d'Amercoeur explained his costume to him, the motives for his visit, and the details of his mission.

After twenty years of noble service in the army, a local gentleman, Monsieur d'Heurteleure had come back to settle there. Shortly thereafter, he married Mademoiselle de Callistie. She was a poor girl from a good family, and very beautiful. The spouses lived in the Hôtel d'Heurteleure. The aristocracy of the town frequented the house and the most assiduous in showing himself there was Monsieur d'Auglieul. He was related by marriage to Monsieur Heurteleure who had been his commanding officer in his young days, and liked him a great deal. Life at the Hôtel Heurteleure was very simple: no noise, few domestics, but an existence that expanded to the proportion of its rooms, the width of its staircases and all the anachronistic ostentation of the ancient dwelling.

Perhaps because of the tedium of that sojourn in a small town that had come down in the world after the agitation of an active profession, but after six years, Monsieur d'Heurteleure and Monsieur d'Aiglieul disappeared one day, without anyone being able to discover their whereabouts. Time passed, enquiries led nowhere. People sensed some mystery. Madame d'Heurteleure wept. Singular rumors spread, eventually reaching the court, where the gentlemen in question were still remembered. The double disappearance had been mentioned one day in the presence of Monsieur d'Amercoeur, who was enthusiastic to clear up the mystery. He had been given full authority to act and had departed.

His first concern was to put on a monkish robe, sure of getting in anywhere with that habit, via doors standing ajar as well the fissures of conscience, and Dom Ricard facilitated the means of his investigation.

His initial enquiries produced no result. Favored by the incognito of his costume and the appearance of his status, they were patient and various. He sniffed around the vicinity of the

167

Hôtel d'Heurteleure, scrutinized the habits of the people, took the pulse their lives. He listened closely to the rumors, still lively, concerning the event. It was all in vain. He asked to see Madame d'Heurteleure. He was told that she was ill; he could not breach the seclusion in which she was sealed.

Every day, he went past the house. He followed the street that went along the sub-basement and stopped in front of the façade. Often, he went as far as the fountain that he had mentioned to me. The fresh water cooled his mouth; on the way back, while going down the steps, he examined the enormous building of stone and rock. He would have liked to apply is ear to it and listen to its mystery; it seemed to him that the flanks of the old dwelling contained the phantom of the secret, which he had come to summon from the silence and return to oblivion.

Finally, discouraged, he was on the point of giving up. He would have taken his leave of Dom Ricard without the old man's insistence, which retained him. The old monk relaxed in the company of that sheep, so dissimilar from the flock that his wooden crosier led through the monotonous pathways of the rule.

One day, at about five o'clock in the afternoon, Monsieur d'Amercoeur, after going out by the old porch, walked through the long grass of the avenue. The moment was melancholy and grandiose, the shadows of the trees striping the funereal pathway, lizards running over the warm stone of the ancient tombs and slipping through their cracks.

With one hand, Monsieur d'Amercoeur tucked up his long monk's robe; with the other he turned the key to open the heart-shaped lock of the medicinal garden, where he liked to walk. He wanted to see it one more time before leaving, to hear the soles of his sandals squeaking on the gravel of the paths, to feel the hem of his robe brushing the box-tree verges.

The symmetry of the plots pleased him; their squares contained delicate plants and curious flowers; little pools nourished aquatic plants, which plunged their rots into the water and blossomed, mirrored there. At the intersections of the paths, faience vases painted with pharmaceutical symbols and devices, with serpents on the handles, contained precious varieties. Above the wall one could see the crowns of the poplars; in the kitchen-garden to one side, separated by tall green trellises, the sound of a rake was audible, along with the collision of a spade with a water-trough and the faint sound of secateurs cutting shoots; here, everything was silence; a flower head bent, flexible beneath the weight of a insect; swallows were flying around; dragonflies were skimming the greenish water; stout serpentine plants were coiling and knotting themselves like caducei.

Monsieur d'Amercoeur was heading for the door to the singular little enclosure when, at the end of the avenue, he saw a black-clad woman coming toward him. She was advancing slowly, as if hesitantly. He perceived inwardly, by a sort of sudden revelation, that the tall dark form could not be anyone but Madame Heurteleure. He slowed down, in order to cross her oath just as she arrived at the small door. Having got there, he put the key in the lock. The noise made the solitary walker shiver. She hesitated. He bent down, as if trying to open it. She tried to take advantage of the moment and pass on, but she found herself face to face with him when he turned round abruptly.

He saw the pale, handsome face, racked by insomnia and grief, the eyes emotional, the lips parted, a hand raised to the breathless bosom.

Then he went in quickly, leaving the key in the closed door, in the iron heart of the lock.

The next day, he was thinking in the little cloister when he was told that a veiled woman was asking to speak to him. She came in. He recognized Madame d'Heurteleure and invited her to sit down on a stone bench. The doves were cooing softly on the capitals of the deserted cloister; their cooing mingled with the suffocation that was causing the penitent's bosom to heave. He made a large sign of the cross over her kneeling form and, with his head lowered and his hands in his sleeves, he listened to her painful confession.

It was a horrible and tragic story. Why did she tell it to him? He seemed to have laid her secret bare. The monk, opening that heart-shaped lock with a key, had seemed to her to be forcing access to her conscience. She saw in that meeting a speech of sorts, and in that gesture a mysterious allusion to, and also the predestined emblem of the deliverance of her soul, imprisoned in the horror of her silence.

Her marriage to Monsieur d'Heurteleure was loveless. She esteemed, while fearing it, his noble character, whose harshness intimidated her confidence and discouraged her affection; years passed. One winter, Monsieur d'Aiglieul appeared in her life and frequented her intimacy. He was handsome, and still young. She gave herself to him: those were days of joy and terror, lived in apprehension of being caught and in the anguish of remorse. Monsieur d'Heurteleure perceived nothing; he was, as usual, often absent—except that he was aging, and another large wrinkle was added to those already hollowing out his forehead.

One evening, Madame d'Heurteleure had retired to her bedroom at about midnight. She felt sad. Monsieur d'Aiglieul had not put in an appearance that day, and he hardly ever failed to come every day. Monsieur d'Heurteleure had gone out on horseback that morning, even though it was raining.

As she was combing her hair in front of a mirror she saw the door open, and her husband came in. He was wearing boots but is boots bore no trace of mud; his coat seemed dusty, and a large cobweb was hanging from his elbow. He was holding a key in his hand.

Without saying anything, he went straight to the wall of the room, where an ivory crucifix was hanging from a nail, took hold of it and smashed it on the floor—and in its place, he hung the large rusty key. He face was pale and violent.

Madame d'Heurteleure sat still for a moment, uncomprehendingly; then, suddenly putting her hands to her heart, she uttered a scream and fell backwards.

When she recovered her senses, the frightful adventure became apparent to her. Her husband must have lured Monsieur d'Aiglieul into some trap. The old dwelling underneath the fortress contained invisible redoubts and eternal hiding-places in its flanks. One scream—her own—still vibrated in her ears, but it seemed to be coming from down below, muffled by the mass of stone, piercing the superimposed vaults, reaching her from the lips from which she was separated forever by the thickness of the walls. She tried to get out; the door resisted; padlocks sealed the windows; the domestics lived some distance away.

The next day, Monsieur d'Heurteleure came to bring her food. He came back every day. The cobweb was still hanging from the sleeve of his dusty coat; his boots rattled on the pavement; the deep wrinkle in his forehead hollowed out further in a pallor of torment and insomnia. Every time he went away again silently, and to tears and supplications he only responded with a curt gesture, pointing to the key hanging on the wall.

Those were tragic days, in which the unhappy woman lived with her eyes fixed on the horrible devotional offering, which grew, becoming enormous. The rust appeared to her to be blood red. She felt herself draining away in the solitude of her despair. The house seemed dead. In the evening, footsteps became audible. Monsieur d'Heurteleure came in once more, carrying a lamp and a basket. His hair had gone white; he did not even look down at the unfortunate woman who had thrown herself at his feet, but never ceased to stare avidly at the redoubtable key.

Then Madame Heurteleure understood the covetousness from which her husband was suffering, the bitter desire that was consuming him—that of seeing his rival dead, of observing his vengeance, of touching the putrefaction that beloved flesh had become—in sum, taking back the key that he had nailed to the wall, substituted for the symbol of forgiveness whose ivory image he had broken, as a sign of the eternal rancor with which he had suspended the inflexible emblem of bronze.

Alas, the thirst for vengeance is never slaked; the desire still remains; there is still a violence and a torment therein that returns repeatedly, until the end of life and in the depths of memory.

Monsieur d'Heurteleure sensed that his solitary torture had been divined, and suffered more in consequence. The black marble of his pride was furrowed with bloody veins.

One night, when Madame d'Heurteleure was lying in bed asleep, she heard her door open quietly and saw her husband appear on the threshold. He was holding a muted lamp in his hand and walked, as lightly as a shadow, without the floor-tiles grating, as if the somber somnambulism of his obsession had made him an imponderable phantom. He crossed the room, stood on tiptoe, took the key and went out again. A fly awakened by the light buzzed momentarily and fell silent. The door was not locked again.

An indescribable start brought Madame Heurteleure upright, Bare-footed, she slipped into the corridor. Her husband went downstairs; she followed him. Having reached the ground floor he continued descending, the steps plunging into darkness. In the depths of the subterranean corridors she heard the footsteps ahead of her. They were in the ancient substructures of the old house. The walls were sweating; they passed beneath arched vaults.

One final staircase hollowed out its spiral in the rock. Down below, a glimmer of light still shone from the wall as the little lamp disappeared. Madame d'Heurteleure listened. A grating sound reached her and the light went out. There was a circular chamber at the bottom. A section of the wall standing ajar revealed a narrow passage. She continued going forward.

At the far end her groping fingers encountered a door, imperceptibly ajar. She opened it. Monsieur d'Heurteleure was sitting on the ground next to his little lamp in a sort of square hole, vaulted and flagstoned. He was motionless, gazing with wide open eyes. He was staring, but not seeing. A nauseating odor emerged from the cellar; visible on the stone, outside the shadows, already green-tinted, was a fleshless hand.

172

Madame d'Heurteleure made no sound.

Should she awaken the wretched somnambulist, whose furious sleep had brought him to this tragic cellar? Should she inflict on his pride the torture of that surprise? No. The vengeance of the outrage was just. Why show him his debasement? She felt pity for the wild eyes that were gazing without seeing, for the tortured face, for the hair whitened by so much silent suffering, and understood that, in order to safeguard that dolor, it was necessary to keep the secret of his nocturnal distress and let him satisfy his terrible desire in peace, in the eternal silence of the tomb, without him ever knowing what invisible hand had walled him up in the face of his sacrilege.

Monsieur d'Heurteleure was still staring. Very calmly, she knelt down and kissed the green-tinted palm that was displaying its fleshless fingers on the floor. She locked the door from the outside, withdrew on tiptoe, and activated the mechanism that moved the wall at the entrance to the passage. She went back up the spiral staircase, the subterranean steps and the stairs to the upper floor and, from the rusty nail in her bedroom, she suspended the tragic key, which swung there momentarily and then settled into immobility, marking an eternal hour.

The doves passed back and forth, flying under the arches of the little cloister. The hour chimed simultaneously in all the town's bell-towers. The poor woman sobbed, and held out the large key to Monsieur d'Amercoeur, dropping it at his feet. He picked it up; it was heavy; its rust seemed very red. Madame d'Heurteleure knelt down, imploring him with the gesture, distraught, her hands convulsive, on seeing him draw away from her.

He went down to the little sunken garden that embalmed the center of the cloister. Flowers grew there between the symmetrical borders of the beds. Large roses garlanded the stone rim of the well. Their thorns clawed at the monk's robe as he leaned over. The water splashed. A tall golden sunflower inclined its honeyed monstrance.

A dove cooed faintly, and Monsieur d'Amercoeur, returning to the penitent, who was still on her knees, murmured in her ear the words of an absolution, which, if it did not release anything from Heaven, at least gave peace to a dolorous soul on Earth.

VIII. The Magnificent House

The house that I built for Madame de Sérences was large and magnificent. The noblest quarries furnished the stone and marble; the wood came from the most beautiful forests. The Architect, a bald and bearded old man, acted according to his ancient precepts. To the science of the building he joined the understanding of the gardens. He excelled at disposing the water features, as many flat as gushing. He knew how to plant arbors, entangle labyrinths and cause the most ingenious weathervanes to rotate on rooftops.

After having chosen the orientation and composed the perspectives, his artistry extended to the interior detail. Behind the aspects of facades he contrived the secrets of apartments: chandeliers hanging from ceilings like stalactites in rustic grottoes, carpets as soft as lawns, wall-hangings as florid as flower-beds, mirrors as pure as pools.

All day he was seen hurrying, jumping over the ditches, scaling the scaffolding, in rain or sunshine, in the wake of gardeners or masons. The impact of spades mingled with the noise of hammers; squared beams were fitted to carved stone. Tall trees, with their branches, arrived quivering, their roots exposed, to be implanted and revive in the new soil that received them. Statues went by, dragged by teams of oxen. And every evening, at sunset, the shadow of the house was increased by the day's work.

The bearded old man organized everything: the positioning of the stones and the adjustment of the woodwork; the gravelling of the pathways and the water-level in the pools; quincunxes and guilloches. He was indefatigable, compass in hand and his plans deployed, happy to be creating once again a work of the architecture that he loved passionately, the fashion for which had passed, those savant symmetries giving way to a preference for the improvisations of disparate taste. His mania, in accord with my desire, strove to hasten the work, which had to be finished by an agreed date.

On that day, fixed in advance, everything had to be ready: the flowers embalming the beds between the hedges of the pathways and the pyramids of holly; the obelisk of yews upright at the round-points; the smile of the statues on their marble faces, their bare feet trampling the garlanded pedestals; the waters impatient to send forth their sprays and overflow their vases, to fill the entire garden with their delightful murmurs. It was necessary that all the keys were in all the doors, the brackets on the walls, everything in its place in its minute perfection, with wines and fruits served on the table—and everywhere, the mirrors that I had wanted to be numerous and beautiful, to reflect in passing the divine smile, nocturnal tresses and graceful deportment of the incomparable Madame de Sérences, whose mysterious beauty was about to behold itself within them, once and forever!

No more beautiful day ever shone. From dawn onwards, the rakes were smoothing the pathways, the watering-cans pearling the refreshed flowers. The atmosphere was mild, pure and light. The bright morning promised a fine late summer afternoon. The warm sun caressed the statues and softened their marble; the pools were sparkling; not a single leaf was to fall, not a single rose to shed a petal; only the strongest had been left, and their vigorous maturity guaranteed their endurance.

At midday I advanced to the gate to greet Madame de Sérences. She got down from her carriage and I kissed her hand. I thanked her for coming and reminded her of her promise. She smiled sweetly. There was a moment of silence, and she handed me the three roses that she was carrying, according to her custom. I took them and, having bowed, I went away from her and the magnificent house. Three times I returned, kissing each one of the three flowers, and each time, I saw that she was looking at me.

Madame de Sérences has walked alone in the avenue. The tall trees accompanied her, one by one, silently. At the end, the view of the gardens opened up. They were truly admirable. The masses of verdure disposed cool shade. Three flute-players responded to one another in the depths of the labyrinth, hidden in the complex shell of the maze. The gushing waters embellished the silence of that solitude, but only the statues have smiled at the beautiful visitor.

The house displayed porphyry columns beneath its fronton.

Madame de Sérences has entered the cool vestibule; the chambers offered themselves, in turn, to her silent stroll. Some of them were simple, others sumptuous, small or large, designed for love, sleep or reverie, for meditation of a joy or reflection on a sadness.

Madame de Sérences has spent the day in the magnificent house. In the rear, a flight of steps descends into a small garden. One single pathway winds around a green lawn in which a square pond lies dormant. Two little earthenware sphinxes are mirrored therein. At the corners, large crystal cornets make the tall hollyhocks that grow there into singular water-flowers issuing from a transparent calyx. Dusk falls delightfully there; the evening will have arrived.

In the high-ceilinged dining-room that table presented a supper of sliced meats, jam and fruits. It is from there, leaving the marks of smiling teeth in a peach, that Madame de Sérences would go upstairs to sleep. All the mirrors would certainly see her, and one of them would reflect her, nude, and keep forever, within its crystal, the invisible image of the woman who had gambled with me, and lost her shadow.

In those days, I was a gambler, and a lucky gambler. According to an old precept of superstition, I never failed to keep my gold in a purse made of bat-skin. I did not believe in the virtue of that eccentricity so much as savor its singularity. I indulged myself with many baroque traits, with a view to adding to my character that which might render it as curious to others as to myself.

Every evening, therefore, I was to be found at a casino or someplace where there was a card game. Private and public gambling were equally in fashion; the casinos were overflowing because the passion for dice and cards, reaching the point of frenzy, brought the most brilliant to the green baize. The hairy fingers of men clenched on the cloth where the diamond-studded hands of women were extended. Anticipation was breathless on charming lips or dribbled from hideous mouths; losses saddened in gracious moues or tight lips. Gold clinked, and one heard in the intermittent silence the rattled of dice-cups or the furtive and ominous dealing of cards.

The gold of winnings infiltrated the surrounding lives, or losses carved out their fissures. Subtle or sly venalities were created, some unexpected, the others spied upon. Holed or cracked, consciences collapsed or crumbled. Gold circulated from hand to hand, slaking desires. There was bargaining, auctioning and merchandising. Everyone was trying to sell something or buy someone. Some made a profit on the intervention, many speculated on the need, everyone cheated on the quality. Every passion could be satisfied, provided that chance favored it.

Languid young men wearing make-up, and virile and cavalier women, negotiated their inverted caresses. The caprices of wealth, its decrepitude and unexpectedness gave to every desire the abruptness of its haste. The luckiest wearied of their good fortune by virtue of the monotony of its duration. Fantasies were exasperated, visibly becoming monstrous. People sought, by virtue of a kind of stupid emulation, to surpass one another in excess, in which the pleasure of doing things counted for less than the vanity of having done them. It was a time of great disorder and singular debauchery; I played my part in it, and the examples I set remained famous.

If we did not see first light rising over the consumed candles of card-games, the dawn caught us drinking wine or

177

making love. We observed, then, the treachery of our double intoxication. Slumbering around us, flesh weary and hair undone, were the cadavers of the phantoms that had lured us. We went away, annoyed.

Every evening, whatever the adventures of the day or the labors of the night had been, brought me back in spite of myself to the green tables. Among the numerous transients who succeeded one another there, I noticed, as soon as I arrived and during my entire sojourn, a female gambler of great beauty. She showed herself to be both assiduous and negligent, always sitting in the same place, respiring the flowers of a bouquet that she never abandoned. Among so many various and alternating fortunes, our luck remained imperturbable, and that continuity of fortune attracted attention to both of us. A circle formed around us, and Monsieur d'Amercoeur was no less envied than Madame de Sérences.

Once, I found myself next to her, and we talked about our duplicate luck, whose permanence astonished us, convincing us to pit our good fortune against one another, to see which streak would give way. The proof having been decided, a time and place was fixed for the confrontation.

It was on a beautiful August night that I sat down opposite Madame de Sérences. The population of gamblers was buzzing over the duel. People were already talking about the outcome before the encounter had commenced. Large sums were wagered. Each of our solitary gestures provoked its reaction and its consequence. Multiple interests depended on the science of our strategies and the hazard of our trump cards.

Madame de Sérences drawing-room, where I found myself alone with her, had three windows overlooking a beautiful garden, whose perfumes reached us. Each of the candles was burning its ace of light. Madame de Sérences placed her bouquet of roses on the table; the most beautiful hung at the end of it broken stem and shed its petals, one by one, in the course of that poignant night.

The slender hands of the dealer shuffled the flexible cards. The game began. The stake, which was considerable, fell to me; doubled up, it fell to me again; then again and again and again. Gold coins piled up, with chips representing others. Madame de Sérences smiled softly. We played for gems; her clear voice named them, one by one: diamonds launched their fires; rubies sparkled; pearls ran drop by drop. She lost. We played for domains, Their sonorous or charming names evoked them as we went: châteaux amid forests at the ends of avenues of oaks or through curtains of pines; houses on river-banks, russet wheatfields, brown terrains, green meadows, farms where bulls bellowed, farms where doves cooed, sands and rocks, mussel-beds and beehives. Madame de Sérences was still smiling.

A silence intervened between us. She had risen to her feet, standing in her green silk dress with one hand on the table. The perfume of flowers came in through the open windows; a pile of gold collapsed on to the carpet; a candle-flame made contact with its holder, which cracked. We looked at one another for a long time. Madame de Sérences blushed, as if she scented the final stake.

With a gesture that made her shiver, I showed her the table, on which I laid down the cards that I held in my hand. The painted faces seemed to me to be grimacing a smile. The bearded kings were mocking the hairless knaves. The halberds of some clashed with the swords of others. The queens respired their variegated tulips. I sensed that I was about to speak, without knowing what I was going to say, and a voice that I recognized as mine murmured slowly, while I gestured an invitation to the beautiful player to resume the interrupted game, in order to conclude it.

"Everything, Madame," I said, "against your shadow."

It was thus that I played for and won Madame de Sérences' shadow.

I constructed the magnificent house, in order to keep the image forever: one of its mirrors conserves in its crystal the invisible reflection on which the doors have closed forever. They will not reopen for me, and the marvelous secret will

return with the ruins of the place that contains it to the eternal
dust to which all beings and things, and their shadows, come.

UNCERTAIN STORIES

The Sealed Pavilion

To Madame Paul Barbier [25]

It was a few lines in a society column, in the section on changes of address, which informed me that the Marquis de Lauturières had left the Château de Nailly and had gone to Neyrol-les-Bains to take the waters. That news, related in the most aristocratic of our periodicals, was of no great importance in itself, and would probably not have attracted my attention had it concerned anyone else by the Marquis de Lauturières and if it had not acquired a particular significance in relation to him. Was it not, in fact, an indication of a profound and unusual perturbation in Monsieur de Lauturières' habitual existence?

For many long years Monsieur de Lauturières had spent all four seasons at Nailly, without ever absenting himself. Whatever the reason for that breach of custom, it must have required very exceptional circumstances, the character of which I could easily guess: Monsieur de Lauturières must be very ill, or he would not have consented to change his residence in the Château de Nailly for that of Neyrol-les-Bains. Only the demands of his health could have imposed that displacement on him, and he must have delayed it to the point of rendering it probably futile—from which I concluded, with a very human indifference, that France would soon count one

---

[25] It seems probable that this dedication to Marthe Barbier, one of Régnier's close female friends, is to the wife of the poet and librettist Paul Jules Barbier, more commonly known as Jules Barbier, rather than the wife of the lexicographer Paul Barbier, but the *Cahiers* are unclear on this point.

183

less great seigneur and veritable savant, and a famous eccentric too.

For there was only one Marquis de Lauturières!

Widowed and childless, having married Mademoiselle Varades, the daughter of the great industrialist, who had brought with her and left behind a considerable fortune, he had renounced thereafter the worldly and sporting life that he had previously led, either in his sumptuous town house in the Avenue Matignon or the magnificent Château de Nailly. There, Mademoiselle Varades' dowry permitted him to be a worthy successor to the Maréchal de Nailly, the victor of Nassingen and Heilkirch, who had constructed the opulent dwelling at the end of the seventeenth century and from whom Monsieur de Lauturières descended via his mother, the last de Nailly, as he himself was the last of his own line...

It is quite commonplace, however, in the social class to which the Marquis belonged to let family interests take precedence over the preferences of the heart, so remarriages are frequent therein. The duty of not letting an illustrious name die out often silences the obscure objections of sentiment. Monsieur de Lauturières did not conform to the custom and did not obey that duty. With his wife dead, the house in Paris sold, and Nailly returned to the silence of its vast apartments and deserted gardens, he departed for a long voyage to Asia, in the course of which he traveled through Persia and India, visited Japan and, more especially and more scrupulously, China, in its various provinces, including the high regions of Tibet. He came back therefrom not in the least consoled regarding his widowhood or any more inclined to contract a further union, but well-versed in Chinese and Tibetan languages and a passionate lover of Far Eastern linguistics and Asiatic antiquities.

To that passion, Monsieur de Lauturières, had never thereafter ceased to devote himself, not with the dilettantism of a man of the world but with the conscientiousness of a scientist. Exceedingly profound and very serious studies, carried out in the austere and complete solitude of Nailly, made him an eminent Sinologist to whom the Académie des Inscriptions would have been glad to open its doors—but Monsieur de Lauturières had not responded to the advances of the savant company, limiting himself to communicating thereto the numerous works and papers that he published.

These publications and communications were very nearly his only relationship with the world of the living. He had progressively renounced all ties of family and friendship and remained strictly confined in the Château de Nailly, from which, as I have said, he never absented himself under any pretext. He had assembled an important library there and a rich collection of manuscripts, access to which he did not refuse to his colleagues in Sinology, when they desired to consult them—for, although Monsieur de Lauturières never knocked on anyone's door, no one was forbidden to come and knock on his. It only stood ajar, however, for brief visits, which, however courteously they were made and received, never led to any intimacy with the master of the place.

Given Monsieur de Lauturières' character and preoccupations, there was little chance that circumstances would ever put me in contact with him. My studies of the amorous secret life of the eighteenth century would have been of very little interest to someone who doubtless preferred to Louis XV the emperors of distant Chinese dynasties of which I did not even know the names. And yet, different as our endeavors were, they nevertheless resembled one another in one respect. Did we not both have a similar curiosity regarding the past? Were we not seeking, each in our own fashion, to decipher its enigmas and pierce its mysteries? Did we not experience as similar attraction toward the unknown? Except that the veil that Monsieur de Lauturières tried to rip apart was embroidered with bizarre and extravagant characters and ancient hieratical figures, while the one that I was attempting to lift was made of a light and supple gauze, behind which appeared the frivolous and smiling grace of the epoch in which I would most have liked to live, and in which I amused myself greatly in imagining that I had lived. Nevertheless, I would have astonished Monsieur de Lauturières greatly had I assimilated the Chinese and Tibetan texts on which he exercised his science to the petty archives in which I was gradually discovering a little of the life and mores of long ago.

It was, however, to that humble research that I owed the opportunity to have recourse to the kindness of the Marquis de Lauturières, and this is how it came about. One day, a dealer in autograph manuscripts, knowing that the historians of "petty history" do not disdain documents of that sort, came to offer me the chance to purchase a rather curious correspondence dating from the eighteenth century.

Written by a man of the Court to a woman of quality, these letters, witty as well as amorously inclined, related certain episodes of life at Versailles, notably the story of the beautiful Comtesse de Nailly, of whom Louis XV was amorous, and whose husband, whom she alerted herself to the passion she had inspired, brought her, without delay and as rapidly as possible, to the Château de Nailly, where he locked himself away with her, jealously, never emerging again until their death.

Of that anecdote, of which one finds traces in memoirs of the era, the author seemed particularly well-informed. He gave rather explicit details regarding the beautiful recluse and her life in the solitary château, and related, among other things, that the Comtesse Sabine—for she bore that name, suggestive of abduction—had had a pavilion constructed at the far end of the gardens, to which she loved to retire in the middle of the day in order to "dream and make music" there, and where she had placed her portrait, painted by La Tour[26] some time before her abduction, "as if she had wanted," the author of the letters added, "to conserve before her the face that had excited the caprice of a king, and which had earned her, by its beauty, the severe exile in which she would be consumed until the futile and perishable marvel reached its end."

---

[26] Maurice Quentin de La Tour (1704-1788) was one of the most famous portrait painters of the era.

Such as they were, these letters, of which I had not succeeded in identifying either the author or the addressee, might
have given rise to an interesting publication—but how much
more interesting it would be if it were possible for me to col-
lect more information about the heroine of that distant adventure and combine it with the reproduction of the La Tour portrait, which might perhaps still exist, along with the mysterious pavilion, and the Château de Nailly! As for the latter, I
was satisfied on that score. The *Annuaire des Châteaux* mentioned it, with the name of its present owner. It only remained
for me to obtain from him the necessary authorizations, in case
my anticipations were justified.

Without allowing myself to be discouraged by what I
learned about the Marquis de Lauturières and his reputation
for eccentricity, therefore, I wrote to him to solicit access to
his family archives and the places where his beautiful ancestor
had lived. The response was so unexpected that, while opening
the envelope that contained it, I had the suspicion that it was
bringing me one of those polite and categorical refusals before
which one can only bow—but after taking cognizance of the
epistle whose crowned device had revealed its provenance, my
gaze fell upon the signature. It was not that of Monsieur de
Lauturières. The châtelain had appropriated in order to reply
to me the pen of his librarian, Monsieur Luc Destieux...

Luc Destieux! But Luc Destieux as the name of a former
friend of my schooldays and youth, of whom I had lost sight a
long time before. The encounter was singular, and Destieux
sincerely rejoiced in the coincidence that had brought us together in such an unexpected fashion, to which he had made
the Marquis party. So he informed me that, on his insistence,
Monsieur de Lauturières had authorized me to visit Nailly,
without, however, hiding from me the fact that the visit would
more than probably be a disappointment for me, and that I
would find nothing in the archives concerning his ancestress.
Dispersed after the Revolution, they had only been partially
reconstituted.

187

As for the pavilion, Monsieur de Lauturières excused himself for to letting me see it. Strictly locked up since the death of Madame de Lauturières, as well as the apartments she had occupied in the château, no one ever went in there. Now, as more than thirty years had elapsed since the Marquise de Laututières had made it into a sort of Trianon, to which she sometimes came in summer to do some needlework or read a book, the La Tour portrait, already much deteriorated at that time, must be entirely effaced by now. The Marquis instructed Destieux to express his regrets at a refusal the reasons for which I would surely understand.

The letter concluded with Destieux's wish that I would carry through my project. The thought of seeing me again gave him considerable pleasure. He was dying of boredom in that solitude, among his Chinese manuscripts and in the company of the aged eccentric. Fortunately, he had his great epic poem in twenty-four parts to distract him, on which he had been working for six years and of which he would read me fragments. A timetable of trains to Nailly was enclosed.

If Destieux's letter did not satisfy me entirely, it did not discourage me totally. I had the vague hope that, once at Nailly, some fortuitous circumstance might permit me to overcome Monsieur de Lauturière's reluctance to let me visit the famous pavilion. I had already had occasion in my life to seek means of overcoming the most insurmountable obstacles. If I could just get close to Monsieur Lauturière, I felt certain I could reach my goal—but the response that he had made to me seemed to signify that it would not be him that my visit to Nailly would be addressed, and that he would leave to Destieux the responsibility of receiving me at the château. At any rate, once in the place, I would act according to circumstances—but for the first time in my life I regretted not being a Sinologist. Alas, I knew no other Chinese people than those that the eighteenth century depicted on its screens and in its *contes philosophiques*. Nevertheless, I decided to attempt the adventure that would, at least, give me the pleasure of seeing the worthy Destieux again and listening to a few fragments of his epic poem—which was not, after all, a run-of-the-mill entertainment.

I found Luc Destieux at the station and recognized him from a distance. He had scarcely changed since our last meeting, although that had been a good few years ago. He had a few gray hairs and the beginnings of a paunch. Apart from that, he was still the same Destieux that I had known as a teacher in a crammer, the editor in chief of a periodical with no subscribers, an insurance salesman and an assistant to a theater manager, before I had lost sight of him and rediscovered him as a librarian to a eminent Sinologist and epic poet in his spare time.

After the benevolent handshake, however, he had me sit down beside him in an elegant tilbury. He cracked his whip and the horse set off at a tranquil trot. At the first upward slope Destieux lit his short pipe.

"Life's strange, you know! I'm damned if I thought I'd see you at Nailly, or even to see you again elsewhere. Oh, I haven't forgotten you, old man, but I'm not much good at maintaining contact with people, you know. I leave it to chance—and I wasn't wrong, since here you are. Oh, I'm glad! You'll stay for dinner and sleep at the château, and you shan't leave until tomorrow evening. There's a good train. That's agreed with the Marquis. He'll stay in his room—he's ill just now, although that doesn't stop him...

"It's true, though, that I'm glad to see you. You haven't aged a bit, although it wasn't yesterday that we met at poor Félicie's Do you remember? Félicie Landret, the 'Félicie of all the felicities,' as we called her? A nice girl—and cheerful and funny, and slim and very talkative. To think that she ended up married to that imbecile La Rupelle...how long ago it was! Damn! We had a good time in those days, while here...well, it gives me pleasure to see another face than that of my Marquis. It's not that he's a bad chap, but he's had his troubles. He's never got over the death of his wife—that's what led him to Sinology. Still, if he took me to China with him, it would be a distraction, but cataloguing his library, making file-cards, copying papers and notes—that's not a life...

"What can you do? It's my living, occupying myself with all these old documents, but as for being interested...the only advantage is that I'm comfortable here from the material viewpoint. No worries, no temptations—so I can work in peace on my epic poem. But we'll talk about that later. All I can tell you, for the moment, it that my *Alexandriad* has been in the workshop for six years. Twenty-four sections...you'll see."

Destieux shook the ashes from his pipe before putting it back in his jacket pocket. Then he went on:

"A rough-hewn block, but flawless! Sculpted—but what hard labor! *Nulla dies sine linea.*[27] Anyway, that's what has permitted me not to die of boredom in that immense deserted château, in close company with the Marquis, absorbed in his memories and working away at his chinoiseries. I had to find something: sniff the wine, run after the women! I preferred writing an epic poem. I began it as a joke and then got into it in earnest. It's exciting, my dear chap...and it might go far, but what a bother! Fortunately, I'm not disturbed. No one to see. From time to time, some old scholar who comes to consult our documents gives the domestics a forty-sou tip, and leaves. Oh, yes, there's Pouthier—Pouthier's the Marquis' agent. He travels Europe to buy him wads of paper, attend auction sales, visit dealers. A decent chap, Pouthier, but he's almost never here. Always on the road, but full of stories when he returns, for the old rogue adores women. His wife is dead. Two children being brought up by an old English spinster. The Marquis puts them up in summer, in one of the château's outbuildings. Two handsome kids. Sometimes the old man asks to see them, considers them, and his eyes fill with tears. What can you expect? He's so lonely, that old Chinaman..."

While Destieux chattered away, the horse continued to trot meekly along the road. It was a fine fresh September day.

---

[27] "Not a day without a line." (Pliny.)

The sky was clear and bright. Meadows extended to the right and the left. The countryside composed one of those simple and harmonious French landscapes that, without attracting attention to any particularly picturesque detail, nevertheless sticks in the memory by virtue of some secret charm of colors and contours. I was about to make that observation to Destieux when, as we passed a distance-marker, he pointed at it with the end of his whip.

"Nailly, six kilometers. We're entering the domain of the beautiful Comtesse."

It was the first allusion he had made to the object of my visit, and I was about to interrogate him, to find out whether I really had to abandon all hope concerning the forbidden pavilion and the invisible portrait, when he anticipated my question.

"In that regard, old chap, I tried again, you know, for the portrait—but nothing doing. The Sinologist is intractable. He even begged me, very dryly, not to take you to the vicinity of the pavilion. Between ourselves, there's nothing very curious about it. I've only been there once, at the beginning of my sojourn in Nailly. That part of the grounds is completely abandoned and not very practicable. To tell the truth, you're not missing much, because the Marquis doesn't allow anyone to go inside. As for the rest, château and gardens, he's told me to do you the honors. It's worth the trip, even if you don't find anything in the archives. Nailly's a beautiful dwelling, and the beautiful Comtesse didn't have much to complain about, after all. But we're almost there..."

In front of us the road continued, white in the sunlight, when the carriage made an abrupt turn to go into a broad avenue, when went uphill, bordered by a quadruple row of exceedingly old trees and preceded by two columns, each supporting a mounted Victory. The horses and figures were in the style of Coysevox,[28] and the seigneurial aspect of the avenue

---

[28] Antoine Coysevox (1640-1720) did a great deal of work on the statuary for Versailles, to which his flamboyant mock-

191

was completed by a monumental wrought iron gate whose gilded pikes rose up sharply at the top of the slope, outlined against the sky between two pillars ornamented with sumptuous trophies of arms and armor, in the same style as the clarion-sounding Victories between which we had passed.

Destieux nudged me with his elbow. "Well, my dear chap, admit that that gate's a smart entrance, with its medallions, on which the Maréchal de Nailly's batons and his military trophies overlap. It's could serve as the frontispiece of an epic poem. But we'll get out here and go to the château on foot. You'll see that my Marquis isn't badly housed..."

The avenue ended in a sort of paved esplanade. To either side of the gate, some distance away, there was a low building with a slate roof, whose windows, ornamented with grotesque figures, were garlanded by climbing roses. While I admired the grace of the two lodges, Destieux uttered a shrill whistle.

At that signal, an old man came out of the lodge to the left and bowed to us. Destieux shouted to him: "It's not worth the trouble of opening the gate, Père Nargouze—we'll go through your house. Take the carriage to the stables. But before that, old chap, look at that!"

And, through the gilded ironwork of the tall gate, Destieux showed me with a gesture what, with a humorous mixture of pride and disdain, he had called familiarly "that."

That! The château built by the Maréchal de Nailly was a magnificent dwelling of the noblest and most majestic proportions. Without being immense, Nailly was grand, by virtue of the beauty of its architectural lines, and the air of solidity, logic and elegant pomp that the great century brought to its conceptions.

In front of the façade shone a water-garden preceded by a large basin ornamented in its center by a group in gilded bronze. That vast open space framed tall clumps of verdure

---

Classical style was admirably suited. The images are the gates of Nailly are presumably similar to the Coysevox Victories that can still be seen in the Tuileries gardens.

that must have formed an entire forest of trees behind the château, pierced by regular footpaths, animated by fountains and statues and surrounded by silence and solitude.

And it was in this ostentatious, noble and sad decor, which time had not altered, in which the seductive Sabine de Nailly—whose youthful grace the memoirs of the Duc de Cambefort and the Abbé Gaillardet had compared to that of Flora, the goddess of spring, had lived the long years of her virtuous exile. It was here in Nailly, far from Versailles— which must have reminded her of it in the murmur of its fountains and the odor of its neatly-trimmed box-hedges—that she had seen her youth take flight, and that beauty fade away, of which she came to contemplate the intact and melancholy image in the La Tour portrait, in the depths of the pavilion to which she retreated in order to "dream and make music." So said the yellowed letters, whose pages, rediscovered by chance, had told me of what had repeated by her contemporaries, moved by her melancholy and slightly amusing adventure that conjugal scruples had forced upon her.

I was letting myself linger on these thoughts when, as if to reply to them, in the great silence, laughter burst forth, youthful, sonorous and merry. It was coming from the lodge with the windows garlanded with climbing roses, which was appended to the ne from which Père Nargouze had emerged in response to Destieux's appeal. As I was about to question the latter, I saw him shrug his shoulders while inhaling a draught from his reignited pipe.

"That's Pouthier's kids, amusing themselves! Ah, that's youth! But come on, what do you think of the old place?"

The silvery laughter had died away in the silence, with which was mingled the distant odor of roses and the murmur of invisible water. The tall gate extended its gilded pikes into the clear sky.

If the Château de Nailly had suffered certain depredations in the Revolutionary era, no apparent traces of them remained. After his marriage to Mademoiselle Varades and before his widowhood, the Marquis de Lauturières had restored it with a great deal of taste and intelligence, and brought the exterior and interior alike up to scratch. Nailly was, in fact, furnished with a sober aristocratic magnificence. The parts of the furniture and the decoration that must have been renewed fitted in perfectly with those that had been conserved. The ensemble was very attractive.

Furthermore, Nailly could still boast numerous souvenirs of the Maréchal. His equestrian portrait was displayed there, showing a large, corpulent man, with leather boots and a leather coat, his *cordon bleu* around his neck, his fleur-de-lys-ornamented baton in his hand, against the background of a landscape and a battle. Other effigies represented him in the costume of the court, hunting attire and battle armor. But the apartments of Nailly were not only decorated by these precious family images; they contained fine paintings beautiful tapestries and a few items of precious Chinese porcelain in their seventeenth- and eighteenth-century mountings. As for the library, which occupied a long gallery, Destieux did not permit me to pause there.

"You'll see that tomorrow, and you can rummage through the Nailly family papers at your leisure. No, not that way—that's the Chinese manuscript room, and it's of no interest to you. Now, let's take a turn around the grounds. I've ordered dinner for half past six, so that we can make a real evening of it."

The dining-room where we ate was small and oval, surrounded by mirrors with gilded stonework frames. Like certain sections of the apartments, it dated from the time of the beautiful Comtesse, who must have had them adapted to her own taste, that château doubtless seeming to her to be old-fashion, too suggestive of the preceding reign.

The meal was exquisite, and did honor to Monsieur de Lauturières' cook—who was female, for the château's male personnel only consisted of a butler and the Marquis' *valet de chambre*, who also took care of Destieux. A housekeeper supervised the maintenance of the house. By way of compensation, five gardeners were employed in the maintenance of the gardens and the pathways in the grounds—where, in any case, Monsieur de Lauturières never strolled. In addition, a kind of steward had overall control of the domain. That was the son of Père Nargouze, who lived with him in one of the lodges at the entrance gate. The old man fulfilled the functions of a porter and looked after the three horses making up the Marquis' stable. One of the gardeners harnessed them, when necessary, and took on the role of coachman.

These domestic details and Destieux's complaints regarding the solitude in which he lived at Nailly took us to the end of the meal. When we had finished, Destieux took me by the arm and led me to his room. To get there, we went up a large stone staircase with wrought iron banisters, which led to the first floor. Like all the rooms in the château, with the exception of the charming little dining-room where we had eaten, it was vast.

While Destieux lit a large lamp placed on a table cluttered with papers and pipes, I went to the window. It opened in the façade of the château opposite the one overlooking the water-garden. Night had not entirely fallen as yet and the moon had already risen over the trees in the grounds, with the result that I could make out their disposition fairly well.

On that side, the Château de Nailly rested on a terrace, from which a double horseshoe-shaped ramp led to a pond surrounded by flower beds, beyond which the masses of trees parted to give way to a rather long and broad canal, which interested at right angles with another to form a cross of water, as at Versailles. The canal was one of the beauties of Nailly. That evening, it was gleaming softly beneath the rising moon and its motionless waters seemed to reflect the silence.

The air was sweet and pure, and it would have been pleasant to smoke a cigar in confrontation with that noble decor of Old France, thinking of all the ancient graces that are no more and its vanished splendors—but I heard Destieux riffling through the pages of his manuscript and coughing, and I tore myself away from my contemplation. Being unable to escape the "epic," the best thing to do was to resign myself to it meekly. So, quitting the window, I came to sit down in the lamplight.

Destieux was waiting for me. Touched by my submission, he placed a box of cigars and matches within arm's reach; then, having put out his unfinished pipe, he pronounced the sacramental words: "*The Alexandriad*, an epic poem in twenty-four parts."

Destieux had no talent; his poem was the inexplicable error of an intelligent fellow. It was a mass of laborious and bombastic verses, a painful sequence of clichés and commonplaces. No invention, no style—a composition of the purest pretentiousness; something false, anachronistic and pointless. How had he abandoned himself to that versifying mania? How had the man I had known, living well and truly alive, strayed into that crypt? For Destieux was no fool. He was not lacking in culture, intellect or seven seriousness, since he was capable of fulfilling with respect to Monsieur de Lauturières a rather difficult function, and acquitting himself well—else the Marquis would not have held on to him for so many years. Why this nonsense, then?

And the strangest thing of all was that he had faith in his work. By virtue of what aberration did he fail to sense its ridiculousness? The stout Destieux, epic poet—what a challenge! The Destieux that I recalled from the time of our meetings at Félicie Landret's, to which he had made allusion, amusing the amiable and generous girl with his buffoonery, his glibness, his slightly coarse, but cheerful and frank verve!

While I was thinking all that, Destieux's voice resonated, measured and monotonous, pronouncing the dismal and flaccid alexandrines. Before that overflow I was downcast but resigned, and fully determined to cover the worthy fellow with praise. What good would it do, in fact, to try to disillusion him? What right did I have to show him the vanity of his work? And if I had attempted it, would I have succeeded? Did he not have a profound conviction, a satisfied pride, an absolute certainty that put him above all criticism? The best thing to, therefore, was to applaud the *Alexandriad* hypocritically—but did Destieux even need applause?

It was after midnight when he stopped reading and, tapping the accumulated pages of his voluminous manuscript with his hand, said to me with a mixture of bonhomie and disarming vanity: "Well, old man, there you are, transfixed! Confess that you didn't expect that! You understand, now, that the thing is in the bag. Just the last four parts, and I can get away from Nailly, the Marquis and the whole shop. I can go back to Paris, make the presses groan. Damn it, what an uproar! No one will say any longer, after my *Alexandriad*, that the French don't have an epic turn of mind!"

I didn't contradict Destieux's opinion, judging it preferable to enter into the game with a partner of that sort. Destieux accepted the unreserved compliments that I thought I ought to address to him with the tranquility of a man who knows what he is worth, but is not unamenable to being told. He listened to me with a benevolent smile, and acquiesced with my praise without astonishment. Then, having smoked one last pipe during that exchange, he offered to take me to my bedroom, and left me there, after making sure that nothing was lacking.

When he had wished me goodnight and I found myself alone, I went to lean on the windowsill. Like that of Destieux's room, it overlooked the terrace and the Grand Canal. The night was infinitely calm. The moon illuminated the beauty of the grave décor of water and trees. Destieux's poor rhymes had ceased buzzing in my ears and, once again, I thought about the distant and melancholy Sabine de Nailly and her mysterious pavilion, which I would never see, and which, out there at the far end of the cross of the Canal, must be mirroring its silvery nocturnal facade in the silent moonlit waves...

Contrary to what is customary in stories of the genre in which I appear to be writing, no sad and gracious phantom visited me in my sleep. All that I can say is that it took rather a long time for me to fall asleep, and that I went to sleep while thinking about the singular taste that dominated my life and of which the excursion to Nailly was a consequence. In fact, if I reflected on what had determined my vocation, I saw it as a form of the curious attraction that the still-living mystery of the past exerts on certain minds. It was that curiosity, that attraction, which had led me to search for the solution of certain petty historical enigmas, which had given me a passion for old documents, places to which memories of olden days were attached or which evoked the faces of yesteryear.

That love for distant and secret things, I found in myself as far back as I could remember. I observed its existence, but I did not know how it had been born. What circumstances determine it in the individuals who are similarly afflicted? How can its future presence be recognized in them? What indications announce it, what events make it specific? Can some people identify its origins in themselves or determine it in others?

Whatever had produced it, in my case, I had obtained considerable enjoyment from the sentiment, and I could only praise myself for having abandoned myself to it. Is it not necessary, in this world, that everyone should have his "hobbyhorse," and was not mine as good as any other? It was easier to satisfy than some and demanded fewer resources than, for example, the research in Chinese and Tibetan manuscripts to which Monsieur de Lauturières devoted himself.

Then again, what had I done, after all, in becoming the "curiosity-seeker" that I had become, except to transpose to determined and retrospective points the disturbance of mystery that torments human beings on the subject of themselves and that of the ensemble and detail of the universe? Who can tell, moreover, whether it was not, perhaps, the same disturbance and the same torment that had driven the Marquis de Lauturières to Sinology, as well as, in his case, the causes that had given him a need to fill, with some occupation extrapolated to the point of obsession, the dolorous solitude in which his widowhood had left him?

The death of his wife, whom he seemed to have loved passionately, certainly must have had a great influence on the destiny of Monsieur de Lauturières and contributed a great deal to the bizarrerie of his existence. It also explained his refusal to permit me access to the mysterious pavilion that contained the portrait of his romantic ancestress. For Monsieur de Lauturières, a more intimate memory than that of the heroine of an adventure of the court of times past was linked to that pavilion, and he did not want anyone to profane the solitude that evoked, for him, not the indifferent phantom of the beautiful lady of long ago, but the ever-present image of a spouse so tenderly adored.

Although, deep down, I found that sentiment respectable, it was nevertheless exceedingly irritating. I admit that I would gladly have defied the Marquis' prohibition, if a means were to presented itself, and I was determined to make one last attempt in that regard on Destieux. My curiosity absolved my indiscretion in advance.

I broached the subject when, the following morning, Destieux appeared in my room to ask me if I had slept well; prudently, however, I did not broach it before having lavished further eulogies on the author of the *Alexandriad* in the subject of his poem. Destieux welcomed them with a proudly modest pleasure. Having paid that diplomatic tribute to his vanity, I came to the subject I wanted to raise.

At the first words, Destieux started laughing. "Oh, my dear chap, I too have thought long and hard about taking you into the pavilion in secret, but there's no way, you see. The Marquis has taken his precautions. The old monster is very familiar with fanatics of your sort, and he knows that they're unscrupulous. So I've already seen Nargouze, the steward, prowling around in the vicinity of the pavilion. He must have been warned to keep an eye on us. Then again, I don't have the keys, and I don't know where the Marquis keeps them. And if we were caught, what a fuss there'd be! He'd send me packing, and then what would become of the last four parts of the *Alexandriad*? I'll only be able to write them at Nailly. One breathes in something classical here, and I wanted to make a Louis Quatorzean work. I know it's annoying to have to renounce seeing the portrait of the beautiful Comtesse, but there truly isn't any means..."

During this speech I had finished dressing and I put my washing and shaving equipment into my traveling bag. A soft morning light came in through the open window. The birds were singing in the trees and a gardener's rake was audible down below on the terrace.

Destieux went on: "I've just been to see him, my Marquis, and he's not brilliant this morning. I think he's changed a lot, and I don't have a good opinion of him. Just as long as it takes to finish my last four parts... In brief, he asked me whether you liked Nailly. Then he talked about the portrait again, and said to me: 'Let your friend console himself; perhaps I'm doing him a great favor. What would he have seen in the pavilion? A more-or-less dilapidated portrait that doubtless won't bear any resemblance to the idea he's formed of my beautiful ancestress. While unknown, she'll continue to occupy his imagination. And make him understand that there's nothing personal about my refusal. If I weren't suffering so much, I'd tell him myself, but I'm not well today, Destieux; I won't work in the library, and you'll have to bring the manuscript that Pouthier has sent me from Amsterdam to me here.' Oh, he's a character, you know! Now, let's make a tour of the archives. Perhaps you'll find something interesting there. My *Alexandriad* seems to you to be a tasty morsel, then, old chap?"

And while we were going downstairs, Destieux declaimed bombastically the opening lines of his poem: "Of Alexander the Great's exploits I sing/Of the conqueror proud who confronted kings..."

Monsieur de Lauturières was right. The archives of Nailly were very poor with regard to the eighteenth century, and none of them contained anything relating to the beautiful Comtesse. It was definitely necessary for me to renounce the possibility of penetrating any further into the romantic adventure whose fortuitous discovery had momentarily piqued my curiosity. Hazard, which had favored me in putting into my hand the letters that had motivated my journey to Nailly, had obviously withdrawn its favor. What good would it do to take my investigation any further? The image of the beautiful exile, which had briefly been on the point of showing itself to me, was definitively effaced from my sight. Why persist in pursuing it any further? Are there not, in the life of every seeker, trails that lead nowhere, at the end of which one is obliged to retrace one's steps?

I had not been following a false trail, but a barrier had loomed up before me and forbidden me the mysterious pavilion that would remain unseen and locked. Monsieur de Lauturières had the key to it, but he refused it to me and had said that I would not decipher the story of his ancestor as he was deciphering the Chinese manuscript that he was in the process of consulting while Destieux and I ate lunch in the little oval dining-room with the stonework-framed mirrors, in which the seductive Lady de Nailly must have looked more than once, during that long retreat, at her melancholy visage and hair, powdered at first by her own graceful hand, and then by that of the years!

The meal ought to have suffered the effects of my bad mood, but I admit that it could not hold up in the face of the naïve and flavorsome vanity of the worthy Destieux—which is to say that the *Alexandriad* redeemed the conversation. That subject, and Destieux's anecdotes regarding our youthful meetings in the home of the hospitable and generous Félicie Landret, lasted us until the time of my departure. Destieux had had my light luggage placed in the tilbury that was awaiting us at the gate, which we were to reach on foot, going through the gardens.

Suddenly, as we were emerging from the château, Destieux nudged me with his elbow and said: "Look, there's the Marquis, behind the window—the second window on the ground floor. No need to bow; he thinks we haven't seen him..."

I darted a clandestine glance at the place Destieux had indicated to me. Vaguely, through the reflection of the pane, I perceived an old man, of tall stature, clad in black, who as holding a half-unrolled scroll in his hand. It was the Marquis de Lauturières, making sure of the departure of the indiscreet visitor.

I pretended not to see anything, and Destieux and I continued to chat as we walked, until we arrived at the gate. When we were outside, I looked back one last time, through the gilded pikes, at the Château de Nailly, to which I thought that I would never return. The same silence surrounded it as the day before. Suddenly, the voices of the same children I had heard before resounded in the lodge with the windows garlanded with roses.

"It's the little Pouthiers, who must be tormenting their English governess," said Destieux, cracking his whip over the horse.

We arrived at the station just in time to catch the Paris train.

The memory of that visit and the petty disappointment it recalled, soon faded from my mind. I relegated the correspondence that had attracted my attention to the beautiful Comtesse de Nailly to the bottom of a drawer. In any case, other subject preoccupied me. It was at that time, in fact, that I undertook, as a consequence of circumstances that it would be tedious to relate, the work that I eventually published under the title *Some Obscure Points in the Memoirs of Saint-Simon*.

I therefore found it easy to forget Nailly and it pavilion, its Sinologist and its epic librarian. The latter in spite of his promise, did not send me news of his epic, nor of himself, and three years went past thus, until the day when I read the newspaper article about the displacement of the Marquis de Lauturières to the waters at Neyrol-les-Bains, from which I concluded—without, as I have said, watching any further importance to it—that the Marquis would have to be very ill to make the decision to renounce, even temporarily, his habitual seclusion. After making that reflection, I had given the matter no further thought, when, a few days later, I received this bizarre letter:

The Comtesse de Nailly will be happy to receive you in her pavilion. Take the 9-18 a.m. train on Thursday and get off at Taillebois station. A carriage will be waiting for you. Exactitude and discretion.

I recognized Destieux's handwriting. My first impulse was to shrug my shoulders. By means of this stratagem, the fellow doubtless wanted to inflict on me the reading of a few thousand alexandrines of his *Alexandriad*, and had found a fine means of getting me to come. It was a bad time. I was working hard and I didn't want to interrupt myself to listen to his nonsense. On the other hand, as it was the height of summer and I felt rather tired, the prospect of a vacation trip and the idea of seeing once again the winged Victories, the gilded gate, the gardens with the silent waters and the noble architecture of the Château de Nailly was not unattractive, even if I had to pay for the pleasure with the imposition of listening to a lecture. In brief, the thought of the brief excursion seduced me, to the extent that on the way to the Bibliothèque Nationale I stopped at the telegraph office at the Bourse to send Destieux a telegram of acceptance.

Having sent the dispatch, I asked myself certain questions about Destieux's missive. To begin with, why instruct me to get off at Taillebois station instead of Nailly? Then again, why was he returning to the subject of the forbidden pavilion? It was scarcely probable that Monsieur de Lauturières' restrictions on that subject had changed. The most plausible hypothesis was that, the Marquis being absent, bored with perishing in his seigneurial solitude, he had thought of me as a means of distraction—which was, all in all, rather flattering.

Anyway, it was too late for me to change my mind, and I would go to Nailly on the twelfth of August.

When I got off the train at Taillebois station, the first person I saw on the platform was Destieux. He was in his shirt-sleeves, for it was exceedingly hot that day. When he had shaken my hand and we were out of the station, he said: "Well, old chap, I'm glad you've come. Are you annoyed with me for having let such a long time go by without sending you any news? But I've been working had! The *Alexandriad* is finished; it's because of that, if fact...but I'll explain it at table, for we're going to have lunch first—not at the château but at an inn. Don't be afraid—the inn's excellent. The cuisine and the cellar are first-rate. We sometimes come here with Pouthier when he's passing through Nailly, to eat a ragout and drink a bottle. It's there, a few paces further on. Anyway, I've had the horse unharnessed and put the tilbury away."

The inn at Taillebois, at the sign of the *Mouton Blanc*, was indeed very pleasant and, when we had been served in a cool basement room and had tasted the impeccable omelet and perfect white wine, I willingly endorsed Destieux's opinion. During the first mouthfuls and sips, he looked at me covertly with a sly and knowing expression, and then suddenly burst out laughing. Rummaging in his pocket, he brought out a large key, which he placed on the table, rubbing his hands.

"You see that key? Well, old chap, it's that of the pavilion, for I'm going to take you to the famous pavilion. Yes, as soon as we've had lunch. But you must have suspected something curious was afoot when I sent you the invitation from the beautiful Comtesse, no? In sum, it's like this. Yes, I've got the key—I've got it because the Marquis is at the waters, where he's taking the cure. So, no danger from that direction. Besides, I've had it now, and I don't give a damn about the Marquis, because, as soon as he gets back I'm going to ask him to find a replacement. The *Alexandriad* is finished, as I've had the honor of telling you, and I'm going back to Paris, where I shall only emerge again from some publishing house. All the same, as I'd prefer the worthy gentleman not to know anything about the adventure, we're taking advantage of a day when Nargouze, the steward, has gone to see his daughter get married in Bourseuil, in the Yonne. So, we won't be spotted. Then again, for safety's sake, I told you to get off at Taillebois. With the tilbury, we'll go back to Nailly under the cover of the forest, as far as the grounds. I've cleared a breach in the wall by which we can easily get in, at the far end of the canal, not far from the pavilion. There's an almost-practicable path. Once there, you have only to take this and you're in tête-à-tête with the Comtesse. Come on, a little *bravo* for your friend Destieux and to your health!"

And Destieux clinked his glass on the metal of the large key that he was holding out to me.

I had taken it between my fingers. It was heavy, beautifully elegant and simple in form, but, all things considered, I felt myself gripped by an unexpected scruple. What we were going to do wasn't very delicate. We were contravening the formal prohibition and the perfectly respectable desire of Monsieur de Lauturières. We were abusing his absence—but, at the same time as that sentiment was born in me, another opposed it: that of the intense curiosity that I had always experienced for places and people surrounded and enveloped by a certain mystery, for that which is enigmatic and secret in the past.

Suddenly, the passionate interest that I had conceived for the Comtesse de Nailly returned, more violently than ever. I had only to introduce that key into the lock that it opened, and the image of that living woman of the olden days would appear to me. I was about to savor the poignant pleasure of seeing her face, and who could tell whether the melancholy smile with which she would welcome me would not absolve my indiscreet audacity? Beautiful romantic shades gladly forgive those who are led to them by the almost amorous attraction that the exercise upon the imagination.

And again I reminded myself of what I knew about that Sabine de Nailly, whose young beauty had charmed her contemporaries and troubled the heart of a king. I reminded myself of Versailles and the Court, the homage and the adulation, the traps and the temptations—especially that set at the feet of the favorite the most beautiful kingdom in the world—and then the retreat from the sin, dazzling as it was, and the fear of herself that had led the imprudent Sabine, like another Princesse de Clèves,[29] to the dangerous, but noble confession of the caprice that she had inspired in the royal fantasy. Then there was the alerted and frightened husband, the flight from Versailles, the premature retreat, the reclusion in that solitary château under jealous conjugal surveillance; there were the years succeeding one another in their similar monotony, the long reveries in the pavilion, before the portrait in which La Tour had represented the exiled beauty in all her seductive glory, before the portrait that showed her the image of what she had been, of that which she was less and less with every passing day, and that which she would never be again.

I was so absorbed in these thoughts that I did not respond immediately to the toast that Destieux had offered to my health, but he had paid no heed to my silence and had not read anything into it. I looked at him. Was I, then, about to make

---

[29] The reference is to the novel *La Princesse de Clèves* (1678), published anonymously but believed to be the work of Madame de La Fayette, in which the eponymous character marries an older man on her mother's advice but then falls in love with a younger one. Instead of acting on her desire, she confesses her temptation to her husband, who begs her not to marry his rival even after his death—an injunction she obeys, dutifully but painfully. Although set in the sixteenth century court of Henri II and featuring many well-known historical individuals, the setting is clearly a disguise meant to excuse an elaborate representation and discussion of the mores of the court of Louis XIV; the Princesse in the novel bears no resemblance to the actual Princesse Sibylle de Clèves. The novel was enormously successful and constituted an important landmark in French prose fiction, inaugurating the tradition of intense psychological analysis that Régnier's prose fiction carries forward.

him party to my scruple and renounce the pleasure that he had so generously prepared for me?

Well, too bad! The opportunity had presented itself and I had not, after all, done anything to provoke it. It was Destieux who, on his own initiative, had organized the expedition. Besides, the time for reflection had passed, and when Destieux got up from the table saying: "Let's go," I followed him meekly...

"Come on, I told them to hitch up the tilbury for three o'clock. We'll need a good horse to get to Nailly through the forest. Oh! Don't forget the key—that would be too stupid."

To go from Taillebois to Nailly one goes through a part of the forest of Senoise. There was an oppressive August heat that day. The sky was clear and scorching, and not a breath of wind stirred the foliage. Flies were buzzing insistently around the rump of the sweating horse. In the silence, modified by the monotonous noise of the wheels, I listened to Destieux talking to me incessantly about printers, publishers, a launch and publicity. As soon as he was established in Paris he was going to busy himself with the publication of the *Alexandriad*, and I divined that he had expended on that hazardous operation all the savings amassed during is sojourn with the Marquis de Lauturières. I also foresaw the amicable eulogistic article that it would be necessary for me to write about the *Alexandriad*, and that prospect rendered me a trifle thoughtful...

Meanwhile, we had arrived in the wildest region of the forest. The height of the trees, the majesty of the fully-grown forest and the solitude of the location had ended up imposing silence on Destieux. Besides, he was obliged to pay attention to where the tilbury was going, for we had left the road and taken a grassy path whose deep ruts were treacherously hidden. The carriage advanced with increasing difficulty as the path narrowed. Branches whipped us in the face and I was anticipating the moment when the impatient horse would refuse to go any further and would unload us into the thicket when an abrupt jolt almost threw me against Destieux. I had closed my eyes to avoid being blinded when I heard Destieux's voice shout: "We're here."

We found ourselves on the edge of the forest, in front of a ditch that was half filled-in and a breach made in the wall of Nailly's grounds. Destieux leapt down from the carriage and tied the horse's reins to the stump of a tree.

"Now old chap, watch out for brambles and look after your calves!"

The part of Nailly's grounds into which we plunged after having crossed the ditch without too much difficulty was in a state of complete abandonment. No trace of pathways remained here, and it was necessary to force a passage though the undergrowth. We walked with some difficulty for ten minutes, protecting our faces as best we could and occasionally tripping over hidden roots. Then it was necessary for us to climb a rather steep bank. Destieux preceded me and, once he had arrived at the summit, he sat down at let himself slide on the seat of his trousers. I did likewise. At the bottom of the descent, my foot encountered the support of a broken paving-stone, through which a bush was growing. I got to my feet and looked around.

We were on the edge of one of the arms of the cross of Nailly's grand canal. At that point it had broken its stone rim and formed a sort of irregular marshy pond, whose shallow and stagnant water had been invaded by filamentous algae and aquatic plants. Tall reeds grew there, immobile in the humid heat, their stems softly tufted. At the extremity of the pool one could make our a kind of terrace, and the steps of a double stairway that had once permitted boats to land and by means of which one went up to the pavilion.

The pavilion was a small edifice with a flat roof edged by a balustrade. Even at a distance, it seemed very dilapidated, the balustrade broken in places, the shuttered of the high windows disjointed, the marble columns mossy and cracked. A heavy sadness weighed upon that isolated demi-ruin in that solitude, at the edge of that green-surfaced lake, which exhaled a warm and insipid marshy odor and lay torpid in a feverish and somnolent silence.

Destieux detached a long bramble that had hooked itself on to his waistcoat.

"It's not lively, your pavilion, is it? No sign of a joyful bubbling fountain! Not surprising, though; no masons or gardeners have passed this way for thirty years, and that's obvious—but the Marquis has forbidden anyone to work here, or even to come into this part of the grounds. So the canal and the pavilion are in a fine state! Watch where you're putting your feet…!"

We followed the edge of the canal, where traces of the ancient paving stones and bordering rim were distinguishable in places. Mosquitoes were buzzing in the warm moisture of the air. Sometimes a frog jumped into the water with a flaccid splash. The spongy ground stifled the noise of our footsteps. As we got closer to the pavilion, its decrepitude became more visible. Finally, we reached the terrace of sorts on which it was built. Destieux had taken out of his pocket the large key that he had taken back from me as we left the inn in Taillebois.

"Let's go round it—the door's on the other side..."

Destieux was preceding me when I saw him stop suddenly with a gesture of surprise and annoyance. He raised his arms in the air and murmured between his teeth: "Oh, this is too much!"

Then he pointed a finger at the object of his irritation.

In front of the pavilion, an old lady was sitting on a fallen tree-trunk, sewing. Nearby were two children. One was a boy about twelve years old, the other a little girl who might have been eight or nine. She was pretty, with beautiful hair tucked under a big straw hat. Her brother—for they resembled one another—made an impression on me with his seeming intelligence. Admirable eyes lent something poetic to his face, which rendered an expression that was simultaneously proud, anxious and passionate even more interesting.

The sight of us seemed to surprise them, and caused the old lady to get to her feet abruptly. The needlework that she was holding on her knees fell to the ground. I perceived then that she was wearing spectacles astride a pointed nose.

Destieux had taken a few steps forward.

"Why, it's you, Miss Spencer! I've caught you at the pavilion again. I strongly recommended to you the other day, however, not to bring the children here again. It's not good for them. This marshy air is unhealthy. It's infested with mosquitoes. Look, there's one about to sting you on the nose! The little ones will catch some sort of fever here and you'll be in a fine pickle afterwards, Miss Spencer! It's stupid, I repeat—but you're more stubborn than a jenny-ass. Permit me to tell you that, Miss Spencer, with all the respect I owe to you." Turning to me, he added: "I've already found Miss Spencer here the other day, with the little Pouthiers. I ask you, is that reasonable?"

And Destieux crushed a large mosquito that had just settled on his cheek.

Miss Spencer had lowered her absurd and blushing English face under the criticism, but she raised it again to reply with an accent that long residence in France had not attenuated: "But it's not only my fault, Monsieur Destieux; it's the children who tormented me to come back to the pavilion. I too find the place unsuitable. Why chose its inconvenience instead of so many beautiful corners of the lovely grounds? I offered them the Orangery, the Three Fountains, the Lovers' Arbor. They insisted. Growl at them, Monsieur Destieux..."

Destieux had turned to the little Pouthiers.

"Truly, Antoinette, you ought to be more obedient to Miss Spencer. I'll write to tell your Papa that you haven't been good. And you, Paul, who are the older!"

Without replying, Paul raised his admirable eyes, in which so much intelligence and anxiety were mingled with so much reverie, to look at Destieux—but Destieux, who had doubtless already decided how to handle the unexpected encounter, was already advancing, shrugging his shoulders, toward the pavilion.

The large key turned in the lock, with difficulty. Instead of opening under Destieux's vigorous push, I thought that the worm-eaten door was about to fall on us. Finally, it yielded, with a groan of its seized-up hinges.

The first room into which we penetrated was a rather large tiled vestibule. The walls, lined with marble plaques, maintained a damp coolness there, even more refreshing after the stifling atmosphere outside. A cellar-like odor was exhaled by the floor-tiles, on which our footsteps resonated, and which, disjointed in places, framed greenish mosses. The infiltrations of the canal must have extended under the pavilion, which doubtless rested on muddy soil, and it seemed probable that someday, thus undermined, the entire edifice, together with its column and balustrades, would collapse limply. I was about to confide this first impression to Destieux, but he was heading toward one of the doors that opened into the vestibule, and I followed him.

The drawing-room into which we entered was even more decrepit, with its rotten parquet, its warped wood paneling and its extensively cracked ceiling. A few old items of fine furniture ornamented it, but in what a state of distressing decay: armchairs whose tapestry upholstery was damp and eaten away, rickety sideboards, lacquer cabinets with scaly panels, all of it taking on a fantastic aspect in the half-light of broken shutters and green-tinted window-panes. And that silence of dead things, in that heavy and humid air, whose coolness was suggestive of the tomb!

And what abandonment, what dilapidation, what melancholy there was in the boudoir that succeeded the drawing-room, that boudoir with extinct mirrors, which no longer reflected anything; in that music room with its obsolete harpsichord and its scattered music-stands, in which a few broken instruments evoked outmoded cadences! What solitude in that sealed pavilion, crumbling among the old trees, at the end of

211

that canal of flat water, which ended in a marsh from which an odor of fever and death rose up!

A call from Destieux made me shudder.

"Nothing much remains of your beautiful Comtesse, old chap!"

The small round room in which I had caught him up, one of whose shutters Destieux had just opened, was better conserved than the others. The parquet, almost intact, was encrusted with marquetry. A large table with a marble top occupied the center. Facing the middle window, an oval frame was fitted into the woodwork. Behind the scratched and tarnished glass, uncertain colors were vaguely discernible, a few indecisive contours, and something like the shadow of an image—something that I considered with a melancholy emotion: the beautiful Sabine de Nailly, twice dead; dead in her perishable flesh, dead in the colored dust in which she had survived for a long time, and which was no more today than the indistinct ash of her form and her beauty.

"Eh? What are you doing here, you little wretch?"

At the sound of Destieux's voice I turned round. Little Paul Pouthier was standing behind us. I saw him raise his eyes to meet ours with the passionate anxiety that I had already remarked therein, but his gaze cleared, with an expression so attentive, so intense and so profound that I felt moved and troubled...

And suddenly, I understood. I understood with all the soul of a curious old man, with all the passion of my life, with all my love of the past, the unknown and mystery. For him, we represented the hazard of a marvelous adventure; we were, perhaps, the key to his future, the revealers of his destiny.

For how long had he wanted to get into this sealed pavilion, into which he had slipped in our wake? How many times had he dreamed of what we were making, for him, an unexpected reality of which he would never lose the memory? The door of the pavilion, mysteriously sealed, around which he prowled and which he had doubtless never dreamed of penetrating, had suddenly been opened before him! The desire of his young imagination had been accomplished with the same facility that one experiences in dreams—and that abrupt realization of his desire had speeded up his palpitating heart, widened his eyes and made his cold hands tremble.

For, having understood, I had taken his hand in mine: the hand of an impassioned child troubled by Destieux's loud, scolding voice—and he understood to, that child, that there was no need to be afraid, that someone was with him who had divined his secret and would protect him. And as Destieux was about to repeat his complaining question, I stopped him, by saying something or other, while caressing the beautiful hair of the little hot head in which was awakening the same appetite for mystery, the same attraction to things of the past, that had been the passion of my life...

Destieux and I went back to dine at the inn in Taillebois before I caught the train again and he returned to Nailly. More than once, listening to Destieux talk about the *Alexandriad* and his schemes of glory, I thought with emotion and melancholy about the anxious and avid eyes of little Paul Pouthier. I thought about them because I seemed to have found in him the image of my distant childhood. I felt a sort of fraternal affection for him.

Did we not belong, both of us, to the same race of beings? Would he not be, as I had been, one of those who experience an obscure love for the beautiful shadows of the past in their secret and distant frames, of those who are attracted to the depths of abandoned parks, to the extremity of dead waters, by the mystery of sealed pavilions, even if they only contain, behind their crumbling walls and their dirty windows, the taciturn disillusionment of solitude and silence?

Marceline; Or, The Fantastic Punishment

To Mademoiselle Madeleine Reclus [30]

You would understand the story that I am going to tell you if you had seen the angry and scornful glance that my wife darted at me when, addressing myself to Signor Barlotti, I asked him the price at which he would be willing to sell me his marionette theater, with the accessories, stage-sets and characters that made it the most delightful, but the most absurd, of playthings.

For three days, the desire to possess that theater of *burattini* [31] had pursued me without let-up, and I had not stopped thinking of the pleasure that I would experience in bringing back to France that baroque and charming souvenir of a journey whose hours had not all been happy—because, I ought to say, of my wife Marceline. Her sulkiness and bad temper had not failed, in fact, to manifest themselves at every opportunity, and on all subjects, and in the light of my irascible companion's continual recriminations, I was forced to recognize that

---

[30] Madeleine Reclus was the daughter of the surgeon Paul Reclus, the owner of the Château d'Orion in Sauveterre (now a hotel). She remains famous by virtue of a portrait painted in 1902 by Ernest Bordes.

[31] The difference between a *burattino* and a *marionetta*, if there is one, is not entirely clear, although it appears that the latter were originally more pretentious in their representations and the former humbler—a distinction lost over time. The etymology of the former term is similarly unclear; it appears to have nothing to do with the celebrated seventeenth century Italian inventor Tito Burattini.

I had been wrong to attempt an experiment that had out contrary to my hopes.

The best thing to do, in view of that failure, was to return home as quickly as possible. On that matter my mind was made up, but on another matter too, it was no less so, and I was firmly resolved not to go back over the frontier without taking with me the seductive little gentlemen of wood and cardboard for which Marceline showed so little sympathy, and toward which mine had been declared as soon as I had made their acquaintance, through the intermediary of the excellent Signor Barlotti. Furthermore, I had a kind of obscure presentiment that they would play a role in my life—and it was that project of purchase that had brought me back to the Palazzo Pastinati.

The Palazzo Pastinati, situated in one of the less frequented parts of Venice, had once been an opulent dwelling. Even though somewhat dilapidated, it still presented a very fine specimen of seventeenth-century Venetian architecture. It mirrored its sumptuous and decrepit façade in a narrow watercourse and conserved a truly grand air with its tall marine door with damp battens, surmounted by the head of a bearded and helmeted warrior.

Once through that door, one penetrated into a vast hall with damp tiles, but of noble proportions, beneath a ceiling of sculpted caissons in which the coat-of-arms of the former masters of the place was depicted. The seigneurial vestibule offered to the gaze an antique sedan chair, beside which a painted wooden statue represented a little lackey holding out a tray to visitors. On that tray where printed cards which bore the words:

CARLO BARLOTTI
Antichità

The Palazzo Pastinati was, in fact, the property of Signor Barlotti, dealer in curiosities. Barlotti had made it into a branch of his shop in the Piazza San Marco and kept a large reserve stock there. That usage made the Palazzo Pastinati the most peculiar place in the world. While obedient to the demands of his trade, however, Signor Barlotti was not lacking in taste. Several rooms in the house having conserved their original decorations in colored stucco, Signor Barlotti had restored them with contemporary furniture. In one of these rooms he had placed three or four live-sized mannequins clad in costumes of the time.

In spite of that effort to bring the Palazzo Pastinati to life, however, Signor Barlotti had not succeeded in freeing it from a certain aspect of fantastic desuetude. One breathed a strange odor of damp and mold there. Footsteps resounded strangely on the sonorous tiles and made the worm-eaten parquets creak bizarrely. With its excessively empty or overly cluttered rooms, its staircases, its doorways and its oddly-angled corners, the Palazzo Pastinati was suggestive of a haunted house.

That impression was further enhanced by the presence of Signor Barlotti. The antiquarian was, in fact, what some would call a freak. His face seemed to be covered by a parchment mask. Very tall and very thin, he stood on long stilt-like legs. Signor Barlotti wore a pince-nez of a copper chain and smoked slender "Virginias" constantly. He was reminiscent of those characters of Hoffmann or Gozzi who are subject to the persecutions of spirits and their malicious tricks.

That resemblance was, however, deceptive. Although he had the air of a revenant, Barlotti did not retreat from anything. He let it be understood that he did not disdain the bed or the table, liked jokes and laughed gladly, albeit cavernously, as he accompanied visitors through his "art gallery," as he called the Palazzo Pastinati. And it was in the course of one of those visits that I had penetrated into the room in which the marionette theater was situated, before which I found myself again that day, and which, beneath Marceline's disapproving gaze, I was contemplating with ardent covetousness.

For as soon as I had seen that little theater, I had felt a crazy desire to acquire it. Immediately, I had understood that I would not quit Venice without satisfying that inoffensive caprice and committing that innocent folly. Whatever price Signor Barlotti might demand of me for his dolls, I was resolved to give him what he wanted, so it was while eyeing the object of my desire with an amorous gaze that I addressed to the antiquarian the question for which he was waiting.

Hardly had I asked it than Signor Barlotti removed his "Virginia" from his lips and his profound and sardonic laughter burst forth.

"Ha ha! You want me to sell you my little theater? To tell the truth, my dear Monsieur, I expected no less of your good taste. Do you know that you have put your finger on the rarest item in my entire gallery, a unique piece, Monsieur, of which I have never seen the like in my whole career as an antique dealer? Yes, look at the finesse of the expressions on the faces. Would not one think they were alive, these *burattini*? Yes, alive, Monsieur—a marvel, a veritable marvel, worthy of a museum! But permit me to consult my notebook."

Signor Barlotti had taken from his pocket a greasy notebook, through which he leafed with his thin finger. In the meantime I gazed at the delightful object, without paying any heed to the repeated signs that Marceline was addressing to me. I only had eyes for my dear little theater and its cartouche, which bore the inscription, in golden letters of the magical words: *Casa di Arlecchino*. Standing in a corner of the room, it fascinated me. Within its framework, encased in a delicate molding that had lost its gilt, the stage opened its minuscule depth against a painted canvas set representing the Piazza San Marco. One could make out the Basilica, the Campanile, the corner of the Libreria and Procuraties.

Against that background, suspended on threads, stood a dozen characters which, as Signor Barlotti had remarked, were truly reminiscent of living beings. The characters in question were those of Italian comedy, the old Commedia dell'Arte, of what were known as Masques, and who charmed Italy and Europe with their wit, their capers, their intrigues, their amours and their extravagant and eternal fantasy, who animated with their poetic and visible presence the parades of old Ruzzante and the sketches of Goldoni and Gozzi.[32] And I never wearied of looking at them, those princes of farce and oddity, grouped in their traditional costumes.

Oh, what an amusing troupe they formed. Signor Barlotti's *burattini*, in their variegated assembly! There was Pantalon, with his red doublet and long black robe, with his swarthy mask beneath his woolen bonnet, Pantalon with his yellow slippers; and next to Pantalon, Brighella and Tartaglia: Brighella clad all in white bedecked with green braid, with his moustachioed mask, his money-bag and his dagger; Tartaglia in a green outfit striped with yellow, balancing large blue-tinted spectacles on his nose. The black-clad Scaramouche was there, with his powdered face, his moustache and painted eyebrows; and the white-clad Pulcinello, black-masked beneath his gray felt hat; and Rosaura and Giacometta; and Coralline in a green silk jacket and skirt, striped with paler green; and the elegant Lelio, all plumes, braid, spangles and frills; and Mezzetin with Colombine; and Arlequin, Arlequin whose bright yellow jacket and trousers were ornamented with triangles of yellow and green fabric, Arlequin with his mask, his hat-band and his black chin-strap, who wore a hare's tail on top of his hat and was gravely saluting with his bat three cha-

---

[32] *Il Ruzzante* [The Peasant] was the nickname of the actor Angelo Biolco (1502-1542), derived from the character he played in many of his improvised sketches and plays, which attempted to revolutionize Italian theater. Carlo Goldoni (1707-1793) brought about a further revolution, substituting middle-class characters and themes for the artificialization that had survived Biolco's innovations, renewed and revived by the Commedia dell'arte, which had emerged and became formalized in the course of the sixteenth century, but Goldoni was sternly opposed by his contemporary and rival Carlo Gozzi (1720-1806), who wanted to preserve a certain traditional flamboyance, and found comic fantasies based on folktales a popular means of so doing.

racters from the Carnaval de Venise, in cloaks, white face-masks and tricorn hats, while in their midst a Centaur proudly displayed his bearded human torso on the body of a horse with horny hooves—yes, a Centaur, who had the singularity, as well as that of being on the Piazetta, of being piebald![33]

And that was the whole of the charming little society, to which was added the inexplicable presence of a mythological monster, of which I was about to become the possessor, for a few miserable gold coins, when the worthy Signor Barlotti lifted his nose out of his notebook and told me the price I would have to pay for the acquisition of the plaything—certainly useless but so very attractive, whatever the severe and disapproving Marceline might think.

I knew full well, of course, that the figure would be extravagant, but even so Signor Barlotti's impudence surpassed my most costly anticipations. Signor Barlotti did not spare me, damn it! He abused and made mock of me. The sensible thing to do, obviously, would have been to reply to his pretensions with a shrug of the shoulders or a pirouette, but Arlequin was looking at me so amiably and Coralline was winking at me so persuasively! Then again, how could I resist Rosaura's smile and Pulchinello's grimace, not to mention that

---

[33] Although I have Italianized Régnier's locational references, I have left the names of the characters in the Commedia dell'arte as he renders them, some of the names being Frenchified (thus, Columbina becomes Colombine, Scaramuccio Scaramouche and Pantalone Pantalon). The resulting admixture is not inappropriate, as the characters in question were subjected to some alteration when they became widely popular in France, where Arlequin [Harlequin in English] became a much more important character than Arlecchino had been in Italy—thus explaining the narrator's emphasis. The one character effectively added by the French, the "sad clown" Pierrot, is scrupulously omitted from the cast of the puppet theater, although his avatar might be detectable in the character of the narrator.

219

Brighella and Tartaglia were joining in, that Pantalon was making signs to Scaramouche and that even the Centaur was tugging his beard and rolling his encouraging eyes! How could I inflict that disappointment on the three Venetian masks that were considering me with their carnivalesque faces of white cardboard?

So, it was with a tranquil voice, as if it were a mere matter of the purchase of some knick-knack that I replied to Barlotti: "Very well, Signor Barlotti, that's agreed. We're leaving Venice in three days. Have it all packed up for the time of our departure."

Signor Barlotti acquiesced. "Come on, Messer Arlequino, bow to your new master."

With the tip of his "Virginia," Signor Barlotti had touched the string of the puppet, who executed a joyful caper.

I turned to Marceline. "It is in three days' time that we're leaving, isn't it, Marceline?"

But Marceline had disappeared. I darted one last glance at my cherished marionettes, as if to implore their help and protection against the discontent that my wife would undoubtedly manifest toward me for what she would call, I had no doubt, "yet another folly," and, preceded by Signor Barlotti, who had reignited his "Virginia," I went through the tiled rooms of the Palazzo Pastinati to rejoin the gondola that had brought us there.

Marceline was already installed there. She made room for me on the cushions and, hardly acknowledging the bows of the honest Signor Barlotti, in a voice that was more than harsh, ordered the gondolier to take us back to the hotel. During the entire journey, she did not say a single word to me. She was decidedly annoyed, and her exasperated expression told me that she would not forgive me for my "extravagance," and that this time, it was "the last straw." How could I have guessed, however, what a snare Marceline would one day make of the strings of all my puppets, in which, having caused me to stumble, she would be caught herself?

I have never had a strong head, and have always lacked the solid will by means of which one can steer through life according to the rules of common sense, with a view to certain of those practical results to which people commonly apply themselves, so my existence was rather disorganized beneath its appearance of monotony and regularity.

Do not, however, deduce from that circumstance that I have committed hypocritical extravagances or obscure misdeeds. No! I am not, by nature, either violent or perverse, and my only deviations arise from the fact that I have always felt incapable of interesting myself in that which preoccupies the majority of human beings. That is why I could not pretend to pass for a reasonable man. Is one reasonable, in fact, when one yields to the deplorable inclination only to see in everything the pleasure and beauty that it might entail, without worrying overmuch about the utility it might possess? If that point of view is adopted, I am obliged to recognize that I have always lived in the most perfect unreason, since I have never been able to regulate my interests, and have always subordinated them to my fantasy.

That disposition only to savor and appreciate what the majority of people consider to be fundamentally vain and undeniably useless was manifest within me at an early age, and I owe thereto the impossibility I found in making a choice of a career. The idea of devoting myself on a daily basis to some practical end and putting myself at the service of some regular occupation was always odious to me. The time that we have to spend on earth is not long enough for us to devote it to anything but ourselves. On that point, there was within me a firm resolution from which nothing could ever turn me away. The mere thought of going against it caused me a sort of internal hilarity. Can you imagine me, in fact, as a physician, an advocate, a civil servant, a manufacturer or a tradesman, spending my days taking pulses, compiling dossiers, scribbling or making deals? To constrain myself to any of those tasks would have required a very different conception of life than the one I had formed, the attribution to reality of a value that it does not have, and never will have for me. It would have been necessary to possess brain very different from mine, all abuzz with chimeras and clouded with dreams.

For I admit unashamedly that I am a dreamer and a visionary. The imaginary plays a more important role in my mind than the real. That is the defect of people of my kind, and they find themselves in consequence placed, so to speak, outside of existence. The truth is, in fact, that I have never been able to involve myself in it seriously. The result of that is that I am a kind of vagabond and nomad. I escape from what surrounds me in distractions that have earned me a well-established reputation as an eccentric and a dreamer. That does not offend me at all, and I accept it with smiling resignation.

Perhaps there might have been, in my youth, means of struggling against that turn of mind, which, without causing it to disappear entirely, would have restrained its excess. On that point I am reduced to hypotheses, for my parents, while perceiving the penchant and perhaps deploring it, did nothing to counter it effectively. Far be it from me, of course, to reproach them for their negligence in that regard. The anxieties that they were obliged to devote to themselves did not permit them to pay the necessary attention to me.

My father and mother, being in delicate health, spent the greater part of their time reciprocally supervising the scrupulous hygienic practices that they imposed on one another with touching solicitude. My parents loved one another tenderly and did not spare me their affection. With that which they gave to one another, their principal concern was to make me happy, and as I seemed to find my happiness in the divagations with which I delighted myself, they scarcely raised any opposition and let me follow their slope. Thus, I lived to the age of fifteen without any serious influence opposing that facility of reverie, that aptitude for chimeras, which gripped me completely.

Add to those circumstances the fact that the existence we led was exceedingly solitary, and unconfused so far as I was concerned with any external interference. Our house, which bore the singular name of the Troublerie,[34] was situated some distance from the town, somewhat isolated in the countryside. It was a charming dwelling, built in the middle of the eighteenth century, surrounded by a vast garden, half-French and half-kitchen, to which a beautiful tree-lined pathway led. Spacious and comfortable, with no pretention to compete with châteaux, it had conserved its original furniture, to which my parents had added a few items from the same epoch.

In spite of its pleasantness, its relative proximity to the town, my mother's exquisite charm and my father's amiability, visitors to the Troublerie were rare, not because they were not received with perfect courtesy, but because they felt that they were somehow superfluous there, so sufficient were my father and my mother to one another. The impression that he gave had extended around them a solitude in which I participated naturally, and which did not displease me. So, when the time arrived to provide for my education, it was with joy that I accepted the decision of my parents. Being unable to resolve themselves to be separated from me by sending me to school, it was agreed that a teacher from the town would come to the Troublerie several times a week to give me the necessary lessons.

It was during one of those lessons, to which I usually only paid a rather mediocre attention, that I was informed about the fatal accident suffered by my dear mother. She had died suddenly in the armchair that she had not quit for several days in consequence of an indisposition that she believed to be slight but which, by virtue of a sudden and unexpected complication, abruptly carried her off. My grief was violent, and my poor father's so frightful that his health, which had always been delicate, deteriorated irredeemably. From that moment

---

[34] This improvisation is not to be found in the *Petit Larousse*, but its implication is perfectly clear; if an Orangerie plays host to oranges, a Troublerie is obviously host to [mental] disturbances.

on, his visible decline was incessant. Soon, he was confined to bed. His conditioned worsened from day to day, and a few months later, I was an orphan.

That event might have led to a complete change in my existence if my uncle, Antoine Brion, whom those sad circumstances had given me as a guardian, had not assumed that responsibility on the sole condition that his own way of life would not be modified in the slightest. Uncle Antoine was my mother's brother. He lived in the town, in a house situated on the ancient ramparts, where he had assembled an enormous library, celebrated throughout the land. That library was his principal occupation, and he did not intend that I should be another, additional to it. Not for an instant did he think of taking me into his home. My presence would have disturbed his habits—those of a confirmed bachelor and obsessive collector. On the other hand, having expressed to him my reluctance to leave the Troublerie and complete my education at a boarding-school, he consented that I should stay there. My teacher, Monsieur Alain Lefougeret,[35] who had no wife and children and no academic ambitions, moved into the house with me and continued his work of enlightenment, while old Ernestine, who had been in my parents' service for thirty years, kept our scholarly household and ensured its smooth running.

These dispositions having been made, life at the Troublerie was organized with an exemplary regularity. Alain Lefougeret was an excellent fellow, full of knowledge and wisdom, but incapable of acquitting any influence over his pupil, for he limited himself strictly to the exercise of his professorial duties and left me free to take from is instruction whatever it suited me to gather therefrom. His task fulfilled, he took no interest whatsoever in me and devoted himself entirely to an immoderate liking for fishing with rod and line. The river the

---

[35] Most of the surnames contained in the story are suggestive, some more vaguely than others; the verb *fouger* refers to what a pig does when rooting for truffles—an implication that will become clear in due course.

passed the end of the garden of the Troublerie was full of fish, and two ponds attached to the property furnished Monsieur Lefougeret with the opportunity to deploy the admirable patience and marvelous expertise of the model angler.

Monsieur Lefougeret had only arrived at the wisdom of making life's pleasure consist of the intelligent observation of a cork after disappointments in his career that had led him to exchange his opposition in the town's college for the kind of retreat that he had adopted at the Troublerie. He declared himself misunderstood, but had renounce his struggle against human injustice philosophically. He had accepted its judgments and no longer allowed himself to bite on the poisoned hooks of ambition. Monsieur Lefougeret was wise, and no longer took bait; he left all that to the scaly people of the waters.

These talents had won Monsieur Lefougeret a great deal of consideration on the part of Ernestine. Without entirely sharing the esteem in which she held him, I greatly appreciated in Monsieur Lefougeret an occupation that guaranteed my liberty. In fact, outside lesson times, Monsieur Lefougeret devoted himself entirely to his lines and bait, and I was able to spend as I wished that time that was not required for the completion of my homework. This leisure permitted me to devote myself to my favorite penchant, to which the solitude in which I lived lent itself. It scarcely suffered any interruption, save for a weekly visit to Uncle Antoine.

On that day, Monsieur Lefougeret abandoned his rods and lines and replaced his fishing-outfit with a severe professorial frock-coat, whose buttonhole was ornamented by the violet ribbon of academic honors. I spruced myself up a bit too, and Ernestine made sure that my cravat was properly tied and my braces extended to the right length. These formalities accomplished, Monsieur Lefougeret and I set out for the town and idled around the streets while waiting for dinner-time.

We paused to look in shop windows. Some attracted our particular attention. Monsieur Lefougeret liked to consider certain exotic fish behind the taxidermist's window, where they served as an ornament, and never failed to cast a glance, at the hat-maker's, at the velvet-covered board to which were attached the ribbons and rosettes of various honorific orders. For my part, my preferences inclined toward the display in Monsieur Tournemain's bookshop, and that of the antique-dealer Père Bricard, for I felt a sympathetic curiosity for the old objects that filled his shop and overflowed on to the sidewalk, and I felt a keen attraction to the volumes garnishing the shelves on which Monsieur Tournemain, his spectacles pushed back over his forehead, inspected them with amicable benevolence.

From that time on, I fact, I developed a taste for reading, and a more attentive educator could have found in that a means of moderating the penchant that was drawing me further and further into the vaporous world of chimeras—but no one thought of directing my reading any more than of alimenting it. Monsieur Lefougeret and my Uncle Antoine knew nothing about me from that viewpoint, as from so many others. The idea of asking Monsieur Lefougeret for advice never entered my head, any more than that of borrowing a book from my uncle. I had understood that his library, the object of his sole passion and the sole pride of his existence, was something inaccessible, indissoluble and secret.

In any case, my uncle had taken care to enlighten me as to his intentions in that regard. After his death, his library would be bequeathed to the town, along with the house that contained it. The public would have access to it, but Uncle Antoine had elaborated with a very particular care the regulations that would be applied to the access in question. Those regulations, which my uncle never ceased perfecting, were an incomparable masterpiece. By means of their sly restrictions and hypocritical precautions, their convoluted prescriptions and its cunning obstacles, they opposed an almost insurmountable barrier to scholars and curiosity-seekers. That web was woven with a veritably diabolical ingenuity. As for the future curator of the treasure, he was also bound by a series of obligations that made his existence the most refined of tortures. Any man who, attracted by the marble plaque bearing the words *Fondation Antoine Brion,* succeeded in obtaining access to the smallest pamphlet, would be exceedingly clever. And, with that thought in mind, Uncle Antoine rubbed his hands together as he reread through his horn-rimmed spectacles the Draconian paragraphs of his famous regulations.

Monsieur Lefougeret's incuriosity and Uncle Antoine's mania had, therefore, made me a humble client of Monsieur Tournemain, and it was in his shop that I furnished myself with the works with which I desired to become acquainted. No one directed their choice, I brought no order to my reading, and I was solely indebted to my caprice for my guidance. Orientating itself by the profession of the titles, it was very disparate and quite adventurous. I asked nothing of my books except that they furnish alimentation for my dreams, and I thus added to my own nourishment that of the most various minds. To my most ridiculous demands, Monsieur Tournemain acceded with a smile.

Not far from Monsieur Tournemain's bookshop was, as I have said, Père Bricard's antique shop. Père Bricard was an old, bearded man equipped with a trunk-like nose and enormous hands, with which he manipulated the heaviest objects as expertly as the most delicate antiquities. Weight did not seem to exist for them, any more than soap—for they bore superimposed layers of dirt and constituted an object of curiosity in themselves. Père Bricard was proud of them; they had served to accumulate in his store-room a formidable host of diverse objects. In Père Bricard's shop one found boxes of engravings, pieces of lace, stubs of tapestry and bits of cloth, items of faience, bronze, furniture, scrap metal and sculpted wood, watch-keys—the debris, fragments and crumbs of the past.

Without my really knowing why, that strange amalgam exercised a certain melancholy attraction on me, which sometimes led me to acquire one of the gewgaws, which I brought back to the Troublerie with a secret excitement.

Uncle Antoine was not unaware my visits to Monsieur Tournemain's shop and my pauses in Père Bricard's. He did not disapprove of them at all. He was "in favor of liberty" and intended that I should live in my own way. The concern that had been the principal one of his own life he found quite natural in another. He thought it ideal that everyone should maintain his independence, and it was to preserve his own that he had not married. The idea of introducing anyone else into his precious library had always seemed inadmissible to him, but, although a bachelor himself, he made no tempt to impose his way of seeing on anyone else.

He held to that rule with regard to me, and reduced the pressure of his guardianship to a minimum. Having provided what as necessary by the adjunction of Monsieur Lefougeret to old Ernestine, he did not take his surveillance any further. I lived at the Troublerie in perfect tranquility and nothing stood in the way of my developing the dispositions that I have already mentioned more than once, untroubled by any necessity to occupy myself with the material obligations of existence. In fact, Uncle Antoine supervised the administration of my property, which was proportionate to my needs.

That last circumstance thus dispensed me from making a choice of a profession or a career. My taste, in any case, did not incline me toward any, and I envisaged the future as an indefinite continuation of the present. I knew full well that Monsieur Lefougeret's lessons would come to a end one day, but I did not conclude from that the expulsion of the worthy Monsieur Lefougeret. There was no reason why he should not continue his exploits as a fisherman at the Troublerie when my education was complete, while I, for my part, would also continue to deliver myself freely to the spirit of chimerical fantasy that was within me.

Several years passed, according to my anticipations, without any notable event, and I attained the age of majority. To mark that occasion, Uncle Antoine invited me to an important ceremony: the surrender of his obligations as a guardian. When the notary had gone, my worthy uncle set aside for once from his habitual indifference, gave me a little speech and interrogated me as to my future intentions.

"I approve, Nephew," he said, when I had revealed them, "and I have nothing but praise for your plans. Your parents would have been happy to know that you would not abandon the Troublerie to travel the world and that you would live there as they lived there. I am also glad that you will not separate yourself from the excellent Monsieur Lefougeret. That proves that your heart is in the right place, and capable of gratitude. I don't doubt that you will be happy, my boy. Is it not a thousand times better to remain in one's own home doing nothing than to waste one's time involving oneself in the affairs of others? There are enough people to get mixed up in those, one way and another, and with the country's. What good does it do to increase the number of civil servants who live at the state's expense or gamble their own resources on more or less advantageous operations? Then again, what the Devil could you do with your ten fingers? How could you employ them? I can't see that you have any particular talent for anything whatsoever. You have neither the mental rigor that judges need, not the loquacity appropriate to advocates, nor the scheming instinct of a tradesman or manufacturer. As for being an artist, there's too much of the scatterbrain and dreamer in you. The artists I know are all infinitely practical fellows—which doesn't prevent them, however, from dying, more or less of starvation. So stay at the Troublerie, my young friend; that is, indeed, where you will do best, and it's the best thing for you to do. And if you ever get bored there, you still have the option of marrying."

And Uncle Antoine added: "I've always kept that last distraction in reserve, but I've never had the time to take it, and I believe that I'll end my days without needing it."

Poor Uncle Antoine, he did not know how truly he spoke. A few months after that conversation, as old Ernestine was in the process of having me admire a basketful of fish caught in the pond by Monsieur Lefougeret's diligent hook, someone came to tell me that my uncle, Antoine Brion, had suffered a serious accident. Having climbed up on his portable ladder to examine a shelf in his library, he had fallen so awk-

229

wardly that his head had struck the corner of a table and he had fractured his skull. He had been found lying on the floor in a pool of blood and had not recovered consciousness. The physician who had been summoned had declared his condition desperate. I had to hurry if I wanted to bid a last farewell to the dying man.

By the time I arrived at the house my poor uncle had rendered his last sigh and I was only able to salute is remains. When I had accomplished that duty, I went to the place where the accident had happened. The fatal ladder, from the top of which my uncle had fallen, was still set up. At the bottom lay the volume of which the poor man had gone in search on the shelf. It was a little old book entitled *Histoire des masques de la Comédie italienne.* I leafed through it. The illustrations therein represented the traditional characters of the comic stage.

I put the volume n my pocket; I wanted to keep it as a souvenir of my worthy uncle, for I knew in advance, by virtue of his testamentary dispositions, that none of the volumes assembled by his care would every belong to me. Having done that, I went to the table with which my uncle's had had collided. Blood could still be seen there, of which a few drops had splashed the papers covering it. I leaned over. There were catalogues there of libraries and auctions, file-cards and a new copy of the famous regulations, which my uncle had so often reformulated before bringing them to their definitive perfection. I read a few of the articles with a sincere admiration, but I noticed that the name of the curator had been left blank. Over that grave question my poor uncle had hesitated, and I experienced a certain melancholy in thinking that he would be unable to resolve it himself.

I have often thought since that if my uncle had had time to fill in that lacuna and indicate that name, many things that occurred in consequence might not have happened. In fact, when the legacy that my uncle made to the town of his library had been accepted by the municipality and it was a matter of appointing a librarian, the choice fell upon Monsieur Lefouge-ret.

On receiving this news, Monsieur Lefougeret manifested some surprise, and a touching reluctance to leave me, to the extent that I was obliged to press him to accept the honorable position to which the voice of the public had summoned him. He could not shirk the flattering mark of esteem that the municipal powers had bestowed upon him.

After putting up an appropriate show of resistance, Monsieur Lefougeret yielded to my reasoning. It was agreed that on Sundays and during vacations, Monsieur Lefougeret would return to the Troublerie, where he would take up his lines and hooks again.

On this generous promise, I accompanied Monsieur Lefougeret to town; I wanted to help him enter into his functions and take possession of the lodgings that had been assigned to him in my late uncle's house. It was when I left him to confront the famous regulations that, having stopped off at the Tournemain bookshop, I learned that Monsieur Lefougeret had slyly and ardently solicited the position of librarian. Yes, during his angling sessions, Monsieur Lefougeret had been rolling secret ambitions around his head.

It was certainly not the quest for money that had driven Monsieur Fougeret to these covert steps. No, he had a nobler end in mind: the prospect of seeing the modest violet ribbon ornamenting his buttonhole exchanged one day for a bright red ribbon.[36] Like all Frenchmen, the worthy Monsieur Lefougeret was unable to resist the attraction of honorific distinctions, and that hope had caused him to abandon the tranquil diversion of angling for the responsibility of imposing, in all their pitiless rigor, Uncle Antoine's famous regulations and torturing the unfortunates who chanced to solicit access to the *Fondation Brion*.

Although I could have taken offense at Monsieur Lefougeret's conduct in my regard, it was impossible for me really

---

[36] i.e., the red ribbon of the Légion d'honneur.

to hold that excellent man's secrecy against him, and I felt that he would be welcome even so at the Troublerie, whenever it pleased him to come back to exercise his skill at the expense of the carp and pike of the pond.

Poor Monsieur Lefougeret—he had bitten a hook! Alas, I was to allow myself to be caught too, by means of fallacious bait.

It was in Père Bricard's shop that I met Marceline for the first time. That event occurred about two years after Uncle Antoine's death.

I had come to town to visit Monsieur Lefougeret, against whom, as I have said. I had not conserved any rancor because of his ambitious aspirations. They had, in any case, not yet been realized, and he bitterly resented what he was beginning to consider as a denial of justice. He consoled himself by applying with a ferocious rigor the regulations that made the rooms of the *Fondation Antoine Brion* a desert into which no one even thought of venturing. On that point, Monsieur Lefougeret waxed lyrical in complaints about the intellectual negligence of the province, to which I only lent half an ear—for, I must confess, I had not made any progress in the attention I paid to real life.

In fact, I had surrendered myself increasingly to my penchant, and my visionary nature was becoming increasingly accentuated. My detachment from reality was truly complete, and that condition rendered me perfectly happy. The spectacle of Monsieur Lefougeret's disappointments would have served, if necessary as a salutary example, and every time he told me the story, I congratulated myself for not feeling any species of ambition for anything whatsoever. My desires went no further than possessing the vague books with which Monsieur Tournemain furnished me, and the vague objects that I acquired from Père Bricard.

I therefore found myself in the later's shop, in the process of riffling through a box of prints, when the event of which I spoke occurred. It was a beautiful summer morning; I had come on foot from the Troublerie, idling and following the ever-capricious train of my thoughts. Having stopped outside Monsieur Tournemain's, I was lingering in Père Bricard's, waiting for the time to go have lunch with Monsieur Lefougeret, when the antique dealer's door suddenly opened and the ringing of the cracked doorbell announced the advent of a visitor.

Ordinarily, I paid no attention to such entrances. Père Bricard's clientele consisted of a few local collectors and passing strangers—who, more often than not, went out again without buying anything. This time, however, the bell's ring caused me to shiver instinctively, and I took my nose out of the box of engravings, which I almost dropped, in surprise and shock.

This time, the visitor was not an aged collector or an insignificant passer-by. The person who had just opened the door of Père Bricard's shop lit up the entire room with a spring-like radiance. The individual in question was the most delightful young woman that I had ever seen. She might have been eighteen, but her age was of no importance; she was youth itself. Not very tall, she appeared so by virtue of being perfectly proportioned. Dressed with a discreet elegance, she was wearing an exquisite dress and a charming hat, and beneath that hat, she displayed the prettiest face that hat ever been coiffed with straw, ribbons and roses. She was blonde, with eyes of a profound blue, a delicate nose, an infinitely agreeable mouth and the most dazzling complexion in the world. Her entire attitude communicated an idea of prudence, decency and reason.

Nothing more graceful than that cheerful apparition can be imagined. My gaze could not tear itself away from her, and, in my delighted astonishment, I wondered what that marvelous luminosity was doing in Père Bricard's somber shop, among so many dusty old things. I soon found out, for the newcomer, after a *bonjour*, politely explained the reason for her visit.

She had not come to buy but to sell. Would Monsieur Bricard care to acquire what she was offering him? In speaking thus, she drew the object in question from a little bag she was carrying I her hand. It was a watch: an old watch with a double case in gold, guilloched in various colors. One desired to dispose of it. The watch did not work well and the watchmaker could not guarantee that it would keep good time. In saying this, the pretty seller frowned slightly. Now, she liked to know the exact time. So, with the money she would get for the antique, she would buy a marine chronometer that she wanted. But she only wanted to sell the watch at a reasonable price, or she would renounce her caprice and give up on the chronometer. Once could be a woman and still possess common sense. Besides, Monsieur Bricard's honesty was well-known.

All that, she stated in a firm and clear voice, like a person sure of herself, who knew what she wanted. She smiled as she spoke, without haste and precisely. I listened with delight, for I never stopped looking at her, without taking account at the time of the character revealed by those words. At that moment, though, I was incapable of any judgment. The seller was so pretty, so blonde, so young, and she expressed herself so persuasively...

Monsieur Bricard could have made the purchase in complete confidence. The watch was not a stolen item. She had obtained it from her grandmother. It was a family heirloom—but too bad. It was necessary to be of her time and make progress with her century. Furthermore, she was not an adventuress. She lived in the High Street, with her aunts, the Mademoiselles Pierrebrune, and her name was Marceline Fontefroide.[37]

---

[37] *Fonte* has more than one meaning, but generally refers to a product of fusion: melted snow, for example, or the metal used in casting a statue or a component of a machine. Its other reference is to a holster attached to the saddle of a horse in which a pistol might be sheathed. Either one, in combination with an adjective signifying "cold," might have given the narrator

During this little speech, Père Bricard examined the watch. He opened the cases, jiggled he hands, and studied the guilloche-work with a magnifying-glass. That manipulation annoyed me. Père Bricard, with his enormous filthy hands and his elephantine nose, exasperated me. What did his insulting hesitation signify, and why had he not precipitated himself upon his drawer in order to offer its contents to Mademoiselle Fontefroide on his knees? Besides, was an object presented by such pretty hands not beyond price?

The one that Père Bricard offered seemed to me to be derisory. That was also Mademoiselle Fontefroide's opinion. She told Père Bricard as much with the most amiable smile, and the haggling began. It went on for some time. Mademoiselle Fontefroide held firm and ended up winning the argument. The business concluded, she carefully counted the bills and coins, slipped them into her little bag, bowed to the merchant with amiable dignity, and left. I had great difficulty in not precipitating myself after her, while Père Bricard muttered: "Not easily to roll over, that little bourgeoise, a sly one, who can defend herself...."

Poor Père Bricard—what an angry glare I directed at him! How had he dared to deprive that charming individual thus of a family heirloom of which she was perhaps more attached than she claimed? Oh, if I had been able to offer her all the chronometers on Earth! But Mademoiselle Marceline Fontefroide did not know me and would not have accepted my present. I knew her name and where she lived though.

Throughout the meal my distraction was complete, but fortunately, Monsieur Lefougeret did not notice. As if in a dream, I saw the entrance of Marceline's dazzling beauty into Père Bricard's shop once again. I heard the ringing of the bell. In the meantime, Monsieur Lefougeret talked, and talked bitterly. The fifteenth of July list of decorations had appeared, and his name was not on it. Injustice had become persecution.

---

pause for thought had he been conscious of the symbolism of names, but his innocence seems boundless.

Monsieur Lefougeret threatened to hand in his resignation. Let them try to find someone else as firm in his application of the famous regulations! He would leave the country! He would get married!

At those words, I shivered. The image of Marceline became more precise before my hallucinated eyes, and it was with a strangled voice that I asked of Monsieur Fougeret: "By the way, who is that young woman, Mademoiselle Fontefroide, who is living in the High Street with her aged relatives, the Mademoiselles de Pierrebrune?"

The early days of my marriage were perfectly and entirely happy. Mademoiselle Fontefroide had accepted my hand without hesitation. She was, moreover, entirely at liberty to dispose of herself. An orphan, as I as was, she had no other relatives save for the aged demoiselles de Pierrebrune, who welcomed my request with favor and viewed the union with pleasure.

I was, in fact, what is called an eligible bachelor. Without being truly rich, I possessed a notable ease, and the Troublerie was an agreeable residence. Those considerations made up Marceline's mind, for I did not have the vanity to believe that my physical attributes counted for much in her decision. Perhaps, however, the promptitude with which I declared myself touched her, and she found my urgency flattering.

The fact is that the day after the encounter in Père Bricard's shop, I sent Monsieur Lefougeret, bewildered but obedient, out on campaign. Fortunately, he knew the demoiselles de Pierrebrune. What he was instructed to say to them was extremely simple. At first sight, as if thunderstruck, I had fallen madly in love with Mademoiselle Fontefroide, and I had conceived an irresistible passion for her—the first that I had ever experienced.

For, I must admit, women had not played any part in my existence until then. The isolated life that I led at the Troublerie, the dearth of relationships I had in the town and the lack of opportunities had numbed my sensibility and had maintained in that regard a tranquil indifference.

To be sure, the idea of love sometimes mingled with my reveries and colored them with romantic tints, but that idea was easily dissipated, for want of any object on which to fix itself. It remained stray and vague, and had never taken on any precise form. In the chimerical world in which I lived, love existed, but it was not incarnate for me in any face or living body. Thus, the encounter with Marceline was a total revelation.

I suddenly understood what it was to love, in the most complete sense of the word, for I experienced for Marceline a desire all the stronger and sharper because it was mingled with curiosity and added to my inexperience. I was in love with her physically and the mere thought of kissing her hand agitated me with a quivering ecstasy. I wanted Marceline, and in order to obtain her, I would have surmounted any obstacle.

Now, it turned out that those obstacles were lacking and that I did not have to put the amorous energy that I suddenly felt to the proof. Nothing separated me from Marceline. An orphan, as I have said, she was wholly disposed to a reasonable marriage. The advantages that I represented materially to her were exactly those that her precocious wisdom was seeking. Furthermore, I did not displease her. What Monsieur Lefougeret had been able to say about my character was quite satisfactory. I was mild, placid and distracted, and those dispositions assured her of an easy influence over me. So the overtures that I had him make were easily accepted. After a visit to the Troublerie, our engagement was settled. We agreed that our marriage would be celebrated with the briefest possible delay. Within a matter of weeks, Marceline would be mine.

That idea filled me with joy and prevented me from looking any further ahead. What I esteemed above all in the marriage was the daily, permanent and exclusive possession of Marceline. To the rest, I hardly gave a thought. I paid no heed to whether our characters were compatible and or humors in accord. Marceline's mind was a matter of indifference to me. What was important was that her delicate body would belong to me—the body that I coveted furiously, with all the ardor of youth, chastity and solitude—and that was what the sacramental "I do" pronounced by that pretty mouth was about to give me...

Love is contagious, and I wonder whether the love I experienced for Marceline did not initially win me some return of her affection. Marceline seemed to accommodate herself to my flame and lend herself to my passion with an amiable and smiling generosity. I gave her continual signs of that passion, and nothing prevented me from anticipating that it would ever be sated. Detached as I was from other realities of existence, what Marceline represented to me was an infinite amusement. My love for Marceline had taken the place of all the chimeras with which I had previously nourished myself, and it required a long time for them to return to play a new role in my mind.

However, a time came when my former preoccupations reappeared. They were too profoundly rooted within me for them to be exiled forever. At first their presence was manifest feebly, then with greater frequency. I certainly loved Marceline as much as ever, but in a somewhat intermittent fashion. Through those interstices, my old reveries infiltrated themselves, and gradually resumed beating their wings within my brain. I welcomed them without suspicion, and even with a certain pleasure. I began reading again, leafing through my boxes of engravings and examining my trinkets. I sometimes let my thoughts turn to the past. I became familiar again with Monsieur Tournemain's shop, and found my way back to Père Bricard's. When I came back from town late, Marceline pointed it out to me, taking out of her handbag the precision chronometer that she had acquired for the price of her old watch.

These urban visits were the cause of the first argument that arose between Marceline and me. One day, she started criticizing, with a certain irony with which I was unfamiliar, the modest acquisitions that I had brought back to the Troublerie. She added to that criticism a few disobliging considerations regarding the life I led, and what she called my "utter uselessness." Without my attaching any further importance to it, that little scene caused me to reflect.

I soon realized that I had been wrong to act in regard to Marceline as I had done and to have built the harmony of our household on the physical attraction for her person that I had experienced madly and still experienced profoundly. That was an imprudence on my part, which was, in sum, reparable. I had counted on an amorous reciprocity on Marceline's part that was not what I had believed it to be. That was a disappointment for my self-respect, but it was necessary for me not to exaggerate its importance, and better for me to be grateful to Marceline for the happiness she had given me than to reproach her for not having obtained as much from me as I had received from her. What was important now was to adopt another line of conduct, more in conformity with the point in life that we had reached, and the knowledge of her character that had been revealed to me.

That character had nothing, as yet, so marked that I could not entertain illusions as to its true nature. The best course to take with Marceline appeared to me to be to seek to convert her to my tastes. That did not seem to be so difficult. I proposed reading material to her, I talked to her about my intimate thoughts, I initiated her into my reveries, my imaginations and my chimeras.

Alas, though, in that fine project a further surprise awaited me. From my first attempts onwards, I perceived that Marceline, instead of following me along the path that I indicated, refused even to set foot upon it, and even distanced herself from it resolutely. I sensed from the beginning a secret and insidious resistance in her, and that resistance was accentuated into a kind of aversion. From indifference to my tastes, Marceline moved on to become hostile to them. Instead of, if not adopting them, at least discussing them, she set about mocking and belittling them, sometimes with disdain, sometimes with acidity.

By virtue of a quite unexpected effect, which I had not anticipated, the practical side of her character came into collision with the chimerical aspects of mine. The latent opposition that existed between us became suddenly visible, and, muted as it was, suddenly attained a point so sharp that it was impossible for me to hide my defeat from myself. Everything that I loved appeared to Marceline to be denuded of any kind of interest, and she was obstinate in remaining deliberately estranged therefrom. She was refractory to all my hopes. The visionary had no hold on Marceline. Caprice and mental fantasy appeared to unworthy of a serious person, which she had the pretention to be, as opposed to the dreamer to whom an unfortunate hazard had linked her destiny.

Soon, as a separation was hollowed out between us that became gradually deeper, Marceline began to mingle with her initial disdain reproaches that seemed to me, to say the least, unwarranted. She criticized me bitterly for the scant attention I paid to the realities of life. She considered me as a useless idler. She wanted me to take up a career, a profession. She went so far as to hold up the worthy Monsieur Lefougeret as an example. The life I led was "no life at all." I could not even take care of my material interests. I was incapable of rendering to the estate of the Troubleries that which I owed to it. I was neither a municipal councilor nor mayor! I was a collector of trivia, a dreamer, a good-for-nothing.

From one day to the next, Marceline became bolder in the sort of animosity that was manifest within her against my most cherished tastes, the tastes that I had wanted so much for her to share, but of which she became increasingly scornful as she revealed her true nature more clearly.

On seeing the opposition between us increase in that way, I experienced a veritable chagrin. I could not resign myself to that dissent and sought a means of remedying it. It was not easy, for I discovered in Marceline every day a stubbornness of which I had had no suspicion. I discovered in her too, alas, an ensemble of ideas, practical, down-to-earth and reasonable, in association with mediocrity, sufficiency and vanity, that desolated me in their unexpected revelation.

And yet, should not certain indications not have warned me about the true Marceline, even when she had been in Père Bricard's shop?—that exchange of an old watch for a frightful modern chronometer! At that moment, however, I was all desire and passion, and had not seen anything in Marceline but a delightful flower of youth and sensuality.

Nevertheless, how could I resign myself to admitting that Marceline was truly an irremediably what she showed herself to be at present? Was it necessary to renounce the desire to associate her with my life and my mind, thus abandoning her to the worst in her? That thought mortified me cruelly, and I racked my brain to find a means of ridding her of what I named, with a sigh, the "demon of mediocrity."

One day, after a bitter argument with Marceline on our usual subject, I had retired to the room that served me as a study and library, when my eyes fell upon the little volume entitled *Histoire des Masques de la Comédie italienne*, which I had taken from Uncle Antoine's house on the day of the accident and kept in memory of him. Suddenly, an idea sprang to mind and I uttered a cry of joy. I had finally found the means: the certain means, the irresistible means.

I would take Marceline to Italy!

Was not Italy the marvelous land of dreams? There, Marceline would live in the midst of favorable influences, which would dissolve that which was mediocre and desiccated within her. She would be unable to resist the poetry scattered beneath the beautiful skies of Italy. Rome, Florence, Naples and the divine Venice would reckon with her down-to-earth nature, and after that experience, of which I ought to have thought sooner, I would bring back to the Troublerie a Marceline regenerated and converted, a Marceline exorcized of her bourgeois prejudices and bewitched by the magical prestige of art, dreams and beauty!

I had counted, as I have just said, on that voyage to Italy to produce in Marceline the change for which I hoped, but alas, I soon had to recognize that I was cruelly mistaken. From the outset of that misconceived displacement, the difference between our respective natures was manifest even more vividly than in quotidian life.

Right away, I perceived that my pleasure in seeing the cities and places celebrated in art and history found no echo in Marceline. Neither the beauty of the landscapes, nor the grandeur of the monuments, not the marvels of every sort, the sight of which filled me with admiration, moved her in any fashion. She felt neither pleasure nor exaltation at such spectacles. She walked through the streets of Rome, Florence and Naples at the same measured and precise pace with which she trod the sidewalks of our little provincial town. She did not understand my curiosity or my enthusiasm, and shrugged her shoulders when I attempted to share them with her. I appeared to her increasingly as an extravagant person and, let us say the word, a kind of ridiculous crackpot. To my admiration Marceline sometimes opposed irony, sometimes simply bad temper. Decidedly, my experiment failed pitifully. Marceline was irreducible. The spell that I had attempted to cast on her did not work; on the contrary, it uncovered certain aspects of her character that only made it clearer to me how much distance there was between us and how little chance remained to us of ever encountering a meeting-point on which we might find support.

Among the things that most exasperated Marceline during the voyage, the most continual was what I spent on it. She did not understand why one would pay money to be transported to places to which one does not have to go, where one does not know anyone, and which are devoid of all interest. She never ceased comparing what one paid out with what one obtained in exchange, and those comparisons occasioned bitter remarks. The comfort of hotels was never justly matched to the tariff. There was a discordance therein which she never ceased to observe and for which she reproached me, as if I were responsible for it.

Certain expenditures irritated her more particularly: the purchases I made of photographs and the admission fees to museums. She criticized my modest acquisitions of postcards and was irritated that I encumbered myself with them, having no one to whom to send them.

The unpleasantness of all these recriminations went beyond their puerility; they revealed to me in Marceline a love of money and an avarice that I had not suspected, and it led me to wonder, sadly, whether Marceline, in marrying me, had only wanted to obtain an easier and broader life for herself than the one she led with her aged relatives, the demoiselles de Pierrebrune: a social advantage for which she had found it a fair price to pay with the matrimonial offering of her charming body.

These reflections would certainly have been more painful to me if I had made them in other circumstances, but they lost some of their edge in the enchantment in which I was living. Moving in that simultaneously brilliant and subtle atmosphere, one can imagine to what extent my mind enjoyed the marvelous elasticity that the air of Italy lends to the most leaden imaginations. So, I abandoned myself to those delights in spite of the worries that were harassing me.

If Marceline obstinately refused to associate herself with my pleasure, was it just that I should renounce it in consequence? Was it not better to bring back beautiful memories of the voyage with which I could nourish myself on my return? If Marceline considered me definitively as a dreamer, let my dreams at least be dreams full of consoling, amusing and picturesque images—and too bad about Marceline and her grumpiness. Had I not given her the opportunity to escape the narrow circle of her paltry preoccupations? She was at liberty not to take advantage of the opportunity!

I wanted to give her one last chance, however, and I had reserved for the last stage of our itinerary a rather long sojourn in Venice. Perhaps Marceline would be unable to resist the charm of that incomparable city completely. There, perhaps, she might feel a little of the emotion that I experienced in thinking about the moment when I would see, over the lagoon, the domes and campaniles of the marine city.

I did not ask much of my poor Marceline, for I had renounced the possibility of ever making her a companion of my dreams and taking her to the regions to which I felt myself increasingly attracted and which I despaired of ever penetrating; my sole ambition was to weaken the hostility that she testified to them in my person. Perhaps Venice would incline her to some indulgence for my chimeras and inoffensive reveries, and she would not remain totally insensitive to the miraculous prestige whose marvelous reality might perhaps reconcile her momentarily to the imaginary world in which my mind liked to play. I was determined to attempt that last experiment, and Marceline consented, albeit with a rather bad grace, to extend our voyage as far as Venice.

We arrived there in admirable moonlight, but I do not want to recount that final disappointment in detail. I do not want to spoil the beautiful memories that I retain of that Venetian fortnight. Nevertheless, I am obliged to admit that Marceline showed herself to be more Marceline than ever. Nothing that delighted me found favor in her eyes. The very structure of Venice appeared to her to be a veritable stupidity. What was that absurd city planted in the middle of the water, that city without carriages or tramways, full of bells and pigeons, but a veritable challenge to common sense and progress? There was no sense in any of it. And what could be more ridiculous than the gondolas, with their rowers balanced on the poop, indulging in perpetual acrobatics?

With respect to everything we saw, Marceline was pitiless. When we traveled the canals, her face expressed a veritable disgust and her mouth was creased in a disapproving moue. And yet, Marceline was charming, and I experienced a melancholy regret that everything distanced her from me thus. Instead of bringing us closer together, that misconceived voyage to Italy separated us irredeemably.

It was, therefore, with an increasing divergence that our sojourn came to an end, and the purchase of Signor Barlotti's

244

little marionette theater brought matters sharply to a head, for, when we had quit the Palazzo Pastinati and returned to the hotel, Marceline burst into violent recriminations against my "folly," and, on her charming convulsed face I saw for the first time, no longer that expression of disdain that I had read there only too frequently, but a veritable anger, and almost, dare I say, a flash of hatred.

The impression that quarrel left on me contributed more than a little to rendering our return melancholy. However, as we got closer to the Troublerie, Marceline appeared to calm down. She seemed to have found the serenity of someone who has made a decision and has reconciled herself to the inevitable. On several occasions, she was even almost pleasant to me. I concluded that the fatigues of the voyage and its inevitable petty inconveniences had contributed a great deal to Marceline's bad moods and nervous exasperation. In spite of that excuse, though, it remained no less true that the attempt I had made had failed.

I observed that again, more at leisure, when we were reinstalled at the Troublerie. I had plenty of time to reflect, for I saw very little of Marceline. She had been gripped, on returning home, with a veritable fever of housework.[38] From morning until evening, she washed, dusted and polished. The duster and the broom pursued me from room to room, but I lent myself to the mania with a good grace. Since Marcelline had found an occupation worthy of her "common sense"—the practical attitude that she took to everything, and opposed to my "nonsense" and "deceptions," it was only fair that she should devote herself to it in total liberty. Does not everyone have, in this world, their choice of diversion and the right to make whatever use of themselves they wish?

For my part, I took refuge in my cherished reveries. I gazed at the photographs brought back from Italy, and, I can certainly say, I looked forward impatiently to the arrival of my

---

[38] Ernestine seems to have vanished from the scene, with no explanation.

245

beloved marionettes. I rejoiced in the fact that I would soon see Arlequino again, and Pantalon, Brighella, Tartaglia, Scaramouche and the piebald and bearded centaur. What charming companions they would be in my solitude! How we would be able to chat together about our dear Italy! I rejoiced in the thought of those discussions and I looked forward with all my heart to the arrival of those future confidants of my chimeras and my dreams.

When I was notified of their arrival, however, I could not help conceiving a certain anxiety. What would Marceline say? Since our return from Italy she had abstained from any allusion to that purchase, of which she had so strongly disapproved. Doubtless she preferred not to touch the sore subject, for when the carrier brought the boxes that contained the characters and scenery of the little theater, she made no comment. She limited herself to asking me, mockingly, where I intended to lodge that little society. I manifested the intention of installing my new friends in a small room adjacent to my study, which served as a lumber-room. It was rare for anyone to go into it.

Marceline made no objection to this plan and contend herself with pinching her lips; then, pirouetting on her heels, she left me alone. She was dressed to go out and was about to leave for town. I had noticed that she went there quite often since we had returned to the Troublerie, but I refrained from interrogating her as to the motive for those comings and goings. Our lives were definitely becoming increasingly separate. We were gradually taking back our liberty.

Detached as I was from Marceline's activities and withdrawn into my habitual dreams, I could not help perceiving that something unusual was happening to my wife. From one day to the next her character became firmer and more decisive, to put it mildly. To be sure, I had never been very jealous of my prerogatives as master of the house, but it was evident that Marceline was beginning to treat me as a negligible quantity. Under various pretexts, she had taken the domestic administration in hand. Several repairs in our farms having to be carried out, Marceline occupied herself with the question and resolved it without consulting me. Gradually, she freed herself from all subjection to me. She assumed the general direction of my affairs and excluded me from any participation in their regulation. She seemed to consider me as incapable of being able to do it and to assume that I was good for nothing except talking nonsense and amusing myself with puppets. She had drawn conclusions from the purchase of the little theater that were not to my advantage.

I perceived that clearly one day when, having gone to see Monsieur Lefougeret, he mentioned it to me in an embarrassed and vaguely reproving manner. I divined that Marceline had called in and had not kept it to herself. She must have told her aunts about it, and, hawked around by her, the story had become the talk of the town. I confess that I was unconcerned about the slander. Tongues could wag as much as they liked without my having the slightest desire to hold against my dear puppets what was being said about me.

They had, in any case, only been a momentary whim on my parts. Once I had taken them out of their boxes and replaced them in their theater, I soon ceased to take much interest in them. I rarely opened the door of the room in which I had given them shelter—or, if I chanced to go in, I only gave them a distracted glance, in spite of the way they looked at me from the end of their strings and the wide-eyed stare that the bearded centaur fixed upon me. My reverie had no need of expedients and interlocutors, being sufficient to itself.

I did not understand what Marceline was trying to achieve by ridiculing me. So, some people from the town having come to visit Marceline and having asked me to show them my "famous little theater," I had received them rather rudely—with which Marceline did not seem at all displeased, as if my ill humor, manifested before witnesses, had been agreeable to her. For Marceline, who had previously lived a rather secluded existence at the Troublerie, had begun to attract society there. She had even adopted a reception day. As the visits bored me, I generally abstained from appearing in the drawing-room. Nevertheless, having come once, I was quite astonished to find Marceline in confidential discussion with Doctor Thibaut.

Doctor Thibaut enjoyed a rather bad reputation in the region. He was the director of a sort of local sanitarium, which had no great reputation, and of which certain stories had gone around that rendered it scarcely respectable. I had heard from Monsieur Lefougeret that there was talk of invalids retained in treatment for much longer than they wished by Dr. Thibaut, who thus lent certain less than innocent assistance to their families. Also placed to his account were clandestine childbirths, substitutions of children and other more-or-less suspect contrivances.

In addition, Dr. Thibaut's appearance did not augur anything good. Very tall and very thin, with long flat hair that covered is ears and whose complexion seemed irredeemably somber, he gave an impression, simultaneously funereal, brutal and sly, that did not predispose one in his favor. A horn-rimed pince-nez with tinted lenses protected his eyes, which seemed charged with transparent bile. On top of all that, he was both obsequious and hypocritical.

What was that equivocal individual—who set about examining me with untoward attention as soon as I entered the room—doing in Marceline's house? He plied me with questions, while exchanging sly knowing looks with Marceline. These affectations annoyed me slightly, and I was on the point, when Dr. Thibaut took is leave, of making that remark to Marceline, but I abstained for the moment, deciding to put it off until another occasion. I therefore reserved my observations, in case Dr. Thibaut repeated his visit.

He did not reappear the following week, and there was no question of confrontation between Marceline and myself, but I soon perceived a further change in her attitude to me. I have said that the period of bitter recriminations that marked the time of our voyage to Italy had been succeeded by another in which Marceline seemed to have decided to envelop me in scornful indifference. She appeared to be ignoring my existence and devoted all her attention to domestic and household affairs. Then, suddenly, she adopted another policy.

Now, she affected toward me an attitude of mute and profound commiseration. Whatever I said or did, she raised her eyes to the heavens with an exasperating expression of pity. She surrounded me with the most irritating and the most futile solicitude. If I quit my armchair, she made as if to rush toward me in order to support me, as if she were fearful that I might fall. At table, she watched each of my mouthfuls carefully, always ready to come to my aid if I were to choke. She watched over all my movements as if the most natural among them risked producing some catastrophe. If I wanted to go out, she studied me with an ill-concealed anxiety; if I were late coming back, I found her on the doorstep of the house, and my arrival seemed to relieve some secret anxiety.

In sum, she dedicated to me the mute attention that devotes to an invalid to whom one does not want to reveal his illness. Several times she got up in the night in order to look in on my sleep. She exercised an indirect surveillance over me for which I could not discover a reason. What did this behavior signify? I asked myself the question in vain, but what is certain is that it irritated me considerably and that I was aggravated by it—but Marceline's machinations were not yet concluded, and I was soon to have further specimens thereof.

One day, I saw a tall fellow who looked like a criminal turn up at the Troublerie, who had a long conversation with Marceline. Where could the rogue have come from and what was that interminable discussion about? I had an explanation when, at dinner time, I found the lanky fellow standing behind my chair and passing the plates, and when, the following day, I found him in the corridor with a broom in his hand. He was a domestic that Marceline had engaged.

I soon perceived that the pretended servant had singular habits. I seemed to interest him keenly, and he observed me with a strange insistence. I encountered him at every turn. He was continually in my path, occupied with feigned tasks, while the truth appeared to be that he was spying on me. I noticed between Marceline and that clown the same knowing exchanges that I had already observed between her and Dr. Thibaut. I thus acquired the conviction that Hilaire—that was the fellow's name—was, behind the mask of a domestic, some sort of nurse that Marceline had placed near me, in expectation of God knows what eventuality.

That discovery, I must say, impressed me rather disagreeably. There was something about the man that I did not like. His face, which I have described accurately enough as criminal, was seconded by a Herculean musculature. Enormous fists hung at the ends of his arms, and his heavy and athletic body reposed on immense feet shod in cork-soled boots. He made no sound as he walked. Like Marceline, he too seemed to consider me with a certain compassion, very rare among servants, and which sometimes caused me to reflect. Might I be ill without knowing it? Had Marceline discerned in me symptoms of some grave affliction? I examined myself carefully, but could find nothing abnormal; nevertheless, I was intrigued by the vigilance with which I was surrounded.

The idea of illness was gradually implanted in my mind, at first intermittently, then with sufficient frequency to become a veritable preoccupation. I paused as I passed in front of mirrors to inspect my appearance therein. I stuck out my tongue; I took my pulse twenty times a day. I listened to my breathing. I took careful note of my slightest impressions of wellbeing or malaise. Marceline considered the inspections to which I subjected myself from the corner of her eye, and Hilaire observed them too. Every morning, when I woke up, he asked me how I was, in a singular tone, as if he expected me to reveal a sudden deterioration in my health. It all ended up causing me a muted anxiety, which decided me to clear the matter up, and one day, I went to town to consult Doctor Bonin.

Doctor Bonin was an aged physician who had looked after my parents, renowned for the accuracy of his diagnoses—a physician of the old school, full of prudence and good sense. I therefore sought him out and, without explaining my situation in detail, asked him to give me a thorough examination. He did so with scrupulous attention.

When he had finished his examination, Dr. Bonin said: "My word, my boy, I can't find any cause for anxiety. Your organs are in good condition, and none of them offers any unfavorable indication. The only thing I observe is a slight nervous disequilibrium. You lead too solitary a life, with an overly charming wife. You need a little open air and altitude. Oh, I'm not advising you to go and shut yourself up in some sanitarium; I'm not a partisan of such places and am not of the school of our famous Dr. Thibaut, who isolates his patients so well that, three-quarters of the time, they're never seen again. No, what I advise you to take isn't a cure but a pleasure trip. Go to Switzerland, install yourself in a good hotel, eat, sleep, walk, pick mountain flowers, drink spring water, breathe deeply and don't think about anything.

"As it happens, I've just given the same prescription to your friend Lefougeret. He needs to get away from his books and his regulations for a while. It's high time. Why don't you arrange to spend a month in Switzerland together? You'll recover there all the better because you aren't ill, and you'll come back with even more pleasure, after that absence, to your charming wife. Oh, my lad, it's necessary to be wise even in marriage."

With these words, the excellent Dr. Bonin sent me away, with an amicable clap on the shoulder, and steered me toward Monsieur Lefougeret's house. When I came out again, our voyage had been decided, and a few days later, having buckled my suitcases and bid adieu to Marceline, who had not manifested any intention to accompany me in that hygienic displacement, I departed for Switzerland in company with Monsieur Lefougeret.

The excellent Dr. Bonin was absolutely right; the real invalid, of Monsieur Lefougeret and myself, was poor Lefougeret. As soon as we arrived at the Grand Hôtel du Mont-Haut,

I perceived that he was in a state of hypochondria of which I feared that nothing could cure him.

The cause of his illness resided in that wretched matter of decoration. Every year, in January and July, it was redoubled. On not reading his name in the lists, the unfortunate experience a veritable crisis of despair. He lost his appetite, slept badly, and became sallow-complexioned and thin in consequence. At the last promotion, his disappointment had been all the greater and his bitterness more profound because, in spite of formal promises, the cross had been suspended on the obscure breast of Dr. Thibaut.

He saw in that denial of justice a veritable persecution. Why was there such obstinacy, in high places, in refusing him a distinction to which those who were its object had no more right than him? By virtue of that treatment, Monsieur Lefougeret suffered in his vanity and his honor. There weighed upon him, in his own eyes, a sort of discredit. During our meals and during our walks, Monsieur Lefourgeret never stopped talking about his grievances.

I listened to them, I admit, with a rather distracted ar. The keen air that one breathed on Mont-Haut, had given me what is known as a "crack of the whip." The hotel was comfortable, particularly frequented by English people and Italians, and one enjoyed absolute liberty there. I had taken my habitual chimeras with me, and nothing distracted me from their company. In the mountain air, they spread their vigorous and iridescent wings and carried me away in their benevolent flight. I was happy again, soothed by not having Marceline's disapproving expression before me or her falsely compassionate gaze. I experienced a delightful rest, scarcely troubled by Marceline's letters. They were rare; Marceline declared herself "exhausted by all the fuss and bother."

What could the absorbing occupations be to which my wife thus made allusion? I confess that I hardly cared, fully occupied in thoughts into which she scarcely entered. Why the Devil had I tried, even for a moment, to associated Marceline with my phantasmagorias? What absurd folly had been going

252

through my head? Marceline and I were hardly creatures of the same species! Was it not better that I had perceived that irremeably dissimilarity? Henceforth, I would not longer attempt that which I had been wrong to try. In any case, had I not committed an imprudence in acting thus?

Why did I want to involve Marceline with my most intimate thoughts and the most secret play of my mind? Why had I wanted to put the keys to my imagination in her hands? Was that not a domain into which no one should penetrate, and which ought to remain forbidden to everyone? Why had I invited Marceline into it? She had not understood either its bizarre order or its vaporous perspectives. The fantasies of my mind, the sense of which escaped her, had caused her a sort of sharp irritation. That imaginary life, in which she did not participate at all, had aggravated her to the point of exasperation. That was the reason for the kind of divorce that had been effected between us.

Obviously I regretted that things were as they were; I had loved Marceline passionately and had suffered in seeing her draw away from me with a disdain that she had not sought to conceal from me. For the moment, however, I had set my regrets aside. I was free from that species of inexplicable commiseration that Marceline testified toward me so ostentatiously; I was liberated from the espionage of the odious Hilaire. That was the main thing—and I delighted in my Helvetian liberty.

I thought about these things vaguely as I walked the beautiful mountain paths. With that exercise, I recovered an excellent wellbeing, with which, on my return, Marceline would no longer have any pretext to sympathize. What would she have thought, on the other hand, about poor Monsieur Lefougeret? He was scarcely following my example. He remained jaundiced and bilious. His hypochondria did not dissipate, and I saw that I would take him back to the worthy Dr. Bonin in very nearly the same state as on his departure. For the time of our return was drawing near; we had already been at Mont-Haut for a months and a half, and it was necessary that Monsieur Lefougeret resume the duties that had become the bane of his life. And to think that he had schemed like a demon to get away from the Troublerie and to have himself appointed to that position as a librarian. Oh, the wretched folly of human ambitions!

It was, however, necessary to leave. I envisaged that event without overmuch displeasure. I would have to submit on my return to the pitting gaze of Marceline, unless she had replaced that habit with some new fad. In any case, though, I was bringing back from Switzerland the certainty that I was no invalid, as Marceline had tried to persuade me with her trickery, of which I still had not divined the objective.

I should add that the prospect of seeing the Troublerie again also gave me a certain pleasure. I loved my old house, with its old garden, half pleasure-garden and half utility-garden, with its arbors, its flower-beds, its espaliers, its hedges and its pyramidal fruit-trees. I loved my house and its old-fashioned furniture, such as my parents had arranged it and as I had disposed it myself; I loved it for the modest trinkets that I had collected there, for all the dreams that I had dreamed there—and I was going to see all that soon. I was going to see my bedroom, with its Toile de Jouy wall-hangings, my library with its huge latticed bookshelves and, as well, I would see once again, if the fantasy took me, my pretty marionette theater, where, between Arlequin and Brighella, the worthy bearded centaur awaited me. I would also see Marceline again...

That idea, I confess, was the last one that presented itself to my mind. As I paused on it, I perceived that it was not disagreeable to me. I did not hold Marceline's various conducts in my regard against her. During those two months of absence, she had become almost indifferent to me, and I expected to continue in that sentiment. Only one prospect bothered me: finding at the Troublerie that Hilaire whom my wife had inflicted upon me, and to whom I had taken a sovereign dislike. As I packed my bags I recalled the fellow's criminal appearance, his enormous fists and his immense feet furnished with cork soled shoes, which gave him the stifled and silent tread of a burglar. Add to that the fact that the unprepossessing individual reeked of sweat and carbolic acid, and you will understand why I resolved to seek an opportunity to throw him out.

After having taken poor Monsieur Lefougeret home and given him a deal of good advice—among others, to reconcile himself once and for all to the ministerial injustice of which he was periodically the victim—I set out for the Troublerie.

I had left my luggage at the station, and I was walking at a brisk pace, the habit of which I had acquired during my mountain walks. It was the end of a beautiful day; a few harmonious clouds were grouped in the sky, and I distinguished chimerical figures in them with which I held a mental dialogue. I have always liked those conversations with the clouds and had always found great pleasure therein. Nevertheless, I hastened my steps, desirous of getting home before nightfall.

I had already been walking for a long time, gripped by my reveries, and I should already have glimpsed the trees of the avenue which led from the main road to the Troublerie. Doubtless I had gone past it. I stopped to get my bearings and uttered an exclamation of surprise. I was just at the point where the avenue led away in the direction of the Troublerie. The avenue was certainly there but the trees were missing. The double row of poplars that had bordered it previously had disappeared without trace.

What could have caused that sudden disappearance? Two months earlier the trees had been there, and I had passed under their shade as I left the Troublerie. Suddenly, I slapped my forehead. Some violent storm must have caused the disaster, unless there had been a violent conflagration. But why had Marceline not told me about it in any of her letters? Then again, some of the trees must have been spared by the scourge. Why had Marceline, without consulting me, had the survivors felled?

Was this, then, one of the absorbing occupations to which she had made allusion? Oh, she had done fine work there! I was furious.

My surprises were not to end there, however. When I arrived at a run at the end of the denuded avenue and the Troublerie appeared before me, I stopped, nailed to the spot. I could not believe my eyes. My house—my beloved house, which I had left two months earlier so charming in its semi-decrepitude—was unrecognizable. The old mossy stones, so softly gray in color had been coated with a hideous yellow distemper, against which chestnut-colored shutters stood out. On the roof, two monstrous weathervanes in cut-out iron offered the view of a zouave smoking a pipe and a canteen-filler carrying a small barrel of eau-de-vie over his shoulder. Furthermore, the entrance door was surmounted by a zinc marquise, dressed in finery and flanked by two brown faience dogs. As for the virgin vine that had garlanded my bedroom window, it had been torn up.

At this spectacle, a dolorous anger took hold of me, and a new dread pierced my heart. What might Marceline had done to the interior of the house? Scarcely had I gone in than I understood that the ravages there had been no less. From the vestibule ripolined in pale green with red edges, I precipitated myself into the drawing-room. The beautiful old furniture that had ornamented it was no longer there. In its place was a prodigious item in the modern Munich style that I shall not describe to you. In my office, my beautiful antique bookshelves had been replaced with pretentious glass-fronted ones. The little room adjacent to it was empty. The marionette theater had been removed therefrom.

The Troublerie, my beloved Troublerie, was now a despoiled and dishonored place where all reverie would henceforth be impossible. Oh, I understood now the mocking smile with which Père Bricard had greeted me when I had passed his shop. Marceline must have sold him all my beautiful old things in order to replace them with these abominations. But why had she done it? What heartfelt malice had driven her? What madness had got into her head?

And confronted by that stupid or perverse vandalism, by my disfigured house, devastated of all those cherished memories, I began to weep like a child.

Instead of extinguishing my anger, however, those tears reignited it, and suddenly, gripping a strong iron-tipped cane that I had brought back from Switzerland, I began striking out around me like a madman. Under my blows, Marceline's trashy goods were smashed to smithereens. When I had smashed everything in my study I precipitated myself toward the drawing-room. My fury increased as I slaked it. On the hideous objects I wreaked the vengeance of the cherished antiquities that had disappeared. I did not weary of lashing out; I could have lashed out indefinitely, gripped by a kind of wild frenzy.

I had just finished disemboweling an armchair when Marceline appeared.

She came in from the garden, where she had been watching out for me, probably attracted by the din. She was carrying a basket full of snails. At the sight of all the debris that surrounded me an expression of triumphant joy appeared on her face.

With one bound I had launched myself toward her and gripped her by the wrist. She dropped the basket of snails, which crashed to the floor with a sound of breaking shells, but at the same time, a heavy hand descended on the nape of my neck. I uttered a cry of dolor and age. The brutal face of Hilaire leaned over mine. The wretch held me with irresistible force, while tying me up solidly by means of a long rope. I struggled in vain, furiously, but the rogue's muscles were more powerful than mine. In a trice, he had me bound and deposited me on the parquet, trussed up like a sausage, in front of Marceline.

She was considering me with her chin in her hand when Hilaire said to her: "That's it, Madame Marceline. The crisis is characteristic. There's nothing more to do now than alert Dr. Thibaut."

At these words, I understood, but my gag stifled my cries of rage. Suddenly, I saw through Marceline's tortuous and implacable schemes; I understood the sinister plan that had formed in her mind; I understood the trap into which I had fallen. The presence of the infamous Hilaire now became explicable, along with that of the infamous Dr. Thibaut. It was them who had helped Marceline realize her perfidious plan. In exasperating me with her disdain and her false solicitude, by the outrage to which she had subjected my beloved house, in provoking the fit of anger to which I had allowed myself to release, Marceline wanted me to pass for a lunatic.

Oh, it had been well planned, and had I not furnished myself the proofs of my insanity? The debris of the broken furniture that surrounded me testified to it. I had been carried away in a fit of temper and had doubtless exceeded the requirements of my torturers. Thanks to the connivance of Dr. Thibaut, I was about be deprived of my liberty, locked in a cell and reduced to a condition of permanent misery. And that scheme was the diabolical work of Marceline. Not only had she never understood the dreamer who had loved her, not only had she refused to associate herself with my dreams, not only had she been an indifferent and disdainful spouse, but she had become an enemy.

How had I not perceived it? Was not that animosity bound to develop? Did we not represent two opposed and incompatible principles: she, the commonsensical, the down-to-earth, the wise; me the chimerical, the nonsensical, the lunatic? Once more dream had been vanquished by reality; love had been powerless to disarm those old rivals. "Oh, Marceline, Marceline," I would have cried had my gag not been so tight, "Marceline!"

My eyes filled with tears, and I felt faint.

When I awoke from my faint I was surrounded by profound darkness. My head was aching and my wrists hurt. My bonds had been slackened somewhat but still retained me rather narrowly. I was lying on a mattress, and at the slightest movement I felt the rope that bound me digging into me. In the state of extreme weakness in which I found myself, there was no prospect of breaking my bonds. Every precaution had been taken to make sure of my person, but my gag had been removed.

I had the idea of calling for help, but what good would that call have done? The infamous Hilaire must be standing guard nearby. I had neither the strength nor the means to try to escape. To negotiate with Marceline would be a waste of time. One does not set up such a trap without a very definite plan. I had no alternative, therefore, but to await, on my prisoner's bed, the arrival of Dr. Thibaut.

I was firmly resolved to defend my liberty and not to allow myself to be locked up without resistance. A person cannot be sequestered thus with impunity in the middle of the nineteenth century. At the last moment, the wretched Thibault would hesitate over the responsibility of so arbitrary an action. I would demonstrate its grave consequences to him. He knew nothing about me but what Marceline had told him, and she must have told him something in accordance with his views.

In order to be victorious in the battle that I was about to fight, however, it was necessary for me to get my strength back. Unfortunately, I sensed that it would be impossible for me to sleep. The thought of Marceline was tormenting me cruelly. Hatred was sliding insidiously into my heart and I ruminated it in silence. No sound troubled the dense obscurity that surrounded me. The house seemed to be asleep.

I had remained thus for some time, absorbed in my reflections, when I seemed to hear whispering. It was coming from outside, probably rising from the garden. I suddenly recognized Marceline's voice, without being able to make out what she was saying—but I distinctly heard the reply that the frightful Hilaire made:

"That way, Monsieur will be locked away tomorrow morning..."

Then the voices fell silent; footsteps drew away and the silence became total again.

I had closed my eyes and I remained motionless, still lying on my back. My pain-racked body avoided all movement, but my thoughts were racing. If I did not succeed in convincing Dr. Thibaut, it would be necessary to escape in order to recover my liberty, for I was resolved to recover it at any price. Obviously, I would be closely supervised, but is not often that a prisoner fully determined to escape cannot succeed in evading the precautions of his jailers. That observation gave me some hope, but I would have preferred to thwart Marceline and put an immediate end to the scheme that the perfidious woman had prepared for me.

As I thought about the snare in which she had caught me my anger surged forth again. An abrupt movement reminded my cruelly of my dire position. The rope that bound me made me suffer. I opened my eyes again. A faint light caused me to turn my head slightly.

The moon, which had just risen, illuminated the place of my detention feebly, and I recognized the part of the house that I was in. It was the grain-loft to which Marceline and Hilaire had transported me. It was vast and let in light through two skylights, which were sufficient to give passage to the vague moonlight. The darkness having been dissipated, my eyes were gradually contriving to distinguish certain objects when a brighter beam penetrated through the skylight situated above my head. Instinctively, my gaze followed that beam, and I uttered an exclamation of surprise. In a corner of the attic stood my marionette theater!

At that sight, a sudden emotion gripped me. I recalled my voyage to Italy, Venice and the Palazzo Pastinati—and Signor Barlotti, the antiquarian...

How immediately Marceline had detested them, those little characters of the Commedia! With what scorn she had looked them up and down, with her hand on her chin, and what an indignant gaze she had directed at me when I had concluded the bargain with Signor Barlotti that had made me master of the variegated troupe! It was them whose purchase had confirmed in her the mute antipathy that she felt for my way of life. Who could tell whether the frightful plan formulated against me, which had reached its conclusion today, did not date from our visit to the Palazzo Pastinati?

Poor marionettes! You shared the hatred that I inspired in Marceline, and I found you relegated, like me, to the grain-loft! You were all there, my inoffensive puppets, suspended at the end of your strings, as I saw you when I went to contemplate you and imagine adventures for you or confide my dreams in you. You were all there: Pantalon with your red doublet and your capacious black robe, your swarthy mask and yellow slippers; Brighella with your white jacket with the green braid, your moustachioed mask, your money-bag and your dagger; Tartaglia and your large blue-tinted spectacles; and you, all black and white, Scaramouche; and you Pulcinello of the gray felt; and you, Rosaura and Giacometta; and you, Coralline, next to Lelio, all plumes, braid, spangles and frills; and you too, Mezzetin, and you, Colombine, and you, multicolored Arlequin, wearing the mask, the hat-band and his black chin-strap, with a hare's tail on top of his hat and wield a bat, and the three lords from the Carnaval, and the Centaur, the piebald and bearded Centaur. Yes, but alas, what can you do to alleviate my distress, so small, so distant, in the moonlight that is now filling the whole grain-loft with its soft silvery light?

I was indulging in these bitter reflections and reiterating the circumstances of my misfortune when I suddenly had a bizarre impression. If my hands had been free I would certainly have rubbed my eyes. I contented myself with opening them wide with an astonishment that you will comprehend.

Was it an illusion of the fever caused by the bruises I had received in the course of my struggle with the brutal Hilaire, a hallucination provoked by the excessive tension of my nerves, or the effect of some trick of the light? It seemed to me, however, that the three Venetian characters standing in front of the theater had just moved. One of them had advanced toward the bearded Centaur, who had also changed his position. He had raised one of his legs and, having turned his head, was presenting his profile to me. At the same time, Arlequin made a movement with his bat.

Was Marceline right? Had I really been afflicted by madness?

I had closed my eyes, and I opened them again. This time, I was not mistaken. The Centaur had just shaken himself, at the same time as Arlequin sketched a caper and Pantalon and Brighella nudged one another with their elbows.

No, I was not mistaken; I was not mad, nor was I seeing things. Mezzetin leaned toward Colombine, Rosaura and Coralline tapped one another's noses with a powder-puff. Tartaglia clapped Scaramouche on the shoulder. Lelio pinched Giacometta. The Centaur flicked his tail and ran his hand through his beard. One after another, all the marionettes stirred at the end of their strings, in the moonlight in which they were perfectly distinct.

My natural disposition as a visionary and the situation in which I found myself inclined me to accept all phantasmagorias; nevertheless, this one surpassed the credulity of which I was capable. There was something supernatural involved in it, which I was ready to admit, but which required confirmation all the same. I therefore awaited some further manifestation of the bizarre life of which the little *burattini* of Signor Barlotti's theater were giving evidence.

Those manifestations were not long delayed. After a few seconds, in fact, a lively discussion seemed to be engaged between the characters on the stage. They moved back and forth, gesticulating. I saw from their gestures that I was the subject of their agitation, and I no longer had any doubt about the significance of the discussion when Pantalon, approaching the edge of the stage, pointed at me with his extended finger, while addressing Arlequin.

That disconcerting spectacle had caused me such surprise that I had forgotten my miseries. A vivid curiosity gripped me. What was going to come of all this? I was addressing that question to myself mentally, when the sound of hooves abruptly resounded on the floor of the grain-loft. With one bound, the bearded Centaur had leapt off the stage. Cautiously, he advanced toward the place where I was lying, and, by virtue of a strange phenomenon, as he approached I saw him grow. Minuscule to begin with, when he reached me, he had attained the natural double height of a horse and a man.

Confronted by this new prodigy, I was literally pinned to my mattress by amazement. The Centaur leaned over me, and considered me for some time. I could make out the slightest details of his face and body. I felt his breath on my hands. Suddenly, he turned round and headed back toward the theater, leaping up to the stage, on two which he dropped his four feet again.

Now, he rendered a report of his mission. Around him, the grouped puppets were gripped by an extreme animation. In the moonlight, I could make out their gestures. The bearded Centaur replied to their questions. I also perceived, to my further surprise, that he had resumed dimensions proportionate to those of the other characters.

I soon observed, however, that the little society seemed to be brought into agreement after a speech from Pantalon that provoked a salvo of mute applause, for they all precipitated themselves toward the edge of the stage in a tumult. Arlequin was the first to jump down, nimbly, followed by Pantalon, who got tangled up in his long robe and nearly fell. Then Brighella, Tartaglia and Pulcinello let themselves down in their turn, while the gallant Lelio helped Giacometta and Rosaura down; the latter extended a hand to Coralline, and Mezzetin lifted Colombine in his arms. Scaramouche came down last, accompanied by the three masked Venetians and the Centaur, who took up a position at the head of the troupe.

As they advanced toward my meager bed, the phenomenon that I had already observed in respect of the Centaur was reproduced in each of them. They grew visibly and attained their natural height. I stared at them in amazement.

Having reached the mattress where I was lying, bound, they formed a line and examine me curiously. I would have liked to reach out to them and implore their help, but the rope with which the vile Hilaire had tied me up prohibited any gesture.

Suddenly, Arlequin, seizing the dagger that hung from Brighella's belt, started cutting my bonds. Gradually, I felt their grip relax, and I recovered the liberty of my movements. Soon, I was able to prop myself up on my elbow. On seeing that, the variegated troupe applauded. In clapping, their wooden hands made a noise that resounded loudly in the sonority of the grain-loft and the silence of the night. The Centaur pranced, stamping his hooves. Arlequin shut him up, raising his bat, and then, with a multicolored bow, addressed a speech to me. I thought I heard the following words:

"Kind Seigneur, Arlequin and his comic troupe present their respects to you and want you to know that we are all at your service. When you brought us away with you from the Palazzo Pastinati, we understood that we would be of serious use to you one day. We knew humanity well enough to know that it is the enemy of fantasy and visions, and we had divined that the Lady Marceline and you were not of the same spiritual family. We have witnessed the plot that she contrived against you, and we have come to deliver you from her wicked enterprise. Oh, good Seigneur, leave this society for which you are ill-fitted, this real world that you have never understood at all. Come into ours; that is the one to which you are suited. Leave Marceline and her supporters here. Come with us. Accept the invitation of this beautiful moonbeam gliding through the skylight. Its silvery path will guide you to our happy Venice. You will take up the cloak and the mask, like the three seigneurs you see here, and will thus be liberated from the servitude of the real, and you will put on your face the white cardboard mask through which one sees life in the thousand colors of fantasy and dream, whose changing and mobile livery I wear in the pieces of my costume."

Further applause saluted Arlequin's words. The noise of clapping wooden hands was mingled with delighted stamping feet, to which the sound of the bearded Centaur's hooves replied. The excited troupe filled the moonlit grain-loft with a deafening racket.

It was at that moment that the door opened and Marceline appeared, lamp in hand. She must have been woken up by the noise, for she was in night attire. Her hair was stretched on curlers; she was wearing slippers on her otherwise-bare feet, and her hand was shielding her face. Her face expressed a satisfied malevolence, and one could sense that she was thinking, in seeing my surrounded by the gesticulating marionettes: *You can't pretend now that you aren't mad!*

She did not have time to express her thought, however. The bearded Centaur had loomed up before her and had planted a big kiss on each of her cheeks, so rudely that she dropped the lamp and fell backwards. Then, calmly seizing the fainted Marceline in both arms, he headed for the little theater, leaping on to the stage with a single bound.

I did not realize what had happened, at first, but when he had leapt on to the boards I understood. Marceline was suspended from a string, head down, swaying gently. Then the swaying topped and she remained motionless.

Arlequin nudge me with is elbow.

"Come on, kind Seigneur."

Before I had time to reply, I felt myself lifted off the ground by a friendly and muscular hand, and the bearded Centaur, who had put my on his back, climbed up to the skylight along the beautiful silver moonbeam that descended therefrom. Behind him came the laughing procession. Arlequin waved his bat, Pantalon wiped the lenses of his spectacles, Brighella and Tartaglia, arm in arm, preceded Lelio, accompanied by Giacometta, Rosaura and Coralline. Mezzetin escorted Colombine, followed by Scaramouche, and Pulcinello brought up the rear, thumbing his nose at poor Marceline—who, reduced to the minuscule stature of a doll, was quivering at the end of her string, in the beautiful moonlight dear to dreamers, poets and lunatics…in the beautiful silent moonlight.

The Glimpse

To Madame Henri Farge [39]

The Palazzo Altinengo[40] that will feature in this story is not the one that tourists admire on the Grand Canal for its Lombardesque façade ornamented with serpentine disks and the Neptune with two tridents who watches over the lintel of its marine door, for the ancient and powerful Altinengo family, one of the most illustrious in the Most Serene Republic, possessed several ducal buildings in the city, built in different epochs and situated in different *sestieri*.

That circumstance is not rare in Venice. Can one not count several Palazzos Grimani, one in San Polo, another in San Toma, a third in San Luca and a fourth in Santa Maria Formosa, to which are added the Grimani della Vida? It is the same for Palazzos Contarini. The Contarini-Fasan has for siblings the Contarini della Serigni, the Contarini della Figure and the Contarini del Bavolo. Three Palazzos Mocenigo sit side by side on the Grand Canal, which also boasts three Palazzos

---

[39] Henri Farge (1884-1970) was a painter and illustrator who produced (among many others) numerous studies of Venice. Régnier met Farge and his wife Madeleine in 1911, long before he became famous, and maintained a close platonic relationship with Madeleine for many years.

[40] The Palazzo Altinengo featured in the story is based on the Palazzo Vendramin ai Carmini, in which Rénier lodged (with his wife and son) in October-November 1913, during his eleventh visit to his beloved Venice, and the last he was able to make before the story's publication in 1917. He only visited the city once more, in 1924.

267

Corner: the Corner-Spinelli, the Corner della Cà Grande and the Corner della Regina.

Now, although all the guides mention two Palazzos Altinengo—that of San Staè and that of San Bernardetto, none point out the third, and it is exactly that last one whose memory is mingled with, I shall not say the most singular and inexplicable event of my life, but the *only* inexplicable and singular event of my entire existence.

There is, at any rate, nothing very astonishing about the fact that the third Palazzo Altinengo had escaped my investigations as a Venetian tourist No one can boast of knowing Venice in its entirety, no matter how many times one has stayed there or how much time one has spent there—no one, except perhaps my friend Tiberio Prentinaglia...

Before getting to the circumstances that led me to spend a few months as a guest in the strange dwelling in question, however, it is necessary that I tell you something about the reasons that decided me, at the end of that September in the 1890s, to take the road to my beloved city once again.

About those reasons I shall be brief, for it is not a confession that I am making here. I have always been reluctant to confide in others, not judging myself sufficiently interesting to solicit their attention. All that I shall permit myself to do is to note in these pages certain facts that I dare to qualify as singular, and which appear even more so by virtue of the unexpectedness of their having as a witness a person of my sort—for nothing prepared me, in fact, for the entirely involuntary role that I was to play in this story.

I am a very ordinary man, who is undistinguished from the average by any special ability, nor by any conspicuous intellectual merit. I have always lived for myself and have always found it quite natural to pass unperceived by the eyes of others. In fact, there is nothing distinctive about me—not even my liking for Venice, which I share with thousands of people, and from which I do not claim to have obtained any advantage. I love Italy, and Venice in particular, modestly and without seeking any luster in consequence. I have never had

any ambition to feature in society columns among the notabili-
ties of the Piazza San Marco or the stars of the Procuraties. No
elegant newspaper has ever signaled my presence on the lagoon at the time of year when high society shows itself off
there. For me, Venice has not been a pretext to put on remarkable suits and sensational cravats, nor a mean of entering into
relationships with the cosmopolitan celebrities of the arts, letters, finance and the aristocracy who judge it useful to their
glory to be seen, once a year, on the Piazzetta, between the
Lion and Crocodile columns.[41]

I will even add that, in default of worldly considerations,
it was not aesthetic curiosity either that led me to Venice—not
that I am any less able than anyone else to appreciate the beauties of an architecture, a painting or a statue. I am neither ignorant nor an imbecile, so I have savored in Venice the pleasures
of that sort that it offers to travelers. Neither the Doge's Palazzo nor San Marco has left me indifferent. I have even acquired
a certain knowledge of Venetian art in its various manifestations. I am not insensitive to the delicate marvel of a piece of
lace or the fragile perfection of an item of glassware. The history of the old Venice of masks and serenades is quite familiar
to me, in its mores and its particularities. I have read the President de Brosses[42] and studied Casanova, but Venice is sufficient for me in itself and I have no need of its past to submit to
the charm of its living enchantment.

---

[41] The Colonna San Marco depicts a winged lion, that being
the symbol of St. Mark. St. Mark was not the original patron
saint of Venice, however, and the Piazza also contains the
Colonna San Teodoro, which depicts St. Theodore of Amasea
battling what Venetians insist on calling a crocodile, although
everyone else thinks that it is a dragon.
[42] Charles de Bosses, Comte de Tournay, wrote a series of
letters from Venice to his family in Dijon, which were published there under the signature "President de Bosses" because
he was the president of the local parliament.

269

Yes—and I think I have made the point—my love for Venice was always a healthy and simple love, a familial love, exempt from snobbery and aestheticism, and also exempt from romanticism: realistic, if one can say that of pleasures that are both spontaneous and reflective.

Venice pleases me infinitely. I love its climate, its color and it light. The kind of life that it permits and imposes is adapted to my tastes. I enjoy a particular wellbeing there amid things that occupy my eyes and my thoughts agreeably. Nowhere do my days go by with a gentler ease, and even solitude is devoid of bitterness there. There is nowhere else in the world where one is one self-possessed and can tolerate oneself with less ennui. The kind of satisfaction that Venice gives me explains why I have led a rather reclusive existence there. During my numerous sojourns, I have made few acquaintances—which was easy for me, not being one of those people whose presence solicits curiosity. Besides which, I have always avoided being in Venice at the times of year when it becomes a fashionable rendezvous, where society beauties, idle snobs and pretentious aesthetes take their places on the Piazza San Marco with the sentiment of accomplishing a ritual of lofty elegance, supreme chic and unparalleled refinement.

On that point too I shall permit myself to insist. I have never felt obliged to live in Venice "differently" than elsewhere, in a particular exaltation or an unaccustomed state of mind. I have never expected to experience any exceptional impressions there. For me, Venice has never been "the City of Dreams"—even though, in writing those words, I feel a hesitation that will be more comprehensible in due course. On the contrary, I ask nothing more of it than its charming, original, gentle reality. To descend from a railway carriage and climb into a gondola seems perfectly natural to me and not suggestive of any astonishment. A gondola seems to me to be a vehicle like any other. I am insensitive to its romantic glamour, but I appreciate the marine elegance of its form, its nautical qualities, while much preferring to wander on foot through the labyrinthine *calli*.

In sum, the fact of being in Venice does not confer any special dignity upon me in my own eyes. I do not derive any pride or vanity therefrom. Venice pleases me; I like it; I submit joyfully to its charm and its prestige, but I only expect from it what it gives to everyone. I am not one of those whom Venice bewitches in advance and on whose finger it places its magical ring, and I have never draped myself in the cloak of Venetian romanticism.

The circumstances that took me to Venice for the first time were, in any case, the simplest imaginable. Old friends of my family, Monsieur and Madame C***, lived there for several years. They had rented the top floor of a Palazzo situated in San Trovaso and had set up house there with all the usual comforts. That floor consisted of a vast gallery accompanied by a number of rooms, all garnished with that delightful old Venetian furniture that one finds today in antique shops. That furniture consisted of bulging chests of drawers, more-or-less baroque sofas and armchairs, cupboards, sets of shelves, and especially of mirrors.

The C***s had retired there by virtue of a taste for tranquility and silence, with the desire to end their days—which did not promise to be long—in peace. Madame de C*** was in delicate health and her husband suffered from incurable infirmities. It was a sudden aggravation of Monsieur de C***'s condition that decided me to make the journey to Venice, but when I arrived there the dangerous crisis had passed, sufficiently for the C***s to keep me with them, with the result that I stayed for a full month as the guest of those charming people, whom I liked very much.

Oh, what a pleasant sojourn, and what god memories I retained of the old Palazzo in San Trovaso and its mild family atmosphere. Monsieur de C*** did not want his incapacity to prevent me from enjoying the pleasures of Venice and Madame de C***, in spite of the cares she devoted to her husband, took responsibility for being my guide. She was an intelligent and educated woman; she did not weary my attention or fatigue my curiosity by overburdening me with visits to

271

churches and museums. Of artistic Venice she only showed me what was necessary to inspire a desire to know it more deeply one day. For the rest, she contented herself with permitting me to accompany her on her habitual walks—and it was thus that I learned the sweetness of living in Venice, neither as a tourist, nor as an aesthete, or as a snob, but as a dilettante of light, color and beauty, as a spectator amused by the charming, bizarre, peaceful and picturesque Venetian way of life.

I had, in quitting them, promised those dear and good friends to come back the following year. I kept my promise, but I did not see them again. A few months after my departure, they both died within a brief interval. I was traveling in Russia at the time and it was there that I learned the sad news. It caused me veritable grief, but that loss, instead of keeping me away from Venice, bound me to it more tightly, although the first time I passed in front of the Palazzo San Trovaso my heart ached as I considered the windows of the now-vacant floor whose closed shutters bore the little strip of adhesive paper that indicates apartments for hire in Venice. Since then, I have never failed, in the course of each of my sojourns, to go and salute in grateful memory the residence of the old friends who had initiated me into the charms of Venetian life and who, as they loved to repeat with an amicable pride, had "Venetianized" me.

I was Venetianized to a point at which I could scarcely tolerate hotel life. The generous hospitality of my friends in San Trovaso had spared me its annoyances and it was to them that I also owed the lodgings that became my habitual pied-à-terre. I remembered having heard them talk about a certain Casa Trigiani, where they had stayed before moving to San Trovaso. That Casa Trigiani, situated on the Fondamenta Barbaro, was occupied by two old spinsters who let out a few rooms there. The rooms in question were clean and habitable, and one of them overlooked a small garden in which a few rose bushes grew alongside a cypress, not far from a bed of scarlet sage. The Sorelle Trigiani had something absurd and alarming about them, which I liked. I became their tenant and it was on hem that I descended every time I came to Venice—which is to say, almost every year for fifteen years.

It was necessary, to interrupt that long and pleasant annual habit, for dire events to upset the course of my existence. In fact, for three years I underwent a particularly painful intimate crisis.[43] All that I can say about that period of my life—for, as I have already stated, this is not a confession and it is facts rather than sentiments that I am attempting to record—is that it was so profoundly troubled that my thoughts did not revert once to the happier times when, in Autumn or Spring, I had spent a few weeks as a guest at the Casa Trigiani.

During those three years. I ceased going to Venice, and it was not until I was convalescent after a cruel illness, by which that harsh sentimental ordeal was completed, that I thought of renewing he links that had attached me for such a long time to the charming city that brought back so many pleasant and inoffensive memories. Perhaps I would be able to rehabilitate myself there more fully to living. I broached the subject with the physicians who were caring for me. Without approving of the project, they did not oppose it. My state of health was not so bad that a voyage was out of the question.

The residue of my illness now consisted of persistent insomnia and nervous apprehension, combined with a sincere disgust for all society and a profound need for solitude. Venice would give me the desired isolation. Why not, I fact, attempt the experiment? The summer, with its heatwaves, was almost over. September was drawing to a close and I would soon find the melancholy and calm beauty of the Venetian autumn on the lagoon. The prospect pleased me. In my mind's eye, I saw

---

[43] Régnier probably began writing this story three years after his previous visit to Venice; it is, however, explicitly set in the 1890s, the period in which he married, but before his first visit to Venice, which was in 1899; during his second, in 1901, he fell ill, and suffered extensively from fever and insomnia.

once again the cypresses in the small garden of the Casa Trigiani. I heard the shrill and amicable voices of the Sorelle, the sound of clogs rattling on the paving stones of the Fondamenta Barbaro, the cries of the ambulant merchants, the warning calls of the gondoliers turning the corners of little *rios*, all the familiar rumor of popular Venice, and, in the sky, the beautiful bells of the Salute and the Gesuati.

My decision was made. It only remained for me to send a telegram to the Sorelle Trigiani informing them of the date of my arrival.

I remember quite clearly having drafted that dispatch immediately after the doctor's departure. I had got up from the divan to accompany him to the door, and when I went back to my desk I picked up the piece of paper on which I wrote the text of the telegram, and then gave it-at least, I believe I did—with two others to my domestic, in order that he might send them. How did it come about that I found that piece of paper a few days later, carefully folded in four and slipped into a pocket of my portfolio? Whence came that distraction?

I did not dwell unduly on the inadvertence that I had committed. It simply proved that the illness had weakened my attentive faculties and reminded me that it was a still-fragile convalescent who was looking out of the window of the railway carriage at the Italian countryside—for it was between Verona and Vicenza, in the train that was taking me to Venice, that I perceived my error. It was too late to repair it; in any case, it could not be of any great importance. Even unalerted, the Sorelle Trigiani would make arrangements to accommodate me. If the room overlooking the garden was not free at present, they would put me in another.

That prospect, I must admit, troubled me slightly. The Sorelle having not replied to my telegram—for the good reason that they had not received it—their silence had seemed unusual to me. I reproached myself for my negligence and conceived a certain ill-humor against myself Then again, in sum, why that hasty and precipitate departure? Why had I not waited until my health was consolidated? What was the urgen-

274

cy? What was I going to do in that distant city, with my poor aching head and my poor troubled heart? Would I find the peace that I sought there, with which I sought to numb my cruel melancholy? Would I not be victim to all the surprises and the caprices of the imagination, incapable in advance of resisting them, submissive to all their traps and all their tricks, exposed without defense to all the dolorous and dangerous phantasmagorias of regret and remembrance?

These reflections rendered the remainder of the voyage rather painful. When the train left Mestre, however, and began to run alongside the stagnant infiltrations of the lagoon, my apprehension dissipated. In those days, the express arrived at five o'clock and Venice appeared to the traveler in all its luminous splendor as one crossed the bridge linking it to the mainland. That approach to the beloved city always provoked an impression of indefinable but profound pleasure in me. If, this time, I did not experience that pleasure in its plenitude, I nevertheless felt a real satisfaction when, on getting down from the train and leaving the station, I saw the water of the canal bathing the steps of the quay, and, above the irons of the lined-up gondolas, the verdigris-stained dome of San Simeone round against the sky.

Suddenly, all the Venice of yesteryear revived in my memory, and it seemed to me, when the oar beat the water and the gondola that was carrying me swerved gently, that I was leaving behind my heavy and dolorous life of recent times and that I was no longer anything but a lightened shadow moving into the silence and the light, toward peace, calm and forgetfulness.

Those thoughts occupied me sufficiently for me to remain almost indifferent to the sweet spectacle of Venice rediscovered. They took me as far as the moment when the gondola reached the steps of the Fondamenta Barbaro, facing the Casa Trigiani. It was still the same old Casa, with its ocher façade and brown shutters, its little door, alongside which hung the copper ring attached by a cord to the bell. I seized that ring with a gesture that I had made hundreds of times. As usual, the

275

carillon resounded inside the house. Immediately, footsteps came down the stairs. The person who came to open the door looked at me in astonishment, considering the suitcase I held in my hand. I asked for the Sorelle Trigiani. A smile replied to me interrogation. Three months before, the Sorelle Trigiani had retired to Vicenza to look after a sick brother; the house was now rented in its entirety to an English family...

In other circumstances, I would have weathered that petty snag easily, but my state of unhealthy sensitivity caused me to exaggerate its importance. That slight disappointment threw me into an anxiety disproportionate to its cause. In Venice there are twenty boarding houses more or less similar to the Casa Trigiani. I had a embarrassment of choice—but that insignificant disappointment seemed to me to be a bad omen. It was like an imperceptible rupture in the ensemble of my habits, whose resumption was supposed to contribute to retiring me to what I had been when they had been created. A thread had given way in the mesh that ought to have enveloped me entirely in its invisible net, and that inconvenience, minimal in itself, impressed me painfully.

There was nothing else I could do, that day, but go to a hotel. The next day, I would set out in search of lodgings. I gave a gondolier the first address that came to mind. It was—I don't know why—the Victoria Hotel that I indicated to him, and soon afterwards I was installed in a banal but sufficiently comfortable room, from which I descended, after having bathed and changed, into a similarly comfortable and banal dining room. It was dinner time, and my intention was to go to bed immediately afterwards, but when the meal was over, having lit one of those long "Virginias" traversed by a straw, whose strong and bitter taste I like, the desire overtook me to take a stroll and I went out.

Scarcely was I outside when I felt a sensation of pleasure. I was almost happy to find myself back in the nocturnal Venice whose inextricable *calli* I had so often roamed. How many times, in fact, had I ventured into the obscure and capricious Venetian maze? I had eventually got to know it so well that I navigated there with almost absolute certainty.

Now, that evening, I soon perceived that I no longer possessed my usual security of orientation. Several times, I was obliged to stop, uncertain of the direction to follow; once, I even went into one of those *rami* without issue, which terminate in a *rio*, before which one is forced to retrace one's steps. These little mistakes caused me an irritation all the more inexplicable because my stroll had no definite objective and I was in no hurry. I therefore continued to wander at hazard. That seemed to me to be the best way to soothe the nervous tension that was tormenting me and was doubtless due to the long immobility of the journey.

I was quite determined to vanquish by fatigue the insomnia the probably awaited me in my hotel room. Then again, such long wanderings were part of my Venetian habits of yore—that once upon a time to which I had returned in the superstitious hope of rediscovering the sweetest hours of my past.

It was getting late, however. I perceived the increasing solitude of the *calli* through which I moving and the *campi* I crossed. Once, it had been that solitude that pleased me the most. I had savored therein what is justly called the "Venetian mystery": the furtive gait of a passer-by, the gliding motion of a gondola, the sound of a heel on the pavement, the splash of an oar in the water, a voice, a song, silence, the lighted windows in somber facades—but today, the nocturnal Venice that I had loved so much made a impression on me that I found it difficult to define.

It was certainly not fear. I had lived in Venice long enough, and was sufficiently familiar with Venetian mores to know that visitors are perfectly safe there. The role of the *vigili*, as the agents of the police are called, is rather restricted. It is limited to arresting a few drunks overfond of "*vini nostrani*" and catching a few thieves now and again. Outside these minor misdeeds, the Venetians are tranquil folk and one can wander in the most remote districts, by day and by night, without any fear of unfortunate encounters. The sole risk is that of going astray and letting oneself fall into some *rio*, and even that inconvenience is diminished by the excellence of the street-lighting, which, while conserving a picturesque semi-obscurity for the city, renders it perfectly practicable for pedestrians.

Fear, therefore, had no part in that malaise, the nature of which remained uncertain, and which had gradually succeeded the initial pleasure that I had felt in treading the sonorous pavements of the *calli*. Was it due to the still-precarious state of my health or was it a consequence of the rather sharp irritation of the incident at the Casa Trigiani? Whatever the cause might be, it was no less certain that an indefinable apprehension had gradually overtaken me. It resembled the kind of anxiety occasioned by entry into an unexpectedly charged psychic atmosphere.

Soon, that insidious anguish became so painful that it caused me to hasten my steps, and it was a veritable relief when, after numerous turns whose direction I had ceased to control, hazard or instinct brought me back to the lights of the Piazza San Marco. That sight rapidly dissipated my anxiety, and it was at an abruptly decelerated pace that I went into the Piazza, which was almost deserted, beneath a sky marbled with large clouds, in the interstices of which stars were studded.

It was then very late and strollers were scarce under the Procuraties. I have always loved Venice at the moment when the famous galleries extend empty corridors with the gleaming pavements in front of the closed shops. Many times, on coming out of the Café Florian, I had wandered there, but that evening, weary from my long walk, I had little desire to play the solitary peripatetic. One the other hand, I was in no hurry to go back to the hotel. I therefore headed for the Café Florian. Open all night, it is hospitable to the belated pedestrian, and offers him the shelter of its panted rooms and velvet-clad booths.

The Café Florian is comprised, as everyone knows, of several contiguous small rooms, variously decorated and reminiscent of drawing-rooms. There was one of those rooms of which I was particularly fond. Its walls are ornamented with mirrors and frescoes kept under glass to preserve them from smoke and deterioration. Those frescoes represent the costumed figures of different peoples. Two of the figures, among others, amused me: a Turk in a turban and a Chinese man with his pigtail. It was beneath the latter that I most gladly sat down on the red velvet, in front of one of those round marble tables whose top turns on the sole supporting foot.

My favorite place was free when I went into the almost-empty room. At the other side of the room two Venetians were chatting while finishing their glasses of water, and in a corner, an old man with a red nose was swigging the final mouthfuls of a small glass of *strega*. I asked the waiter for an alkermes punch. Before he had brought it the two conversationalists got up and left. The man with the red nose saluted them with his hand. The waiter did not take long, however, to come back with the punch I had ordered. It is a pink-colored drink with a taste that is simultaneously aromatic and insipid. I sipped it slowly.

My malaise dissipated and changed into a sort of wellbeing. That release was welcome. I had definitely done the right thing in going into the old and dear Florian, where I had spent so man evenings, and coming to sit beneath the Chinese man. I half-turned toward the face of the fresco. The Chinese man was considering me with a mocking bonhomie, and seemed to be congratulating me for having paid him a visit before going back to the hotel, at which I had decided to stay for the least possible time. The first thing in the morning, I would set out in quest of lodgings to replace the Casa Trigiani.

The names of several family boarding-houses came to mind: the *pension* Domenico in San Gregorio, the *pension* Cimarosa in Campo San Vitale, and others. But would I enjoy the same tranquility there as at Casa Trigiani? It might be necessary for me to be subjected to annoying neighbors. Why not, instead, rent rooms in some old Palazzo? I could furnish them summarily and live there in total liberty. My sojourn would be long enough to be worth the trouble of that petty installation.

That idea pleased me. If chance favored me, I would surely be able to discover some picturesque dwelling in one of the solitary districts in which Venice is all the more charming for being more itself. There, perhaps, in the silence and the calm, I would recover some of the sweetness of existence...

While I reflected thus the man with the red nose had disappeared. Passers-by in the Procuraties were becomes increasingly rare. Sometimes one of them paused momentarily, darted a glance inside the café and went on, humming a tune or tapping his cane on the resonant paving stones. I was watching them distractedly when my attention was suddenly attracted by a tall silhouette standing in front of the window waving its arms.

An instant later, the flap of his coat nearly knocking over the empty glass left by the man with the red nose, my friend Tiberio Prentinaglia sat down beside me in the velvet-lined booth and shook my hands, exclaiming: "In Venice! In Venice! And he didn't tell me he was coming! Me, his dear Prentinaglia! In Venice! Since when?"

If I call Signore Tiberio Prentinaglia a friend, it is because he adjudged himself to be one with so much force and conviction that it had been necessary for me to conform with an amicable determination as definite as it was despotic. To tell the truth, I had known Prentinaglia for a number of years, but that acquaintance, with the title that had followed it, had been made less by my choice that that of the remarkable person in question. I was resigned to the necessity, for it is one, of anyone who visits Venice regularly to know Prentinaglia. Prentinaglia made provision to render it inevitable. He made it a point of honor that no foreigner should escape his friendship, but he was able to render it very agreeable. One became Prentinaglia's friend because he wanted it, and remained so because one would not want it to be otherwise. In any case, in Venice, Prentinaglia is an indispensable man.

Tiberio Prentinaglia is a large fellow, thin and gangling, a true Venetian of the time of the Most Serene Republic, the time of Gozzi and Casanova. Clad in ample garments, covered by an overcoat, with a large felt hat, he has a long and jaundiced face, furnished with a large nose, close to which are two keen and ferrety eyes, and which dominates a thin and sinuous mouth, simultaneously loquacious and secretive. By that face Prentinaglia seems masked. It gives him a theatrical appearance in which there is verve, finesse and mystery. One senses that he is supple and subtle, even though he puts on a show of being vehement, with prudence underneath his fluency. On top of that, there is something bizarre, strange and a little crazy about him. A character from comedy, and also some fantastic tale, he seems to be compounded of several superimposed individuals. There are contrasts in him, but what nuances bind them together!

Prentinaglia is both superstitious and incredulous, visionary and practical. The play of oppositions that he presents could be continued in that manner for a long time. In sum, and once and for all, he is an amusing fellow, about whom one could easily argue, but always come back to the conclusion that he is a man of the world who knows Venice better than anyone—its past as well as its present, its art and its scenery, its mores then and now, down to the smallest stone and the most fugitive reflection. Let us add the least of its people, for nothing and no one escapes his vigilance and his curiosity. When one sets foot in Venice, one belongs by right to Prentinaglia, and one cannot complain about it, for he is an infinite resource, ready to serve you as a guide and introducer, to help you visit the city or get to know its society, to regulate walks and to arrange meetings, to give you all the information that you might need. He is the living chronicle of Venice, an intermediary as obligatory for the purchase of a painting as the acquisition of an umbrella. He knows the ins and outs of everything and everyone.

281

A Venetian in Venice, he lives there and therein, for it lives in him, with all the honesty in the world. He follows a hundred professions without having any definite one. He is the agent of the thousand ingenious or absurd schemes that comprise Venetian life. He is principally occupied in the sale of property and is something of an expert in art and antiques. He furnishes palazzos for rich foreigners. His operations also extend to the mainland; he does business in Mestre, Fusina, Dolo, Mira, Stra, Padua and Treviso. From all that he earns enough to live in an elegant palazzino furnished in the Venetian style, in which the knick-knacks are for sale if one asks—and yet he loves those knick-knacks, for my friend Prentinaglia is a man of taste and erudition. I remember visits in his company to the Archives and the Academy in which he charmed me with his reliable and exact knowledge. He has made several important gifts to the Musei Civici, including an admirable theater of marionettes representing characters from the Commedia and the Carnival.

He is one himself, and no less amusing. One can imagine him parading in the *tabaro e baüta*, with the white mask over his face and a tricorn hat over his wig. He does not lack wit, but his fluency occasionally runs out of steam. He is animated and excited, and then falls into long silences, as if the puppet-strings have been cut. What does he think about during those moments of absorption? Some commercial scheme? Some amorous intrigue? Is he planning one of those practical jokes that he sometimes plays—for that is another of his character-traits—or making up one of those fantastic stories that he loves to tell, by which he ends up frightening himself? For he is, as I have said, superstitious; he believes in the Devil, in phantoms, in revenants, in "spirits"—as did the good Carlo Gozzi, on whom he wrote a well-documented study. He boasts about knowing the Kabbalah, and that Gnomes and Salamanders have no secrets from him. He even claims that he is capable of constructing "the pyramid," as Casanova did for Senator

282

Bragadin and his friends.[44] Perhaps Tiberio Prentinaglia is something of a sorcerer, but he is, all the same, a useful fellow and an agreeable eccentric who brings imagination and virtuosity to the solution of the difficulties that life throws up.

Such was the individual who came to sit down beside me under the Chinese man in the Café Florian. If I have taken the trouble to describe him in detail, it is not because he reappears frequently in this story. He will scarcely be glimpsed again until the epilogue of events in which I cannot say that he was mixed up, but to the determination of whose sequence he nevertheless contributed. Besides, even if he only represented hazard therein, that would justify the rather extensive sketch that I have drawn of the companion of my old Venetian life I rediscovered that evening.

To get back to his sudden appearance in the Café Florian, where we used to run into one another so frequently, it seemed to me to present an opportunity to get me out of difficulty. Prentinaglia would certainly be able to give me the address of some palazzo where I might rent the apartment I sought. Before telling him what I wanted from him, however, I felt that it would be necessary for me to reply to a few preliminary questions.

Prentinaglia had already repeated the one he had asked me on arrival: "How long have you been in Venice?"

"I arrived today."

That response appeared to reassure Prentinaglia from two points of view: that of my sentiments in his regard and that of his impeccable vigilance. That I might have been in Venice for several days without his knowing and without my having sought to see him would have outraged his friendship and mortified his curiosity. Take note too that, during the three

---

[44] Cassanova often posed as an occultist for the fraudulent purposes, both amatory and pecuniary; he claimed in his *Memoirs* to have built Kabbalistic "pyramids" for Bragadin in order to get him to speak to the father of a girl he wanted to marry on his behalf; as usual, the plan went awry.

years that I had not come to Venice, he had not enquired about me. One only exists for Prentinaglia when one is in Venice. Once departed, one no longer exists until one returns. I had returned, and returned to existence. He testified to that by a sigh of relief and satisfaction.

"Excellent—and for a long stay, I hope?"

I made an evasive gesture. There was only one project about which I wanted to talk to Prentinaglia. What point was there is bringing up the rest? What good would it do to confess my distress to him? What could he do against my illness? It would have required someone exceedingly ingenious and subtle to invent something capable of taking me out of myself. With what exorcism could his Kabbalah furnish him to break the dolorous spell that held me prisoner? All that he could do for me was procure me the retreat I desired, where I thought I might recover the illusion of my inoffensive Venetian past—that past in which he was mingled and in which he represented certain agreeable and picturesque hours, those in which we met almost every evening "under the Chinese man" in this same Café Florian, with Otto von Hohenberg and Lord Robert Sperling.

That memory gave me the means of cutting short Prentinaglia's questions. Did he recall that spring when, during my last sojourn in Venice, we all met up—Hohenberg, Sperling, he and I—to exchange news of the day? In those days, Hohenberg and Sperling were both in love with the shade of Catherine Cornaro, the Queen of Cyprus, and were disputing her favors.[45] Fortunately, they had reconciled over a few bottles of Giacomuzzi.

---

[45] The Venice-born Caterina Cornaro (1454-1510) became Queen of the old crusader kingdom of Cyprus by marriage, and Cyprus was annexed by Venice when her husband died in 1489. She was allowed to retain her title as an honorific, and subsequently acquired a reputation as a patroness of the arts, but her portraits do not suggest that she was a great beauty.

That allusion to our Florianesque[46] little group made Prentinaglia burst out laughing.

"Do I remember, my dear friend, do I remember! Alas, poor Hohenberg! His family ended up getting annoyed with him and summoning him home to his castle in Bohemia. They cut off his allowance. He had to sell the little palazzo, bid farewell to the worthy Carlo and old Pierino, renounce his box at the Theater and go back to that devil of a schloss, full of subterranean passages and dungeons about which he told such fine stories. Poor Hohenberg, how bored he must be out there, where he's doubtless trying, in front of a tankard of beer, to forget the disdain of the inexorable Queen of Cyprus! By contrast, though, Sperling has settled in Venice for good. Shortly after your last departure he bought the Casa degli Spiriti and has restored it magnificently. You'll see it, my dear fellow."

The Casa degli Spiriti is a palazzo situated near San Alvise, on that part of the lagoon known as the "dead lagoon," where the tide has almost no effect. It is a large square building, which remained uninhabited for a long time because it was reputed to be haunted.

"And how is Sperling getting along with the spirits?"

At that question, Prentinaglia became suddenly thoughtful. He stroked his nose with a serious expression. Often, Prentinaglia's gravity was only a feint that served to prepare for some comic effect, but this time, he seemed sincerely grave. He darted a circumspect glance around the room to make sure that no one was watching us. At that late hour, the Florian was empty, but Prentinaglia lowered his voice anyway.

---

[46] This adjective would normally derive from the French fabulist Jean-Pierre Claris de Florian (1755-1794), second only to Jean de La Fontaine in that capacity. It is possible that the Café Florian is named after him, although Florian is a fairly common forename—but probable, in any case, that the echo is intentional on Régnier's part.

"My dear chap, I don't know how Sperling is getting along with the spirits, but you're wrong to joke about such things, for very extraordinary things happen here. Take Prentinaglia's word for it, one might believe that we were back in the times when the worthy Carlo Gozzi complained about the occult tricks of which he was the victim.[47] It's enough to make the most skeptical person reflect."

He seemed to be entirely serious, but I was suspicious of his penchant for practical jokes.

"Come on, Prentinaglia, explain yourself."

Again he looked around, as if to make sure that no indiscreet ear was listening to us—but was that a genuine preoccupation, or a mere maneuver designed to pique my curiosity?

Finally, he came to a decision, lowered his voice again and said, in a confidential tone: "You know I don't like to raise certain subjects with the incredulous, but I've said too much to leave it there. Well, yes, extraordinary things are happening here. Judge for yourself. You're not in a hurry to get back to your hotel?"

I shook my head negatively. He continued: "You know Taddeo Talventi, the director of the Musei Civici? He's a cold, taciturn, meticulous man, devoid of imagination—of which we do have a few in Italy. Three days ago, he summoned me, having, he said, to consult me about an embarrassing situation. You recall, don't you, that in room IV of the museum—the one that contains the Persian tapestry donated to the Venetian Republic by Shah Abbas[48]—there's a display-case containing

---

[47] The famous playwright's *Memorie Inutili* [Useless Memoirs] (1797-98), though far from useless, are generally considered somewhat unreliable, and not simply because of their complaints about occult persecution.

[48] Abbas I of Persia, known as Abbas the Great (1571-1629) sent a diplomatic mission to Europe in 1599 to seek support in his war against the Ottoman Turks; it was received by the Doge as well as numerous other heads of state, causing a sen-

a small porcelain bust? You know the one I mean: a charming little bust of the *settecento*, so expressive and alive!"

Prentinaglia emphasized the word "alive."

I did, indeed, remember, perfectly. I had often admired the little trinket, which had struck me by virtue of its artistic quality. The man represented, doubtless some Venetian patrician, necessarily attracted attention. He face was narrow, gaunt and distinguished, with a long nose and a sensual mouth. Everything about the individual suggested voluptuousness and amorousness. He must have been passionate about ornamentation, food, flowers and women, but above all, there was an insatiable curiosity in the expression of the face. About what had that Venetian lord been so curious? Secrets of the heart or secrets of State? What finesse there was in that attentive and ardent physiognomy! What kind of life had he lived? What adventures had he had? What name had he borne?

More than once I had interrogated Prentinaglia about the origin of that bust. Prentinaglia, I recalled very clearly, had made enquiries of the director of the museum, but no one had been able to tell him anything. No one even knew when the bust had been added to the collections. The label had doubtless gone astray. The catalogue contained no indication. All that anyone had been able to say was that the object had been in the display case for a long time. As for the individual's identity, the same ignorance. The unknown man seemed to be amusing himself with that in his enigmatic and delicate smile.

All those details returned to mind with Prentinaglia's interrogation.

"Yes, certainly, Prentinaglia my friend, I remember the bust. It's one of those faces in which the best of old Venetian finesse can be read, so diplomatic, so shrewd, his love of elegant, passionate life... What's happened to the bust?"

"What has happened, my dear fellow is that it's gone."

"Gone!"

---

sation and initiating some moderately useful contacts, for which Abbas was duly grateful.

287

Tiberio Prentinaglia nodded his head affirmatively. "Yes, gone. A week ago, it disappeared, and all attempts to find it have been fruitless. Taddeo Talventi summoned me and told me about it. You'll agree that it's strange. The display case is intact. The lock hasn't been touched. No trace of a break-in—none—and yet the bust is no longer there..."

Prentinaglia fell silent and looked at me, as if to judge the effect of his revelation. He went on:

"Well, my dear chap, I told you that there are mysterious things happening here, incomprehensible and inexplicable, as in the days when our Carlo Gozzi reported in his memoirs the strange intrigues on the part of occult powers of which he was the victim. And don't tell me that the affair of the bust is of a natural order and will be cleared up of its own accord one day...no, the investigation has been conducted scrupulously, but it has produced no result. Oh, I assure you that Taddeo Talventi doesn't play tricks..."

I studied Prentinaglia attentively. The story he had told me was certainly strange, but was it true? Was there not some invention on his part? Was he trying to put one over on me? But why? He did not seem to be joking.

Suddenly, he took off his felt hat and passed his hand over his forehead several times. While he was silent and seemingly absorbed in his reflections I took out my watch. It was two o'clock in the morning. All of a sudden, I felt exhausted by fatigue. The impression of malaise that I had experienced during my after-dinner walk came back again.

Finally, Prentinaglia broke the silence by rapping sharply on the table to wake the waiter, who was dozing in the next room. While the man was depositing coins in the little saucer serving that purpose, Prentinaglia said to me: "Come on, my dear chap, we must go home, for I'm taking the express to Rome tomorrow where I'm going to meet Lord Sperling, with whom I'm making a tour of Sicily. So it's lucky that I ran into you this evening! But why the devil have I told you all these strange things? Bah! You're not superstitious, are you?"

288

As he said that, Prentinaglia looked at me with an almost irksome attention. Did he want to take account of the effect that his story had had on me? Doubtless my face disclosed the state of malaise that I was in, for he took me by the arm.

"And that fool Prentinaglia forgot, my poor friend that you've just spent twenty-four hours on a train, and is keeping you here to chat! What a torturer! I'll walk you back to your hotel. Where are you staying?"

"The Victoria—but I'll only be staying there just long enough to find somewhere."

And as we turned the corner of the Frezzaria, while we walked, I told Prentinaglia about the incident at the Casa Trigiani and the plan I had made. He listened to me while letting the tip of his cane trail along the pavement. We arrived thus at the door of the hotel.

"Several rooms...a quiet quarter...yes, I see what you need and I might know somewhere—but how I regret that unfortunate departure, and not being here to help you! At any rate, I'll send you an address tomorrow morning, with information for the location of furniture. Besides which, I'll be back in a few weeks, and we'll meet again 'under the Chinese man.' Sperling will be delighted to know that you're here. Well, my dear chap, sleep well. No bad dreams—and may our Venice be kind to you."

Whether because of the fatigue of the journey, or a certain nervousness due to the incidents of that first night in Venice, I slept quite badly: a slumber both heavy and incomplete, from which I woke up the next day just in time to hear someone knock on my door.

The porter had brought me a letter. I recognized Tiberio Prentinaglia's eccentric handwriting and the seal on the envelope. The ring whose imprint it bore was formed by a cornelian engraved with Kabbalistic symbols. It had belonged to some adept of the occult sciences, of which there had been many in eighteenth-century Venice. The jewel in question was perfectly adapted to the appearance of a sorcerer that Signore

Prentinaglia liked to put on and was one of the facets of his multiple personality. For the moment, however, what interested me above all about him was his perfect knowledge of Venice, thanks to which I did not doubt that he had discovered suitable lodgings for me.

It was with that thought in mind that I broke the conjuratory wax.

Prentinaglia had written:

My dear and very dear friend,

Since you desire to be entirely Venetian, I advise you to go as soon as possible to number 796 Fondamenta Foscarini. Ring the doorbell of the old Palazzo Altinengo ai Carmini. Signora Verana will open the door to you and show you the rooms she has to let. I don't know anything more seductive in the Venice of the settecento. *With the few necessary furnishings, your* mezzanino *will be worthy of the gallant Casanova himself and the visionary Carlo Gozzi. This is the address where you will procure what you need. Signora Verana will render you all the necessary care. As soon as I return I shall come to see you in your lodgings. As for the date,* Non so, *as we say in Venetian. I shake your hand in the French fashion.*

Your very devoted,
Tiberio Prentinaglia.

I folded up the piece of paper. I confess that I felt a little disappointed, at first, without knowing whence that disappointment came. After a few minutes of reflection, I discovered its cause. Prentinaglia had given me the information requested, but he letter made no allusion to our conversation of the previous evening. Not a word about the bizarre story of the bust that had disappeared in mysterious circumstances. At any rate, the essential thing was the address that he had given me, and which I repeated several times as I prepared my shaving equipment: *Palazzo Altnengo ai Carmini, Palazzo Altinengo...*

I knew of two Palazzos Altinengo in Venice, but I had to admit that I did not know of the existence of the one identified to me by Prentinaglia, which he said was situated near the Carmini. On the other hand the church of the Carmini was familiar to me, especially by virtue of its proximity to the *Scuola* of the same name and Tiepolo's charming paintings. More than once I had rung the doorbell of the *Scuola* and given the custodian the one lire bill that permitted one to enter the edifice, climb the staircase to the stucco vaults and contemplate on the ceiling of the great hall the holy and voluptuous figures whose Tiepoloesque grace gave the place the simultaneous appearance of an oratory and a ballroom. The church and the *Scuola* had often attracted me to that quarter of Venice, the popular character of which I liked, especially accentuated by the Campo Santa Margherita.

That *Campo* is, along with that of San Polo, one of the largest in Venice. It is not distinguished by any particularly interesting monument, but I liked its paved extent and the surroundings of poor houses and shops: little groceries, shops selling faience and vulgar fabrics. I liked the bands of ragged children, animated in their frolics, the women with long shawls who traversed it, the merchants of fried fish and *calamari*, the sellers of polenta in the open, its noisy comings and goings, in which tourists only rarely mingled, the majority going to the Carmini and the *Scuola* by gondola, via the canals.

It was not by that means that I counted on going in search of my Palazzo Altinengo. On the contrary, I promised myself the pleasure of a long walk on foot. I would no longer experience therein, I hoped, the singular malaise that had gripped me the day before, during my nocturnal ramble, of which a kind of physical anxiety still remained to me, to which the fresh air and sunlight of a beautiful would doubtless put paid.

I decided to begin with lunch in a restaurant. The one to which I headed was a short distance from the hotel, and when I had ordered a plate of scampi and a bottle of Valpolicella, eaten the delicate crustaceans and drunk a few glasses of the sparkling wine, I felt in perfect mental equilibrium. I had been unused to that impression for a long time, and I attribute its return to the pacifying atmosphere of Venice. Had I not been right to seek shelter in the hospitable and silent city?

These thoughts occupied me until the moment when, my bill being paid, the waiter brought the *candela* closer so that I could light my Virginia, from which I had carefully extracted the straw. After taking the first few puffs I consulted my watch. It was time to set off, via the paved trail of the *calli*, for the Carmini and the Palazzo Altinengo. I therefore got to my feet and, via San Fantin, San Maurizio and the Campo Morosini, reached the Ponte dell'Academia, which crosses the Grand Canal, with a magnificent view.

That view is familiar to me, of course, but it always excites my admiration and I never see the noble curve of that magnificent avenue of water without being moved by its beauty. That sentiment was so powerful that I had some difficulty continuing on my way. It took me through one of the quarters of Venice that I liked best, and in whose narrow *calli* and tranquil *fondamenta* I had often strolled. Today, though, I was not in a mood for idling; a kind of haste pressed me to arrive at the Palazzo Altinengo that Prentinaglia had indicated to me. Thus, I headed for the church of the Carmini by the most direct route.

Once there, it was not difficult for me to find the Fondamenta Foscarini. It runs alongside the *rio* de Santa Margherita and begin within sight of the church. It is a narrow quayside with a parapet, bordered by rather shabby houses of modest appearance. Two buildings, however, were distinguished from the rest, and were evidently former palazzos fallen from their antique splendor and let out in parts. One of them, the Foscarini, had given its name to the Fondamenta; the other was the Altinengo, of lesser dimension but equally dilapidated.

Constructed in the eighteenth century, it had three upper floors above a *mezzanino*. The façade, coated with grey roughcast, was flaking in places, but the beautiful lines of the architecture and the harmony of the balconied windows still testified to what the edifice had once been. A sort of portal, with columns surmounted by stones vases, preceded it. On one of the columns, juxtaposed bells corresponded to different floors of the palazzo. That of the entresol bore the name of Signora Verana.

Before tugging the iron ring of that bell-rope, I retreated as far as the parapet to get a better view of the Palazzo Altinengo, which, according to Prentinaglia's indications, was to become my lodging. Only the windows of the *mezzanino* displayed the paper strips advertising apartments for hire; the other floors appeared to be occupied. On the balconies of one of them, ocher-colored awnings were displayed; from another, flower-pots reminiscent of salad-bowls were suspended. The closed shutters of the *mezzanino* were painted pale green. The general appearance of the dwelling, wretched and scarcely attractive, attested to an advanced decrepitude, but I had confidence in the taste of my friend Prentinaglia, and, deliberately, I pulled the bell-rope that ought to put me in the presence of Signora Verana and give me access to the Palazzo Altinengo.

After a grating noise, a carillon resounded, distant and cracked. I waited for a little while. No one came. The portal remaining closed, I rang again. No response. Signora Verana was obviously hard of hearing. I took a few steps back and considered the façade of the palazzo again. The sun, which had been veiled by a cloud before, was shining brightly now, and laid bare all its decrepitude in all its misery.

That observation, which ought to have sent me away, on the contrary, pleased me strangely. Suddenly, I felt an inexplicable attraction to that broken-down and dejected palazzo—which I attempted to rationalize. It was simultaneously so noble and so pitiful, that Palazzo Altinengo, so leprous and so morose! And what a silence surrounded it! The Campo in front of the church of the Carmini was deserted. There was no one on the bridge. On the *rio*, two large empty barges were moored, groaning faintly on their chains. In the jade-colored water, the heads of vegetables were floating. All that had something humble and mysterious about it, and formed a frame so appropriate to the old decaying palazzo, which seemed ready to totter on its crumbling foundations.

No, I would not live anywhere else in Venice, in spite of the obstinacy of Signora Verana in not responding to my appeal. Once again, I rang without result; finally, irritated, I tugged the rope of the bell corresponding to one of the other floors. Too bad for the tenant I was disturbing thus!

I had been lucky, for on one of the convex balconies, beneath an ocher awning, an old man leaned over. From the height of his improvised podium, the old man explained to me that Signora Verana was in Mestre today, but that she would definitely be back the following morning. That news reassured me, for between now and tomorrow no one would rent the apartment that, without knowing why, I already considered as mine. I was disappointed, for I would rather have gone into the Palazzo Altinengo immediately. That urgency, moreover, astonished me slightly. Since my illness and my chagrin, life had no longer been anything for me but a sequence of actions devoid of interest, repeatedly indifferently; this was the first time I had experienced a desire.

I could no more help the fact that Signora Verana was in Mestre than I could stand there indefinitely contemplating the closed door—all the more so because the sky was darkening and the clouds, scattered at first, were joining up to become a misty blanket. Having darted one last glance at the Palazzo Altinengo, therefore, I walked at hazard through the nearby *calli*, while reflecting on the strange interest acquired for me by the façade of the dilapidated building, to which the indicative and kabbalistic gesture of my friend Tiberio Prentinaglia, the great expert in apartments for hire and connoisseur of mysterious Venice, had directed me.

A few drops of rain extracted me from those reflections, which I must have been following for some time, for I only interrupted them some distance away from the Carmini, beside the church dedicated to San Giovanni Decollato, whom Venetian dialect makes into San Zan Degola. I realized then that I was only a few steps away from the Musei Civici. Why not take shelter there to let the downpour pass? If it continued, the *vaporetto* that made a stop at the Fondaco dei Turchi, where the museum is located, would take me back to the Piazza San Marco.

All of old Venice lives again in the rooms of the Musei Civici, and I had spent many hours in the past examining the thousand objects that comprise its repertoire, evocative of ancient Venetian mores: prints, weapons, fabrics, costumes, items of furniture, bindings. That day, however, after the merest of glances around the main hall, where the image of the Peloponnesian Morosini stand amid trophies and flags, I headed with a sudden haste toward the display case where I had more than once admired the little bust of the Venetian gentleman, about whose mysterious disappearance Prentinaglia had told me the previous evening.

Curiously, I leaned over it. The place allocated to the bust was empty, but none of the objects that surrounded it was missing. Still the same vases in Basano or Nove faience, the same white porcelain cups decorated with tiny gilded landscapes. The only absentee was the mysterious patrician with the enigmatic smile. Into whose hands had it fallen? Why had the thief, out of the many precious objects the museum contained, chosen just than one? What could the reason for the singular larceny have been?

For it had surely been stolen, and Prentinaglia had been wasting his time trying to mystify me with his fantastic stories. What motive had he been obeying? I was slightly resentful of his absurd ramblings. He must think me very credulous—but I was not at all disposed to allow myself to be troubled by such nonsense. The hypothesis of a theft doubtless seeming too simple to my friend Prentinaglia, and he had substituted another that pleased his imagination more.

That theft, however, even as a theft, remained interesting, because of the inexplicability of its motive, which denoted a very specific intention. Had some determine collector employed that means of appropriating the curious object? What relationship could it have to the supernatural events of which

Venice, according to Prentinaglia, had been the theater, and on the subject of which I remained very skeptical?

I had reached that point in my reveries when they were interrupted by the nearby cough of one of the keepers. My long pause before the display case had attracted his attention. The brave man had surely been given orders to keep an eye on the visitors, and I must have seemed suspicious to him. Just as long as he did not, in an excess of zeal, have me arrested! My visit to Signora Verana the following day would have been compromised, and the mischievous Venetian gentleman would have done me a bad turn. I had done nothing to warrant him exercising his malice against me. He had given enough proof of it by his mysterious disappearance to have no need of any further exploit.

These thoughts amused me while I went back to my hotel on foot, and were still occupying me when, after dinner that evening, I went to sit down in the Café Florian.

I did not find myself alone there, even though none of my old companions—Prentinaglia, Sperling or Hohenberg—sat down beside me "under the Chinese man." Without suspecting it, I had brought my Venetian unknown with me.

I saw once again, distinctly, his delicate and sly physiognomy, and interrogated his image curiously. What had he done in life for him to have retained therefrom that simultaneously complacent and melancholy smile? Of that eighteenth-century Venice, with which his mode of dress and the form of his wig attested that he was contemporary, he must have known all the pleasures, all the graces and all the refinements. He must have loved and been loved. Had love been sweet or bitter to him? What had he been thinking as he walked under the same arcades of the Procuraties, wearing a tricorn hat, his face covered by a white cardboard mask?

Of all that he had done and all that he had been, however, nothing now remained but that fragile bust with the mocking eyes and he slender mouth, that enigmatic bust to which the nonetheless singular fact of its disappearance added something even more enigmatic.

This time, Signora Verana was at home, for the response to my ringing the bell was the grating of the chain that operated the lock of the great portal. It opened slightly, and I pushed the batten. I found myself in a narrow courtyard. At the far side I perceived, beneath an arch, the beginning of a broad stone stairway. To the right, there was another door, low-set and painted in the same pale green as the shutters of the *mezzanino*, behind which I was not long delayed in hearing heavy muffled footsteps. Soon afterwards, a hand lifted a latch and I suddenly found myself in the presence of Signora Verana.

She was a woman about sixty years old, short and thick-set, dressed in black, with a square face, sunken eyes, a jaundiced complexion and gray hair. She seemed suspicious and taciturn, and looked at me with a curiosity devoid of benevolence. At the name of Prentinaglia however, her face brightened with a smile of sorts and she sketched a sort of bow that was not without dignity—after which the conversation began.

The Signora listened to my explanations, her eyes lowered. When I had finished, as best I could—for my Venetian is not impeccable—Signora Verana smiled again. Evidently, I was now more sympathetic to her, and it was almost with interest that she relied.

"Signore Prentinaglia is correct; the *mezzanino* is for rent—but did he also tell you that the rooms have not been occupied for a long time, and that you'll be very isolated, without any communication with the rest of the palazzo?"

The *mezzanino*, in fact, as Signora Verana explained, formed an entirely separate apartment. One went into it through the green door on whose threshold we were negotiating. The staircase visible at the back of the small courtyard gave access to the other floors. It was to one of those floors that Signora Verana would retreat if she let the *mezzanino*, one of whose rooms she was occupying temporarily. Nevertheless, she would not refuse, in case it was rented, to take responsibility for the tenant's housekeeping, in spite of the inconvenience of the service.

All Signora Verana's explanations, though scarcely inviting, did not discourage me at all. On the contrary, that dearth of neighborhood, that solitude, pleased me as much as the sight of the dilapidated and crumbling Palazzo Altinengo had pleased me. Nevertheless, I wondered why, out of all the apartments for rent in Venice, Prentinaglia had told me that this one was suit me particularly.

Most of the time, these fallen palazzos in the popular quarters do not retain any of their old interior decoration. The antique-dealer has passed that way, and the Altinengo ought to have been similar, whatever Prentinaglia had written in his letter. Moreover, its external appearance and situation had nothing remarkably picturesque about it. And yet, I did not doubt that Prentinaglia had had his reasons for sending me to Signora Verana. At any rate, it was necessary for me to visit the *mezzanino*.

Signora Verana acquiesced to my request. Not without politeness, she excused herself from preceding me to show me the way.

Once through the door a rather gloomy staircase presented itself, whose worn steps I felt beneath my feet. As I climbed them I noticed the saltpeter staining the walls. It was as if the Palazzo Altinengo were advertising in advance that it was damp. And it was still the warm season! What would it be like in the winter months? I was about to make that observation to Signora Verana when she stopped before a closed door.

From the landing, I examined that door with a certain surprise, mingled with a certain hope, for it was quite beautiful, in natural, knotty wood, marvelously veined and patina-encrusted, strengthened by copper plates. While Signora Verana grappled with the recalcitrant lock, I noticed something shiny on the brown and black floor-tiles. Among the little marble cubes that formed the *pavimento*, a nacreous fragment had been inserted. That eccentricity interested me. It reminded me of Prentinaglia, and I began to understand why he judged this Palazzo Altinengo worth of a visit and why he had pointed me in the direction of Signora Verana's *mezzanino* for rent in the distant and solitary quarter of the Carmini, with its little nacre disk set on its threshold, like a beauty spot from some Venetian visage of yesteryear!

The vestibule into which we penetrated was rather vast. The walls were decorated with brown arabesques and stucco tracery on a pink background. On the ceiling, similar ornaments framed medallions whose subjects I could scarcely make out in the semi-darkness. All of that, it goes without saying, revealed a state of extreme decrepitude. The paint was flaking off the walls and the stucco of the moldings was cracked, but the ensemble had that kind of simultaneously elegant and shabby grace that provides the impoverished and melancholy charm of old Venetian dwellings.

From the vestibule, several doors in the same knotty and veined wood gave access to the various parts of the dwelling. The one for which Signora Verana headed opened into a charming room of sizeable dimensions, similarly rather dark, in which I nevertheless immediately remarked a magnificent fireplace in antique green marble. I could see it more clearly when the Signora had opened the disjointed shutters of the windows overlooking the Rio Santa Margherita. Save for the fireplace, the room offered nothing very remarkable. Shreds of paper hung from the walls. To tell the truth, it was uninhabitable, and I began to suspect that I would never be able to install myself in the Palazzo Altinengo. So it was with considerable urgency that I followed Signora Verana into the adjacent room.

That second room, infinitely better conserved than the preceding one, presented a curious and original décor. To be sure the ceiling was cracked and the wood paneling had lost the hangings that once covered it, replaced by a layer of paint, but those empty panels were surrounded by stucco banderoles and surmounted by medallions displaying mythological figures finely modeled by hand. On the mosaic *pavimento* a garland of fruits and flowers unfurled, flowing from four horns of plenty in the corners.

The ensemble of that decoration was in charming taste and delightfully colored. Unfortunately, I could not see any easy means of exploiting it, and the best thing to do seemed to me to be to carry away the pleasant memory and looking for somewhere other than that baroque but overly uncomfortable *mezzanino* in which to set up home. I was about to explain that to Signora Verana, but she had disappeared, and I heard her opening the shutters of the room into which she had preceded me, and on the threshold of which I came to a sudden halt.

Oh! This time, I understood my friend Prentinaglia completely.

It was a sort of drawing-room, almost square, with two windows, between which stood a yellow marble fireplace, surmounted by a mirror with a gilded spiral frame. The tint of the marble and the old gold were complemented by the color of the walls. They were painted in a delightful shade of amber yellow, like honey, and from that background, in an exquisitely soft mildness of hues, white stucco moldings projected, forming symmetrical arabesques. Those arabesques, admirable fantastic in their design, on each of three sides of the room, framed large panels of white faience, on which were depicted, in gold and black, scenes of chinoiserie. To the right and left of each of these pictures were two smaller ones, in thin stucco frames.

The same décor of chinoiseries was continued on the ceiling, completed by a fresco depicting birds, flowers and insects. The *pavimento* was incrusted, here and there, with fragments of nacre, and in one of the corners of the room stood a full-length mirror in a yellow marble frame, reflecting it in all its sumptuous and ludicrous fantasy, and in all its unexpected and charming mystery.

To be sure, I had admired more than once in Venice the delicate stucco-work in which Venetian decorators excelled, but I had seen nothing similar to what I had before my eyes, nothing that attained such beauty in fantasy. Mirrors, arabesques, figures faiences—all of it formed an ensemble of a unique grace and refinement. It created an impression of surprise and mystery to encounter that unexpected marvel in the depths of such a wretchedly poor old palazzo, so irresistible decrepit, with its gray façade, its moldy shutters and its decayed and corroded appearance. Oh, Prentinaglia had accurately divined the attraction that the décor would exert on me in directing my search toward this ancient palazzo lost in this distant quarter of Venice! What place could be more propitious to shelter my solitude with its silence and its remoteness, to soften it with this atmosphere of gilded honey, to occupy it with these arabesques, favorable to the unfurling of dreams, and to amuse it with these Chinese figures, who would be the minuscule and obliging interlocutrices of my melancholy leisure.

I had turned to Signora Verana.

"All this will suit me perfectly, Signora Verana. Would you care to draw up the tenancy agreement for me: I'd like to move in as soon as possible."

Signora Verana, who had not pronounced a word during my visit, agreed to my request with a nod of the head. That mutism seemed to me to be a good omen. Since the Signora would take responsibility for my service, I would not have to dread her loquacity. That taciturn person would be the ideal housekeeper—and housekeeper was the correct term, for la Verana, by virtue of her reserved manner, differed from the common run of servants. Certainly, she did not have the absurd gentility of the good Sorelle Trigiani, but in default of the thousand attentions that the dear old ladies had heaped upon me, I would at least find, in this matron with the unprepossessing but honest face, respect for my habits and the indispensable cares.

There were still a number of rooms belonging to the *mezzanino* on the far side of the vestibule. I had to follow Signora Verana there. It was in one of them that she was temporarily resident, next door to a small kitchen. She explained to me briefly that, as soon as I moved in, she would withdraw to the home of friends who lived on one of the upper floors. I would, therefore, as she had warned me, be entirely on my own. She

301

would only come in to perform the fairly simple services that I required of her.

Save for that room, which was very nearly habitable, all of that part of the palazzo was in a state of extreme dilapidation and truly seemed to be on the brink of ruin. My domain concluded with a fairly large room from which an exterior staircase gave access to a garden planted with vegetables and a few trees. At the far side of the garden stood a bizarre construction, a sort of small temple with columns on the fronton: the former Casino of the Palazzo. I cast a rather indifferent glance over all of that. I was in a hurry to see the stucco drawing-room again.

A ray of sunlight made it even more beautiful and gilded. An atmosphere of luminous sadness filled it, and I felt myself griped by an indefinable emotion. Would I not be an intruder in this place? Was I not going to disturb its abandonment? By what right, after all, did I dare to introduce myself into its mysterious silence?

At any rate, I would not be a very troublesome intruder! I would not be bringing with me either the noisy joy of youth or the laughter of health. I played so little part in life, and yet, it was to try to live again that I had returned to Venice to seek in my past something to connect to my present misery! A vain attempt, a chimerical hope. It was scarcely a living person who would welcome into the peace of his semi-death that old Palazzo Altinengo.

And all of a sudden, in the tall mirror, standing in its marble frame, I saw myself, distant and vague, as if my image had abruptly entered into the mute reflected region of ghosts...

It took me a week to make provision for my summary installation in my new lodgings. My first concern was to have them completely and scrupulously cleaned. Signora Verana took care of that by means of two aged neighbors, who carefully dusted the walls and washed the mosaic floor-tiles with abundant water. While the two women busied themselves with that task, I occupied myself with the equipment of my corner of the palazzo with the necessary furniture.

Thanks to the addresses that Prentinaglia had left when he departed, I was able to hire a very proper iron-framed bed with a new mattress, and a dressing-table with all its utensils. The indispensable linen I bought. As for the other furniture, the idea of uglifying my fantastic domain with vile modern objects being repugnant, I addressed myself to the honest Lorenzo Zotarelli.

Zotarelli is a Venetian antique dealer. Previously recommended by my friends the C***s, who had found him satisfactory, I had had no complaints. Certainly, not everything that Zotarelli sells is, strictly speaking, antique, but if he does not admit that openly, he has in front of suspect pieces a smile so broad that one can, with a little practice, be informed as to their authenticity. If the buyer does not understand the advertisement and persists in his project, Zotarelli does not go so far as to oppose it. That would be too much to ask of him. Every profession has its own morality, and Zotarelli has that of his. So much the worse for ignorant amateurs and presumptuous connoisseurs! Zotarelli is, therefore, from his own viewpoint, a very honest man—and, moreover, an excellent and amiable useful man.

In the Spadaria, behind the Piazza San Marco, he has a cramped shop heaped in a disorderly fashion with glassware, faience, lace and small trinkets, but in the vicinity of Santa Maria Formosa another store serves to shelter bulkier objects. I had already had recourse to his good offices many times, for, without being a collector, I had not neglected to accumulate a few Venetian antiquities during my various sojourns in Venice. It was, therefore, entirely appropriate that I should have recourse to him on the present occasion, in which it was a matter of him selling me the old furniture I needed, with the promise to buy it back on my departure.

When I went into the shop in the Spadaria, Zotarelli was unpacking one of those Venetian glass centerpieces formed of an assembly of vases, statuettes, balustrades, columns and porticos, which transform the table at who center they are placed into a fragile and charming miniature garden. Absorbed in this delicate operation, he did not see me come in, and I was able to examine him at my ease—which I had never done before, for my attention was usually more devoted to the objects on sale.

Zotarelli appeared to me as a small, stout man with a large head and agile hands. I was admiring their dexterity when he noticed me, which caused him to utter an exclamation of welcome, soon followed by the customary dialogue, in the course of which I naturally told him about my intentions with regard to the Palazzo Altinengo. That I had become its tenant seemed to surprise him slightly, for he looked at me in a strange fashion. When I mentioned Prentinaglia's name he sketched a grimace, which I noticed and attributed to some quarrel between them. At any rate, Zotarelli did not follow his grimace with any comment, and offered to take me immediately to his store in Santa Maria Formosa.

When I had chosen the various items of furniture that seemed to me to be the most suitable, Zotarelli said: "I'll send all this to the Palazzo Altinengo ai Carmini, then, to Signora Verana?"

So he knew Signora Verana. That seemed to be a good opportunity to obtain some information about the person in question. Who was she? Could she be trusted? How, and under what authority, did she come to be renting out a floor of the dilapidated palazzo?

Zotarelli, who was usually loquacious, replied to my questions evasively and prudently, as if he were holding something back. La Verana was from a good family that had fallen on hard times. He had known her parents. She was probably a very respectable lady, but he knew very little about her. And Zotarelli assumed the expression that he wore in the presence of suspect objects. His attitude intrigued me. Why so much reticence?

When I pressed him further, he ended up saying: "I don't know any more. Go ask Signore Prentinaglia, damn it, since

304

he's the one who sent you there, to the Palazzo Altinengo! Enough! I believe I recall that this Verana was once the housekeeper in Lord Sperling's home in the Casa degli Spiriti. Since then, she's left the place. It's said that she would have liked to open a family boarding-house in the Palazzo Altinengo, but the Palazzo is badly situated and would need too many repairs. And then... You, don't you need anything else, then?"

Evidently, my determination to live in that solitary and decrepit Palazzo, far from the most frequented quarters of Venice, the Piazza San Marco and the Spadaria, surprised the excellent Zotarelli. Without permitting himself any direct observation, he obviously disapproved of my plan. Zotarelli regretted seeing his furniture emigrating to the distant *mezzanino* on the Fondamenta Foscarini. He promised nevertheless to send the items the following day, but I noticed that, although he was normally so obliging, he did not offer to bring them himself or to help me install them. Zotarelli had some prejudice against Prentinaglia, Signora Verana and the Palazzo Altinengo that I could not understand. Venetian souls are complicated and secretive, however, and I knew that I would get nothing more out of him.

I still had a few things to do before dinner. I wanted to buy shawls of the kind sold in the shops of the Rialto for the two old ladies who had cleaned my future lodgings. I was therefore heading in that direction when I suddenly felt tired. A kind of dizziness stunned me, and I thought I was going to fall over. At that moment I was in front of the church of Santa Maria Formosa. An empty gondola was going past on the *rio*. I made a sign to the gondolier, who came to the foot of the steps. The roaming *rampino* used his hook to secure his position. Once I had slumped on to the cushions, I felt better, but the alert proved that my strength had not yet returned. The warning I had received on the evening of my arrival should have rendered me more prudent. A tour of the lagoon would put me right. Nothing is more restful for overtaxed nerves.

Such excursions have always been one of my most cherished Venetian passions. For them alone I used the gondola, which I scarcely employed otherwise, preferring pedestrian rambling. For the moment, though, I was incapable of walking through the *calli*. My malaise would have been exasperated by that, whereas it was already being soothed by stretching out on the cushions and by the rhythmic sway of the supple boat. The one I had taken was truly excellent. It was *premiata*, as is said of those gondolas whose *barcaroï* have won prizes in the regattas. This barcarole was a tall, slim and elegant fellow, a skillful rower—as I perceived as soon as he plied his oar. Thus, we rapidly covered the distance that separated Santa Maria Formosa from the Fondamenta Nuove, where the Rio dei Mendicanti opened into the lagoon and the powerful and noble arch of its marble bridge curved between the sky and the water.

I love going into the lagoon via the Rio and the Ponte dei Mendicanti. As soon as we had passed under it, the whole extent of the waters appeared, flat, calm and harmoniously tinted. No part of the vast marine mirror that surrounds Venice is smoother and more peaceful. The tide is hardly sensible in that part of the lagoon, which is known as the dead lagoon and which bathes, in order to justify its name further, the Isle of the Dead, the red San Michele with the crimson crenellated walls, like a fortress of sleep.

It is also that lagoon with the somnolent waters which surrounds with its eternal silence the other islands that form with San Michele, on the insular flank of Venice, its northern archipelago: Murano, where the glassworks are; Burano, where the agile fingers of lacemakers weave the celebrated arabesques of Venetian fantasy; Torcello and Mazzorbo, where fever is endemic;[49] San Francesco in Deserto, whose

---

[49] Torcello was the first of the Venetian islands to be settled and was for a long time the most populous and most important, but the change in sea level that created the "dead lagoon" turned it into a swamp that proved to be an ideal breeding-ground for malarial mosquitoes, rendering it virtually uninha-

Franciscan cypresses are reflected in strangely solitary water. That whole ensemble is singularly melancholy, although the play of light on the lagoon is sometimes strangely iridescent. I have contemplated prodigious festivals of color there, but it is more often dominated by an impression of sadness without bitterness, misery without regret and solitude without anguish, so peaceful, monotonous and silent is it.

That day, I must say, the sight of those things was excee-dingly melancholy. A sort of mist, of an extreme delicacy, floated between the sky and the water. It enveloped San Mi-chele with its light, moist tissue and made Murano into a kind of phantom isle. It was not a day for venturing far and going to savor in the middle of the lagoon the particular sentiment that one experiences there in similarly misty dusks, when one feels that one is not in the world of the living there. In any case, it was getting late, so I instructed the gondolier simply to go around the city and re-enter it via the Canareggio. He com-plied with the order immediately, and the gondola continued gliding smoothly under the regular impulsion of the oar.

I listened with half-closed eyes. I listened to the man's footsteps on the carpet at the poop, the various sounds of the water and the wood, with reassured attention. It was a distrac-tion from the indefinable malaise that I felt once again, that species of anxiety without cause, which might easily have resembled fear. And yet there was nothing that might motivate that absurd sensation.

Nevertheless, as we moved over that motionless water, my internal disquiet increased. In vain, by way of diversion, I tried to think about precise things: the furniture chosen at Zo-tarelli's, certain details of the ornamentation of the Palazzo Altinengo, even what I was going to eat at dinner. In spite of everything, the same impression continue to grip me to the point of suffering. It was so strong that I was driven to speak

---

bitable. The smaller island of Mazzorbo experienced similar problems.

to the gondolier in order to try to break the anguish that was oppressing me, and I turned toward him abruptly.

He doubtless interpreted my gesture to mean that I was asking him where we were, for, pointing to a square building that was looming up in the mist at the point of Venice that extended furthest into the lagoon, he called out to me as he leaned over his oar: "That's the Casa degli Spiriti, Signore."

We were, indeed, in front of the Casa degli Spiriti. It had scarcely changed since I had last seen it, before Lord Sperling bought it, doubtless to install his psychic research laboratory far from indiscreet eyes and ears—for Sperling was an adept of the occult sciences. Already, when I had known him, he had been very preoccupied with such questions.

In spite of its new purpose and its new owner, the Casa still presented very nearly the same appearance. The exterior had not been modified; the façade was still coated in the same yellow roughcast. Lord Sperling had limited himself to reestablishing certain formerly bricked-up windows, repairing a few damaged balconies and reconstructing the tall chimneys, hooded in a manner reminiscent of a turban, so characteristic of Venetian dwellings. It was, however, mostly in the interior that he must have effected the restorations the Prentinaglia had mentioned.

It was possible that the Casa—a former Palazzo Salvizzi—had conserved decorations that Lord Sperling could have had taken out. He was not lacking in taste, nor in curiosity, and in the times when I had kept company with him and we found ourselves at the Florian under the Cinaman with Hohenberg and Prentinaglia, I had seen him buy old furniture enthusiastically, with a view to a future installation in Venice. At that time he was living in a hotel, leaving his acquisitions on deposit with the merchants. He had doubtless had them extracted to ornament the rooms of the Casa, whose garden, which overlooked the lagoon from a previously-abandoned terrace, now displayed carefully-pruned trees and rose-bushes that overflowed the balustrade and hung down almost to the water.

In spite of that flowery terrace, the Casa degli Spiriti conserved a scarcely welcoming aspect, to which the mist lent a character of mysterious singularity. Lord Sperling had certainly found a propitious location for his endeavors. No one would disturb him there in his incantations and experiments. The fact that Sperling had been a disciple of William Crookes left no doubt as to their nature.

In the epoch of the Chinaman, as I have said, Sperling was already inclined to curiosity regarding the beyond. I had often heard him relate the surprising results obtained by the English scientist: strange phenomena such as levitation, the transport of objects, the manifestation of mysterious flowers, and materializations recorded on photographic plates. After having studied the theory, Sperling had wanted to move on to the practice. Hence, the purchase of the Casa degli Spiriti, whose popular nickname doubtless seemed to him to be a good omen.

All the "miracles" that Crookes obtained by courtesy of borrowed mediums, Sperling intended to seek by the same means. From that point of view, Venice had no lack of resources, and I wondered whether Signora Verana, who, Zotarelli had told me, had been in Sperling's service, might have played a role in his psychic experiments, and whether, after all, the unusual disappearance of the bust from the Musei Civici might have some connection with the phantasmagorical games whose existence the superstitious Prentinaglia had suggested to me during our encounter in the Café Florian.

All that was, at any rate, unimportant. Was not the essential thing that Prentinaglia had told me about the Palazzo Altinengo and that Signora Verana carried out the duties that she had undertaken for me punctually? As for the charming bust in the Musei Civici, whether it had disappeared from its display case because of some thief or the artifice of some sorcerer, it was no concern of mine! The fine Venetian aristocrat that it represented must have been taken by one evil means or the other. He must have had many adventures while alive and this one was unlikely to displease his ironic and smiling shade.

As I reflected on these things, the gondola reached the entrance to the Canareggio. Behind us, the lagoon extended its misty and crepuscular waters, from which rose an odor both saline and muddy. In front of us, the first lanterns were being lit and there were lights on both banks in the windows of the old palazzos, so picturesque in their populous living decrepitude. The silence of the dead waves was succeeded by the multitudinous rumor of an animated quarter. We passed heavy barges and rapid *sandolos*.

Gradually, with each stroke of the oar, we reentered into life and I experienced an undeniable relief, to the extent that when we arrived at the Rialto, I signaled to the gondolier to set me down. I wanted to go back to the hotel on foot, after having bought in one of the shops on the bridge the two Venetian shawls that I intended to give to the two old women who, under Signora Verana's orders, had helped with the cleaning of my *mezzanino* in the Palazzo Altinengo, of which I would soon be taking possession.

It was the day after that excursion on the lagoon that the furniture sent by Zotarelli arrived at the Palazzo Altinengo. I had gone to the Palazzo in advance to receive them and to decide exactly where I would put them. Having done that, I leaned on the windowsill to await their arrival.

The weather that day was very bright and very mild, and nothing remained in the sky of the previous day's mist. I no longer felt the malaise I had experienced. In any case, was it not necessary for me to get used to such alternations of profound depression and relative health? I ought not to forget that I was still, if not an invalid, at least a convalescent, who lacked, to assist his cure, the violent desire to live that succeeds grave physical crises and which is such a powerful assistance in similar cases. All that I could hope for in Venice, therefore, was a sort of acceptance of existence, a sort of acquiescence with its melancholy monotony.

To arrive at that state of joyless peace and indifferent calm, the old Palazzo Altinengo was about to lend me its silence and its solitude. I had sensed right away that it would be hospitable to me and that it was, in some sense, destined, by virtue of the immediate attraction that it had exerted upon me. Perhaps, one day, if that attraction turned into a durable attachment, I might even envisage installing myself here permanently—but for the moment, it was still no more than an improvised encampment.

At about two o'clock I saw the large boat containing the furniture sent by Zotarelli approaching. Heavy and round-bellied, it landed at the steps of the Fondamenta. Zotarelli had sent me two men to unload it. One of them handed me a letter in which the antique dealer apologized for not coming in person. He wished me a happy sojourn in my new lodgings, but that wish did not seem to me to be formulated without a certain irony. The worthy Zotarelli definitely "had something against" the Palazzo Altinengo, as they say.

I folded up his note and occupied myself giving my orders to the porters. I must admit that they set about their work with a promptitude that is not habitual in Venetians. They seemed to be in a hurry to finish the job, and while placing the furniture in the indicated positions they darted furtive glances to the right and the left. When the work was done and they had pocketed their tips, they ran downstairs and regained their boat, which I heard drawing away over the water of the canal with powerful strokes of the oars.

This is how I had made use of the three habitable rooms of the mezzanino. In the room with the green marble fireplace I had installed my dressing-table. In the one with the mythological medallions my bed was hidden behind a tall screen with two sections, fabricated with one of those old Venetian papers that have the charm of an antique fabric when faded. A large wardrobe, a table, a few armchairs completed the furniture, in company with a convex chest of drawers painted with fruits and flowers, which matched the mosaics of the *parvimento* very well. For the stucco drawing-room, in which it was important, above all, not to allow anything to mask the décor of the walls, I had chosen at Zotarelli's one of those large lac-

311

quer tables of which many were made in eighteenth-century Venice. On a yellow background, Chinamen and pagodas were designed in black and gold. A comfortable rococo sofa and four armchairs constituted the seating. That was all. For lighting, there were four large Bassano candelabras and brackets in smoked Murano glass, which I had placed above each of the little panels of stucco and faience that accompanied those of larger dimension, whose bizarre and charming beauty comprised the principal ornamentation of that strange place, where a carnivalesque China mingled with the Venice of the era of masks. As for the fireplace, it was sufficient in itself, with its yellow marble and its mirrors, amid their stonework decorations.

Signora Verana had helped me to move in, silently. On arrival, I had paid her the rent for the first quarter, and, her zeal doubtless augmented thereby, she offered to help me redistribute the contents of my trunks in the wardrobe and the chest of drawers. While she was busy with that I studied her more closely than I had hitherto.

Signora Verana was evidently a rather bizarre creature, with her thickset body, her square jaundiced face and her deep-set eyes—whose gaze, when it fixed on you, was so sharp that it seemed to transpierce you, as if you were no-existent and offered no consistency to its acuity. Yes, Signora Verana was a singular individual. Traces were distinguishable in her of a status superior to the one in which she now appeared to find herself. What adventures had she passed through before ending up renting a stranger a few dilapidated rooms in an old run-down palazzo, and accepting an ancillary role with regard to that tenant?

To be sure, she had already done the same for Lord Sperling, as Zotarelli had told me. I was on the point of asking her about that, but I changed my mind. Signora Verana's principal virtue was her taciturnity, and there are taciturn individuals who, if encouraged, easily become chatterboxes of the worst sort. The Signora, by virtue of her function, was about to become involved in my quotidian existence, so her silence was too precious for me to do anything that might serve as a pretext for her to depart therefrom. I therefore abstained and swore to refrain from asking any questions. I limited myself to agreeing once again with Signora Verana the services that she would undertake to perform for me.

She would take care of the cleaning the apartment and the laundry, and would furnish the morning chocolate. For my meals, I expected to go to the restaurant. A little trattoria I knew in the neighborhood would free me from the need to go as far as the Piazza when it seemed too far to walk. If I did not want to go out, Signora Verana would prepare what was necessary: eggs, pâtés and a glass of Chianti. All of that having been definitively settled, Signora Verana showed me where to find the supply of candles; then, having garnished the candelabras and the brackets, she cast one last glance around and left.

I was now alone in my new lodgings, and that desired moment was pleasant. The attraction that had drawn me toward the old Palazzo Altinengo persisted, in spite of Zotarelli's disapproving expressions and reticence. Nevertheless, I had no illusions about the inconveniences of such a dwelling. I knew full well that it would be uncomfortable, especially as the season advanced. Venetian palazzos are difficult to warm and the one I was going to live in promised me a few numb fingertips. The windows were badly fitted and the old doors in curl-grained wood let in numerous draughts. Moreover, the extreme decrepitude of the building threatened damp from which nothing would be able to spare me, but to which I resigned myself in advance.

I even envisaged the descent of my *mezzanino* into the canal. The foundations must be in a very poor state and certain depressions of the *pavimento*, bulges in the walls and cracks in the ceilings were warning signs—but I had confidence, in spite of everything, in the vigilance of the Venetian municipality. Venice is the city where one sees more bent-over, dejected and moribund houses than anywhere else in the world, which only se to stay upright by some miracle of equilibrium. The

Palazzo Altinengo had doubtless been realizing that miracle for a long time, and would doubtless realize it for a long time yet, under the surveillance of a discreet but knowledgeable local authority. And what did it matter, anyway? The risk left me quite indifferent. What did it matter to someone who accorded little importance to life and asked nothing of it, in sum, but rest and forgetfulness?

From that point of view, had I not found in the Palazzo Altinengo a place that suited my desire for solitude and silence? Had I not come to Venice in search of isolation and tranquility? To be sure, I had promised my doctors to observe certain precepts of hygiene, to mingle my rest with a little exercise, but I already sensed that I would have difficulty conforming to their prescriptions. The painful and insidious feelings of malaise that I had experienced several times since my arrival scarcely disposed me to movement and walking, while everything in the décor that was about to surround me inclined me to a sedentary existence and to indistinct dreams in which the hours passed without overburdening one with the weight of their heavy wings, charged with regrets and memories.

And I imagined, not without pleasure, slow days and slow evenings spent in the stucco drawing room with the ingenious arabesques and chimerical chinoiseries, which the great fires of Autumn and the light of candles would illuminate with their tremulous reflections the figures and the pagodas of the faience panels, would brighten the spiral moldings and the unevenness of the stonework, and cause the enigmatic fragments of nacre in the mosaic of the *pavimento* to glitter.

It was in these reflections that I waited for the time to light the candles. I was curious to see the effect that their light would produce on the faiences and stuccos, and I confess that my expectations were surpassed. In the candlelight, the stucco drawing room was even more admirable. It was filled with a kind of gilded atmosphere of incomparable softness. Every figure, every ornament, every spiral and every piece of stonework seemed to participate in that luminous diffusion. Only the tall mirror, upright in its yellow marble frame, opposed its metallic, cold and strangely refractory surface thereto. It stood there like a doorway open to another world, and, in a real dream, one could see therein, in reversed perspective, that same stucco drawing room, with the same arabesques and the same figurines, but situated at a distance of centuries, in an inaccessible and mysteriously nocturnal retreat.

The first fortnight of my sojourn at the Palazzo Altinengo passed without any noteworthy incident. In the morning, Signora Verana brought my breakfast. It comprised skillfully-warmed chocolate, buttered toast and a few clusters of black grapes of the variety known as *Fragola* because it has a rather pronounce flavor of strawberries. As for my midday and evening meals, I took them in one of Venice's numerous restaurants. I alternated between the Vapore, the Capelo Nero, the Città di Firenze, the Anticho Cavalletto and even the Bella Venezia, whose somber space, with the half-paneled walls and odor of wine and salt water, I liked. I went to the Florian on a regular basis to drink a cup of black coffee and sit under the Chinaman, but what was that Chinaman by comparison with the magnificent mandarins and delicate princesses who ornamented the faience panels of my gilded stucco drawing room?

Although the weather was fine I did not feel much like walking. The troubles from which I had suffered since my arrival were not renewed, but had left in their place a vague fatigue, a sort of physical reverie, sometimes annoying but ordinarily rather mild. That state had its mental equivalent. My former chagrin was still resident in my thoughts, but they tormented me more dully, either because time had attenuated them, because they had been deflected by the change of location or because the physical and mental exhaustion they had induced in me deprived me of the strength to nourish them. It seemed to me that my former life became gradually remote. I felt as though I were becoming a stranger to myself, and during the long says I spent in the stucco drawing room, sometimes I almost forgot the personal circumstances that has brought me there.

That monotonous and solitary existence was sufficient for me and I felt no need to vary it, not any need for society. One or two brief visits to Zotarelli, with a view to completing my furniture, and a few words exchanged with Signora Verana constituted my entire relationship with other human beings during that fortnight. As for my friend Prentinaglia, I would scarcely have given him a thought if the curious story he had told me at the Florian had not come to mind more than once.

More than once! I should say often—but I judged the persistence with which the adventure of the vanished bust presented itself to my memory quite natural. My present existence, denuded of all events, lent itself thereby to mediation on subjects of that sort, and I willingly accepted the one my reverie provided as an inoffensive aliment. I did not make any effort to limit the role that the "Prentinaglian" story played in my imagination. Perhaps, though, if I had reflected on it more attentively, I would have been astonished by the interest that I attached to the sleight of hand to which the worthy Prentinaglia, for unknown reasons, had delighted in giving a phantasmagorical character.

And yet, the fact was easily explicable. On the evening when Prentinaglia had told me, in the Florian, about the ostensibly mysterious disappearance if the bust from the Musei Civici, I was in a particularly sensitive state of mind. The fatigue of the journey, the bizarre impression that I had experienced on seeing Venice again, the sensation of malaise and the anxiety of that first contact disposed me to what Prentinaglia's words had incrusted in my memory, and they remained there more sharply and more profoundly written than they merited. Moreover, the turn of his story had contributed to its imposition in my memory.

At any rate, whatever Prentinaglia's objective had been in acting thus—a taste of mystery or the pleasure of mystification—I must confess that he had succeeded in his purpose. Since my installation in the Palazzo Altinengo, the incident of the vagabond bust had become the subject, with increasing frequency, of my idle dreams during the hours I spent in the stucco drawing room, sitting in one of the rococo armchairs, with my elbow on the lacquer table and my gaze straying from the arabesques on the wall to the tall mirror, which, in its yellow marble frame, reflected in such a strange distance the sumptuous and melancholy décor in which the grace of the old Venice of yesteryear and its intimate fantasies survived.

At first, when that singular occupation intruded upon my thoughts, the details of the bust's disappearance were the primary object. I imagined the various plausible hypotheses that explained how the coup might have been achieved; I framed some that would not have been unworthy of our best detective stories—but I carefully excluded anything fantastic therefrom, for, as I have said, I was not inclined to admit the supernatural interventions to which the excellent Prentinaglia had allowed me to understand that the event in question was no stranger. I gave no credit to such nonsense and preferred to calculate the ruses by which a clever thief might have been able to appropriate the charming work of art, which had always seduced me by the quality of its manufacture and by the physiognomy of the individual it represented, so lifelike and original.

Gradually, that individual came to be substituted for the adventure that had overtaken his effigy. Who could that anonymous Venetian have been? How had he lived? I had already asked those questions when I contemplated the mocking, voluptuous and delicate face of the unknown person in the display-case at the museum, some time before, but I repeated them with a more marked persistence and a more passionate curiosity, and as I addressed those interrogations to myself more frequently, a rather bizarre phenomenon occurred within me that I shall try to render comprehensible.

When my friend Tiberio Prentinaglia had mentioned the disappearance of the bust to me in the Florian, its image had been designed in my mind's eye with perfect clarity and precision. I saw once again the ironic and intelligent face, the form of the nose and mouth—the whole face, with the expression of its gaze—but the representation I formed at that time had not surpassed what can normally be formed of an object previously considered on numerous occasions with attention and interest by someone endowed with a god visual memory. To tell the truth, there were twenty individuals, painted or sculpted, in various museums as familiar to my memory as the Venetian gentleman whose mysterious escapade reminded me of his features.

At present, however, I had to admit that it was no longer the case, and that the primitive image of the unknown individual of the Musei Civici was subject to curious deformations.

The term "deformation" is not exact, however, and inadequate to express my meaning. The image was not *de*formed so much as *re*formed, and now appeared to me to have attained such precision that it was doubtful that the bust itself could have been taken by the modeler to such a degree of reality. The face of the unknown appeared distinctly to me in a surprising verity, and—more bizarrely still—I saw it as if I were looking at it with the aid of a magnifying glass that had returned it to its natural dimensions.

That first phenomenon was not, moreover, the only one I observed. Another, no less disconcerting, was combined with it: that the bust, in its enlargement, was completed by certain other body-parts. Sometimes, it was continued by the arms, displayed the lower abdomen, and even the rump. Sometimes, it even rested on its legs. The phenomenon remained intermittent, but quite frequent. I had before me, not only a bust but an almost-entire person.

I say "almost entire" because, by virtue of a caprice that I cannot explain, he never appeared to me in his integrity. He never formed for my sight a total appearance; on the other hand, though, the parts that I distinguished were always remarkable in their clarity, while remaining fragmentary. When my unknown was manifest standing on his feet, one or both of his arms was lacking. Sometimes, only one arm and one leg were visible.

These particularities, which ought to have seemed strange to me, hardly astonished me at all, so used had I become to such visual games. They should, however have

318

caused me to reflect and realize that the phenomena were emerging from an abnormal sensitivity and a rather unfavorable nervous condition.

If I had reasoned thus, I would have had to conclude that the existence I was leading at the Palazzo Altinengo was not the one I needed, and that I would have done better to conform more exactly to the advice of my physicians. It would have been necessary, according to their recommendations, to combine the prescribed rest with moderate exercise and not to allow my hours of inactivity to go by in vague reveries, as I was doing. I had, however, conceived a taste for that sort of existence and I emerged less and less frequently from that stucco drawing room in which hazard had furnished my imagination with a companion, whose presence animated my solitude.

It was therefore with some annoyance that one day, in the late afternoon, as the light was beginning to fade, I perceived that Signora Verana had forgotten to renew he drawing room candles, and that, to complete the frustration, the supply that she always maintained was completely exhausted. As I have said, I had no means of communication between my apartment and the lodgings that Signor Verana occupied on one of the upper floors of the Palazzo. No bell linked me too her—and it was quite possible that she was not at home.

Often, at very various times, when I was standing at the window, I saw her going out or coming in, enveloped by a long mantle and wearing an implausible hat. In that accoutrement, carrying a sort of shopping-basket under her arm, head bowed, back stooped and hugging the walls, she resembled some card-reader or palmist hastening to an appointment. It might very well be the case today, therefore, that my housekeeper was absent on some exclusion or visit—for she must have relatives, and the habitual silence she maintained in my presence might be compensated elsewhere by the inexhaustible gossip that is the distraction of old Venetian woman, sometimes stopping them at the corner of a *campo*, at the turning of a *calle* or on a bridge, in animated and mysterious dis-

319

cussions, uninterruptable by the elbows of strollers or the jostling of passers-by.

If that were the case, there was only one course of action that remained to me; the simplest thing to do was to go and buy some candles myself at the nearest grocery. That grocery was, at any rate, only a short distance away, facing the church of San Pantaleone. I therefore went into my bedroom to fetch my hat and overcoat—for it was beginning to get cold in those late October days, and I had asked Signora Ventura the day before to provide me with some firewood and to place it in one of the uninhabited rooms of the Palazzo. Now, observing Signora Verana's negligence with respect to the candles, it occurred to me that she might not have carried out my orders any better on the subject of the wood, and I decided to make sure of that immediately. Thus, from the vestibule, I headed to that part of the *mezzanino* in which I had asked the lady to have the logs designated for heating piled up in the rooms that I rented.

I had not gone back into that part of the Palazzo since the day when I had entered it with Signora Verana and had become her tenant. The state of abandonment, decrepitude and dilapidation of those deserted rooms struck me even more forcibly than before. The ceilings were buckling in a disquieting manner, the woodwork crumbling to dust, the damp plaster falling away in chunks, the mosaics of the *pavimento* coming apart. The atmosphere was impregnated with an odor of saltpeter and mold, and light penetrated bizarrely through the gaps in the disjointed shutters. At certain windows they were lacking completely, or no longer consisted of more than a few semi-rotted slats—which provided sufficient light for my investigation.

Passing from room to room, I arrived in the one overlooking the garden, without discovering what I sought anywhere. I would be entitled, I thought, to reprimand Signora Verana for that, and was about to go back to the vestibule when—I don't know why—my attention was attracted by a door that stood ajar. Perhaps it was there that Signora Verana had established her woodpile.

It was a sort of cubby-hole with a very low ceiling, of exceedingly narrow dimensions. A small window with dusty panes lit it feebly, but enough to permit the remains of wood panels to be seen on the walls. On one of the panels the molding formed two juxtaposed frames, and in one of those frames a painting remained, which must have been a portrait, although it was so badly flaked that nothing could be distinguished by a few patches of color. The canvas that the other frame had contained, detached at the top, hung down lamentably, inverted. It could hardly be in any better condition than its neighbor—but it was easy enough for me to find out.

To be sure, the second painting had suffered similarly, and a great rip had almost torn it in two, but it seemed that the individual it represented ought to be fairly distinct. At any rate, an inscription that was quite well preserved ought to tell me his name. Bringing my eyes very close to the canvas I was, indeed, able to read the words: *Vincente Altinengo, nobile Veneziano MDCCLXII.*

It was definitely the portrait of one of the former owners of the Palazzo, doubtless the one who had fitted out that sumptuous and seductive mezzanine and had ordered the construction of the astonishing décor of stuccos and faiences. The date indicated was concordant with the style of the decoration that I admired every day. I was therefore in the presence of my predecessor in the place decorated by him with so much luxury and taste, and I felt a keen curiosity regarding the living appearance of the Venetian gentleman who had prepared for my solitude the melancholy and mysterious retreat to which I had come in search of the silence of my heart and the forgetfulness of life.

I had taken my handkerchief from my pocket and I wiped away the thick coat of dust that covered the canvas. Having done that, I replaced it in its frame by means of an old nail that I found in the woodwork within arm's reach. Then I stepped back a few paces—but scarcely had I raised my eyes to the painting than I uttered an exclamation of surprise.

I had known the person that I had before me for a long time! I knew that gaunt and meager face, with the long nose, the ironic gaze and the ardent, disillusioned smile. I knew that expression of finesse; I knew the projections of that powered wig over the forehead. No doubt was possible.

Yes Vincente Altinengo and the unknown man represented by the little bust from the Musei Civici were one and the same. The resemblance between the painted portrait and the modeled effigy was striking, and a singular hazard permitted me to identify them with one another. The unknown man of the Musei was the Altinengo of the old frame. But why had that curious revelation been reserved for me? The astonishment of it held me back against the wall, immobile, my eyes fixed on the eyes that were considering me from the depths of the past, with a gaze that was both distant and near: an almost living gaze.

My first impulse was to go to impart my discovery to Signore Talventi, the director of the Musei Civici. Hazard had, in fact, put me in possession of an interesting datum of Venetian iconography—but I knew from Prentinaglia that the worthy Talventi had been powerfully affected by the disappearance of the little bust. What good would it do to renew his regret by telling him that the boarder who had parted from his company so irreverently had borne the name Vincente Altinengo?

That was not the only reason that inhibited me from putting my plan into operation, and also prevented me from writing to tell Prentinaglia about the curious coincidence that had acquainted me with the name of the vagabond of the Room IV display case. The true motive for that double abstention was that, in the days following the event I have just narrated, my health suffered one of those sudden depressions that I have already described several times. I fell back into the state of anxiety I had suffered before and had already attempted to analyze. I presented no symptoms of illness, however. My appetite was normal, my sleep, without being good, sufficient. There was nothing but that persistent impression of an indefinite anguish.

I ought to add that the anguish in question had no relationship to my anterior pain. It was as if the bitter chagrin thereof had been extinguished by the great physical crisis that I had undergone before coming to Venice. I knew now that my sentimental life was broken and that nothing would ever repair the disaster, and I accepted that destiny without rebellion, since, in spite of my dolor and despair, I had not had the courage to put an end to my torment. It was not, therefore, some sharper remembrance of the past that was causing my present recrudescence of neuroticism.

It seemed natural, therefore, to attribute it to the change of season. Save for a few fogs and a few rain showers, the month of October had been rather fine, but several days before the temperate had dropped noticeably. It was that same circumstance which, my having instructed Signora Verana to buy some wood, had been the cause of my discovery. The apartments of the Palazzo Altinengo were in great need of being heated by vigorous flames. The large fireplace in the stucco drawing room lent itself to that purpose admirably. I resolved to carry out the experiment.

To aliment their furnaces, the glassmakers of Murano use long and heavy logs which come from the nearby Alps. The dimensions of the tall yellow marble fireplace permitted their use. They burned there with sparkling flames and embers as precious as gems. The luxury of the fire fitted in marvelously with the gilded luxury of the stucco, faience and stonework, and it spread through the entire atmosphere a sort of warm wellbeing that I greatly appreciated in the near-unhealthy condition in which I found myself.

That condition and the attraction that the first fires of autumn had for me contributed to keeping me indoors even more than usual. If I went to the restaurant for lunch, I could not resign myself to returning there in the evening at dinner time. I preferred to remove from the cupboard a few of the meager provisions that I had asked Signora Verana to place there, and improvised a light meal on a corner of the table. In that fashion, I only went out of the Palazzo Altinengo once a day, and that excursion often did not take me as far as the Piazza. I was content to go to a little local trattoria, which cut short my absence and brought me back to the Palazzo rapidly.

It was during these excursions, short as they were, that the malaise of which I have spoken manifested itself more readily, but the indefinable anxiety resultant therefrom diminished immediately I neared home. Sometimes, I came back to the Campo Santa Margherita and the Carmini almost at a run. As soon as I perceived the dilapidated façade of the Palazzo Altinengo, its convex balconies, its dismantled shutters, its dirty window panes and its portal with its two columns, surmounted by sculpted vases, my apprehension diminished.

And yet, nothing summoned my back to my lodgings. I would find there neither a friendly smile, nor a beloved face, nor a familiar footstep, nor a cherished voice: nothing of that which ordinarily welcomes us on returning home. No remembrance inhabited the sparsely-furnished rooms of the dwelling that hazard had made into the refuge of my melancholy solitude. In spite of that, I hastened to come back when the anguish chased me through the narrow Venetian *calli* that I had once loved so much. It was there that I found sanctuary, my heart beating rapidly and my legs heavy.

They incidents were repeated often enough for me to reach the point of no longer exposing myself to the risk. Gradually, I renounced my meals at the trattoria and, from that moment on, my existence became totally sedentary. Once I had washed and dressed in the morning, I left my room with the mythological medallions and mosaic garlands and shut myself away in the stucco drawing rom. Signora Verana lit the fire in the large yellow marble fireplace. Long logs deposited on the *pavimento* furnished me with enough fuel for the day and part of the night, for I stayed up quite late. My time was spent in a sort of indefinite reverie in which I forgot the passage of time.

Signora Verana was the only person who troubled my solitude, and I scarcely perceived her presence any longer. I did not receive anyone at the Palazzo Altinengo. Prentinaglia and Lord Sperling, still absent, were doubtless prolonging their voyage to Sicily. Not once had Prentinaglia given me any sign of life. Nevertheless, the doorbell sometimes rang. The postman occasionally brought me a few letters from Paris. I had not been able to do otherwise than send my address to my physician, Dr. F*** and two or three friends. The postman deposited the letters in a basket made for that purpose, which hung at the end of a rope from the widow of the vestibule into the little courtyard—a Venetian custom that I had adopted.

At any rate, I adapted myself very well to that almost absolute solitude. Although I was obliged to confine my existence strictly to the Palazzo Altinengo, it would not have been very different if my health had permitted me to frequent the parts of Venice where one "runs into people"—by which I mean the Piazza and its cafés—as I had in the early weeks of my sojourn. I had always avoided cultivating relationships in Venice. My Venetian acquaintances were limited to Prentinaglia, and Lord Sperling. As for Parisian faces, the present season was a sufficient safeguard against them. Parisians are September people. By mid-October, the most obstinate have departed. In November, Venice becomes Venetian again.

I would certainly have taken advantage of that security had my mental and physical dispositions been different. I would have enjoyed the *calli, campi* and *rii* of the city and the lagoon, in their charming and melancholy beauty, so seductive at the end of autumn. I had a thousand precious memories that it would have been pleasant to renew. I knew Venice well enough to know that its various enjoyments are inexhaustible. I knew their magnificence and their intimacy, their famous aspects and hidden corners, their glories and secrets. But I felt incapable of trying to renew those impressions of yore, for the

325

moment. Later, perhaps, I would be able to return to a less secluded existence.

In the meantime, was not the best thing to do not to leave the Palazzo Altinengo any longer?

Why impose on myself these futile excursions which always terminated in a crisis of infinitely painful anguish? Was it not better to spend my days by my fire, reading or daydreaming, in that baroque and pleasant stucco drawing room, where the silence was only broken by the crackling of logs or the indefinable and imperceptible noises that are their mysterious confidences and secret insinuations?

As soon as I had come to that decision and had renounced any opposition to it, I experienced an immediate relief. My anxieties dissipated. Liberated from the kind of apprehension that troubled them, the hours began to pass with singular facility, so easily that I soon gave up reading. I no longer opened the few familiar volumes brought from Paris. I scarcely glanced at the letters I received. As for replies, they remained at the stage of vague plans, which I put off from day to day. I had not given any more thought to the intention of writing to Prentinaglia to tell him about my interesting discovery in the matter of the Musei Civici bust and its identity, curiously demonstrated by the discovery of the portrait in one of the abandoned rooms of the Palazzo Altinengo. The story of the bust's disappearance, which had intrigued me momentarily, ceased to interest me. I scarcely thought about it any longer, and it no longer provided fuel for my imagination.

In that respect, I also ought to note a rather curious detail. During the time when that story preoccupied me, when I happened to think with a certain intensity about the unknown man of the Musei Civici, he presented himself to my memory with an extreme precision, but the image that formed of him later was subject, as I have said, to certain modifications, the principal ones consisting of the image being magnified to almost natural dimensions and the completion of certain parts of the individual—without, however, my being able to represent him in his entirety.

Now, at present, those phenomena of optical illusion had almost completely ceased, and that cessation, by a noteworthy coincidence, dated from the day when hazard had informed me of the name of the unknown painted on that old canvas relegated to a corner of the Palazzo Altinengo. The bizarre connection by which I was living in a part of his own Palazzo, instead of augmenting the interest that I had formerly had and more recently devoted to that personage, long enigmatic from my viewpoint, has dissipated all my curiosity in his regard. The questions that I had often asked myself on the subject no longer presented themselves to my mind since I had found out that the gentleman of the bust was Vincente Altinengo, whose portrait was finishing flaking away in the damp of the dark little room in which Signora Verana's negligence had led me to him.

One thing, however, rendered me sympathetic to him. I knew that he had taken it into his head to decorate with delightful and baroque stucco the drawing room that had become the décor of my life. I have already indicated to what degree, from the moment when Signora Verana had introduced me into the *mezzanino*, that bizarre and magnificent room had seduced me with its Oriental theme, its color and its ornamental detail. Now, that seduction had not ceased to increase. It was the sole distraction of my sedentary existence.

How many hours I spent minutely examining the interlacement of the arabesques, the contours of the moldings and the dispositions of the *pavimento*! I knew the exact locations where the fragments of nacre were encrusted among the cubes of the mosaic. I knew all the tricks of daylight or candlelight on the charming panels with gilded faces. I knew how the princesses and mandarins were illuminated, according to the hour: their gleams and reflections. I would have been able to draw them from memory, as well as the subjects on the ceiling and the stonework that framed the little widows in their rococo compartments above the fireplace.

Out of all the curious and singular decoration, however, one item had come to be particularly interesting to me. I have already aid that the stucco drawing room had three doors, all in a beautiful coarse and curl-grained wood, two of which opened to the vestibule, opposite the windows. The third, which gave access to the room with the mythological medallions, was opposite the full-length mirror that I have already mentioned, which simulated a fourth by symmetry, in its own marble frame.

That fourth, artificial door was thus composed of a great mirror, which constituted by its dimensions a masterpiece of Venetian industry. With time, it had acquired an indefinable and admirable appearance of deep subterranean water, and the images that formed within it took on a sort of crepuscular obscurity—something distant and mysterious. Light reflected from it as if veiled. Everything therein appeared grave and distant, in retreat in an extraordinary beyond.

These details had ended up exerting a veritable fascination upon me. During the long hours of daydreaming that consumed my days of solitude, my gaze kept coming back, with an ever more investigative attraction, to the strange perspective that sank deeply into that marble frame and reproduced, along with my own person, all the antique and absurd décor of faience and stucco, constructed according to his whim in the old Palazzo that still bore his name by His Lordship Vincente Altinengo—of whom a double hazard that one could almost qualify as fantastic had revealed the enigmatic and mocking face and vigilant gaze to me, in the bust from the Musei Civici and the portrait in the cubby-hole!

The evening on which the "event" occurred that was the first manifestation of a series of facts that were, to say the least, strange, was an evening like any other. To prove to myself that I have a perfect consciousness and the most precise memory of what happened. I shall give the exact date; it was, therefore, on the seventeenth of November that it took place.

To that precision, better to establish that I had not lost the sense of reality, I will add the circumstantial detail of the day. I had begun it at the usual time—which is to say, rather late in the morning. Signora Verana's comings and goings in the stucco drawing room woke me up. La Verana took advantage of my sleep to tidy up the drawing room, open the windows, prepare the fire and deposit my breakfast on the table. Having done that, she knocked on my door and lit a fire in my dressing-room. At that moment I got up, put my pajamas on and went to drink my cup of chocolate; in the meantime, la Verana made my bed and brought hot water. I did not see her again until one o'clock in the afternoon, when she brought down the meal that I served for myself and whose residue she took away when she brought me dinner.

That day, everything passed as usual. One I had got up, I went into the stucco drawing room. A fire was blazing in the fireplace; I added a log to it, for it was cold in spite of the beautiful day that it promised to be. Through the windows, the sky showed clear and blue. The air must have been pure, because the bells of the Carmini and the nearby churches were ringing with a clear and lively sound. I amused myself recognizing each of them by its timbre. I distinguished these of San Sebastiano from those of the Frari and those of Arcangelo Rafaele. The bells of the Carmini, one of which is slightly cracked, sounded so close by that I no longer paid them any attention, but more distant bells sometimes reached me, brought by the wind, of which I was unable to be sure of the presumed provenance. The air of Venice is very capricious. It is veined by aerial currents, just as the city is patterned by marine canals.

The sole incident of the day was a dispute between boatmen at two o'clock. Two heavy barges had collided on the Rio Santa Margherita, one laden with fruits, the other transporting planks of wood: primitive, black, round-hulled vessels each with a red ornament painted on the prow. The impact was rather severe and, while seeking to draw apart, the boatmen insulted one another copiously. One might have believed that they would come to blows, but the quarrelers limited themselves to heaping sonorous curses on one another, with which a large dog on the boat with the planks mingled its furious barking. In the blink of an eye, the Fondamenta Foscarini, the Campo dei Carmini and the bridge were covered with spectators: children, women in shawls and passersby. The dispute was becoming more exasperated when it suddenly came to an end, for no reason at all, or perhaps because the two fellows had exhausted their vocabularies of insults. Either way, the separated barges resumed their silent progress. Only the dog was still yapping periodically. The crowd dispersed, and everything became tranquil on the deserted *rio*.

The reestablished calm was untroubled until nightfall. During those hours, I no longer heard the familiar sounds—the gliding of gondolas or barges on the *rio*, footsteps on the paving stones of the Fondamenta, the voices of women and children, the cries of ambulant merchants, the whistles and sirens of ships of the canal of the Giudecca, with which are mingled the mysterious vibrations of things that are like hiccups in the respiration of silence. It was thus until the moment when I got up from my armchair to light the candles in the brackets, which had been renewed, as usual, by Signora Verana.

I have already said that I awaited that moment every day with a certain impatience. Certainly, I liked the play of natural light in the noble and charming décor of my stuccos, but I preferred the nocturnal caprices. The Chinese scenes on the faience panels, with their princesses and their mandarins, their palanquins and their pagodas, their birds and their flowers, then took on all their bizarre charm. The old gilt became animated and the entire room filled with an atmosphere of mysterious luxury. In the mosaic on the floor the fragments of nacre glittered softly with marine phosphorescence. The flames of the hearth were added to those of the candles, and I followed their movements with an attention and a curiosity that never grew weary.

In spite of the pleasure I experienced in that contemplation, however, it was toward the large door in the mirror that my gaze soon turned. Now, on the evening of which I am speaking, everything had happened as usual. In the fireplace, flames were consuming the wood; the candles were burning in

330

the brackets and the tall mirror was reflecting, as usual, in its distant and obscurely illuminated profundity, the magnificent and bizarre décor of the strange room, even stranger for being seen thus. For some time already I had been savoring the attraction of that spectacle, scarcely interrupted by my brief meal, and after that diversion I had fallen back into my habitual reverie, which I usually prolonged until the exhausted candles gave me the signal to retire.

It was one of the candles that extracted me from the somnolence into which I had let myself slip, with my eyes open. Doubtless shorter than the others, it must have been slipped into the packet by mistake, for its sputtering caused me to notice that it was almost entirely consumed, and that its dying flame risked crackling the glass disk of the bracket. I therefore got up in order to go snuff it out.

It was placed directly to the right of the false door. At the first step I took, I had the impression of something unusual. I had before me the reflected stucco room. I could see the panels, the brackets, the fireplace and the furniture—but I could not see myself therein. The mirror, which offered me the surrounding objects in their distant exactitude, did not present me with my own image.

The surprise that the observation of that absence caused me held me motionless momentarily, and then I took another step. The reflected drawing room was still devoid of my presence. I went closer, enough to be able to touch the glass with my hand. I could not see my hand, or my face, or my body. The mirror took no more account of me than if I had become an inconstant shade, transparent and immaterial. It only displayed the brilliant and baroque décor in which I was a nonentity.

And yet, I was alive, and thoroughly alive. I was breathing; I was moving. I was not dreaming. It really was me who was standing in front of that glass portal, in which I had often seen myself among the objects that it reproduced faithfully in its distant depths. I was the same, and nothing around me had changed. The candles were burning in their brackets, the fire reddening in the hearth. The Palazzo Altinengo was still the Palazzo Altinengo, Venice was still Venice. And yet, it was necessary for me to recognize that I had suddenly become an exceptional being and that that day, which had seemed to me to be like all the others, marked my entry into a paradoxical existence, as if that mirrored door had been the emblem of the magical arcade by which one penetrates into the world of mystery and the inexplicable, on the threshold of which I now found myself, without anything ever having seeming to have predestined me for it.

I was, in fact, not at all prepared to become, in my own eyes, a fantastic individual. I had never dreamed that any such adventure might befall me. My mind is not at all inclined to supernatural curiosities. I had always lived a life that had nothing marvelous about it, in the stronger sense of the word. My pleasures, my chagrins and my occupations had always been those of the common run of men—and all of a sudden, I found myself transformed into the hero of some Arabian tale!

That transformation ought to have caused me a profound impression of surprise. On the contrary, instead of being moved by it, I accepted it with a facility and an indifference that would have been explicable had the phenomenon in question been isolated, for I would have been able to attribute it to a temporary visual disturbance. But that was not the case. The occurrence was repeated in circumstances too identical for it to be possible for me to conclude that it was an exceptional illusion.

The next day, in fact, as soon as I got up, my first concern was to go confront the mirror that had shown itself so strangely refractory to my reflection the previous evening. Meekly, it presented me in its glaucous depths. Having carried out that experiment, I began my day in the customary fashion, after asking Signora Verana to procure me a small hand-mirror—which she brought me during the afternoon.

When she had gone I continued reading and daydreaming by the fire, while sometimes darting a glance at the magical door. Each time, I could see myself therein. The daylight faded, however, and the moment approached for lighting the candles. Without haste, I proceeded with the operation. I made a tour of the room, then returned to the portal. In its mirror, it no longer reflected anything but the empty drawing room.

Three evenings in succession, I repeated the experiment. During the day, the large mirror accepted my image, but in the evening, it excluded it. The small mirror purchased for me by la Verana behaved differently. It never refused to reflect me. The phenomenon could not, therefore, be caused by a visual disturbance. It remained something stranger.

Why, when evening came and the candles were lit, did the glass panel with the false door repeat every detail of that which surrounded me, except that there was no place for me therein? Why that exception to a physical law—an exception that had no cause, save for a mysterious intention for which I could not divine a reason?

It was not until the fourth evening that I began to take account of what was happening. On that fourth evening, to the phenomenon that I have faithfully reported was added an even stranger event.

As on the preceding evenings, having lit the candles, I had come back to sit down in my armchair next to the fireplace. I had been there for a short while, with my head in my hands, when I was alerted by a sort of instinctive curiosity that something interesting was in preparation. What? I would not have been able to formulate that to myself, but I had a very clear impression of it—so clear that my gaze turned toward the mirrored door, certain that it was there that the unexpected event I anticipated would be produced.

I was not mistaken, for, in the depths of the reflected stucco room, a form became manifest, still uncertain, as if vaporous, but which was not mine, for it was moving while I was standing still. That human form replaced my absent image; I became more aware of that as it became more distinct. Gradually, it became sufficiently so for me to be able to make out the individual who was appearing to me thus.

Enveloped in a long cloak, he wore a tricorn hat with short culottes and a periwig, but his face was not visible. A kind of mist covered it, while the rest of the body stood out clearly in gray. The man was standing upright in an attitude of indecision. One might have thought him a traveler returning home after a long absence. Suddenly, he made a gesture and raised a hand to his face.

I perceived then that what I had taken for a mist was one of those carnival masks that the Venetians of yore had worn, but beneath that mask, before he had taken it off, I had already divined my nocturnal visitor's identity. Should I not, in fact, have expected his coming, advertised by so many indications? Since the first evening of my arrival in Venice, when I was in the Florian, installed under the Chinese man listening to Prentinaglia's tales, had he not already been prowling around me? Was it not him who had wanted me to come and live in his own Palazzo? Was it not him who had revealed his name to me? Had he not chosen me, among everyone else, in whom to manifest himself?

And all that, I now sensed so clearly that I experienced no surprise in consequence. Was it not just that he should recover possession of his own drawing room with the beautiful stuccos? Before him, I could only bow, saying: "Greetings, Vincente Altinengo, greetings! Be welcome in this dwelling, which is yours!"

Now that I could make out his face, his mask having been removed, there could be no further doubt. Vincente Altinengo was very similar to his effigies, his bust and his portrait. It really was Vincente Altinengo who was standing before me, in the depths of the mirror from which his image had evicted mine. It was him whose feet were posed on the mosaic floor with the fragments of incrusted nacre, and who stood there, colorless, imponderable, almost still immaterial—and his presence seemed to me so simple and so natural that I did not seek to comprehend the meaning, the intention and the mystery of it.

Vincente Altinengo did not appear in the same fashion every evening in the mirror of the tall door. Although he still awaited the hour of the candles, he did not always show himself, as he had the first time, enveloped by a cloak, wearing a tricorn hat with a mask on his face. Sometimes, he was seated, with his elbow on the table; sometimes, he had his back to the fireplace; sometimes he was standing by the window as if he were looking out. Quite often, he was striding back and forth, with a reflective air.

These various attitudes were not the only change produced in him. There was another, more sensible from one evening to the next. In fact, the consistency of the apparition was gradually modified. At first, as I have said, the shade of Vincente Altinengo seemed somehow immaterial, imponderable and was, furthermore, colorless in its gray vaporousness; soon, however, it seemed to me that it was gaining weight and that its substance was solidifying. At the same time, it became colored by increasingly real hues, still faint but already distinct from one another. As this transformation took place, Vincente Altinengo lost his illusory appearance. After a certain lapse of time, I could distinguish the color of his garments and the quality of the fabrics. The hands and face were very nearly those of a living person.

I observed this progress curiously. With an attentive and already familiar curiosity, I contemplated that taciturn companion. I watched him come and go in the depths of the full-length mirror. He lived there alone, as I lived myself; we were separated from one another by a thin sheet of glass, face to face in our reciprocal isolation.

That situation went on for a certain time. In the meantime, the apparitions of Vincente Altinengo, at first rather brief, became longer and longer. Often, during his first manifestations, the phantom had had a certain difficulty in forming himself, and when he had attained the degree of perfection that he was able to reach he dissipated gradually and decayed before disappearing. Now, he reached the appearance of reality much more rapidly and maintained himself there until the moment when the candles began to go out.

Although I had easily taken my part in that singular presence, one question came to mind nevertheless. Was Vincente Altinengo aware of my existence? Was I visible to him as he was to me?

Thus far, no indication had permitted me to suppose so, but a moment came when it was possible for me to think differently. That evening, Altinengo was walking with his hands clasped behind his back, and his entire person was particularly distinct. Suddenly, he stopped, turned abruptly toward me, made a gesture of surprise, and then resumed his march—but he seemed preoccupied. Evidently, Altinengo had been troubled by something, and perhaps it was me who was the cause of his disturbance.

That idea returned to me on the following evenings, for Altinengo's anxiety was only increased. It was manifest in a marked agitation, in the glances he darted toward the part of the room where I was, in certain gestures and attitudes. Altinengo was watching me, sometimes overtly, sometimes clandestinely. Sometimes he got up abruptly from the armchair in which he had just sat down, took a few turns around the room, then stopped still, his eyes wary and his ear cocked. Several times, I saw him rub his eyes, like someone seeking to dispel an optical illusion. One evening, however, I had no further doubt, and this was the circumstance that gave rise to it.

That evening, Altinengo had been striding back and forth across the room for some time when I saw him suddenly head toward one of the doors. By his gestures I understood that he was introducing a visitor, and that, although the visitor remained invisible to me, I was no less able to take account of the object of his visit and the subject of the conversation. It obviously concerned me.

Altinengo explained the unusual phenomena that he had observed. He replied to his interlocutor's objections. The latter was probably trying to convince him that he was the victim of an illusion, but Altinengo shook his head, like a man who does

336

not want to listen to reason. Altinengo and I existed for one another.

That persuasion had for its consequence, on my part, a violent desire to communicate with that being, so close to me and so far away—and it seemed to me that Altinengo was experiencing a similar sentiment. What was astonishing about that reciprocity? Had not a mysterious hazard but us in one another's presence: me, the Parisian of today; him the Venetian of yesteryear? Were we not, therefore, responding to some profound intention of destiny? Were we not obedient to secret coincidences that wanted that old abandoned Venetian Palazzo to be our meeting-place? A strange adventure for which nothing had prepared me, but which I welcomed without astonishment...

Why should I not accept it, since it presented itself in such conditions of facility, so naturally? It was not the result of any conjuration or any sorcery. A few sparse petty facts had led me insensibly toward it. Why refuse it, since it came to me? And then, as a guest of Vincente Altinengo, was it not simple politeness to extend my hand to his shade?

And Altinengo thought the same; I had now acquired that certainty. Thus far, he had stayed determinedly at the back of the room, but from one evening to the next he came closer. I could see him now at close range. For hours we stared at one another, face to face. Only that thin sheet of glass interposed itself between us, and we sensed that it would not be long delayed in breaking.

That event was necessary, certain, inevitable. But which of us would provoke it? Would it be Altinengo or would it be me? Would it be the phantom or the living man? Which of the two would be the bolder?

And with our gazes, we were asking one another that question while, standing upright, we stood there face to face, each of us on one side of life, while behind us, by candlelight, the magnificent and baroque décor of the old stucco and faience gleamed in its iridescent gilt; while, above our heads, the ancient Palazzo Altinengo loomed up on its corroded foundations in all its shaky decrepitude; and while, in the surroundings, mysterious nocturnal Venice superimposed itself, fragile, complicated and marvelous, upon its own reflection, doubled by the mirror of its circular lagoon and its waters, insinuated by a thousand canals into its architectural mosaic: Venice, above which shone, like one of those fragments of nacre in the *pavimento*, the horned disk of some sparkling moon...

And, from one evening to the next, the inevitable event became more imminent. It was my sole thought, and it occupied me entirely. I forgot everything except Altinengo entirely. I forgot myself. If anyone had asked me why I was in Venice, in the depths of that old Palazzo, what circumstances of my life had brought me there, I would certainly not have been able to reply. But no one interrogated me. No one came to distract my solitude.

Only the vague quotidian words spoken by Signora Verana broke the silence that surrounded me, while the high winds that raised and swelled the autumn tides roared outside—those tides while gorged the canals of Venice with water, mounting the steps of the quays, penetrating beneath the marine doors and invading the vestibules of the palazzos, while the breath of the tempest shook their tall chimneys and the wooden frameworks of their terraces.

Tides so high, sometimes, that they cover the harbor wall and overflow the Piazzetta, making the Piazza San Marco into a lake, on which the little waves raised thereon seem to be sailing, like a *Bucentaur* of marble and enamel, the Byzantine vessel of the Martian basilica,[50] saline tides blowing from the

---

[50] The *Bucentaur* was the Doge's ship of state, employed in the annual Ascension Day ceremony that wedded Venice to the sea between the fourteenth and eighteenth enturies; the last of the four ceremonial vessels was destroyed by Napoléon Bonaparte to symbolize his conquest of Venice in 1798. The reference to a *basilique martienne* [Martian basilica] is puzzling, and is probably a misprint, the intended adjective being

open sea, which the Lion, on its porphyry column, aspires with its avid nostrils, by virtue of which its wings of bronze palpitate in imaginary flight.

But what did all that matter to me?

Only one thing mattered to me. Who—Altinengo or me—would make the decisive gesture that we were both expecting—for we both desired it.

Our faces were almost touching, our eyes attracting one another with a infinite curiosity, our hand seeking one another.

Would it be me? Would it be Altinengo? Or would it be some hazard that would take responsibility for realizing the miracle?

The slumber from which I awoke was a singular sleep. It seemed to me that it had lasted for a very long time—much longer than nightly sleep lasts. Profound and absolute, it had been a complete cessation of my entire being. Everything within me had been asleep: my body, my blood, my thoughts and my memory. From the depths of that slumber, I rose up slowly, as if from an abyss, in a continuous ascension. Now, I touched the surface; I became a living being again. I was not yet alive, but I was going to live. Soon, I would be able to open my eyes, move my foot or my hand, move myself, and speak.

In silence, I gazed. I was lying in a bed. Around me were the ripolined walls of a succinctly-furnished room. I was wearing a coarse cotton chemise. Something was around my head: a bandage. Where was I, then? What was I doing in this bed? Why this white cell? What had happened?

I made a gesture and encountered a bell-pull. A young nurse appeared and approached me. She took my wrist, smiling.

---

derived from San Marco rather than the planet, but it might be worth noting that Percival Lowell's depiction of Mars, elaborately criss-crossed by canals, was often stigmatized by sceptics as the "Martian Venice."

"Ah! Our dear invalid is much better today. Does he need anything? I'll go fetch the doctor anyway—he's in his study. He gave me strict instructions...."

I stopped her. "What I need first of all, Mademoiselle, is to know where I am."

The young woman started laughing. "That's true. You're in Dr. Bellincioni's clinic, in the Giudecca."

More than once, while walking in the Giudecca, I had passed the small yellow house with the tall hooded chimneys that displayed a large red cross inscribed above the door. Once, I had even gone in to examine the garden that was perceptible from outside on the far side of the vestibule.

"But why am I in the doctor's clinic?"

"Wait a moment—the doctor will tell you that himself, Monsieur."

Doctor Bellincioni was a large, jovial and friendly man, with a clean-shaven face. Without replying to my questions, he set about examining me. His investigation appeared to be satisfactory, for, once it was terminated, he sat down unceremoniously at the foot of the bed, rubbed his huge hands and said: "Well, well, my dear Monsieur, that's perfect. You're now out of danger. The wound hasn't scarred over, but the abnormal phenomena have completely disappeared. The shock must have been rude, and you've been badly stricken."

I raised myself up on my pillows. "But what shock, Doctor?"

"What shock? That of the heavy mirror door that detached itself from its frame and fell on your head, breaking into shards! It was those shards and the impact that inflicted the serious wound from which you're in the process of recovering. You'll come out of it all right, Monsieur—but permit me to tell you that the person who suggested that old Palazzo Altinengo to you as lodgings didn't make a very fortunate choice, for not only did the door that wounded you fall apart but the day after your accident, a part of the wall crumbled and the pavimento subsided. When you went into it, the Palazzo was in a dangerous state of dilapidation, and it could not resist the high tide and the wind that was blowing a gale. It nearly collapsed into the canal in its entirety. At any rate, the municipality has evacuated it, and it's going to be demolished."

I was listening to the doctor attentively. He continued: "The accident must have occurred during the night. What is curious is that the other inhabitants of the building heard nothing of the racket. It's true that your apartment as rather isolated and that there was a high wind that night. In the morning, when she came in, your housekeeper, Signora Verana found you unconscious, lying in a pool of blood. The lady had the good idea of having you transported to my clinic. She has come several times to obtain news of you, as have a worthy antiquarian named Zotarelli and one of your friends, Signore Prentinaglia, who returned from a voyage the day after your accident. He was very distraught, and interrogated me at length about the circumstances that led to the accident, but I have not been able to enlighten him. Perhaps you will be able to do better than me, and perhaps you will remember what happened between you and that diabolical door, which—take my word for it—nearly served you as a passage to the other world. But that's enough for today; we mustn't chat too long. Get a few hours rest before your dressing's changed this evening."

I followed Dr. Bellincioni's advice and, after having thanked him for his kindness, set about reflecting.

Ought I to accept Dr. Bellincioni's version of events? Had hazard put an end to the hallucination of which I had been the victim for weeks? Like my own body, had the fragile shade of Vincente Altinengo been struck by the abrupt collapse of the door? Was it by accident that our mysterious colloquy had been interrupted? Had the marvelous adventure on whose threshold I had believed myself to be standing been arbitrarily terminated by the stupid wound that had prevented me taking it to its conclusion? Had it continued in the abnormal slumber that had astonished and worried Dr. Bellincioni?

Had I, during that time, joined Vincente Altinengo in the mysterious domain from which he had wanted to emerge and into which he had wanted to draw me? Whatever might have been the case in that regard, I had, alas, lost all memory of it. Thus, the last chance that had been given to me to escape from my sad life had vanished.

Perhaps Vincente Altinengo, in the same room with the stucco and faience décor, had once suffered melancholies similar to mine, and perhaps he had come to bring me the consolatory word that I would never know. But might not all of that have been the dreams of my poor cracked head, which would make Dr. Bellincioni smile if I took it into my head to confide in him?

That evening, when the doctor had changed my dressing, rather painfully, and adjusted the bandage, he said to me, with a satisfied expression: "Well, the wound is healing well, very well, and if Signores Zotarelli and Prentinaglia come to obtain news of you tomorrow, I'll let them come in to see you for a moment."

Signore Prentinaglia was the first to be introduced. He precipitated himself upon my bed and kissed my hands frantically.

"Oh, my friend, my very dear friend, how I have reproached myself! For in the end, it's my fault. It's your Prentinaglia's fault that all this has happened. Yes, was it not me who told you about that accursed Palazzo Altinengo? Oh, your poor head! I shall never forgive myself!"

And, while striking his breast with one hand, he pointed to my bandage with the other. He was standing up, dressed, as always, in his vast overcoat, with his jaundiced theatrical face. On his finger shone the kabbalistic ring with which he had sealed the letter in which he had given me the address of the Palazzo on the Fondamenta Foscarini, and that of Signora Verana. What did that taciturn Verana with the sly gaze and this Prentinaglia with the mask-like face have in common? And that madman Lord Sperling, with his Casa degli Spiriti? Prentinaglia had returned to Rome with him and had left him traveling to Milan for a conference on psychical sciences—but soon, they would be together again under the Chinese man in Florian's.

Negligently, Prentinaglia added: "By the way, old chap, do you remember the story of the Musei Civici's little bust, whose disappearance I mentioned to you? Well, it has resumed its place in the display-case. One morning, he was discovered there, still smiling, beneath his periwig—but the trickster who carried it off must have dropped it, for a rather visible crack was observed thereon. It's being repaired now...but I'm tiring you, my friend. *Au revoir* and *à bientôt*. I shall come back."

And Prentinaglia, his felt hat and his overcoat disappeared, while in his farewell gesture, I saw the cornelian ring with the mystical symbols gleaming...

When he had gone, I felt a trifle weary and half-closed me eyes. I was alone in my white room. The great silence of the Giudecca surrounded me.

With my mind's eye, I saw the Fondamenta Foscarini again, the old Palazzo with its gray façade and green shutters, its ocher awnings and pot-bellied balconies, its stairway with worn steps and saltpetered walls, the little mosaic landing incrusted with a single fragment of nacre, the vestibule, the room with the medallions, the stucco drawing room with its moldings, its fireplace, its faience panels with gilded figures. I saw the tall mirrored door again in its marble frame, in which the mysterious shade or morbid illusion of Vincente Altinengo, Venetian, had appeared to me in the profound distance of its reflection, as if to welcome the present guest of his ancient dwelling to the world beyond.

And, with a gesture of farewell, while the bells of the Redentore and Santa Eufemia smashed the crystalline air with their sound, I saluted his image one last time—which seemed to reply to my salute with its mocking, melancholy and enigmatic smile, and which I have never seen again.

Addendum:
The Last Chapter of "Marceline"

"Truly, my dear Jacques, you can boast of being insupportable yesterday evening! I don't know what insect had stung you, but you were in a very bad mood and your behavior was odious. I believe you had drunk too much Chianti at dinner and absorbed three small glasses of grappa in the evening, but that was no reason to spoil, as you did, that magnificent moonlight. The Piazza San Marco was so beautiful, in that silvery light, and the lagoon...!

"And instead of enjoying so much beauty, the divine calm of the heavens and the waters, you had that stupid quarrel with Marceline about buying marionettes. Fundamentally, your wife is right. What will you do with that clutter when you don't look at it any more, as you will? It's all very well in the Palazzo Pastinati, but at home, in the Troublerie...trust your old Lefougeret.

"And now, get up. It's after noon. I think you've been ruminating your misdeeds. As for Marceline, who's annoyed with you, but only slightly, she'd told me to tell you that she's lunching at the *Anticho Cavalleto* with Dr. Thibaut, your bête noire. Oh, I know you don't like him, but he's an excellent fellow. That he doesn't know much about Venice, and that it annoys you, I'll admit, but he's leaving in two days. Put up with him, as you put up with your old teacher Alain Lefougeret, whom you had the bizarre idea of bringing with you on this Venetian voyage. Come on! Get up. We're lunching at *Vapore* and then we'll go to the Palazzo Pastinati to tell Signor Barlotti that you've changed your mind about buying his marionettes. After which we'll rejoin Marceline in the garden of the Giudecca and you'll be nice to her. That's settled."

Monsieur Lefougeret was sitting on the foot of my bed and considering me with is benevolent smiling face, while I rubbed my eyes and restored order to my tousled hair, while looking at my clothes, thrown at random on to the parquet of my room, into which slid a warm sunbeam, and into which penetrated, though the open window, with the marine odor of Venice, the noises of the canal and the street: the plash of oars, the impact of heels on flagstones—all that which, in Venice, renders the vast silence that surrounds it even vaster.

Then, suddenly, I burst out laughing, thinking that the worthy Lefougeret would never know what a grotesque character he had become in my nocturnal phantasmagoria, just as poor Dr. Thibaut would be unaware of the odious role he had played, with his faithful domestic Hilaire. And Marceline, my beloved, pretty and reasonable Marceline, would never suspect that I had transformed her into a malevolent doll, which a piebald and bearded Centaur, to the applause of Pantalon, Brighella, Scaramouche, Arlequin and *tutti quanti*,[51] had hung head down on the end of a string on the enchanted stage of Signor Barlotti's marionette theater!

All that appeared to me so odd and comical that I threw back my bedclothes and leapt across the room, capering around Monsieur Lefougeret—who, astonished by my hilarity and my gesticulations, repeated indulgently: "My poor Jacques, my poor Jacques! I believe that you still have Chianti and grappa in the brain. Come on, get dressed and come and eat a *fritto misto*,[52] accompanied by a modest bottle of Nocera. I have spoken."

And Monsieur Lefougeret, with a noble gesture, held out my yellow pajama suit, which the play of the sunlight, reflected from the painted ceiling of my room, covered with changing gleams, like the costume of an Arlequin.

---

[51] "and all the rest"

[52] A mixture of fried foods (fish, in Venice).

ADDENDA

The Widowhood of Scheherazade

For A.M. [53]

Speech is not its language...
Madame de Staël

Scheherazade had slept badly that night. The day had been weighed down by blazing sunlight, and the air had been so penetrated by it that it felt as if one were breathing in a kind of burn, whose ill-effects nothing could temper. The lightness of the most transparent muslins seemed an unwelcome burden, and the winged caress of fans remained powerless to refresh the overheated shade.

In vain Scheherazade had stripped off, one by one, the veils not demanded by decency. In vain she had freed herself of the inconvenience imposed by her necklaces and bracelets. In vain she had let her most precious rings slip on to trays, with a clink of gold and a click of gems, including the magic ring that Sultan Shariar had placed on her finger himself on the evening of the thousand-and-first night, as a testimony of love and a guarantee of security: the ring whose sacred talisman rendered her henceforth inviolable and set aside forever the threat of the trenchant blade of the sword and the mortal grip of the silken cord.

---

[53] Régnier was acquainted with many people with these initials, but one storyteller he met at around the time this story was written and with whom he became quite friendly was Émile Herzog, who wrote under the pseudonym André Maurois, to whose wife, the former Simone de Caillavet, he took quite a shine.

Having retreated to the most secret and best ventilated summer-house in the gardens—the one that was made entirely of crustal and above which intersected the flexible plumes of three great water jets, which ornamented it with a sparkling fluid crown—Scheherazade had seen the hours of that torrid day go by ponderously, in the regular tears of clepsydras and the successive grains of sand-glasses, without anything bringing relief to the overwhelming languor of her impatient lassitude. Even her favorite white doves with the crimson throats, in brushing her weary face with their amorous wings, had scarcely caused her mouth and eyes to smile momentarily.

Exhausted by that torpor, Scheherazade had not even had the strength to think about the marvelous story that she would relate to Sultan Shariar that evening, when, the sun having set, they would meet on the highest terrace of the palace in order to savor the furtive nocturnal alleviation beneath the starry sky.

Just as the day had been unbearable, the evening had been scarcely less so, and Scheherazade, before trying to obtain a little sleep, had recalled its disagreeable circumstances without any pleasure. Not the least of them had been the indifferent and distracted fashion in which the Sultan Shariar had listened to the quotidian tale. Scarcely had Scheherazade begun to speak than Shariar had turned his attention away from the storyteller's words to his own thoughts.

By the manner in which the Sultan passed his hand through his black beard, which was beginning to be streaked with silver threads, it was obvious that those thoughts could not be offering any enjoyment to Shariar's mind. Scheherazade had seen the Sultan's dark eyebrows frown. Several times, he had even put his hand impatiently upon the ruby-studded hilt of his sword and fidgeted with the agate hilt of his dagger. In spite of the ingenious twists and turns of Scheherazade's tale, which was the story of a genie enclosed in a bottle, Shariar's face had remained taciturn beneath his diamond-bedecked turban. Not only had he not reached out to Scheherazade, as he normally did, to thank her for her tale, but he had even neglected have her brought the customary cup of snow so that she might quench her thirst. Was that forgetfulness not proof, in Sultan Shariar, of great preoccupation?

Shariar's attitude had afflicted Scheherazade's vanity. Scheherazade was proud of her prowess as a storyteller and of the artistry she brought to her stories, whose renown had spread beyond the limits of Bagdad throughout the world. The name of Scheherazade was universally famous, and her celebrated adventure was related everywhere. Women, especially, professed an enthusiastic admiration for her. Was she not the honor and the pearl of their sex, and the marvel of their intelligence? Had she not been able, by virtue of her talent, to impose herself on Shariar's cruel whims and put an end to them? By her delightful ruse, by her ingenious cunning, she had thwarted the mortal trap to which she had been exposed. Was she not a magnificent and charming example of feminine superiority? All that had earned her a renown to which she was not insensible.

And that evening, Shariar had wounded her susceptibility. He had been negligent. He had forgotten to thank her for all that she had done for him. When one has the privilege and the good fortune to hear a Scheherazade tell a story, one ought to be all ears. How can one risk missing the least of her words? What was the meaning of the pensive expression, the frown beneath his turban, the fidgeting with the sword and the dagger, the adoption of a distracted and preoccupied appearance?

That was a veritable insult, and, like all authors. Scheherazade was irritable and rancorous. She had been extremely vexed by Shariar's behavior, but what had completed her irritation was that Shariar, when she had stopped speaking, had not asked her the questions that he never failed address to her concerning the events and characters in her tales. Decidedly, Shariar had been a recalcitrant listener, and when the tale was finished, without paying any further heed to Scheherazade, he had surrounded himself with spirals of smoke from his long pipe, while from the depths of the garden, beneath the stars, came the plaint of fountains, and mischievously furtive bats fluttered around his somber turbaned face.

The silence of Sultan Shariar had lasted until the appearance on the terrace of the grand vizier Kerendar. Kerendar was an individual that Scheherazade did not like at all. Shariar listened to him, and more than once, he had opposed Scheherazade's costly fantasies. For example, he had criticized the construction of the famous crystal summer-house crowned with water-jets, and various other amusements of the Sultana.

Kerendar explained these oppositions and criticisms by reasons of State. The great and glorious wars waged by Sultan Shariar had cost a great many men and a great deal of money. The kingdom was decimated and the treasury had run dry. All that had not made Shariar very popular. He was accused of not being sufficiently sparing with either the gold or blood of his subjects, and squandering them to satisfy his ambitions and his pleasures. The people of Bagdad were murmuring and complaining.

Kerendar had been alerted to these murmurs and complaints, for he maintained a powerful and perspicacious police force. It kept him up to date with what was going on in the kingdom, and also in the city and the palace. Scheherazade's actions and gestures did not escape Kerendar's investigations. The surveillance that Kerendar carried out reassured Shariar's jealousy, but made Scheherazade's hair prickle. Not that she had any intention of being unfaithful to Shariar, but it had not displeased her to be surrounded by tender tributes and sweet words. Now, the vigilance of Kerendar deterred the most audacious; no one dared look at her in his presence. The sight of a handsome face is an innocent pleasure, however, and Scheherazade had liked to see a few of them demonstrating that they were charmed by her beauty. Shariar's somber face was not extremely diverting, so far as she was concerned.

As Kerendar had spoken in a hushed voice to Shariar, Shariar's face had become even more somber. His hand had clenched on the ruby-studded hilt of his sword. The news that Kerendar brought was not, in fact, very agreeable. Emissaries sent to various parts of the kingdom had returned with the most worrying news. The raising of taxes was provoking disturbances. In certain places, people had gone so far as to maltreat the agents of the revenue. In addition, the peasants were hiding their crops and the merchants concealing their produce, counting on the price increases that famine would produce, its imminence having been advertised. Many inhabitants were leaving the country and several regions were becoming deserted. There was general discontent leveled against a Sultan who spent his nights listening to stories instead of working for the relief of his people.

Scheherazade, who, like all women, had keen ears, did not miss any of what Kerendar said. Thus she learned that a conspiracy had been formed in Bagdad to make an attempt on the Sultan's life. The conspirators were planning to get into the palace, break down the garden gates and finish Shariar off by means of fire and the sword. This criminal company had numerous members, linked to one another by formidable oaths and directed by fanatical leaders. Bagdad was infested by these intrigues, which would have presented a real danger if Kerendar's police had not been watching them and keeping track of the threads of the plot. The grand vizier was in a position to nullify these deadly threats, provided that he did not lose sight of them for an instant, but it would cost considerable sums of money. It was therefore necessary to restrict all the resources of the State to that purpose, and not to employ a single dinar for any other. If he were given the means, Kerendar would answer for everything.

During this speech, Shariar had never ceased tugging the points of his beard,, and he had left the terrace with his hand on Kerendar's shoulder, without a glance for Scheherazade, who was not long delayed in retiring to her apartment.

Once she was in her own room and sure that Shariar would not come to look for her that night, she had sent away her women and had lain down on the perfumed leather of her cushions. The nocturnal air had lost a little of its ardor and it was easier to breathe. The murmur of fountains and the scent

353

of roses came in through the windows, mingled with the silvery rays of a belated moon.

The silence was only troubled by the calls of the sentinels who, yataghans drawn, were guarding the garden gates. Briefly, Scheherazade thought about going down there. She sometimes liked to walk there at night and to admire the slumber of the aviaries. The beautiful birds that filled them slept with their heads beneath their wings and Scheherazade was amused by their decapitated silhouettes. She had been deterred, however, by the fatigue of putting on her curved slippers again and had contented herself with thinking about the boastful magpie that had amused her so much when she was a child.

That magpie was the joy of her father's poor cobbler's stall. How it jabbered away, that magpie, while the worthy man hammered and stitched the leather! Scheherazade often thought about her father's stall. It was there that she had grown up, clad in rags that she already arranged coquettishly while sucking a slice of water-melon. It was there that she had heard the various people who frequented the stall talking. The city's news was circulated there, with abundant commentary.

Her father's tongue had been as cutting and pointed as his awl, and he did not disdain amusing his clients with his anecdotes and apologues. It was in that humble and credulous audience that she had acquired the taste for the tales that had played such an important role in her singular history. While very small, she had made her contribution to all that palaver, and her infantile imaginations and inventions had amused that facile popular public.

By that means she had attracted the attention of Ibrahim, the old carpet-merchant, to whom her father had sold her, and who had taught her about love, without her experiencing any for him. Ibrahim had not been her only teacher in that matter, and others had completed his lessons. She had not obtained any pleasure therefrom. The faces that had leaned over her had scarcely shown her youth or beauty, but her complaisance had allowed her to eat better, to dress better, to ornament herself

354

with a few jewels, and enabled her to come to the aid of her family's poverty. In those difficult times she consoled herself for her tribulations by imagining marvelous adventures in which she attributed the leading role to herself.

It had been thus until the day when the rumor reached her ears of the strange proof to which Sultan Shariar submitted the storytellers who strove to distract his insomnia. She had known the bloody risks that the imprudent ran, but had conceived a secret desire to make the dangerous attempt. So, one day, she had presented herself at the palace to be inscribed on the fatal list. It had not taken long for her name to be called. She could still see the high terrace, and the Sultan, attentive to her stories, so astutely interrupted and left in suspense.

She thought about the strange fortune that had come to her. Not only had the trenchant sword not fallen on her neck, but the Sultan's black beard had brushed her face and his heavily-ringed hands had caressed her body. The cobbler's daughter, the little storyteller of the Thousand-and-One Nights, had become the favorite Sultana of the great Sultan Shariar. All Bagdad envied her power, and her own story was even more marvelous than all those she had recounted...

While she mulled over that brilliant past, Scheherazade had felt her eyelids grown heavy. Gradually, sleep, long unfaithful, came to her, with the first light of dawn. Soon, poor Shariar would wake up in order to occupy himself with affairs of State, while she, who had no such concerns, could sleep for a long time, idly, as if she were still in the depths of her father's stall, the cobbler's little daughter.

But Scheherazade was not to get much sleep that night. Scarcely had she closed her eyes than she seemed to hear unusual sounds. The palace filled with bizarre noises: running footsteps in the gardens and resounding on the staircases. Soon, those noises were mingled with cries. A strange disorder was manifest everywhere. What was happening? Were the people of Bagdad in revolt? Was there a fire or an earthquake? Had enemies suddenly attacked the city? Was she dreaming, prey to some nightmare? Was it one of her tales, continuing in her sleep?

No! That man standing by her bed, his turban unknotted, his arms raised, was neither a phantom nor a spirit. Scheherazade recognized that olive complexion, that long nose, those oblique eyes. It really was the grand vizier Kerendar standing before her, haggard, stammering and gesticulating, whose blood-stained hands were dripping red drops on to the marble pavement!

Sultan Shariar had just been assassinated in his bed. His own dagger with the agate hilt had been plunged into his breast and his own sword with the ruby-studded hilt had served to cut his throat. His guards lay at his door, their tongues hanging out and cords around their necks. As for the murderer, who had disappeared without leaving any trace, he would never be found.

A muted discontentment reigned in Bagdad, and the death of Sultan Shariar was the proof of it. On entering his master's bedroom in the morning and seeing the tragic spectacle offered to his eyes, Kerendar had attempted to bring help to the Sultan, but all help was futile. Kerendar had only been able to ascertain Shariar's death, and had run to warn Scheherazade.

Scheherazade was very popular in Bagdad because of her beauty and her talent, and Kerendar offered to have her recognized as the reigning Sultana. Nothing was easier, and our man would be able to arrange everything, provided that Scheherazade promised to maintain him as grand vizier and appoint him to govern in her name. If not, power would pass into the hands of the Atabeg of Mossoul, and Scheherazade would be locked up until her dying day in a safe place, unless her days were cut short by other means.

Scheherazade had no ambition, but she liked her comforts. The thought of leaving her palace, her gardens, her summer-houses, her fountains, her rose-bushes and her aviaries was painful. Then again, would not this royal adventure complete her marvelous destiny?

Shariar's death caused her little grief, and the prospect of being absolute mistress of her actions was rather pleasant. Henceforth, she could live as she pleased, without having to distract a doubtless generous but demanding master with her body and her words. She would be able to sleep all night without having to stay up late to amuse her insomniac listener she would be able to come and go as she liked, rest or remain silent, and above all, not tell tales any more. What a relief not to be obliged to invent those fabulous stories, of which she was beginning to get weary!

All these considerations led her to accept Kerendar's proposition. He took care of everything, with remarkable dexterity. Shariar's funeral was followed rapidly by the coronation of Scheherazade, who soon had the grand vizier Kerendar hanged for the murder of Sultan Shariar, even though no proof had been found of his participation in the crime. A guilty party was necessary, though, and Scheherazade had taken a dislike to Kerendar since he had scared her by appearing so abruptly before her and waving his bloody hands in that ridiculous manner.

The first phase of Scheherazade's reign was fortunate—which is to say that the people of Bagdad continued to suffer exactly the same evils, paying the same taxes, supporting the same injustices and the same miseries, but that the state of affairs that had caused Shariar to be detested caused Scheherazade to be adored. Peoples are like that. Their lot is uniformly pitiful and their happiness only ever imaginary. Scheherazade thus inaugurated a happy reign.

This was repeated to her so often that she began to be astonished that her own happiness was not equal to that of her people. The disproportion was vexatious. Thus, when Scheherazade had slept for as long as she wished, when she had ornamented herself with all the jewels of Shariar's treasure, when she had shown herself to the people and been greeted with cheers, when she had rebuilt her palace, replanted her gardens, changed the location of the summer-houses, the fountains and the arbors and hanged the grand vizier Kerendar, she perceived that she was no happier than when Shariar was alive. When evening came and she went up on to the terrace of her new palace, something was lacking. She felt idle and uncertain.

Scheherazade had the habit of rationalizing her impressions. Having reflected long and hard, she realized that the stories she had told every evening to Shariar had maintained her mind in a fortifying and ingenious activity. It had been necessary for her to invent a subject and imagine circumstances. Now the game was over, the consequence for her had been a sort of intellectual torpor that was nothing less than a discreet form of ennui. Bow how could she remedy that condition?

She could not group her retinue and her guards around her to form an audience; she detested their complaisance and was suspicious of their applause. There remained the resource of writing stories, but she knew that stories lose a great deal in being written down. Hers, marvelous as they were, would lack the sound of her voice, the grace of her gestures, the mischief and mystery of her smile and her eyes. Her universal reputation as a great storyteller would be at risk of being lost.

These observations increased her ennui. The days seemed long and the approach of night made her agitated. To distract herself, Scheherazade could have had recourse to pleasure that are no less lively for being silent, but she knew almost all of the pleasures that can be attained from physical embraces, and love cannot be improvised any more by sultanas than by cobblers' daughters. Then again, when all honors are bestowed upon one, when one is adulated, respected and feared, it is very difficult to be loved.

Scheherazade often went to her crystal summer-house—the only one she had conserved from the old gardens—to meditate upon these things. The sound of the water-jets lulled her thoughts and it seemed to her that their fluid voices were telling her an improbable story—but alas, the voice of water is not a human voice.

Suddenly, Scheherazade shuddered. A sudden idea had occurred to her. Would it not be amusing for her, who had told so many tales, to hear them told in her turn? Why not try it? Certainly, unlike Shariar, she would not have boring tellers decapitated; she would content herself with having their ears cut off to punish them for not having charmed hers. Scheherazade was not cruel; she was even slightly repentant about having poor Kerendar hanged. She was wiser now, but wisdom has its hours of ennui. She would definitely summon storytellers. The news would be published in Bagdad the next day...

It was, and it had a tremendous effect. The marvelous story of Scheherazade, the cobbler's daughter who had become the favorite Sultana of the great Shariar, had made stories very fashionable, and that fashion had given rise to an infinite number of storytellers. There was scarcely a household in Bagdad in which tales were not being told. The evenings resounded with fabulous stories, full of twists and turns and prodigies. Assemblies, or academies, had been formed which met on certain days to listen to the new compositions of the members of the association. These societies had instituted competitions and were giving out prizes. This resulted in singular vanities, ardent rivalries and animosities that extended as far as hatred. These cenacles were bitterly jealous of one another.

In brief, a veritable literary fury had taken hold of Bagdad. One can imagine the effect produced by the appeal for storytellers launched by the Sultana and the invitation issued to them to come to distract her. The competitors disposed to subject themselves to the proof could have their names inscribed by the chief steward of the palace. The clause about the ears being cut off in case of failure was slightly worrying, but the vanity of Bagdad's storytellers was so powerful that none of them would admit the possibility of having to submit to such an outrage. Was their talent not a guarantee of the fortunate outcome of the adventure? The most modest was convinced that, as soon as Scheherazade heard his tale, she would be impressed and would reward him magnificently. The order in which the storytellers would perform was decided by drawing lots.

The first one favored by the draw was Mardouk. He was a short man, ugly and pretentious. He had an infinite self-esteem, so he did not doubt that when Scheherazade had heard him, she would keep him there and attach him to her person. He was, therefore, full of admirable self-assurance when he presented himself at the palace. In spite of his rivals scorning him and judging him a minor talent, they were nevertheless a trifle anxious. Women have such bad taste that one can never be sure of the justice of their choice, and their caprices foil all anticipations. As for Mardouk, he was certain that he would succeed. That was evident in the fashion in which his twisted legs limped up the stairway that led to the terrace of the palace where Scheherazade was waiting for him.

Mardouk had dressed up for the occasion. He had had the best tailor in Bagdad make him a suit that showed him off to his advantage and he was wearing a voluminous turban surmounted by a spray of feathers. With his hair freshly cut and his beard perfumed, he was animated by a vast pride. In fact, the colleagues in his association had insisted on accompanying him as far as the palace gate, and a large crowd of people had joined them.

It was with this imposing procession that Mardouk presented himself at the palace. When he had been admitted, the crowd had not dissipated. A great animating agitated the groups. Arguments blew up regarding Mardouk's talents. The night had worn on, and the conversations had not ceased—but they suddenly fell silent when the great bronze gate of the palace opened abruptly and Mardouk was seen to reappear. His robe in disorder and his turban unrolled, he was holding his severed ears preciously in a piece of cloth.

Mardouk's example did not discourage his rivals. Every week, the individual selected by lot went up to the high terrace of Scheherazade's palace. She listened carefully to the story he told, but was obliged to recognize that she obtained no great pleasure from it. The marvelous inventions that had delighted her so much when they were born in her own mind appeared to her devoid of interest when she heard them from someone else's mouth.

How monotonous these adventures are, with their marvelous lamps, their enchanted jars, their genies, their monsters, their treasures, their voyages, their grottoes, their magic spells and everything that pleases the poor human imagination! How vain and tiresome it all is! So much so that Scheherazade, after a certain number of trials and twice as many severed ears, became discouraged, and let the storytellers leave without demanding the auricular forfeit that she had the right to claim from them. What good was all that nonsense and trickery to her? Would no one be capable of soothing her ennui?

Weary, she started sending the storytellers away before they had even unpacked their nonsense. Wounded in their vanity, the latter did not hesitate to attribute their failure to causes that relieved its bitterness. Venomous tongues spread sly and malevolent rumors throughout Bagdad. It was repeated in whispers that the Sultana, weakened in mind and lowered in intelligence, was no longer in a fit state to appreciate the fine tales of Bagdad's storytellers. Comic songs and epigrams were composed on her account, in which she was vilified.

To distract her from these disappointments, Scheherazade wandered in her gardens. They seemed to her to be extremely empty. The sound of footsteps repeated by an echo made her shiver. In vain the fountains launched forth their water-jets, in vain the flowers spread their perfumes, in vain the birds sang. Scheherazade felt melancholy and abandoned. The respect that surrounded her, in showing her the extent of her power, caused her to see its futility. She had almost got to the point of missing the perfunctory and bearded kisses of Shariar, his solid embraces and coarse voice, which had sometimes praised her beauty.

Sometimes, Scheherazade thought about traveling, of touring her realm. Standing on the highest terrace of the palace, she gazed at the horizon. The river flowed through the city, its majestic and monotonous course reflecting the minarets of the mosques. Beyond it, an immense landscape extended all the way to the distant mountains. She watched the eagles soaring in the sky and the flocks grazing the verdure of meadows irrigated by the fertile network of canals. Sometimes, she perceived a caravan on its way to Bagdad. Might it not be bringing, at the rhythmic pace of its camels, unexpected news, a rare gem, a unique presence, a marvelous face? And she dreamed, regretfully, of the time when life had made misery for her, and the unknown—when, as the little daughter of a cobbler, she had eaten the rinds of water-melons heaped up in the detritus of markets, while vermin pullulated in the rags that covered her young bare skin so poorly.

It was on one of these days of sadness that Scheherazade was notified of the arrival of a great caravan. From the depths of the land of the Garamides, crossing the deserts of the Bogdiane,[54] it had reached Bagdad at the expense of a thousand fatigues and a thousand dangers, to offer the Sultana presents addressed to her by the king of that land. The men who composed it did not resemble those of Bagdad, either in their clothing or in their faces.

Among them was one who had the reputation of a celebrated storyteller and asked to attempt the proof. He was tall, and left his face carefully veiled, like a woman's. He was said to be of a great race and a princely family. He solicited the favor of telling a story to the Sultana. To this request, Scheherazade had shrugged her shoulders. What was the point of repeating a futile experiment yet again? What did the presumptuous stranger expect? This one, as an example, she would not spare. To punish his audacity, she would not have his ears cut off, but his head. So much the worse for the man who was told that she would await him the following day!

---

[54] I have left these two terms as they are in the original, although it is possible that the author is thinking of the Garamantes, a tribe once reputed to live in the southern Sahara.

It was a hot and luminous night, like the one on which Shariar had been assassinated. The stars were shining and the moon had risen. Scheherazade, lying on her perfumed leather cushions, listened, as on that previous night, to the murmur of the fountains, while respiring the odor of the roses. She felt strangely troubled. She would have liked to bathe her feverish body in icy water to extinguish its unquiet ardor. As soon as she had finished with the presumptuous stranger, she would plunge into the subterranean swimming bath whose waters came from a spring so profound that they had the sparkling transparency of diamond—but before then, she gave the order for the storyteller to be introduced. He appeared instantly.

He was, indeed, tall of stature, and seemed elegant and robust in his build. Am ample robe enveloped him entirely and his face was covered by a veil. Instead of prostrating himself at the Sultana's feet he stood upright before her. She considered him curiously. What words were about to emerge from that secret mouth?

Scheherazade suddenly felt interested. Suddenly, it seemed that the leather of her cushions had become delightfully cool, that the stars were brighter, the moon more silvery. The air had a particular savor. The fountains were murmuring more harmoniously, the roses were more sweetly-scented. Abruptly, in the shadows that were suddenly divine, a nightingale began to sing.

The stranger remained silent, and veiled. Scheherazade was silent too, her heart palpitating, and she lowered her eyes.

When she raised them again, the man had removed his veil and was gazing at her, his face bare, with a finger placed on his lips. He was handsome—as handsome as happiness and the dawn—and he continued to maintain silence; and yet, Scheherazade heard emerging from that taciturn mouth the mute words of the most marvelous of tales: that of Love, spoken in the silence, which contains all the beauty of death and of life.

Paradise Regained

To Alexander Arnoux [55]

The assertion that Eve's tomb is in Arabia, and the claim that Adam lived no longer than nine hundred and thirty years, are quite mistaken. The truth is quite different, but legends endure, and I dread that what I am about to tell you might not be believed. I am, however, drawing on as reliable a source as I can...but let us get on with it without further delay.

Thus, contrary to what is falsely reported, our original parents are not dead. In creating them, God, according to the vulgar expression, "done a good job" and endowed his two creatures with an exceptionally robust constitution. They emerged from his hands so perfectly conformed in strength and health that death has had no purchase upon them.

Adam and Eve have vanquished the efforts of time. They are still alive, and very much alive. With a steady tread they have traversed the centuries and have arrived in ours. Their demise was a false rumor, to which it would have been easy for them to give the lie, but they did nothing about it, for their long experience of existence has given them a taste for privacy. Fortunately, all trace was lost of them to the point of their being declared dead. They enjoy their incognito and defend it jealously against any indiscretion.

Having traveled various regions of the world and after having resided in many places under borrowed names, Adam and Eve have ended up settling in a little village in the heart of

---

[55] Alexander Arnoux (1884-1973) was a poet, novelist, playwright and essayist to whose works Régnier was presumably sympathetic, although he does not seem to have known him personally—he is not mentioned at all in the *Cahiers*.

France, the name of which I have been asked not to divulge. Adam and Eve fear curiosity more than anything, and that of the era in which we live is infinite. The supposedly-informative press is particularly avid for sensational news and if it discovered that our original parents had become simple villagers, their door would be besieged by reporters and photographers. They would be bombarded by more or less absurd questions, some of which might be very painful for them. Imagine some dolt interrogating Adam about the extraction from his side to which Eve owed her birth, or some insensitive idiot making allusion in front of Eve to the murder of Abel by Cain. Think about the information that would unfailingly be demanded of them about the serpent and the apple, or the angel with the fiery sword stationed at the threshold of the earthly paradise. The life of these venerable exiles would become impossible, and such importunities would compromise their tranquility. Their great age requires careful management; they know that, and are therefore extremely regular in their habits.

Adam is a fine old man and Eve a charming old lady. They have the occupations of their age and sex. She still knits and reads without spectacles. Adam wears spectacles, but that does not prevent him being a fine angler. Eve is very home-loving and contentedly silent, while Adam is something of a chatterbox. While Eve remains at home and takes care of the housework, Adam goes out, and does not disdain a chat with the village gossips. He often makes people laugh, but his bonhomie is innocent of any unwonted familiarity. He is very popular, and his fellow citizens have asked him to stand for the local council. He refused, but people often consult him and have recourse to his enlightenment. He is very wise, loves to be of service, and dabbles a little in medicine. She excels notably in jam-making, and her pickled gherkins are justly reputed.

Adam and Eve make up an old household, highly esteemed in the region. They are often held up as an example. Their modest house is surrounded by a small garden, which one of their neighbors, knowledgeable about seeds and planting, cultivates for them. Sometimes Eve invites the worthy man to drink a glass of anisette or cassis. Adam also invites him to smoke a pipe with him.

They have very few other visitors. At long intervals, however, one comes whose arrival gives rise to a veritable upheaval; that is the day when they "put the little pots in the big ones." Eve spruces herself up and Adam goes to meet the traveler at the railway station.

He is a vigorous bearded fellow with a big nose. Tall in stature, but a trifle stooped, he walks with a long stride, leading on a stout staff and making the pavement resonate with his hob-nailed boots. He has an olive complexion and wrinkly eyes. Wisps of gray hair protrude from his battered felt hat, reaching down to his shoulders—which gives him the air of an artist, a musician in an orchestra or a mace-bearer.

He talks loudly, with a marked accent, and always seems to be in a hurry, to such an extent that Adam can hardly keep up with him when they return to the house. When he has set down his staff and taken off his felt hat he sits down, but soon gets up again, and scarcely ever stops pacing back and forth. As the vulgar saying has it, he "can't keep still," so his visits are of short duration, to the great regret of Adam, who has a considerable affection for him, and Eve, with whom he flirts gallantly.

When he goes away, his hosts deplore the destiny that obliges him to leave them and not to stay long anywhere. Certainly, travel does one good, but it must eventually be painful to have neither a trunk nor a hearth, to be forever climbing mountains and descending into valleys, always a nomad and always on the road, with one's boots and his staff. Adam and Eve mourn wholeheartedly for that poor Monsieur Ahasverus, commonly known as the Wandering Jew, who drags the dust of the entire world on his boots.

"God the Father," Adam sighs, "has been very hard on him. At any rate, I scarcely praise my creator any longer; he's been quite severe with us, hasn't he, Eve?"

At these words Eve lowers her eyes, for, like Adam, she misses the earthly paradise—but it's agreed between them that as little as possible will be said about that subject, so full of sweet and sad memories. That is all the easier for them because they have everything that Monsieur Ahasverus has told them during his brief visit on which to comment. Indeed, his interminable travels around the world have brought them up to date with many things. Monsieur Ahasverus had seen a great deal and learned a great deal, being endowed with an excellent memory. He knows a thousand stories, each more amusing that the rest. His conversation alternates between literature, the fine arts, music and the sciences. Politics is by no means foreign to him, and he has the most extensive views on finance.

Adam never fails to ask Monsieur Ahasverus for advice as to where to put his money, and he finds it good, but the latter's conversation is not always concerned with such elevated subjects. He has been witness more than once to the follies that love causes humans to commit, and knows many anecdotes that he relates with infinite wit, as humorous as they are instructive, lewd and scabrous—which, if they make Even blush, put Adam in a good mood. So Monsieur Ahasverus' visits are awaited with impatience by our original parents and are one of the favorite pleasures of their retiring life, from the honest monotony of which they provide a distraction. Monsieur Ahasverus makes them find the day short and causes them to stay up late.

It was during one of these visits to his old friends that Monsieur Ahasverus, who was in fine form that evening, told them the great news that the newspapers were spreading all over the world. The worthy Adam, who scarcely read the papers was still unaware of it, so what Monsieur Ahasverus told him fell upon him like a thunderbolt.

A scientific expedition organized at the expense of the Panbiblical Society, had rediscovered the location of the earthly paradise in Mesopotamia. Better still, it was not merely the vestiges of the celebrated garden that still existed...

In spite of a certain amount of insignificant degradation, it had remained in an extraordinary state of conservation. Eden had escaped the ravages of time and contact with civilizations. Its appearance had not changed since the epoch when its gates had been closed and access to it had been forbidden. The location of the original sin had remained miraculously intact. An International Company had been formed to exploit the marvel, and it offered conditions of transport so advantageous that they were within the range of the most modest purse. Furthermore, the easy terms of payment rendered the voyage accessible to everyone. The travelers were assured of perfect comfort. Special guides presided over the visit and furnished the necessary explanations.

The inauguration ceremony had been a worldwide success. Delegates from all the monotheistic nations had represented the elite of believing humanity. Now the business was launched, and it was good business. The shares had already gained significantly in value. They were quoted on all the respectable stock exchanges. Monsieur Ahasverus had come to warn his old friends about the "rush" that was about to take place. He was one of the leading shareholders in the Company himself—as was only appropriate!

Scarcely had Monsieur Ahasverus fallen silent than he regretted having said anything, on seeing Eve burst into tears and Adam wipe a discreet tear from the corner of his eye. Neither of them had been able to master the emotion that the news they had just heard caused them. Although, as I have said, with a common accord, they avoided talking about it, they both experienced a profound regret for the lost Paradise.

In spite of so many years having gone by since they were expelled therefrom, they retained a marvelous memory of the garden of Temptation and Sin. Was it not there that they had admired together the beauties of light and the mystery of darkness, listened to the murmur of waters, respired the perfume of flowers and tasted the succulence of fruits? Was it not there that they had known one another carnally? To be sure, it was also there that they had incurred the punishment for their

368

disobedience, but in spite of the sad events that had distanced them from it forever, the marvelous garden remained in their memory nonetheless, as having been the witness of their innocence and happiness before being that of their sin and fall.

Before resounding with the echoes of Jehovah, the echoes there had repeated the words of their tenderness. How many times had they not relived in thought the happy times when they had been the first man and the first woman in that Eden, of which everything still remained present to them. And now, all of a sudden, they had learned that it had been rediscovered, and that if they wished, they could go to see the places so long regretted, and where they would encounter to welcome them the living shadow of their youth.

As soon as Monsieur Ahasverus had taken his leave of them, had put on his old felt hat and, with staff in hand, resumed his everlasting journey of eternal wandering, Adam and Eve rapidly took cognizance of the project they had formed spontaneously. As soon as they had made the mutual confession, they set about making arrangements for the long journey that would take them from their little village to Mesopotamia. Thanks to the information given to them by Monsieur Ahasverus, everything was easily and rapidly organized. They agreed not to weigh themselves down with heavy luggage and contented themselves with simple suitcases, as befit modest tourists traveling second class.

Adam went to the Company headquarters to buy the tickets, and also to buy a certain number of its shares with his savings. Having done that, on the appointed day, Adam and Eve, arm in arm, were seen heading for the station, from which a train took them to Marseilles, and to embark on the steamship that would take the pilgrims of the rediscovered Eden to their paradisal destination.

Once aboard, Adam and Eve were slightly surprised by the small number of passengers. They had expected more, but they were told that the previous departure had been so overloaded that it had been decided to limit the available places. Besides, it was a little late in the season, for the Mesopotamian summer is very hot. The flood would begin again when the season of intense heat had passed.

The truth was that the publicity put out by the Panbiblical Society and the advertisements of the Company for the Exploitation of the Rediscovered Paradise had not produced as much effect as had been hoped. Monsieur Ahasverus had allowed himself to be carried away by his Oriental imagination, and had given the affair proportions that it did not have. The profusely-distributed prospectus had not provoked the expected enthusiasm.

Who, in our eminently rational century, is still interested in the old stories about the beginning of the world, the tree of the knowledge of god and evil, the apple, the serpent, the angel with the flaming sword, the wrath of Jehovah and the misadventures of our original parents, poor people who knew nothing of printing or electricity or universal suffrage?—all things infinitely more important than the discovery in some remote region of Asia of the old abandoned garden that had been the Earthly paradise The result of this indifference was that the steamship had departed half empty. Adam and Eve were allowed to dine at the captain's table and to benefit, without any supplementary charge, from one of numerous unoccupied first class cabins.

Adam and Eve's voyage was therefore made in excellent conditions and the steamship dropped anchor without difficulty in the depths of the Persian Gulf, in a little harbor from which an autocar service would conduct the travelers to their final destination.

On coming ashore, Adam and Eve had felt their emotion increase. The moment was approaching when they would see the places full of memories once again. So they exchanged occasional tender glances and squeezed one another's hands clandestinely. Meanwhile, the country they were traversing became gradually hotter, turning to desert. Adam and Eve bore the scorching temperature courageously, which only eased slightly as they approached the banks of the Euphrates. Its muddy flow ran between sandy banks.

370

Finally, they arrived at a sort of encampment, where large wooden stalls had been set up, one which were inscribed—in Hebrew, to add a little local color—the word *Eden*. At the sight of it, Adam and Eve felt their hearts beat precipitately. The autocars came to a halt and the visitors got down, for they had been told that the program included a buffet lunch before the visit to the Garden, which was only a short distance away behind the high sand dune that hid it from view.

While they headed for the dining room Adam and Eve consulted one another. Would it not be better, while everyone else was having lunch, to go out there on their own? There would then be no witnesses to their emotion, and they could abandon themselves to it without constraint. Having decided to do that, Adam and Eve took the indicated route.

The ardent sun warmed the track, which ran through sandy terrain. They walked slowly, for the beating of their hearts made their tread heavy. They climbed the shiny dune in that fashion and, having reached its summit, stopped. A kind of sheltered valley was visible within an enclosure sealed by a red brick wall, which the highest trees surpassed by a cubit. There was a door in the wall. Adam pointed it out to Eve with a gesture.

It was, indeed, standing there that they had seen, on looking back, the angel with the flaming sword who had expelled them from the garden on the day when they had eaten the forbidden fruit. Eve had placed a hand on Adam's shoulder and they had gone on, leaning on one another. How many times during their long exile, had they supported one another mutually like that? And it was in the same way that they went into the enclosure.

There as a profound silence there. Sometimes, Adam and Eve paused momentarily and their eyes met, but neither of them said a word. Sometimes, Adam wiped his forehead, for the heat was extreme. Everything bathed in a fiery atmosphere. No breath of wind animated the heavy air. On a fallen tree-trunk, Adam and Eve sat down. Taciturn, heads bowed, they looked at their feet. Then they continued their mute march under the blazing sun.

They wandered for a long time like that, until they heard voices—those of a group of travelers who, having finished lunch, were advancing under the escort of a guide. That functionary wore a braided helmet and was speaking with a thick German accent. The visitors numbered no more than a dozen, the other tourists having preferred to wait until the intense heat had diminished, a few saving themselves for a nocturnal visit by moonlight.

Among those who had braved the midday temperature were a protestant pastor and his wife, two Americans with clean-shaven faces who were smoking short pipes, a terribly-bearded Russian, an old lady with blue-tinted spectacles, one Swiss, three Italians and two journalists who were taking notes and making puns. The guide, who was sweating copiously, was hurrying the company along, in haste to refresh himself, and steering the little group toward the exit.

Adam and Eve did not join them. Remaining apart, they watched them draw away. When they had all gone, Adam cast a long gaze upon the deserted garden, between its red walls, over the poor vegetation, and over the tree of the knowledge of good and evil, which raised up its cracked trunk in the harsh light. Turning to Eve, with a melancholy smile, he said: "And to think, my poor love, that this is what we missed so much!"

Eve's only reply was a little gesture of disillusionment, and they both thought about their distant humble house, which they had left, in response to the fallacious appeal of memory, and about their modest garden, which was perhaps not an Eden, but in which it was so nice to take a cup of coffee under the arbor—and they experienced a great desire and a great haste to be at home.

When they got back, they learned that the Company formed for the touristic exploitation of the Rediscovered Paradise had been declared bankrupt, and that the shareholders would only find their shares worth the price of the paper. They heard that Monsieur Ahasverus had sold his in the nick of time.

SF & FANTASY

Henri Allorge. *The Great Cataclysm*
Guy d'Armen. *Doc Ardan: The City of Gold and Lepers*
G.-J. Arnaud. *The Ice Company*
Cyprien Bérard. *The Vampire Lord Ruthwen*
Aloysius Bertrand. *Gaspard de la Nuit*
Richard Bessière. *The Gardens of the Apocalypse*
Albert Bleunard. *Ever Smaller*
Félix Bodin. *The Novel of the Future*
Alphonse Brown. *City of Glass*
André Caroff. *The Terror of Madame Atomos; Miss Atomos; The Return of Madame Atomos; The Mistake of Madame Atomos*
Félicien Champsaur. *The Human Arrow*
Didier de Chousy. *Ignis*
Captain Danrit. *Undersea Odyssey*
C. I. Defontenay. *Star (Psi Cassiopeia)*
Charles Derennes. *The People of the Pole*
Georges Dodds (anthologist). *The Missing Link*
Harry Dickson. *The Heir of Dracula*
Jules Dornay. *Lord Ruthven Begins*
Alfred Driou. *The Adventures of a Parisian Aeronaut*
Sâr Dubnotal *vs. Jack the Ripper*
Alexandre Dumas. *The Return of Lord Ruthven*
Renée Dunan. *Baal*
J.-C. Dunyach. *The Night Orchid; The Thieves of Silence*
Henri Duvernois. *The Man Who Found Himself*
Achille Eyraud. *Voyage to Venus*
Henri Falk. *The Age of Lead*
Paul Féval. *Anne of the Isles; Knightshade; Revenants; Vampire City; The Vampire Countess; The Wandering Jew's Daughter*
Paul Féval, *fils. Felifax, the Tiger-Man*
Charles de Fieux. *Lamékis*
Arnould Galopin. *Doctor Omega*; *Doctor Omega & The Shadowmen*
G.L. Gick. *Harry Dickson and the Werewolf of Rutherford Grange*
Edmond Haraucourt. *Illusions of Immortality*
Nathalie Henneberg. *The Green Gods*
V. Hugo, P. Foucher & P. Meurice. *The Hunchback of Notre-Dame*
Michel Jeury. *Chronolysis*
Gustave Kahn. *The Tale of Gold and Silence*

Gérard Klein. *The Mote in Time's Eye*

Jean de La Hire. *Enter the Nyctalope; The Nyctalope on Mars; The Nyctalope vs. Lucifer; The Nyctalope Steps In*

Etienne-Léon de Lamothe-Langon. *The Virgin Vampire*

André Laurie. *Spiridon*

Gabriel de Lautrec. *The Vengeance of the Oval Portrait*

Georges Le Faure & Henri de Graffigny. *The Extraordinary Adventures of a Russian Scientist Across the Solar System* (2 vols.)

Gustave Le Rouge. *The Vampires of Mars*

Jules Lermina. *Mysteryville; Panic in Paris; To-Ho and the Gold Destroyers; The Secret of Zippelius*

Jean-Marc & Randy Lofficier. *Edgar Allan Poe on Mars; The Katrina Protocol; Pacifica; Robonocchio; Tales of the Shadowmen 1-8*

Xavier Mauméjean. *The League of Heroes*

José Moselli. *Illa's End*

John-Antoine Nau. *Enemy Force*

Marie Nizet. *Captain Vampire*

C. Nodier, A. Beraud & Toussaint-Merle. *Frankenstein*

Henri de Parville. *An Inhabitant of the Planet Mars*

Gaston de Pawlowski. *Journey to the Land of the 4th Dimension*

Georges Pellerin. *The World in 2000 Years*

J. Polidori, C. Nodier, E. Scribe. *Lord Ruthven the Vampire*

P.-A. Ponson du Terrail. *The Vampire and the Devil's Son*

Henri de Régnier. *A Surfeit of Mirrors*

Maurice Renard. *The Blue Peril; Doctor Lerne; The Doctored Man; A Man Among the Microbes; The Master of Light*

Jean Richepin. *The Wing*

Albert Robida. *The Adventures of Saturnin Farandoul; The Clock of the Centuries; Chalet in the Sky*

J.-H. Rosny Aîné. *Helgvor of the Blue River; The Givreuse Enigma; The Mysterious Force; The Navigators of Space; Vamireh; The World of the Variants; The Young Vampire*

Marcel Rouff. *Journey to the Inverted World*

Han Ryner. *The Superhumans*

Brian Stableford. *The New Faust at the Tragicomique;The Empire of the Necromancers (The Shadow of Frankenstein; Frankenstein and the Vampire Countess; Frankenstein in London); Sherlock Holmes & The Vampires of Eternity; The Stones of Camelot; The Wayward Muse.* (anthologist) *The Germans on Venus; News from the Moon; The Supreme Progress; The World Above the World; Nemoville*

Jacques Spitz. *The Eye of Purgatory*

Kurt Steiner. *Ortog*
Eugène Thébault. *Radio-Terror*
C.-F. Tiphaigne de La Roche. *Amilec*
Théo Varlet. *The Xenobiotic Invasion; Timeslip Troopers* (w/André Blandin); *The Martian Epic* (w/Octave Joncquel)
Paul Vibert. *The Mysterious Fluid*
Villiers de l'Isle-Adam. *The Scaffold; The Vampire Soul*
Philippe Ward. *Artahe*
Philippe Ward & Sylvie Miller. *The Song of Montségur*

MYSTERIES & THRILLERS

M. Allain & P. Souvestre. *The Daughter of Fantômas*
A. Anicet-Bourgeois, Lucien Dabril. *Rocambole*
A. Bernède & L. Feuillade. *Judex*
A. Bisson & G. Livet. *Nick Carter vs. Fantômas*
V. Darlay & H. de Gorsse. *Lupin vs. Holmes: The Stage Play*
Paul Féval. *Gentlemen of the Night; John Devil; The Black Coats ('Salem Street; The Invisible Weapon; The Parisian Jungle; The Companions of the Treasure; Heart of Steel; The Cadet Gang; The Sword-Swallower)*
Emile Gaboriau. *Monsieur Lecoq*
Steve Leadley. *Sherlock Holmes: The Circle of Blood*
Maurice Leblanc. *Arsène Lupin vs. Countess Cagliostro; Lupin vs. Holmes (The Blonde Phantom; The Hollow Needle)*
Gaston Leroux. *Chéri-Bibi; The Phantom of the Opera; Rouletabille & the Mystery of the Yellow Room*
Richard Marsh. *The Complete Adventures of Judith Lee*
William Patrick Maynard. *The Terror of Fu Manchu*
Frank J. Morlock. *Sherlock Holmes: The Grand Horizontals; Sherlock Holmes vs Jack the Ripper*
P. de Wattyne & Y. Walter. *Sherlock Holmes vs. Fantômas*
David White. *Fantômas in America*

SCREENPLAYS

Mike Baron. *The Iron Triangle*
Emma Bull & Will Shetterly. *Nightspeeder; War for the Oaks*
Gerry Conway & Roy Thomas. *Doc Dynamo*
Steve Englehart. *Majorca*
James Hudnall. *The Devastator*

Jean-Marc & Randy Lofficier. *Royal Flush*
J.-M. & R. Lofficier & Marc Agapit. *Despair*
J.-M. & R. Lofficier & Joël Houssin. *City*
Andrew Paquette. *Peripheral Vision*
R. Thomas, J. Hendler & L. Sprague de Camp. *Rivers of Time*

NON-FICTION
Stephen R. Bissette. *Blur 1-5. Green Mountain Cinema 1*
Win Scott Eckert. *Crossovers* (2 vols.)
Jean-Marc & Randy Lofficier. *Shadowmen* (2 vols.)
Randy Lofficier. *Over Here*

HEXAGON COMICS
Franco Frescura & Luciano Bernasconi. *Wampus*
Franco Frescura & Giorgio Trevisan. *CLASH*
L. Bernasconi, J.-M. Lofficier & Juan Roncagliolo Berger. *Phenix*
Claude Legrand, J.-M. Lofficier & L. Bernasconi. *Kabur*
Franco Oneta. *Zembla*
L. Buffolente, Lofficier & J.-J. Dzialowski. *Strangers: Homicron*
Danilo Grossi. *Strangers: Jaydee*
Claude Legrand & Luciano Bernasconi. *Strangers: Starlock*

ART BOOKS
Jean-Pierre Normand. *Science Fiction Illustrations*
Raven Okeefe. *Raven's L'il Critters*
Randy Lofficier & Raven OKeefe. *If Your Possum Go Daylight...*
Daniele Serra. *Illusions*